BENJAMIN ASHWOOD

BENJAMIN ASHWOOD BOOK 1

AC COBBLE

Cobble Publishing LLC

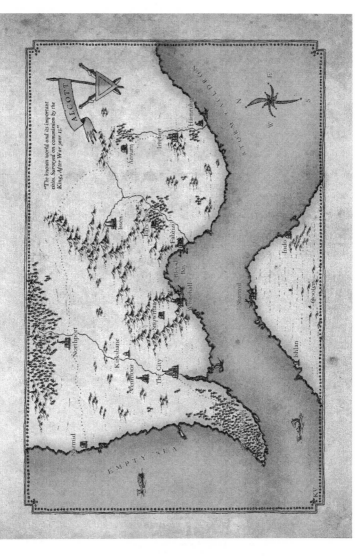

"The known world and its important cities. Surveyed on commission by the King, After War year 15."

ALCOTT

1

HERO

THE TRICKY THING about living in a society that allows you freedom is that everyone else has it too.

Some people can't handle that. They can't accept their neighbor making a different choice than they did. That's the tricky part, letting someone else have the freedom to choose. A choice isn't really a choice if there is only one option. It's inherent with real choices—with true freedom—that everyone can make their own decisions. For us to be free, we have to come to terms with that. We have to understand that not every decision is ours to make. Not every decision is a good one.

People call me a hero. They say that because I fought for them. Let me tell you, the fighting was the easy part.

The hard part, the part that really mattered, is what happened after. That's what I want to be remembered for. Not because I fought. Not because I killed. Not because I survived. Remember me because I tolerated. Remember me because I accepted. Remember me because I understood that I'm not here to make your choices.

If I had done that, if I had been just one more dictator sitting atop a golden throne, then it would have been for nothing.

I didn't free you from your oppressive rulers. I freed you from yourselves.

I'm sorry if you don't like it.

Unattributed lecture series notes
37 A.W. City University

2

FARVIEW

BEN PEERED into the dense fog. The mist blanketed the forest in an unnatural silence. The only sounds were the coughs and nervous shuffling of the men stretched out around him. The men were in a ragged line that quickly disappeared into the impenetrable wall of white.

He imagined the men on the ends of the line could easily slip off unnoticed and head back to town. He tried to remember who was out there on the end and pictured if they were the type to leave their neighbors to this task alone. Dale Catskin was one of them, he thought. He wasn't the type to be out here any longer than he had to.

His reverie was broken when his friend Serrot emerged like a wraith from the fog and moved silently toward the men. Serrot waved an all clear and the men passed it down the line in hushed whispers. They started moving slowly forward again.

Serrot fell in next to Ben and adjusted his grip on his bow. He was clutching it with an arrow nocked and had a long hunting knife strapped to his belt. Ben knew that in normal circumstances Serrot would never have his bowstrings out in this damp.

The hunt they were on had all of them acting skittish. His friend wanted to be ready.

"Did you see anything?" whispered Ben.

"No, I made it up to the stream and it's all clear," answered Serrot with a shrug. "I'm not sure how I'm supposed to see anything in this fog. Hopefully when we get up on the ridgeline, it will have burned off some. It's only another two leagues."

Serrot was acting as their scout. He hunted small game and deer in these woods and could pick up a track better than any man in Farview. They had been friends since Ben moved to Farview years before.

Ben ran his hands along the smooth ash of his quarterstaff and wished for the hundredth time he'd asked to borrow a real weapon. He was good with the quarterstaff. Last year, he'd placed second in the tournament at the Spring Festival. For this though, he wanted something more substantial, he wanted something with an edge.

Serrot hissed, "What if we can't see it in this fog? I don't want the damn thing dropping down on top of me. Old Gamson told me they can fly. He's seen them swoop down behind a man and take his head off without a sound. I can't believe that tight ass on the Town Council wouldn't hire a hunter for this!"

Ben glanced to his left where Alistair Pinewood, Ben's adopted father, was walking with his true son Brandon. Everyone knew who the 'tight ass on the Town Council' was.

Years before, Ben was adopted by the Pinewoods when his real father passed away. Alistair had assumed ownership of the Ashwood family timber holdings to cover unpaid debts. Taking responsibility for Ben in the bargain was one of the few times the rest of the Council got their way and made Alistair bend.

Outstanding debt to Alistair was not unusual in Farview. He was by far the wealthiest man in town and earned much of that wealth by lending to his neighbors. The 'tight ass' moniker came because he didn't always see eye to eye with the rest of the town on what he should contribute to the common good.

Ben had a unique view of what life was like with the Pinewoods. They had money, but it didn't make them any happier. Ben's friends never understood that. Watching Alistair and Brandon walk together now, Ben didn't miss the connection the younger Pinewood had with the older or the gold and property he would eventually inherit. Alistair was a cold, hard man. The short time Ben had with his real father was better than a lifetime of that.

Ben sighed and forced himself to pay attention. He responded to Serrot, "Old Gamson claims to have seen an awfully lot for someone who's never been more than ten leagues outside of Farview. A demon this small can't fly. When they're this small, they don't even have wings. It's like hunting down a rabid dog."

At least Ben hoped it was like that. He hadn't seen any more demons than Serrot had.

In fact, it had been years since anyone in Farview had seen a demon. In the stories, there were big ones who could rip an ox in two. But Ben talked to some of the men down at the Buckhorn Tavern who'd actually been on demon hunts long ago and it didn't sound too scary. The ones they saw weren't more than a yard tall and weren't any more dangerous than an angry bear. Reason for caution certainly, but nothing the men couldn't handle. Sending for a hunter for something like that was unnecessary. Still, with this fog, Ben wished again that he'd brought a weapon more lethal than his quarterstaff.

As the day wore on, the thick fog stubbornly remained floating throughout the forest. It was the early days of spring and this high in the mountains the air still carried a bitter chill. Ben rubbed his arms and strained to see further into the murky white. The eerie silence was unnerving. He couldn't help but wonder where the normal birds and forest creatures had gone.

He was peering so hard into the mist that he missed seeing a tree root which caught his foot and nearly sent him sprawling. He uttered an embarrassed swear and stole a glance at Serrot, who was effortlessly gliding around obstacles. Serrot spent nearly every waking moment in these woods and moved in them as naturally and silently as the animals he hunted.

Ben hoped Serrot knew what he was doing. He was counting on him to be ready in case the demon came at their section of the line. The tactics for hunting a demon this size were fairly simple. Demons fed on life blood and had a supernatural sense for when it was near. A smaller demon would rarely attack a large group of men on its own, but if stumbled upon, it would not be able to resist charging. So, the men spread out in a loose formation and stalked through the forest. When the demon was attracted, they would let the archers wound and slow it down, rush in with spears to pin it, and then finish it with an axe or sword.

The demon would sense their life forces long before they would see it, but a demon is not a cautious creature. It would make no secret when it began its charge. The stories said it would bellow a challenge as it rushed toward its target. With plenty of visibility and skilled archers, there was little danger with a young, small demon.

The topic of demons is not exactly dinner table conversation, but they are a fact of life and Farview is like any small town. There were always plenty of men at the local tavern to tell a story or two. Generally accepted knowledge of demons and how to face them was passed down with the same care and assurance as crop cycles and telling a proper weather forecast.

Because he was largely ignored by Alistair Pinewood, Ben had the freedom at a young age to spend far too many bells at the Buckhorn Tavern hearing those stories. For many of the Buckhorn regulars, young Ben became something of a tavern mascot. They delighted telling him about demons, hunters, grumpkins, hobgoblins, wyverns, mages, the long-lived, and other stories that seemed mythical to a boy in Farview who hadn't seen anything more dangerous or exciting than logging accidents and the Spring Festival. Ben was certain that the most exciting and vivid storytellers, like Old Gamson, didn't have any more experience with these things than he did, but he could never resist hearing about a good adventure.

And finally, he was getting to live his own adventure, even if it was turning out to be a bit boring.

For the last month and a half, many of the farmers who lived on the outskirts of Farview had reported mysteriously losing livestock. Rumors ranged from mountain lions, to bandits, to refugees, to theft by jealous neighbors, to every manner of magical creature.

Last night though, Farmer Ell rushed into town calling for a full meeting of the Town Council.

Still in the middle of the square, he claimed he'd seen what was taking their livestock. Ell said he saw a small black shape no larger than a sheep dog dragging away one of his pigs. He started running across the yard and when he was halfway to the creature, the full moon came out from behind a cloud and there it was—small curved horns on its head and wing buds on its back—it couldn't be anything other than a young demon.

The Town Council immediately called for a posse to track the demon down first thing in the morning. Ben spent the rest of the night thinking about what it would be like to see one of the creatures he'd only heard of in stories. It wasn't nearly as exciting as seeing a wyvern or meeting a long-lived, but still, it was something.

At least, it seemed exciting before they started trooping around in the cold damp forest all morning without seeing anything other than drifting mist.

No one really knew where demons came from. Usually when first spotted, a demon would be small, weak, slow, and confused. As they fed on life blood, they grew in size, strength, and speed. Most dangerously though, they grew in intelligence. A demon the height of a man is incredibly deadly and there were stories where dozens of trained warriors couldn't take one down. When faced with the threat of a grown demon, a town like Farview would hire one or more professional hunters. Hunters were men and women who made a vocation of hunting down demons and other dangerous prey.

Ben shifted his grip on his staff and kept walking. They didn't have a hunter with them. It was up to Ben and the other men from town.

There were around sixty of them in the posse, nearly a quarter of the healthy men in Farview. Ben could only see the closest five or six though as they made their way through the gloom. Massive pine trees loomed out of the mist and disappeared into the curtain of white above them. The silence of the forest was oppressive. Moisture dripping off the pine needles was the only sound that accompanied the ones the men made. Ben glanced at Serrot who was at home among these trees and could see that he was nervous too.

Serrot saw his look and whispered, "It's about five hundred paces down the slope until we get to the stream. There's a clearing there and we can regroup before pushing up to the top of the ridge. Up on the ridgeline we'll get better visibility.

"I hope you're right," muttered Ben.

Alistair Pinewood dramatically grunted and glared at them. When he caught their attention, he hissed, "Stay focused!"

This section of forest was part of Alistair's timber holdings so no one objected when he declared himself the leader of the posse. It had been years since he spent much time in these woods, and as far as Ben knew, he'd never encountered a demon. Ben had to admit though, Alistair was able to use his influence to gather such a large group of men quickly.

As they continued the advance, another sound faintly intruded on Ben's conscious. They were approaching the clearing and he could hear the rushing stream. Alistair curtly motioned

Serrot forward to go scout out the clearing as the rest of the men hung back amongst the trees.

Demons were said to avoid water, so they did not expect it to be near the stream, but a demon in a clearing with this little visibility was dangerous. Even a young demon could gain a lot of speed across open ground. If it was at full speed, they would have little time to react in the fog. Back in the trees they would be somewhat protected because the confused creature could not take a straight line of attack.

Serrot adjusted his grip on his ash bow and drifted off to make a circle of the area. The fog swirled around his legs as he disappeared to Ben's right. In moments, Serrot reappeared on the left. He nodded to Alistair that it was clear to move forward.

Alistair whispered up and down the line, "Move toward the stream and we'll take a break there."

As the men gathered by the water, Ben watched the snow melt swollen creek rush by. It poured over heavy rocks, tumbling branches, and other debris caught up in the seasonal torrent. In four leagues the waters would pass through Farview, and on the other side of town, they would meet more mountain streams to form the Callach River. From there, the river ran by Murdoch's Waystation and, if followed far enough, eventually all of the way to the coast and the port city of Fabrizo.

Serrot nudged Ben and handed him a bite of tough salted jerky. Ben glanced around and saw that most of the men were digging into their belt pouches for something to eat or taking long pulls on their water skins. The way some of the men gave a face afterward made him suspect there was more than water in those skins. He dug into his pack and pulled out a small loaf of bread and wedge of hard white cheese. He broke the loaf in half and passed it to Serrot in exchange for another handful of jerky.

It was only mid-morning, but already it felt like they had been out there all day. For any resident of Farview, a four league hike up into the mountains was not a great difficulty, but the constant need for vigilance and the stress of attempting to peer through the fog was taking its toll on the men.

Alistair must have sensed the strain as well because after conferring with his head logger William Longaxe, who spent even more time in this particular valley than Serrot, he allowed the men a quarter bell before standing up and calling everyone closer.

"All right. Will says there is a shallow crossing about one hundred paces upstream. We'll head up there to cross over, spread out again, and make our way up to the top of the ridgeline. From there, we'll work back toward town. None of us want to be out here after dark. If we haven't seen the thing by then, it's probably moved out of this part of the forest."

As they crossed the stream, Ben was finally glad of his quarterstaff. Even at the shallow crossing, the water came above his knees. The slippery footing risked dumping him in the creek. He had his boots slung over his shoulder to keep them dry and leaned on his quarterstaff to help keep his balance. He couldn't help smiling to himself as he heard a splash behind him and a series of loud curses. At least one man was going to have a long, cold walk home.

Ben was in the first group of men to cross and sat down with both of the Pinewoods while William Longaxe and the miller's son Arthur stood guard. Will seemed completely at ease despite the mission they were about, but Arthur nervously shifted his grip back and forth on the long boar spear he had found somewhere.

Several more men made it across the creek while Ben finished pulling his soft calf high boots back on. Alistair was already up and directing some men to put their shoes on. Others were tasked with holding positions and guarding the crossing as if they were a small invading force landing on foreign soil. As soon as Ben was up, he was sent to stand between Brandon Pinewood and Arthur, halfway to the tree line.

About a quarter of the men had made it across the stream with another quarter crossing. The remaining men mulled around on the far side waiting. Ben glanced back at Serrot who was on the other side after completing a final scouting trip on that bank. Serrot was bent down checking the string on his bow, clearly worried about the damage the moisture was doing.

Ben was still staring across the stream when he heard a sharp crack behind him. His blood ran cold. He spun around, raising his quarterstaff, but couldn't see in the fog past the first few pine trees. His mind raced, trying to find a natural explanation for the sound. He knew that all morning these woods had been dead quiet.

Arthur stammered, "Isn't it supposed to bellow a…"

At that moment, they heard a bestial shriek that rattled their bones. A heavy black shape shot out of the gloom, heading directly for them. Brandon barely had time to raise his axe when the creature swept by him, raking its talons across his leg. He screamed in agony.

Ben had no time to worry about Brandon though—the thing was almost on top of him!

Out of pure instinct, he swung his quarterstaff in front of him and made solid contact with the demon's shoulder. It felt like he had just swung at the side of a building. His quarterstaff shot out of his hands with the impact. It was just enough to turn the demon from its path, though, and it went crashing straight into Arthur.

Ben watched in horror as Arthur sprawled onto his back with the demon on top of him. Ben dove for his fallen quarterstaff. When he rolled to his feet, he could see he was too late. The demon had ripped out Arthur's throat and was greedily slurping the gushing fountain of blood.

Will Longaxe burst out of the shroud of fog with his axe raised above his head and took a mighty swing at the creature. Ben blinked in disbelief as the demon darted to the side and the axe whistled by, catching nothing but cold air. Will stumbled off balance. The demon, which came barely waist high, surged forward and slashed across Will's stomach. A shower of gore slapped onto the wet ground.

Suddenly, an arrow sprouted on the thing's back, right between its two tiny wings. It bellowed in rage and turned toward the new assailant. Ben saw Serrot standing on the far bank nock another arrow and take aim.

Ben knew he had little time before the demon finished with Arthur and turned back on him. His quarterstaff was useless against the monster. He tossed the staff, ran to Brandon's side, and started dragging him back toward the stream and the rest of the men.

He could see Alistair Pinewood and the others standing wide eyed and stunned by the creek bank.

"Get back. Get back! It won't cross the water!" Ben shouted.

Ben had a tight grip on Brandon's jerkin and dragged him across the wet, bumpy ground in a stumbling half-run. He couldn't spare a glance behind him, but knew the demon was coming because Serrot and the other archers were frantically launching arrows behind him and screaming for him to hurry.

Ahead of him, the rest of the terrified men dragged a frozen-in-shock Alistair through the water. None of them stayed behind to help protect Ben's retreat.

Ben knew he could not hope to pull Brandon through the rushing torrent and maintain his balance. If he tried the shallow crossing with Brandon, he'd likely get them both killed if the demon pursued. In his panicked rush, he saw the deep pool of water below the shallows and prayed that everything he heard in the stories was true.

Serrot winged another arrow a hand past Ben's shoulder. Ben

knew he had no time left. With all of his strength, he slung Brandon around in front of him and launched both of them head first off the creek bank into the water. The icy chill blasted the air out of his lungs as he plunged beneath the surface. He lost his grip on Brandon's flailing body and pushed off the rocky creek bottom with both feet. He came up coughing and glanced at the far bank. Serrot and the other archers were still rapidly firing off arrows, but the look of intense terror was gone from their faces. He was too afraid to look over his shoulder and see where the demon was.

Ben felt Brandon thrashing around under the water by his feet and pulled him to the surface. They started awkwardly swimming toward the safety of the far bank, Ben half-pulling Brandon and both of them half-drowning.

They'd been washed several hundred paces downstream by the time they made it to the other side. Most of the men ran to meet them. Several strong hands reached down and dragged them from the water.

Ben lay on his stomach, hacking up what felt like half the Callach River while the men gathered around Brandon. Through their legs, Ben could see Edward Crust, Farview's resident baker and doctor, kneeling beside Brandon and wrapping a makeshift tourniquet around his ruined leg.

Crust glanced up at Alistair. "I think he'll make it, boss. It will be awhile before he walks again, if he ever does, but he'll make it."

Ben's head sank down on the carpet of damp pine needles that covered the floor of the forest. He breathed a sigh of relief. His heart was still hammering inside his ribcage, but he would live, and he'd saved Brandon's life.

TWO WEEKS AFTER THE ATTACK, the entire village was still on edge. In a community the size of Farview, the loss of two people was felt by everyone, and despite Ben's heroic efforts, they were worried that there would be a third casualty. Brandon Pinewood survived the brutal gashes the demon left on his leg, but a few days after the attack, he came down with a fever that Edward Crust did not have the skill to cure.

If it wasn't for the demon still roaming the forest, Brandon's injury and Alistair Pinewood's black grief would have been the talk of the town.

When the battered group returned, there was an emergency Town Council meeting. Alistair demanded a new hunting party form to avenge his son's injury. Cooler heads prevailed, though, and Alistair instead offered to personally finance a contract with a hunter. Since that meeting, he had barricaded himself in his estate and refused to speak with anyone other than his daughter Meghan and Edward Crust. The rumor was that he spent each day by Brandon's bedside in an alcohol-fueled haze, slowly working his way through his prodigious cellar.

Despite the drama with the Pinewoods though, news and speculation about the demon was all that anyone was talking about.

After the initial attack, Serrot and the other archers peppered the creature with a quiver full of arrows. It disappeared back into the fog, dragging the bodies of Arthur and William Longaxe with it. They knew the demon still lived because farmers continued to wake up to dead livestock. The farmers on the outskirts of town began keeping their animals in at night or moving them to farms south of town where attacks had been less frequent. Just two nights past, the creature smashed in Nathan Rockfield's barn door and slaughtered every one of his cows. Since then, everyone slept behind barricaded doors. No one was venturing out after twilight. Even during the day, people were moving about in groups and keeping their weapons nearby.

The storytellers had gone silent at the Buckhorn Tavern. They all knew what came next. As the demon continued to kill, it would grow in power. Eventually the size of the town would no longer be a deterrent. At that time, it would kill or be killed. Ben was not sure how the town would survive. Even two weeks ago, the demon had been faster and stronger than any of them expected. It survived an attack on sixty men and left only injury and death in its wake.

After the emergency Town Council meeting, Serrot and another man were sent at first light to Murdoch's Waystation to find a hunter. They returned four days later with news that there was no one at the Waystation willing or able to take the contract. They left a plea with Murdoch himself to look for a suitable person and offered ten gold coins to anyone who could slay the demon.

While there was no one currently at Murdoch's to take the contract, the Town Council had hope that someone would take it soon. Murdoch's Waystation was not really a town so to speak, and had few permanent residents. It sat at the intersection of the Callach River, the Fabrizo Road, and the Kingdom Highway. Anyone travelling in that part of the continent of Alcott was likely to stop at Murdoch's.

As long as anyone could remember, there had been a Waystation there. Murdoch was just the most recent proprietor. Over the centuries, it had turned from a small roadside inn into a bustling mercantile hub for traders who did not want to travel all the way to the coast at Fabrizo, or up into the small mountain towns like Farview.

It was common for merchant trains to spend a few nights at the Waystation until they could work out a deal with another merchant who came from the other direction. That way, both parties saved a great deal of travel, which directly padded their bottom line. It was also common for all manner of individuals and adventurers to stop by for supplies, news, or work. In that part of the world, Murdoch's was the central meeting point and Farview's best hope for finding a skilled hunter.

TEN DAYS PASSED since Serrot returned from Murdoch's with the bad news, but even with the impending threat of a demon attack, life moved on in Farview. Food had to be put on the tables, children had to be praised or scolded, and shops had to be tended.

Ben was back to work following a few days of exhilarating fear and celebration. After word spread of his part in fending off the demon and saving Brandon Pinewood's life, he spent several happy nights at the Buckhorn Tavern. He got slapped on the back and accepted countless pints of lager in exchange for just one more description of what the demon looked like up close, how fast it moved, or how he knew to dive into the water.

Of course, once he found out about Brandon's fever, the joy leeched out of his celebration. Even though they were never tight like real brothers, Brandon was the closest thing Ben had to one and it felt wrong to celebrate while his life was hanging by a thread. Privately though, Ben was still intoxicated by the thrilling mix of fear and excitement that had coursed through his body during the attack. To his friends, he adamantly proclaimed that he was done with adventures. However, in his heart, he felt like he had discovered something new about himself.

BEN SHOOK his head to clear it of thoughts about the demon. He pulled another bag of hops out of the storage cellar and tossed it next to a large kettle. He knew he should focus on his work and helping out however he could in town, but he couldn't stop remembering how he felt during the attack.

The liquid in the kettle, called wort, was coming to a roiling, healthy boil. Ben expertly gauged the timing before dumping the bag of hops into the mix. Soon, he would take the kettle off the fire and cool it in the cellar. By evening, the cooled liquid would be poured into one of his copper fermenting tanks along with several other kettles of wort. It would sit for about a week. After the week was up, the tanks would be full of strong, dark ale.

In normal times, Ben brewed about four barrels a week for the Buckhorn Tavern and the few residents of Farview who preferred to drink their ale at home. This week, Ben was filling up every one of the copper tanks and wishing he had more. Sales at the Buckhorn had doubled since the demon attack, and people who had never asked for a barrel of beer before wanted one now. He supposed that it was only natural. People had always turned to a pint of ale to spread some cheer or get through a difficult time.

A year before, shortly after his eighteenth birthday, Ben had taken over the brewery. The previous brewer passed away without an heir, and like many of the businesses in Farview, he owed money to Alistair Pinewood.

After giving Ben a little seed money for supplies, Alistair let him run the brewery in exchange for half of the profit. Ben loved the work and because of his frugal lifestyle, he was able to save a little money every week. He had competing visions of paying off Alistair and either owning the brewery or purchasing back his father's old timberland. He was torn, though. He didn't want to give up on his heritage, but when he was honest with himself, the prospect of spending the rest of his life chopping down trees had no allure.

Still, working in the brewery was bittersweet. It was located in the yard behind Farview's timber mill. The same mill Ben's father had taken a loan to build. The one that along with their timberland, Alistair took as collateral on the unpaid loans when Ben's father passed.

Now, Ben lived in a small apartment on the second floor of the mill and crossed the yard every morning to the little shed that housed the brewery. It wasn't a bad life though, and he couldn't complain.

Many people in the town blamed Alistair for their troubles, and because of that, Alistair led a secluded life. After getting to know him, Ben didn't blame Alistair. It was unfortunate when it happened, but many of the people who lost businesses would not have had money to start them if it wasn't for Alistair's loans.

Ben sighed and got back to work. He was brewing as quickly as he could, but he had to be patient and wait for the brew to mature. Only then could he transfer it to the empty barrels he stacked up outside the brewery and deliver the final product to his customers.

Ben splashed his face with water from a trough outside of the timber mill and headed toward his second-floor room. Climbing the steps to his door, he saw Serrot jogging toward him across the timber yard.

Before he came to a stop, Serrot breathlessly blurted, "Ben, have you heard? I thought I'd see you down at the Buckhorn. Where have you been all afternoon?"

"Heard what?" asked Ben. "I've been working all day. I've got more orders than I can possibly fill right now. What's going on?"

"The hunters finally made it," explained Serrot. "They just set off to find the demon."

Ben could only gape in disbelief. Aside from the demon itself, this was the most exciting thing that had happened in Farview in years and he was missing it! Then it dawned on him. "Wait. He's heading into the forest now?"

It was early evening, and already the shadows were growing longer in the timber yard. Out in the forest, under the trees, it would be nearly dark already. Hunting a demon in the dark was pure madness.

"Is he crazy? It's suicide going out there this late!" exclaimed Ben. "This fool is going to get himself killed and we're going to have to find another hunter."

Serrot grinned and said, "It's not just one. There were two of them that went. One of them is a woman, and the other is a blademaster! They seemed pretty confident when they left. Barely took the time to drop the girls off at the tavern."

"Girls? What girls? And a blademaster!" Ben's head was spinning. Blademasters were stuff of legend. He was only half sure it was even a real thing.

He was trying to process all of it but Serrot was already going on again, skipping from when the group arrived to what the girls were eating at the tavern to the woman hunter.

"Wait, wait," pleaded Ben. "Tell me from the beginning. And don't leave anything out!"

"Okay, I don't know everything, but this is what I pieced together from what I saw and the talk at the tavern. A few bells ago, five strangers walked right into the middle of town. There were two men, a woman, and two girls. They walked up to the Buckhorn Tavern and asked Blevin Beerman if there was still a demon problem." Serrot continued breathlessly, "Of course, that sent everyone scrambling. It wasn't but a few moments before Alistair turned up and plunked ten gold coins on the table in front of them. The blademaster and the woman said that they accepted the contract. They asked if the girls could stay in the tavern, then they had Alistair walk them to the edge of the forest and point them toward where the last attack happened. The two girls and the other man are at the tavern now. The man doesn't say much, but the two girls are dressed like highborn ladies."

"Well, what are we waiting for? Let's go see them!"

AT THE BUCKHORN TAVERN, they found they were not the only residents of Farview interested in the strangers. It seemed like the entire town was packed into the tavern or milling around outside. Ben and Serrot pushed their way into the low building and weaved through the crowd, trying to get closer to see the strangers. They were still enjoying a little respect and celebrity for their role in the fight with the demon, so the crowd grudg-ingly parted until they were almost on top of the table where the strangers sat with Alistair and Blevin.

Ben had to agree with Serrot. The two girls were indeed dressed like fine ladies. Their clothing was simple, but the quality far surpassed anything that Ben had ever seen. They wore dark trousers and dark vests over white blouses. Their hair was swept back in loose ponytails, and it took a second for Ben to realize that while they were dressed nearly identical, they looked very different. One was fair-haired and had a scattering of freckles, while the other's hair was a dark brown, nearly black, with a pale complexion and rose-colored cheeks and lips. Both girls were stunningly beautiful.

They were nothing like the fine ladies in stories, always dressed in elegant dresses with reams of sparkling jewelry, but there was no doubt in Ben's mind that these girls came from high bloodlines.

He was so enraptured with the two girls that he hardly noticed the man with them. When he did notice him, he was surprised. Serrot said two members of the group were hunters, and one hunter was a woman. Ben had assumed that the second man must be some sort of assistant, but this man looked deadly and disreputable. He could have stepped out of one of the grittier stories, except, instead of playing the hero, he looked like the bandit. He was nothing like what Ben would expect to be accom-panying two ladies.

The man had shoulder-length unkempt dark hair that he brushed back from his face with one hand. With his other hand he held a half-empty pint. Judging by the empty pitcher in front of him, it was not his first. Next to the pitcher on the table was a wide leather belt with two heavy long knives resting in battered sheaths. Behind him leaned a longsword with a worn wire-wrapped pommel. Ben was no expert, but from what he could tell, these weapons had seen extensive use. The man wore a light leather and chainmail jerkin as comfortably as if he was born in it. Ben could see no badges of rank or sigils proclaiming an allegiance.

As Ben was studying the man, he started when he realized the man was returning the look. He took a step back under the man's direct stare and glanced to his side to make sure Serrot was still with him. This was not the kind of man that you wanted to meet alone.

Blevin suddenly noticed Ben as well and effusively called out, "Ben my boy! Come, sit down! These kind folks were just complimenting you on your wonderful ale."

The two girls turned to Ben and smiled. His knees went weak. He had never met even one girl this beautiful and graceful, much less two at the same time. The girls in Farview were like candles next to these bonfires.

Serrot had to give him a little push from behind to prompt him to move forward and take the remaining seat at the table. He was in between the man and Alistair, and directly across from the two girls.

"I normally prefer wine, but this really is wonderful ale," the dark-haired girl stated. "Rhys tells me it is one of the best he's had in this part of the continent, and Rhys is a man who knows his ale."

Ben smiled at the girl and nodded at the man who must be Rhys. "Thank you sir. I appreciate the compliment."

The man took a long pull on his pint and rumbled, "Ben. Would that be Benjamin Ashwood? The same one who fought off the demon and dragged this man's son to safety?" He looked at Alistair who had his head bowed, ignoring the conversation around him.

"Um, yes, sir. My name is Benjamin Ashwood. I don't know if you could say that I fought off the demon. I just acted on instinct and tried to get Brandon and I out of there."

Both girls were now beaming at Ben. He felt a flush coming on.

"Getting away is one thing," remarked Rhys. "Getting away dragging an injured man is worthy of respect. Fights a demon and brews this good an ale. I wouldn't have thought to find it in a town like this. Barkeep, bring us another pitcher. This man drinks on me tonight."

Rhys leaned forward and stretched out his hand. Ben took it and winced as Rhys gave a crushing squeeze and shake. "I assume you do enjoy your own product," Rhys added with a smirk.

Blevin shot up from the table and shuffled off behind the bar. The movement broke the spell on the rest of the room and people started heading toward the bar to purchase their own pints or drifting off to other tables, pretending they weren't desperately trying to hear what was said at Ben's table.

The dark-haired girl leaned forward and murmured, "I believe this is the first time I have ever seen him shake someone's hand. My name is Amelie, this is my companion Meredith, and of course you just met Rhys. Tell me Benjamin, is the tavern always this crowded?"

"No ma'am. At this time of day there are usually only a handful of regulars here. These folks are all here to see you." He didn't know if that made Farview sound like some backward mountain town to these people, but it was the truth. "And please, call me Ben."

"Well Ben, in that case, please call me Amelie," she replied with a grin.

"Yes ma... I mean, yes, Amelie." Ben cursed himself as a fool.

He was saved from further embarrassment because at that moment, the crowd parted and a strange man and woman entered the room.

The man was obviously the blademaster. He had a clean-shaven head and wore loose, flowing clothing under light leather armor. There was an elegant curved falchion strapped on one side of him and a thin dagger on the other. He walked like a stalking animal rather than a man. Stamped on his scabbard was an intricate sigil denoting he was a recognized blademaster. It was said to be a rare honor. They said a true blademaster achieved skills that were beyond the reach of mortal men. At least, that's what Ben heard from the stories.

The woman was confusing though. She wore a practical travelling dress that was nearly as fine a cut as Amelie and Meredith's clothing, but she wore it like it was a uniform. While the girls' clothing was sensible for travel, they wore it with a certain grace. This woman was all about the business at hand. Like the girls, she wore no jewelry and her hair was pulled back in a tight bun. She seemed to have permanent frown lines around her mouth. The only weapon Ben could see was a small belt knife that he wouldn't want to fight a rabbit with, much less a demon.

He supposed that in the company of the blademaster she had little to fear from the demon. Maybe she was some type of healer or scholar, he wondered.

Alistair finally looked up at the arrival of the two new comers. "Did you finish it? Did you kill the demon?"

The man pulled a small pouch off his belt and, in a quiet voice, answered, "Yes, we found and killed it. Here are the horns as you requested."

He placed the pouch in front of Alistair who snatched it up, loosened the ties, and looked inside. If Ben didn't know better, he could have sworn that he saw tears in his adopted father's eyes. Alistair nodded wordlessly at the man, pushed back his chair, and left without speaking.

The man and the woman sat down in Blevin and Alistair's vacated chairs. Ben realized he was the only local left at the table.

The woman scooped up the ten gold coins Alistair left behind and looked at the two girls. "We rest here tonight and leave at first light. It is done and we've already wasted enough time on this foolish errand."

Amelie met the woman's look and replied, "I believe if you ask any of the residents of this town if it was foolish, they would disagree. In fact, Ben, do you believe it was foolish for us to come here and deal with this demon? Will the people be grateful for what we did?"

"Y-Yes, I think the people will be grateful," Ben stammered while trying to ignore the pointed look from the woman. He was confused by what they were saying and didn't like being called out. The woman had volunteered to come to Farview and take the contract, hadn't she?

"Stupid girl, these people don't know who you are or who they feel grateful to." The woman glared at Amelie as she continued, "So what if we did save a few people here? You jeopardized our timeline by insisting we take this detour. You must learn to overlook immediate and unimportant concerns to focus on the long-term goals. If we stop to fix every problem in the world, we will never get to the city before summer."

"We have plenty of time to make the city," retorted Amelie. "I know we cannot fix every problem in the world, but we did fix this one. Even if they do not know it, these are still my people."

"They haven't been your people for a long, long time."

The argument was broken up by Blevin, who came sloshing up with two fresh pitchers and several mugs which he deposited on the table. "Anything else I can help you with, madams and sirs? We have a roast lamb turning on the spit and my wife is making a stew. I apologize, we are out of wine. We drank the last bottle a month ago. I do have some apple brandy," he offered.

Rhys looked up at the mention of apple brandy but the woman shot him a glare. "The lamb please, Master Blevin. And that will be all."

Ben wondered if he should somehow extricate himself from the table, but Rhys filled up a mug and pushed it in front of him. "Drinks on me, remember?"

The blademaster then reached over and offered his hand to

Ben. In an accent that Ben could not place, he said, "Saala Ishaam, at your pleasure."

~

BEN QUIETLY SIPPED his ale while the conversation continued around him. Amelie and Saala were discussing their travel plans with occasional input from the woman and Meredith. Rhys had the bulk of his attention on emptying as many pitchers as Blevin would bring him. He was primarily focused on refilling his own mug, but regularly topped off Ben's as well. Before long, Ben was having trouble following the conversation. He had a warm feeling from too much ale and had never heard of many of the places they were discussing.

Rhys also kept him distracted by asking questions about the ale, Ben's skill with the quarterstaff, and Ben's encounter with the demon. He felt embarrassed speaking about how he struck the demon in front of people with such obvious martial skill.

Strangely, the girls and Rhys didn't ask Saala Ishaam or the woman about the demon. They knew they had left, and they knew that the demon had been killed, but they didn't seem to care about the details. Who were these people where a battle with a demon was not conversation worthy?

As the night wore on and the pitchers kept flowing, Ben soaked in the strangeness of the situation. No one else in Farview could say they spent a night drinking with two ladies and a real blademaster.

Ben tried to keep up with the discussion and memorize every detail. He doubted he would ever have a chance to meet people like this again, but a thought kept nagging at the back of his head. Why had the woman gone with Saala? She seemed to be the leader of this group, which did not match with his picture of her as a healer or a scholar. And why had Rhys not gone? Based on his attire, he was a man of action and violence. In fact, he was

AC COBBLE

exactly what Ben would imagine a lone hunter or adventurer to be.

The woman could also be a highborn lady he thought, though her stern demeanor and the way Amelie acted toward her did not fit. Possibly she was a merchant, but where were her goods, and why would a merchant get involved in hunting down a demon? His head was full of ideas, but none of them made sense.

Belatedly, Ben realized he was past his capacity for ale when the room started to slowly spin.

"Excuse, me, I'm going to go get some fresh air," he mumbled.

Saala gave him a small smile and Rhys a knowing wink, but the women ignored him. As Ben stumbled his way out the front door of the tavern, he saw how late it had gotten. Most of the crowd from earlier had left, including Serrot and Ben's other friends. He did see Alistair had returned and was in a deep discussion with some farmers in the far corner of the room. Making deals to replace slain livestock or some other way to capitalize on the disruption from the demon, Ben supposed.

He made his way around to the back of the tavern to relieve himself and breathed deep of the crisp mountain air. He hoped the cold air would sober him. He still had so many unasked questions for the strangers.

After finishing his business, he came back around to the front and paused next to Blevin's rain barrel. Blevin left a ladle to scoop water for customers who'd had a little too much to drink inside. Ben took a long drink and leaned back against the rough-hewn logs of the tavern. He ran his hand along the wall and thought about how this tavern had been here a long time. Long before Alistair Pinewood had finished building the timber mill that Ben's father started. The tavern was built back when all of the buildings in Farview were built with rough logs. It wasn't worth the price to float them down to Murdoch's, have them cut into boards, and shipped back up the mountain.

He was still lost in thought when another man came stumbling out of the tavern and headed toward the barrel. As he got closer, Ben realized it was Alistair and that he had also partaken a little too freely.

Alistair splashed his face with water and had the ladle tipped up before he realized Ben was there. He sat the ladle back and coughed wetly to clear his throat. "Ben, I didn't see you. Exciting night, huh?"

"Yes, sir," responded Ben. "I think it's about the most exciting night we've had in Farview."

"You mean aside from the night my boy got killed?" growled Alistair with a steely glare.

Ben grimaced. He hadn't meant any offense. Alistair was in no mood to hear anything but his own troubles. Brandon's injury must be worse than anyone in town realized if Alistair was already talking like he was dead.

"Sorry sir, that's not what I meant. I just meant that I've never heard of a man like the blademaster being in Farview, or the rest of them, high-born ladies or whatever they are." Ben shrugged uncomfortably. Telling Alistair about his excitement seemed like a crime when Brandon was in such bad shape.

Alistair snarled. "I don't care if they're highborn ladies or King Argren's own daughters! I had enough when I had to talk to them earlier. The girls with their noses stuck in the air, the men acting like we don't know what the hell we're doing, and that bitch woman trying to control everything and everyone around her! Who does she think she is?"

Ben blinked in surprise. That was it—control. Nothing else made sense.

"Alistair, she's a mage!"

"What? That is crazy. You've had too much to drink and this demon is getting ideas into your head, boy."

"Think about it, Alistair. She went after the demon with no weapons, she's got a blademaster following her orders, and she bosses around two ladies. What else could she be?"

Alistair stood stunned. A mage in Farview was unthinkable. In the stories, the mages were the hidden hand behind the thrones of the land. They were never mentioned as fighting demons or other mundane heroics. What reason would she have to be in Farview? Ben was certain as soon as he said it though, she had to be a mage.

"Ben, do you know what this means?" Alistair asked excitedly.

"No…"

"If she's a mage, Ben, then she can heal Brandon!"

Alistair spun and ran back toward the door, nearly tripping over the step as he rushed inside. Ben stood in shock. It was true. There were stories about mages who were said to have incredible powers to heal wounds that far surpassed the skill of even a trained physic. But it was also said in the stories that mages never worked for free—and that their payment was rarely in gold. They could perform great, mysterious feats, but they always collected something in return.

THE NEXT MORNING, Ben awoke with a pounding head. He lay on the small cot in his room and winced as a pair of birds burst into song outside of his door. He judged by how much light was coming in under the door that it was mid-morning. He knew he must have woken up with worse hangovers. At the moment, he couldn't recall when.

He stumbled outside to the water trough and plunged his head in. The cold water sent a shock through his body and he came up gasping for air. He filled a tin mug he kept hanging outside and sank down onto a rough-hewn bench and leaned against the timber mill. His head fell back against the wall and he stared up at the clear, cloudless sky. His stomach rumbled in hunger, but the thought of stoking the fire and making porridge or frying eggs seemed like an enormous effort. The thought of eating the handful of hard dry biscuits he had in his tiny pantry was even worse.

He reflected on the previous night and his mind still swirled with unasked and unanswered questions. He'd followed Alistair into the tavern where Alistair was already begging for the help of the woman in front of a stunned crowd. The woman did not deny she was a mage, but she did not admit it either. She simply said she'd look at Brandon's injury and see if she could help.

Rhys and Saala exchanged a worried look then Rhys said he'd go with her. Saala and the two girls quickly retired to their rooms.

Ben and several of the other town folk hung around the tavern, anxiously discussing what it meant to have a mage in their midst. After a bell though, it became apparent there would be no more news that evening.

The stories were all clear that when a mage cast a spell, they expended themselves somehow. They were also clear that a mage would never expend that energy without recompense. From what he could gather, they sounded somewhat self-serving. He guessed they were limited in either what they could do or how often they did it.

As Ben sat thinking on what he knew about mages, it slowly occurred to him that his pounding headache should be much worse. His room was above an operating timber mill. This time of the morning, there should have been the sound of saws cutting raw logs into boards, the crashes and bangs of lumber being moved around inside, and the constant swearing of the mill workers. The only sound he could hear was the chirping of birds.

He groaned and stood to change into fresh clothing and to go find out what was going on. After last night when he nearly missed seeing the blademaster and mage, he wasn't willing to sit and let the news come to him, even with a pounding head.

BEN JOGGED the short distance from the mill into town and he slowly started to feel better. The light exercise got his blood pumping and relieved some of the pressure in his head. As he made his way to the town center, he saw where all of the mill workers had gone. There was a crowd gathered on the green and they all seemed to be shouting toward the small lodging house that was next to the Buckhorn Tavern.

Ben spied Serrot on the outskirts of the crowd and made his way to him. "What's going on? It looks like half the town is here."

"I'm not completely sure. I just got here, but they're saying that the woman mage is trying to kidnap Meghan Pinewood."

"What! Do they have her in there? Is that why everyone is here, to try and rescue her?" Ben glanced around and saw that there were some weapons in the crowd. But even with half the town here, and many of them armed, he didn't like the odds of going up against a blademaster and a mage.

"I'm not sure. Meghan is in there and Alistair is with her. You were with them all night last night. What happened?"

"Nothing that foretold this," replied Ben. "They were more focused on their plans than anything going on in Farview. After the first couple of moments, they mostly ignored me. At the end of the night when we found out the woman was a mage, she did go to the Pinewood's estate to look at Brandon. Something must have happened then."

While they were talking, the crowd was growing restless. Alistair Pinewood was known by everyone in Farview but loved by few. His daughter Meghan, on the other hand, was loved by everyone who had ever met her. While Alistair was cold, businesslike, and a hoarder of gold, Meghan was caring and always willing to help those in need. When someone in Farview was facing hard times, they went to Meghan Pinewood first. There weren't a lot of people in the tight knit community who would turn their back on her if she was in need.

Ben grabbed Serrot and pulled him along into the crowd. He

had to get closer and find out what was really happening. Ben couldn't reconcile the people he met last night with the idea of kidnapers.

As they pushed their way to the front of the crowd, they found Blevin Beerman pacing back and forth on the porch of the lodging house.

"Blevin, what's going on in there?" shouted Ben.

"I don't know! About two bells ago, Alistair and Meghan came bustling on up here. Meghan looked like she was packed to leave and Alistair was beside himself. Right as they were going in the door, he saw me and yelled to get everyone I could, that they were taking his daughter."

The men around Ben and Serrot shouted in anger when they heard Blevin speak. They'd obviously heard the story several times now and were getting more and more worked up with each telling. Soon, they would work themselves up to doing something stupid. Something was not right, but this didn't sound like any kidnapping that Ben had heard of. Meghan and Alistair walked in on their own.

Ben shared a look with Serrot and could tell he was thinking the same thing. "Come on, let's go in there and find out what's really going on before something happens that we all regret."

The crowd settled down a little bit as Ben and Serrot crossed the wide planks of the porch and opened the stout pine door of the lodging house.

The situation was clear as soon as they entered the room. Meghan was there with a heavy travel pack just like Blevin had said. She was Ben's adopted sister, and he could read her every expression. She had a determined look on her face and maybe some worry, but certainly no outright fear. Whatever was happening, it was clear to Ben that she had decided to be a part of it. The five strangers were also there and outfitted for a journey. Alistair was sitting on a chair in the middle of the room with his head in his hands. He looked up as Ben and Serrot entered. Angry red framed his eyes.

"They're taking her Ben," he sobbed. "I thought I had lost one child. I found a way to save him only to end up losing the other."

Meghan stepped forward and pleaded, "Father, you are not losing me. I have to go for a time but I will be back. I will be fine."

"Back? Back when? Everything you know will be gone. I will be dead!" Alistair wailed.

Meghan shot Ben and Serrot an apologetic look and placed her hand on her father's shoulder. "I will be back."

The woman lifted her pack and growled, "I've lost patience with this. We're losing daylight and have a schedule to keep." She looked meaningfully at Meghan. "We're leaving now."

Alistair shuddered in another wave of sobbing. Ben had never seen him like this, even when he thought Brandon was on death's doorstep. Where was Meghan going that he thought he would never see her again? Alistair was a man who was used to controlling every aspect of his own life and many of the lives around him. What had shaken him so that he lost control like this?

Meghan, the woman, and the rest of the party started strapping on their packs, adjusting ties, and settling their gear to leave.

Alistair shot up from the chair and shouted, "Wait, wait!"

He turned to Ben and demanded, "Ben, you must go with them. Escort her to the city, stay with her, and come back when you know she's safe. However long it takes. Brandon doesn't have the strength for it yet. You're the only one I can trust."

Ben looked around the room. His head was spinning, but it was slowly starting to come together. The travel plans Saala and Amelie had been discussing and Alistair's frantic despair at Meghan leaving. He had not had the time or the clear head to consider everything last night. The woman being a mage was the last puzzle piece. They were going to THE City. In the stories, the City was rumored to be the seat of power of all Alcott's mages.

Not even Old Gamson claimed to know where the City was. It was like wyverns, something told to entertain children. Serious people doubted the City existed at all.

But despite that, Ben could tell from the looks on Meghan and Alistair's faces, they were convinced that it did indeed exist. And Meghan was planning to go there.

Ben was still considering the implications of the mythical City being real when Rhys winked at him and said to the group, "He did fend off a demon and save that kid. I don't think he'll slow us down much."

Meghan added breathlessly, "Ben, you should come. Think about the adventure!"

The woman shook her head and glared around the room before shrugging. "Fine, but he's not my responsibility."

She looked at Ben and instructed, "We'll stay at the Waystation tomorrow night and leave in the morning. If you are there, you can come with us. If not, we'll leave you behind."

With that, she cinched tight one final strap on her pack and barked, "We've wasted enough time in this town. We're leaving. Now." She then headed out the door. Meghan spared one last look at Ben and her father. Then she too was gone with the rest of the party behind her.

THE THREE REMAINING men in the room sat in stunned silence. The strangers were a whirlwind that had turned their world upside down. A mage, a blademaster, and the City. Suddenly, Farview seemed like a very small place.

Serrot was the first to speak. "Ben, are you really going with them?"

From his expression, Ben could tell that Serrot would have left in an instant. The thrill of adventure was almost overpowering. But, as badly as he wanted to go, Ben realized it was impossible.

"I can't. Who would tend to the brewery? I don't even know how long I'd be gone or where they're going! And how could I afford to eat and stay at inns? It's expensive to travel and I don't have that kind of money."

Alistair shook himself and pleaded, "You have to go. Those people don't care about Meghan. She's been a sister to you. You have to take care of her!"

Ben hesitated.

Alistair saw his chance. "The brewery is yours. You go with them and bring back word that she's safe, and it's all yours. I'll even take care of your travel." Alistair stripped off his belt pouch and spilled the contents on the oak table. A pile of gold, silver, and copper coins with a smattering of tin bits lay there. It was more money than Ben had ever handled, and by a quick count, it was at least four times more than he had saved behind a loose plank in the back of his room.

The thought of owning the brewery free and clear had always been a dream, but one he was not sure he'd ever achieve. Coupled with the prospect of travelling outside of Farview and seeing the world, he didn't even consider the dangers and unanswered questions before placing a hand on the pile of coins.

"You better move fast, Ben. If they're leaving the Waystation in two days, you need to get packed. You get what you need and I'll meet you west of town at the Callach Road." Serrot slapped him on the back as they both ran out the door. "I'm going to miss having you around here but damn if you don't have all the luck. You, the open road, and two beautiful highborn ladies to keep you company."

Serrot guffawed and shook his head as he turned across the green toward his family's cottage. Ben started trotting back to his room, already planning what he would need for a long journey and how much of it he could actually fit into his rucksack.

3

THE ROAD

BEN QUICKENED his pace as night fell. He had descended from the mountains by the Callach Road, which followed the river of the same name. Closer to Murdoch's, the terrain was heavily wooded and the deep shadows were ominous for someone who weeks before met a demon in a similar forest. Before the demon, Ben was comfortable in the woods, but it would be a little while before he had any desire to be alone in them after dark now.

Back in Farview, he had given little thought to his decision to follow Meghan and the strangers on this journey. Alone on the road with nothing but his own thoughts for company, he was questioning his decision. He thought back to the series of events that led him to be marching at night on this deserted road to accompany people he did not know to a place he recently wasn't sure he believed in.

The strangers were in Farview for less than a day and their visit was a blur. There were still unanswered questions. Why had Meghan agreed to leave and why these five seemingly disparate strangers were travelling together? He nearly stumbled as he came to the disconcerting realization that he didn't even know the mage's name.

When he left Farview, none of these questions seemed important. His entire focus was on preparing to leave and wondering what else was out there. If mages and the City were real, what other truths lay hidden in some far-fetched story?

Ben barely had time to say goodbye to Serrot before he left. They met just outside of town on the Callach River Bridge. Serrot gave Ben a cheesecloth-wrapped package of food his mother had thrown together when she heard Ben was leaving. He also gave Ben his favorite hunting knife. It was nearly the length of Ben's forearm and forged of high quality steel. Serrot spent several silver pieces on it, it was the most valuable thing he owned. Ben almost refused, but he could see that would have upset Serrot. He regretted he did not have an equal gift to give in return. Instead, he asked Serrot to look after the brewery for him and promised he would make it up to him when he got back.

That meeting already seemed ages ago and in a different life. He knew he'd miss Serrot and his other friends, but he decided that until the end of this journey and until he returned home, his life was the road and his focus would be ahead.

It was three bells after dark when he finally saw the lights at the Waystation. He'd been pressing hard since before daylight and his legs felt like he was moving heavy logs instead of numb feet. A day of hard work was not unusual for Ben, but marching that long was a difficult day for anyone. With only half a day on the road yesterday, he didn't have time for anything else. He was spurred by fear that he would arrive at the Waystation and somehow miss his companions.

He started down the final hill before the Waystation and saw its scale laid out in front of him. Even though the only permanent residents were Murdoch, his family, and his employees, the huge inn and surrounding buildings were larger than anything in

Farview. The Waystation was built to accommodate several merchant trains at once and had the space to do so. There were horse corrals, a wagon yard, a barn, a timber mill, a warehouse for merchants to temporarily store their goods, and a general store that supplied travelers and small towns for fifty leagues in every direction.

The inn itself was a massive log structure that included a tavern, quarters for all of the Waystation staff, and could sleep two hundred guests. It was likely only a quarter full at this time of year. During the fall harvest, it was said you had to pay up to five coppers for a bed. No one from Farview ever visited then, of course.

In the wagon yard, Ben saw there was at least one merchant train there and as he got closer, he could tell from the raucous noise pouring out of the tavern that they were cutting loose. He could hear a fiddle, drums, and some type of pipes. From outside, he couldn't tell if they were playing together or just playing. Whatever they were doing though, it was popular with the crowd. Enthusiastic, off-key singing broke out when they started a new verse.

Ben was greeted with a wave of sound as he strode up the creaky pine-plank steps and into the open door. It was early spring, and this far down the mountains, it was pleasantly cool outside. Inside, it was unpleasantly warm with roaring fires at both ends of the hall. One was in an actual fireplace and had an elk turning on a spit. The other was in an open pit on the floor and involved a game where drunken men leapt over the flames.

A serving girl appeared at his side and explained, "Aye, a strange one that. Last spring the fools lit up a bonfire outside and started jumping over it. Murdoch had 'em bring it inside, wrote out some rules, and sales of ale are up twenty percent. I don't understand it," she said with a shrug. "Take a seat lad and I'll be by in a moment for your order."

A spray of bright orange sparks soared upward as a leaping

man caught a flaming log with his foot. Laughter and jeers rang out as the man tumbled to the ground, rolling quickly away from the heat. Another man tossed a fresh log onto the blaze and the fallen man was doused with half drank ales when he stumbled to his feet cursing. Ben smirked when he heard the crowd calling for the man to buy a fresh round for the remaining competitors who'd just soaked him. Murdoch writing out the rules and the spike in sales of ale wasn't that great of a mystery.

After a quick scan of the rest of the room, he found Rhys, Saala, and the girls at a table watching the progress of the game. Rhys kicked out a chair as Ben approached and drawled, "Glad you made it. Take a breather and get some ale and stew if that wench ever comes back. It's all fish and wine down on the coast."

Saala rolled his eyes at Rhys and shook his head. "I'm sure she'd be back more often if you didn't inquire about 'extra services' every time she came by."

Rhys grinned and took a swig of his ale.

"C-Coast? What coast? I thought we were taking the Kingdom Highway," stammered Ben. On the lonely walk down the mountain, he thought he'd figured out which way they were headed. Apparently he was wrong.

Saala replied, "We'll head toward Fabrizo. From there, we'll take a ship across the bay to Whitehall. From Whitehall, we'll cross the Snowmar Pass, go down the Sineook Valley, and follow the Venmoor River to the City. It would take an extra month to go by the Kingdom Highway."

The three girls smiled at Ben as he sat down and the woman scowled, which Ben took to be her permanent expression.

"Now that you've decided to join us, let's get a few things straight," the woman said. No pause for pleasantries with her. "First, my name is Karina Towaal. You should refer to me as Lady Towaal. Second, I am in charge of this group, and as long as you accompany us, you will follow my instructions. Fail to do as you are told and we will leave you behind."

Out of the corner of his eye, Ben saw Meghan grinning. He surmised she had also gotten this talk recently.

"Third," continued Towaal. "Our task is to deliver these girls to the City unharmed. Your part in that enterprise is to remain out of my way. Do you understand and agree to these conditions?"

"Yes Lady Towaal," answered Ben.

Lady Towaal leaned back, apparently saying all she wanted to and having no further interest in conversation. The girls, on the other hand, were excited to have a new companion and gushed about how happy they were he was joining them. Ben couldn't help a smile from forming on his face while watching Amelie and Meredith talk. A long journey in this company suited him just fine.

It was already late and they planned an early start in the morning, so Ben shoveled down a bowl of hot stew. Saala and Rhys said he could share their room. The girls were in an adjacent room.

As they were in the hall going to the rooms, Meghan caught his arm and whispered in his ear, "Meet me back in the common room in a quarter bell."

Ben threw his travel pack on the bed and made an excuse to Saala and Rhys to duck back out of the room. He went to wait for Meghan. As he waited, he watched the rest of the common area. The music had died down from the raucous beat that had been playing earlier and now only the fiddler was playing. The man was talented and slowly slid his bow to produce a mournful, bittersweet tune. Ben noticed several more groups heading toward the hallways that led to the rooms. The serving staff scurried around, wiping off the tables and straightening up chairs and benches.

The men who had been jumping the fire had returned to their tables but were still drinking heavily and laughing loudly. He guessed they were the guards for the merchant train. He imagined they spent long boring days on the road and this must be their most comfortable stop in weeks. There was a scattering of other folk in the room, but this late in the evening most of the serious travelers had gone to bed.

He was still watching the guards when Meghan quietly sat down beside him.

"Ben, I want to talk to you before we leave and this goes any further. I appreciate what you're doing, but I am fine. You don't need to do this and it's not too late if you want to turn back. Just tell my father we already left when you got here. You don't owe him anything."

"I-I'm not doing this for Alistair," he mumbled abashedly.

"Oh no, Ben!" exclaimed Meghan. "You have to know that I love you but like a brother. You can't do this for me!"

Ben's face suddenly felt flush. That was not what he meant at all, but he didn't know how to explain it. "No Meghan, it's not like that. It's just that, well, I always thought I would spend my life in Farview. I always thought the most excitement I'd have was competing with the staff in the Springtime Festival or out hunting with Serrot. This is a chance for me to go out and see the world. This is my chance to really do something."

She smiled at him. He wasn't sure if she believed him or not, but it was the truth. He cared about her, and he wanted to make sure she was safe, but he knew that Saala or Lady Towaal could protect her on the road far better than he could.

"Well, in that case, I'm happy to have you with us. Karina, I mean Lady Towaal, says that it's a two month journey to the City. It will be good to have a familiar face with us."

"Meghan," Ben asked tentatively, "what happened back in Farview? Why are you going to the City?"

"It's for Brandon." She sighed. "Lady Towaal healed Brandon but she only did it after I agreed to go with her. She said she sensed great potential in me and that she would heal him in exchange for twenty years of my service."

"Twenty years! Wait. Service doing what?"

"I am to become an Initiate of the Sanctuary," murmured Meghan.

Ben sat back, stunned. The Sanctuary was part of the myth of the City. It was said that the Sanctuary was a fortress in the middle of the City that housed the mages. It was also said that the Sanctuary was a sort of school.

Meghan kept going, "Lady Towaal says that I will be an Initiate for several years. After that, I will serve the needs of the Sanctuary until the remainder of my twenty years are up. At that time, I'm free to stay or go as I please. Ben, I will be a mage!" Meghan breathlessly finished.

Ben realized that, just like him, she was excited about the possibilities of a life outside of Farview. She may have agreed to this deal to save Brandon's life, but Lady Towaal did not need to force her. She wanted to go and she wanted to do this thing. He sat in silence, contemplating how this girl who was like his sister was going to change into something that he had thought only existed in stories.

"Ben," said Meghan. "I feel like we have so much more to talk about but we've been here too long. We need to get back to the rooms."

Right then, two hairy-knuckled fists smacked down on the table. "Lass, if this boy got you back to his room, he wouldn't know what to do with you. Why don't you come on back to my room instead?"

The man looked to be one of the merchant's guards. He wore a stained leather jerkin and had a bushy black beard that was in serious need of a comb. His eyes were glazed over from too much ale and he reeked of stale sweat. He was a monster of a man, nearly as wide as Ben was tall. His arms were like tree trunks sprouting out of the wood table.

Meghan stared in shock but managed to reply, "No thank you, sir. We are fine."

"Ah, lass, 'fraid that wasn't meant to be a question," rumbled the man. "It's been a long trip all over half of Alcott and this place don't even have a proper whore. But don't you worry. The boys and I will pay you good copper and you might even enjoy it. We ain't here to steal your virtue, just want to rent it for a bit." The man leered down at Meghan and smiled, showing he was missing his front two teeth.

Meghan tried to stammer a response.

The big man clamped one hand around her arm and said, "Now, now, lass. You ain't my wife, so there's no need to go arguing."

Ben shot out of his chair and shoved the man away with all of his strength.

The man drunkenly stumbled backward against a table and slurred, "Hey, why the roughness? You can have your turn too. Right after me and the boys get done. Course, if it's a fight you want..."

He lurched forward, and before Ben knew what was happening, the man backhanded him across the face. Ben felt like he'd been hit in the head with an iron bar and went crashing down to the ale-soaked, sawdust-covered floor.

His vision spun with bright lights but Meghan's scream jolted him to his senses. He looked up and saw the man drag her to her feet and try to wetly kiss her face and neck. She was not going easy, and was kicking and clawing at the man. He was far stronger than her though and had one hand locked around her waist. With the other, he grabbed a handful of hair.

For Ben, the world turned red. He didn't know if it was blood running into his eyes or if it was rage, but he felt an energy burning through his veins that he'd only felt once before, when the demon attacked. He sprang to his feet, snatched up a sturdy wooden chair, hauled back, and smashed it across the man's back with all of his might.

The man fell down onto his knees. Meghan shrieked in terror, scrambling away. Ben yelled at her to run and turned to go with her. His heart sank when he felt a hand grip the back of his tunic. He spun around. With all his weight behind it, he launched his fist straight into the bearded man's face. The man's head snapped back, but he didn't lose his grip on Ben's tunic. The big man blinked rapidly, shook his head, and spit a thick globule of crimson red on the floor. He laughed in Ben's face and his eyes lit up like lanterns.

"Lad, you're a feisty one," snarled the man. "This is more fun than I've had in weeks."

He then pounded his fist into Ben's gut, blasting the air from his lungs and causing him to dry heave as he felt his knees turn to water. But Ben didn't fall. The man was holding him up and lifted Ben above his head as easily as Ben would lift a small sack of hops. The huge man hurled Ben across the room. He went sailing over one table and bounced off another before thudding to the ground at the feet of the man's companions.

Ben took a painful gasp of air as he looked up at the merry faces above him and heard the man call out, "Hold his arms. I think the kid made me bite off a bit of my tongue. I'm going to take a piece of his in exchange."

Two burly men dragged Ben to his feet as he thrashed around. He saw the first man spit another blob of crimson and wipe at the stream of blood running down his chin. The man pulled a razor sharp knife from his belt and winked at Ben. He strode forward, tossing the knife back and forth from hand to hand and chuckling wickedly.

Ben could not take his eyes off of the blade. The fire light flickered across its edge as it spun between the man's hands. Ben struggled to gain enough breath to shout for help from the inn's bouncers, or anyone, but he was still winded and gagging from the punch to his gut.

Suddenly, a hand shot into Ben's field of vision and axed into the bearded man's throat, dropping him like a sack of potatoes. The two men holding Ben let go and shouted in disbelief, one charging forward and the other reaching for his sword. Ben slumped helplessly to the ground and watched as Saala swept effortlessly forward and smashed his elbow into the charging man's face. The force of the blow sent the man crashing flat onto his back where he lay motionless.

The third man had his sword free and leapt over Ben toward Saala. As he pulled back for a swing, Saala stepped in close. Saala gripped and twisted the man's sword arm with one hand while the other chopped down onto the man's elbow, causing an audible crack. The man shouted in pain and dropped his sword. Cradling his broken arm, he slunk away from Saala.

Saala calmly stooped down to pick up the fallen sword. He ignored Ben, the man with the broken arm, and the unconscious body of the second man. The big bearded man had rolled onto his side and was gripping at his throat and kicking his feet as he struggled to draw a breath. Saala knelt and plunged the point of the sword into the oak floor just inches from the man's face. The man froze like a startled deer. All sounds seemed to stop except for the harsh wheezing of painful breath.

Ben struggled to hear as Saala softly spoke to the man. "The girl told me what happened and what you intended to do to her. Slightly harder and instead of injuring you, I would have crushed your throat. You would be dying right now. I want you to know this, to know that it would have been easier to kill you. I made an effort to spare your life. I want you to think about this moment every time you talk to a woman for the rest of your life. If I ever hear that you attempted to force yourself on another woman, or even if a woman complains about your company, I will return. I will kill you as easily as I mounted the steps to this inn."

The bearded man whimpered in response.

With a clatter of weapons and shouts, the two portly bouncers finally arrived, shoving their way through the loose circle that had formed around the fight. They were both brandishing heavy, iron-bound, oaken cudgels and raised them as the larger one spoke to Saala, "Hey now, there ain't no fighting at Murdoch's. You got a problem you settle it out on the road or we crack your head open and take your purse for our trouble. Murdoch don't give a damn about whatever feuds your master got. Around here, you cause trouble, you pay for it." The bouncer gave a nasty grin as the pair split up, attempting to circle Saala.

"From the looks of things, you've already caused plenty of trouble." The man turned toward his partner and said, "What does it look like to you, Mord? Two silvers' worth of trouble?"

Mord held a silent grin and cracked his cudgel against a table, causing the man with the broken arm to give a pained, sympathetic whimper. Mord glanced quizzically at the injured man then frowned as he reevaluated the scene. "Mert—" he started.

Saala rose to his feet and interrupted in the same soft tone he always spoke in. "You, sirs, are too late to prevent this. I have almost finished doing your job for you. These men accosted a female companion of mine in your inn and you failed to protect her. If any damages are to be paid to Murdoch, it will be by these men. And if my companion asks it, I will have recompense from you also."

Saala then raised his foot and swiftly brought his heel down with a sickening crunch onto the bearded man's hand. The man's hoarse shriek filled the silent common room. Saala glanced down at the bearded man, who was writhing in pain clutching his hand. "I trust the loss of function in this hand will be all the reminder you need?"

When Saala returned his gaze to the bouncers, Mert swallowed hard and gripped his cudgel with both hands. He was a tough, hard man. He had been in his share of scuffles with equally hard men, but he had never encountered someone who stood so coolly and completely devoid of fear after being threatened by him and Mord. And this man wasn't even armed. Mert glanced at Mord and saw him nervously licking his lips as he surveyed the wreckage.

Mert was saved from responding when Rhys drunkenly stumbled into the center of the men. "Well, there you two are! What the hell have you been up to? I was halfway asleep 'fore I realized you weren't there and thought you'd gone off to have another pint without me!"

The two bouncers took a step back in silent, unspoken retreat.

Rhys barreled on, "Ben, how long have you been lying there? Passed out drunk, huh? You better not be thinking you're sleeping in the same bed as me if you're smelling like the damn barroom floor."

Rhys kicked away a few shattered pieces of a chair and hauled Ben to his feet. "Let's get you off there 'fore I decide I'm gonna throw you in that river out back. Serve you right, not being able to hold your liquor and all." Rhys gave Ben a sly wink before clapping him on the back and pulling him toward the hallway where they were staying. Ben saw the girls had clustered around Meghan and were pulling her down the hallway already. "Ah, don't feel too bad. Believe me, I've fallen asleep in worse places."

Rhys droned on as he guided Ben to follow the girls down the hall. Saala haughtily eyed the room one last time before following. The crowd stood, surveying the damage and watching Mord and Mert in disbelief. Murdoch ran a relatively peaceful place, as far as roadside taverns go, but the place had its share of action. No one had seen the two bouncers cowed by anything less than near open warfare—and even then they only paused to bring backup.

≈

THE NEXT MORNING, Ben winced at a sharp twinge in his side as he spooned down a warm bowl of oatmeal. He was fortunate that despite the hearty beating he'd taken, he hadn't suffered any incapacitating injuries or broken bones. The bumps and bruises would make for a few unpleasant days on the road, but he'd suffered as bad sparring with the quarterstaff.

Meghan got the worst of it. She'd kept a straight enough head to run for help as soon as she was free, but despite her lack of physical injuries, she had been deeply shocked by the sudden brutality of the world outside of Farview. At home, no one would dare lay an unwanted hand on a woman. Out in the world, even a crowded common room was unsafe.

During breakfast, Meghan kept silent while Amelie and Meredith hovered over Ben, inquiring about how he felt and complimenting him on his bravery. Privately, he knew bravery played no part. He'd reacted on instinct without considering the consequences. If Saala had not arrived when he did, Ben would have been left in much worse shape. He'd profusely thanked Saala last night, but the blademaster took the entire incident in stride and seemed more concerned about Ben's injuries than the ugly violence he'd visited on the merchant's guards.

Lady Towaal had barely spoken the night before. She'd been in the common room when the fight ended, but made no move to intervene. Ben wasn't sure if that was because she arrived too late or if she had other reasons. She professionally checked Ben's injuries before instructing Saala and Rhys to have him ready for travel in the morning. She wasn't at breakfast, but the girls said she was up and out of the room before they'd woken.

Ben gulped down the last few bites of oatmeal when he saw her striding in the door and across the room. Without preamble she barked, "Everyone ready?" When the group nodded in assent, she continued, "Good. We're wasting daylight. I inquired about supplies with the quartermaster and bought enough rations for a few days. Rhys, he's holding it for you to pick up. I also got this." She held up a plain sword and scabbard hanging from a worn leather belt and tossed it on the table in front of Ben. "If you're going to be travelling with us, you'll need to learn to defend yourself. Saala or Rhys can instruct you."

Ben stared in disbelief. He never thought he would need to own a sword. Being trained to use it by a blademaster was something that wasn't attainable even in his dreams. He ran his hand across the smooth wooden hilt and steel cross-guard. He marveled at the weight when he lifted it. He slid the blade a hand's length out of the scabbard and tested the edge with a finger.

Rhys snorted in mirth. "You ought to be able to teach him not to cut himself by the time we get to Fabrizo, right Saala? First things first, why don't you show him how to belt the thing on."

Saala solemnly replied, "I'm not sure I'm much of a teacher, but I will try."

DESPITE BEN'S ENTHUSIASM, the lessons progressed slowly. Each night on the way to Fabrizo, they would take two or three bells for sword practice. The first lesson was grim foreshadowing of how stern a teacher Saala could be. He was an absolute perfectionist when it came to the sword, and Ben soon realized his imagination of dramatic sword fights had little to do with reality.

Ben's daydreams involved him swinging across decks of sinking ships, fending off pirates in overlong contests of stamina and cunning before defeating an evil character with a masterful stroke. But according to Saala, a sword fight rarely lasted more than several heartbeats, and if it did, it was generally due to rank clumsiness of the combatants. When Ben pressed, Saala admitted it was possible that in the rare contest where there were two skilled, equally matched swordsmen, it could possibly take a little longer. But he was firm in stating that this was no concern of Ben's since any skilled swordsman would dispatch him with ease. And Saala made sure to provide numerous object lessons to drive the point home.

~

THE ROAD to Fabrizo would take them several weeks to travel. It was sparsely populated with little towns the size of Farview or smaller along with the occasional hostel. They frequently stopped at these places for fresh supplies, but Lady Towaal usually pushed them to keep moving. They spent most nights on the road. Aside from her constant concern about speed of travel, she claimed most of the small town inns were filled with vermin and that she'd rather spend the night in the open than any of the frequently ramshackle places they passed.

Ben was happy to spend the nights in the open. He was used to going on overnight hunting trips with Serrot in the mountains around Farview. The early spring weather was cool but comfortable. Bedding down in the open also provided him plenty of time for sword practice with Saala and thankfully fewer witnesses. The ones he was traveling with were plenty.

His first lesson in using the sword came on the first night out of Murdoch's. They made camp a good stone's throw off of the road on a small hill. It was clear of the pine forest that filled most of the flat space in the area and had good visibility up and down the road. This section of the Callach Road was well travelled and this close to Murdoch's there was little concern for bandits, but it didn't hurt to be prepared.

As soon as they dropped their gear, Rhys built a small cook fire, Amelie and Meredith started preparing dinner, and they all watched Ben and Saala practice.

"Tonight we will work on two things. First, the most basic aspect of swordsmanship. Second, the most fundamental." Saala pulled a long branch out of Rhys' pile of firewood and walked over to where Ben was standing. "Hold your sword up and defend yourself."

Ben raised his sword with both hands. Before he could react, Saala flicked the branch against Ben's blade and sent it spinning out of his grasp. "Your grip is too loose. Try again."

This time, Ben gripped hard on the wood pommel of his sword and was ready for Saala's blow. Again, the blade flew from his hand as soon as there was impact. Because he was gripping so hard, he felt the shock run up both his arms.

"Too hard. A steel blade against yours, and your entire body would have been ringing. In between those two is correct. Try again."

A third time Saala brought his branch against Ben's sword. Even prepared as he was, Ben barely managed to hold onto his blade. He grimaced as he heard the girls laughing over by the fire. He wasn't sure what he expected, but so far, sword play was not as dashing as he hoped.

"Better," remarked Saala. "Not good, but better."

Saala spent the next two bells positioning Ben's fingers on the pommel and showing him various grips for different strokes. Primarily the difference was one-handed or two-handed, but there were nuanced differences between how to hold the blade for a backhand stroke or a forehand one. During this time, every few strokes, Saala would step back and swipe at Ben's blade, sometimes as a surprise, sometimes with warning. Ben only held on about half the time and Saala stopped commenting on the results. Before long, the tree branch was covered in chips and scars where Ben had managed to meet it with some force.

As the hand grips changed for different strokes, so did the footing. Saala would kick Ben's feet until they were in the proper position. Sideways with one-handed grip, strong hand forward, sideways with two-handed grip off hand forward, centered with two-handed grip, neutral position, and on and on.

Saala explained, "Holding onto the sword is a basic need of course. Having the right footing is fundamental. Without the right footing, nothing else I can teach you will matter."

After two bells, Ben's arms were aching with the effort of keeping his sword point up. His hands were blistered and would have been bleeding if Saala had not wrapped rags around them. He was barely keeping his grip one out of five times.

Saala scolded, "You are getting worse. That is enough for tonight. We will continue again tomorrow night and every night until you are sufficient."

It had an ominous ring to Ben's ears. They sat down with the group and dished out the last of the rice, beans, and sausage the girls had cooked. It had been a fairly easy day of travel, mostly downhill with only a few rolling hills to deal with. The next day would be the same.

Ben was battered and bruised from the fight the night before and the sword practice with Saala, but he was in high spirits. He felt like he was on the cusp of something amazing, camping out on the open road in good weather, with good company and the promise of adventure. He couldn't think of anything he'd rather be doing.

Lady Towaal and Meghan were the only ones who didn't seem to be in a good mood and had both retired to their bedrolls early. Lady Towaal had her perpetual frown. Meghan was still upset and quiet about the events the night before. Rhys produced a small silver flask and stretched out with his head on his pack, quietly staring up at the sky. Swaying pine trees framed a clear, starry night.

Ben was left around the fire with Amelie, Meredith, and Saala. Since Lady Towaal was not paying attention, now was his chance to find out what this strange group was doing together.

In between bites of dinner, Ben casually asked, "So, Amelie, what is your part in this journey?"

She looked at Saala, who just shrugged, before answering, "I'm going to the City also. Like Meghan, I will become an Initiate at the Sanctuary."

"Oh, I am so sorry! Were you forced to go too?" asked Ben.

"No, I, well, no... I am not being forced." She hesitated then finished, "It's complicated."

Obviously there was more to it than she was letting on, but Ben didn't want to spoil the opportunity to talk, so he didn't press. He turned to Meredith and asked her, "Meredith, are you also joining the Sanctuary?"

She blushed and replied, "No, I am only accompanying La...I mean Amelie."

Ben smiled and nodded. He caught her slip, but again, played it slow and didn't comment. At least one of them really was a lady. Was Meredith also a lady or some sort of assistant? He scooped another spoonful of rice and beans and thought that everyone's role was starting to come together. A lady would have bodyguards, even if she was travelling with a mage.

Amelie spoke up to take the attention off of her handmaiden, or whatever she was. "What have you heard about the City, Ben?"

"Not much really," he answered. "Just what the stories tell. No one from Farview has ever travelled that far, and the merchants that come our way mostly trade in this area. I'm sure what I know is more fantasy than reality."

"The City is a place of fantasy. I have never been there myself, but I have spoken with people who have." She snuck a look at the back of Lady Towaal, who was lying a good distance from the fire and wrapped tightly in her bedroll in the cool night air. "The Sanctuary is there, of course, and it's a major commercial and political center. The City is where kings meet. At least, that's what they say. The markets there are said to be full of exotic items from places you've never even heard of. My mother has a device from there that she places in the bath and within moments the water is as hot as if the maids just brought it in."

Ben blinked. Nothing like that had even been mentioned in the stories. The idea that someone would use magic for something so—practical—was a little disconcerting.

Amelie sighed and continued, "Not that I will be likely to see any of the markets. As an initiate, you spend most of your time studying."

Ben stuck another thick branch in the dwindling fire and asked, "How, I mean, what happens at the Sanctuary?"

"They train us to be mages. In exchange for payment or more often service to the Sanctuary, they will teach us what they know." Amelie grinned at Ben. "It's not as exciting as you think. Real magic is nothing like the stories. There are no rain storms called out of a clear blue sky, no speaking with animals, and I'm told there is definitely no flying."

"No flying? Then it hardly seems worth it!" exclaimed Ben with a grin.

Amelie chuckled and Ben watched tension drain out of her body. He hadn't noticed it before. Despite her brave face, she was scared of what was coming. He didn't know if it was the training itself or the mysterious circumstances she was in, but Amelie was definitely dreading something that was to come.

They turned the conversation to lighter topics and started to wind down for the night. Ben was burning to know more about the City, but they had a long way to travel, and his thoughts skipped toward the other places of story he would see. They would be in Fabrizo in two more weeks, and that was a place some residents of Farview had actually been to. It was still exotic for Ben though, and it seemed more real.

THE NEXT TWO weeks continued like that. They slowly came down from the mountainous terrain near Farview and Murdoch's into rolling hills and flat coastal plains. The weather got warmer, but stayed pleasant. For Ben, it was some of the best days of his life.

The journey was along a broad well-travelled road and was mostly downhill. At the end of each day they would make a quick camp. Ben and Saala would work on sword practice and the girls would cluster around Lady Towaal with their heads together. Rhys turned out to be a capable hunter and would leave to scout the area, collect firewood and return with rabbits, birds or something else to supplement the dry goods they'd brought with them.

Saala never commented on it, but Ben could feel himself improving with the sword. His arms were getting stronger and he rarely lost his blade when Saala struck it. He could not move with anything close to the grace that Saala had, but he was more comfortable with the blade and had progressed to learning defensive forms. The girls no longer laughed at his clumsiness. That was most important.

Without pressing them, Ben slowly drew more information from his companions during the quiet nights around the campfire. It turned out they all had some mystery though.

Rhys was always friendly and willing to talk, but when Ben probed for more detail on something, Rhys kept on in a rambling, distracted way that eventually led away from the answer and into another topic. Ben found out that Rhys wasn't in the employ of Amelie like he initially suspected, the man had come with Lady Towaal. He was a resident of the City and the only thing he liked to talk about were the alehouses, of which he had encyclopedic knowledge. Before the two weeks on the road was up, Ben felt like he knew more about the City's drinking establishments than he did about the Buckhorn Tavern in Farview.

Ben liked Rhys, and he was a great travelling companion because of his endless entertaining drinking stories, but Ben felt there was more underneath the surface. Rhys was the only one who ignored Lady Towaal's pointed suggestions and glares, despite the fact that he apparently worked for her. He also carried what looked like a well-used long sword and two wicked long knives, but never participated in Saala and Ben's sword practice.

Amelie was the next most talkative in the group, but she also kept her secrets. The difference was that on the second day, she flat out told Ben she didn't want to talk about her family. He respected her intentions, but over time, he was able to draw out small details and paint a picture in his mind. She was from the city of Issen, and Ben got the impression she was somehow related to the lord of that city. She was going to the Sanctuary at the behest of her father. Lady Towaal had arrived in Issen with Rhys in tow to take her. Amelie's father sent Saala along to keep her safe until she was officially enrolled as an initiate.

Meredith kept silent and seemed to struggle with her role in the group. Over the two weeks, it became clear she was Amelie's handmaiden, but Amelie admonished her to not act like it while they were travelling so they wouldn't raise suspicion. Meredith wasn't going to study at the Sanctuary, so she didn't need to listen to Lady Towaal's lectures each night, but she listened many times anyway. The other nights she would assist Rhys with the camp and the cooking. Unlike Amelie and the others, she had a little chip on her shoulder when it came to Ben and Meghan. She was from a big city and lived in a palace with lords and ladies. She made it clear she considered Ben and Meghan country bumpkins.

Lady Towaal herself had very little to say to Ben. To her, this trip was business and she had no interest in making friends, particularly with a boy from a small town in the mountains. She wasn't rude, just direct. Aside from the lessons with the girls she rarely spoke at length to anyone, she just made imperious directives to the group as a whole. She'd glare around the fire and bark out something like, "We leave at first light." Ben found it was easy to follow her commands and pretend she wasn't there the rest of the time.

Saala and Meghan were the only two that didn't seem to have secrets. Ben would walk with Meghan while they were on the road, but the two of them rarely spoke. Farview was too recent to reminisce about and neither of them knew what to expect in the future. They both enjoyed the comfort of a familiar face though. Both of their lives had been turned upside down.

Saala's natural state was silence, but he readily answered questions when Ben had them. Ben quickly found out that he didn't know what to ask. Saala said he spent most of his time travelling and he didn't keep a permanent home. The concept was foreign to Ben. He found the idea of hitting the road and moving toward a new horizon each day to be invigorating.

The most interesting piece of information Ben got from Saala was how he became a blademaster. A large part of Ben was still that boy who sat on the edge of his chair in the Buckhorn Tavern picking apart every word of a story about blademasters and their adventures. The opportunity to get the real details from an actual blademaster was a thrill he wouldn't have believed possible.

Saala said he was from a wealthy family in the country of Ooswam. Ben was afraid to admit to Saala he had never heard of Ooswam. Saala caught on and explained it wasn't part of Alcott—the continent they were on—it was far south of Fabrizo and Farview, past the Blood Bay and the South Sea. Ben kept to himself that he didn't know enough geography to know what that meant either.

Saala explained that when he was young, his parents sent him to a boarding school where the sword was one of the subjects. In Ooswam high society, poetry, painting, music, and swordplay were all pastimes of the wealthy. It was expected that young members of society would become adept at all of these skills. Saala admitted he had little to no skill in poetry or music, but he had surpassed all of his peers with the sword. Ben gathered there had been some sort of falling out between Saala and his family and he left Ooswam to travel the world and learn the sword from masters anywhere he could find them.

The actual process to become a blademaster, it turned out, was quite simple. One just had to defeat a current blademaster in front of reputable witnesses. Once you defeated a blademaster, you had the right to wear a blademaster's sigil on your weapon and scabbard.

"Wait. What's to prevent anyone from putting a blademaster's sigil on their blade or buying a blade with one on it? How would anyone know?" asked Ben.

"Remember," Saala explained, "to become a blademaster, you must challenge and defeat one. Most of these challenges take place in the colleges with referees and medical personnel standing by. The contest only goes until one combatant yields, but it is not required to be like that. A challenge can happen anywhere at any time. Without the necessary skill, one is not likely to survive long wearing the sigil in public."

THE CLOSER THEY got to the coast, the more frequently they passed through small towns. Most were close to the size of Farview and each seemed to have its own commercial specialty. Rhys explained that the towns supplied merchants in Fabrizo with goods that they shipped across the Blood Bay to other large cities. There was one town that specialized in lace and several that made various types of glass. The glass is what Fabrizo was known for. According to Rhys, the glass makers they were passing were among the best in the world.

They had little time to stop and explore these towns because Lady Towaal pushed them hard to make Fabrizo. She did allow a few stops to eat as their supplies were dwindling. Ben found Rhys had been correct when he said back at Murdoch's that it was mostly fish and wine on the coast. But for Ben, it was an incredible experience. They ate spicy fish stews unlike anything he ever had in Farview. Alistair Pinewood maintained a wine cellar, but he was one of the only ones in Farview who did so. He mostly kept it for himself except for the rare special occasion when he felt like sharing. Usually, it was on his own birthday.

Ben began to think of himself as somewhat worldly, travelling with such experienced companions and trying new things, but the small towns clustered near the coast did nothing to prepare him for the wonder of Fabrizo itself.

They awoke the last morning on the road camped on sandy soil under massive moss-hung oak trees. The air was heavy and had an odd tang to it. In a rare friendly moment, Lady Towaal mentioned it was the humidity and a combination of mud and saltwater in the Bay. They'd be in Fabrizo by early afternoon, and Ben couldn't wait.

As the day wore on and they approached the city, the oak trees faded away and were replaced by tall, thick marsh grasses. The road was busy with merchant trains coming and going from the city as well as travelers like themselves. Ben observed them closely but was disappointed to see that aside from small changes in their clothing, these people could have grown up in Farview and would not have been out of place.

The little towns almost ran together as they got closer. They passed through several of them in the last few bells before finally finding something new. In the distance, over the tall grasses, Ben could see large buildings rising up. He hopped up and down trying to catch a better glimpse, but stopped when he saw Amelie grinning at him.

Rhys noticed as well. "They're warehouses, grain silos, and the like. The merchants store their goods there. It's too expensive in the city. There's also housing for the dock workers, sailors, and the rest of the grunts." Rhys slapped him on the back and continued, "That's where I'd recommend you spend your time in most big cities. Those people know how to have fun, but I think you're going to enjoy Fabrizo. Nothing quite like it."

4

FABRIZO

Ben tried to stop himself from staring as they passed the hustle and bustle of the warehouse district. Most of the wagon trains turned off to head toward the massive cluster of buildings. The huge structures dwarfed anything Ben had ever seen. Murdoch's could easily fit several times over into the largest ones. There were also towering poles bobbing in the distance and Ben realized that they must be ships. Farview had only a few small boats people used for fishing and carrying supplies on the Callach River. He knew about ships, but he couldn't fathom the size of one that stuck out above the tallest of the warehouses.

He was brought back by the clatter of wheels on stone as the road turned from hard packed sand to large stone blocks. The merchant trains had turned off toward the warehouses but smaller wagons and carts joined the flow on the road. The merchant trading must take place in the warehouse district, he thought, but a city still needed goods and supplies. He noticed many of the small carts were carrying food and other things he suspected they couldn't make in a city.

Half a league past the warehouse district he was still craning his neck to see over the marsh grasses and catch a glimpse of the city itself. There were slender towers in the distance but he couldn't see anything the size of the warehouses.

He was focusing so much on looking toward the towers that he was surprised when they came to the causeway. It was flanked by two sturdy stone buildings and a company of bored-looking guards.

He turned toward Rhys. "Shouldn't there be city gates or something? There are always gates in the stories. And where *is* the city?"

Rhys adjusted his pack strap and answered, "We've got another half a league on the causeway. Why bother with gates when you have a natural moat? The city itself is on a hundred little islands out in the Bay. Makes it hard to attack. Probably the only reason it's still an independent city state and not a part of the Alliance."

Ben wasn't sure what the Alliance was, but he did remember hearing stories about Fabrizo being an island city. He thought it was some sort of exaggeration or that there were islands nearby. He didn't realize the entire city was literally a bunch of little islands.

The guards at the foot of the causeway barely looked up when they walked by. The foot traffic going over was steady and Ben supposed his group didn't look like much of a threat. They made their way onto the stone path and started toward the city. The road was worn deep with ruts from the wagon wheels that constantly passed this way. Ben could see they had dumped sand to fill the ruts in the road which must have been easier than replacing half a league of stone.

From the causeway, some buildings were finally visible. There were a few towers poking up but the rest of the buildings were only a few stories high.

They passed from the tall marshy grasses into open water that gently lapped against the pilings of the causeway. Once in the open, the city spread out before them. It was made up of many islands all connected by arcing bridges. In between the islands, Ben saw small boats darting about and outside the cluster of buildings there were larger barges.

The sight was like nothing he had imagined. He'd pictured towering city walls and soaring buildings all guarded by imposing gates. While there were no walls and no gates, he could see why Rhys said it would be hard to attack. An attacker would need to assault each island individually, then cross a narrow bridge to get to the next one. It would be an ugly mess. If the defenders were determined, nearly impossible.

At the end of the road, the causeway spilled into a large square that was surrounded by market stalls and paths leading off into the rest of the city. The square was dominated by a towering obelisk in the center and a sprawling palace opposite the causeway.

Ben gawked at the menagerie of people, animals, and goods in the square. Lady Towaal bore through the center of the chaos like it wasn't there. He scrambled to follow behind her. They turned down a side street, crossed several bridges and passed through narrow alleys before entering what Ben took to be an inn. But it was unlike any inn he had seen before. There was no loud music, no raucous drinking, and no gambling, just a handful of people sitting quietly around tables in hushed conversation.

The innkeeper bustled up to Lady Towaal and bowed over her proffered hand. "So glad to have you back." He eyed the group. "Three rooms this evening? Baths? Dinner? How many nights will you be with us?"

"Yes, yes, all of that, Master Cranston. We'll likely be here a few days," Towaal calmly answered the innkeeper.

"Sauza!" he barked, "Show the ladies to two front rooms and have Zin prepare the baths. This way, sirs, this way."

Rhys shared a grin with Ben and they followed the efficient seeming Cranston up the stairs toward the street side of the building. A girl appeared and took the girls deeper into the inn.

Ben realized the 'front' of the building must actually be on the water.

The place exuded a sense of age and wealth. The walls were painted a deep crimson that matched the colors the staff was wearing. The steps were well made but worn. There was a rich paneling of some type of wood framing the crimson walls. Ben did not recognize the wood, but he could tell at a glance the candles ensconced along the hallway were expensive. They gave off a pleasant scent of oil and sandalwood. He was thankful he could share a room with the other men and that Towaal hadn't asked him to contribute. He wasn't sure if his coin would get him more than a night or two in this place.

The room itself was snug but comfortable looking. They barely had time to set down their gear before Cranston disappeared and returned to take them to the baths. He dropped them off and vanished again. In the bathing room, there was a series of large copper tubs. Three of them were filled to the brim with steaming hot water.

Rhys was first to strip down and gave a big sigh as he lowered himself in. "There are at least a few things they do right in Fabrizo. Enjoy it, boys. We've still got a ways to go, and it's not all going to be as nice as this."

Saala paused to collect a towel and bar of soap off a rack at the side of the room and plunged into his own tub, dunking his head under the water and coming up grinning. Beads of water rolled off his shaved scalp.

Ben noticed a complicated system of pipes and valves leading from the tubs to a tank and stove in the corner then back into the wall. He'd never heard of anything like this, but decided they must somehow heat the water with the stove and pump it into the baths. He was walking over to investigate, and was considering the possibilities to adapting this system to brew beer when Saala splashed and sent a sheet of water his direction. "Rhys is right, get in."

~

RHYS QUICKLY CALLED for chilled wine and the men emptied a pitcher before they finished bathing. Over the billowing steam from the baths, they discussed the next stages of the journey.

From Fabrizo, they would book passage on a ship to travel across the Blood Bay to the city of Whitehall. Saala thought it might take a few days to find passage as tensions were rising between the two cities.

King Argren of Whitehall was raising pressure on the leaders of Fabrizo to join his Alliance of Nations. Publicly, King Argren said it was to counterbalance the power of the Coalition that had formed in the east, but Saala explained rumors were flying that it was merely a naked power grab by the king. Fabrizo, unlike the other powerful cities along the Blood Bay, was ruled by the Merchants' Guild. Because their power base was commercial instead of political, they saw no reason to join The Alliance.

"And why would they bow to Argren? He's got the armies, but they've got the money," snorted Rhys. "They'd be fools to join him."

Saala gave Rhys a meaningful look. "Some of our party may not feel that way."

"Oh, I know what she's about," replied Rhys. "There's a reason they sent Towaal all the way out to get her. It's a dangerous game her father's playing."

"I don't think her father's the only one playing games," murmured Saala.

Rhys chuckled and sunk lower into his bath. "You may be right there. I say we leave them to their games. I'm for gold, girls, and grog." He sloshed his wine mug up in a mock toast. "Here's to doing our jobs and keeping it simple."

Saala raised his mug in response and replied, "If you say so."

Ben remained silent throughout the exchange, hoping they'd continue to ignore him and say more. He was realizing that there was more to this trip than simply travelling to the City. He'd wondered why Amelie wasn't travelling with a large entourage or acknowledging Meredith as her handmaiden. If she was on some sort of mission on behalf of her father, then maybe secrecy was paramount.

Before dinner, Ben pulled Meghan aside and told her what he'd heard. She had similar suspicions, but neither of them had much real information.

"Let's keep it between us," he said. "I like all of them, but we don't know them, and we don't know if we can trust them."

Meghan nodded in agreement. "We're part of this group now whether we like it or not, but no reason we can't look out for ourselves."

DESPITE THE SERIOUS thoughts and concerns, Ben couldn't help but enjoy dinner. It was an experience unlike any he'd had before. His first shock when they sat down in the common room was the silverware laid out on the table. He picked up a heavy fork and, with a start, saw it was made of actual silver. The idea that someone would make something so utilitarian as a fork out of currency was crazy. It was an over-the-top display of wealth that was beyond even the Pinewoods in Farview.

The rest of the meal was just as bizarre. It was a series of small plates that just kept coming. The first dish was a simple pasta and tomato sauce, but that was the last thing Ben recognized. There were vegetables floating in alternating sweet and spicy sauces, tiny meat filled pastries, steamed beans that curled strangely when poured out of a heated pot, thin wafers he thought might be bread that seemed to melt on his tongue, baked fish, grilled fish, lightly fried fish, and even pieces of raw fish.

A whirlwind of staff floated in and out of the room in an intricate dance, collecting the prior course and dispersing new dishes. The thread of conversation from earlier in the day had completely fallen off and everyone focused on the meal. The vast array of dishes, flavors, and textures meant there was little room for anything else.

Ben was seated next to Amelie who did her best to show him the proper way to eat each dish and explain where it was from. The fashion in Fabrizo was to bring in foods from a variety of cultures. The art was in creating complementary pairings and menus. As the meal went on, Ben started to notice not just how the flavors interacted with each other, but how the texture and color of each dish was a play on the previous one.

By the time it was over, several bells after it started, it was late evening. Ben felt like he was stuffed to the point of exploding. The entire group was worn out from the trip. The rich meal, coupled with being clean for the first time in two weeks, meant an early night for all of them.

THE NEXT MORNING, Ben slept in and woke to find Saala and Rhys already out of the room. He headed down to the common area and found Lady Towaal and the girls sitting over a light breakfast.

In her usual brusque tone, Towaal said, "The men left to find a ship and arrange passage. The girls and I will take advantage of the day off and begin talking about their studies in earnest. You are on your own for the day but return here by nightfall and be ready to depart at a moment's notice."

Amelie chimed in, "You should check out the Fish and Stranger's Markets. Also, we need some ribbon for our hair. I'll want to tie it up on the ship. If you see something, could you pick it up for me?" She slid a few coins across the table. "Use it for the ribbon and you can spend the rest on something you need."

Ben scooped up the coins and was surprised to see three

thick silver marks. Unless the price of ribbon was very different in Fabrizo, it was far more than he would need. From Amelie's grin, he realized she knew that as well and probably knew he had very little of his own coin to spend. He bowed his thanks and caught Meghan's eye. She looked more than a little jealous.

He winked at her and exclaimed, "Enjoy your studies, girls!"

THE PROSPECT of spending the entire day exploring a city like Fabrizo couldn't wait, so he dashed up to his room to gather his coin purse and sword then swept out of the inn without stopping for breakfast.

The night before, he had been overwhelmed with everything he saw. He had barely registered the street outside. In the early morning sunlight, he found that it was filled with wall-to-wall buildings painted in a rainbow of different pastels. Many of the buildings were accented with extensive, bright tile work. They were all about three or four stories. The first levels were packed with a wide variety of shops. There were narrow staircases in between many of the shops. He surmised they must lead to the upper levels where people lived.

The streets were teeming with early morning traffic. He saw people running the same types of errands they would do in Farview that time of day. There were women carrying wicker baskets filled with produce, workmen pushing wheeled carts, and proprietors outside the shops calling out their wares. Most of them were dressed in the style of Fabrizo, loose trousers and billowing shirts. It must have been more comfortable in the heat and humidity. There were a few people on the street who were foreigners like him, but none seemed too out of place.

He was tempted to stop in some of the more interesting-looking shops along the street, but he was more excited to explore the city itself. He picked a direction he thought was the opposite of how they came in and started off.

At the end of the street, he found a stone bridge spanning a broad canal. He paused at the top of the bridge and saw the waterways were just as busy as the streets. There were several small boats darting about and a few barges. All of the buildings had pilings or docks on the water where the boats could tie up. Right by the bridge, there was a trio of workmen unloading heavy-looking sacks from one of the barges into a shop that must have been a bakery, judging by the delicious smell, though it was almost overpowered from the scent of saltwater, fish, and refuse.

Seabirds flew overhead, their calls competing with the shouts from the workmen. Underlying it all was the constant lap of water as waves splashed against the buildings. Ben was intoxicated by the mix of sights, sounds, and scents that washed over him.

He spent several long moments paused on the bridge overlooking the water then kept on deeper into the city. The place was a confusing maze of canals, bridges, and streets. Some were broad enough for three or four wagons to pass abreast, and some were so narrow he had to turn sideways to pass through. He was lost within moments but he thought he remembered the way to the inn from the large palace the night before, so he wasn't worried.

He found there was some sense of organization in that several of the streets seemed to have their own specialties. There was one street filled with gem cutters, several with different types of blown glass, and other streets for tailors, herbalists, cobblers, furniture makers, and so on. One street that made him pause was the armorers.

Suits of chain mail, scale mail, helmets, greaves, maces, axes, spears, knives, and more types of swords than he ever imagined were displayed all along the street. Each shop opened up with more goods inside. Ben slowed his walk and his eyes greedily lingered over some of the finer-looking weaponry, but he knew there was nothing along there he'd be able to afford.

In his dreams he often imagined himself heavily armed and armored, confronting a demon or some mythical beast, but the stunning array of equipment went beyond his imagination. The variety of swords alone was beyond counting and there were other edged weapons he couldn't figure how one would even use.

He eventually moved on after receiving some pointed stares from the shopkeepers. He wasn't familiar with the customs in this place and didn't want to cause trouble, though theft couldn't have been common—at least not on that street.

The smell was the first thing that let him know he was near the Fish Market. The entire city had a distinct scent of salt and fish, but the odor became much more powerful near the market. He noticed that the buildings were a little rougher, which made sense because who could stand to live near that. The paint was peeling or chipping on many storefronts and the cobblestones weren't as even as he'd seen in more prosperous areas.

On the outskirts of the market, there were several shirtless, intimidating looking men who at first he took to be thugs. They were lounging around in small groups paying little attention to passersby. He caught a few of them eyeing him as he walked. He adjusted his belt and felt the reassuring weight of his sword on one hip and his hunting knife on the other.

It wasn't until he saw a pair of them hurrying by with a wheelbarrow filled with fish that he realized they must all be porters for the shopkeepers and fish buyers. The fish wouldn't last long in the heat of the day. It made sense it had to be moved quickly. Once he caught on, he saw there was a steady stream of barrows being pushed in from the docks and an equal stream leaving the market.

The market itself was bewildering. He expected to see a variety of fish that were new to him, but there were creatures here he couldn't even describe. He stopped to stare at one stall filled with cases of wiggling masses and heard the keeper bellow, "Urchins, live urchins! Get 'em while they're fresh. Caught this morning just off the Horn. Live urchins! Come on, lad, you buying or what? You keep blocking the traffic and you better be buying. Fresh live urchins!"

Ben hurried on. He wasn't sure what an urchin was, but it certainly didn't look like something he wanted to eat.

He'd been exploring the market about half a bell when he heard a familiar voice and turned to see Master Cranston haggling with a shopkeeper over a pile of long, shiny-scaled fish. Cranston's helper Zin was in tow, carting a wheelbarrow half-filled with sea creatures. Ben spent a few heartbeats trying to guess which ones he'd eaten the night before. Most of what was in the barrow didn't resemble anything he remembered eating—or would want to eat again.

He shouted out, "Master Cranston!"

The innkeeper turned with a scowl on his face before he recognized Ben, then instantly adopted a beaming smile.

"Yes, yes, you're the boy who came with Lady Towaal, right? How are you enjoying our city? First time is it?" He barreled on before Ben could think of a reply, "The Lady Towaal, did she send you out for something? Anything I can be of service with?"

"Uh, no, sir. Just out seeing the city," responded Ben.

"Excellent, you've come to the right place. Fabrizo has the best Fish Market anywhere on the Blood Bay. Best anywhere in the world, some say, and I don't know enough to disagree with them. Come along with me."

Cranston bounced around the market like he owned the place, Ben and the overworked Zin pulled along in his wake. From the reactions of the shopkeepers, Ben saw Cranston was one of their best customers. He seemed most interested in odd choices, he kept repeating rare and was obsessed with freshness. His thoroughness was assuring to Ben, who figured he'd be dining on many of these selections later that evening.

The innkeeper maintained a constant stream of questions and comments, only pausing to closely inspect a particular fish or quickly turn and do a count of what he'd already purchased. He questioned Ben closely on Lady Towaal's needs, which Ben wasn't sure he was qualified to answer, but from the questioning, he realized Towaal must be something of a regular and occasionally passed through with small groups of young people. He decided her job with the Sanctuary was some type of recruiter for new Initiates.

Cranston also paused at several stalls and picked out samples for Ben to try. It wasn't until then that he remembered he'd skipped breakfast that morning so he hungrily snapped up what was offered. Cranston himself frequently spit out the samples, "These damn fish mongers don't even know how to cook their own goods. Phef!" He glared at one poor shopkeeper. "You fried this! A fish this delicate should be sautéed with butter."

Ben thought the samples were pretty good, straightforward and simple, but a gourmand like Cranston must be used to classier fare.

Before long, Cranston was done in the market and said he was heading across town for other supplies. He sent Zin back to the inn with stern instructions on what to tell the cook.

"Master Cranston," Ben asked, "which way is the Stranger's Market?"

"Ah, yes, for a boy like you with a head full of adventure, that is the place to go. Watch your purse, lad, and watch out for the women. Wouldn't do, Lady Towaal catching you talking to the wrong types."

Cranston quickly spouted out directions that somehow made perfect sense. Three bridges, left at the little fountain in the plaza, down the spice sellers alley, and over the yellow bridge. There were no street names in Fabrizo so simple directions worked best.

~

THE STRANGER'S Market was nothing like the rest of the city. It was situated on its own island and looked to be the largest one in the group. Unlike the other islands, this one had no permanent structures. Instead, it was packed from bridge to bridge with a confusing mix of temporary structures. There were narrow walkways weaving in between tightly packed canvass stalls, a hodge podge of tents grouped together in uneven clumps, open spaces covered in carpets and goods, massive tents nearly as large as the commons in Farview, and shops set up in the backs of handcarts.

A wave of odd sounds washed up from the market. Exotic animals, strange music, and vendors cries in a variety of accents and languages all blended together into the cacophony of commerce.

The goods for sale were just as disorganized and even more varied than the temporary structures. There were fabrics made of materials he had never seen before, oils and potions promising cures to any ailment, beads, glassware, jars stuffed full of bizarre items that were frequently difficult to identify, strange fruits and other food items, clothing, spices, odd mechanical devices, boxes, bags, jewelry, and unfamiliar animals.

He stumbled across a tent stuffed full of wire cages with small furry creatures in them. He was staring, trying to identify what the creatures were when the one-eyed proprietor slid up next to him. "Monkeys. You like? They do your bidding for you. You never have to work again. Five silver for untrained. Two gold for fully trained."

"Uh, no thank you," mumbled Ben in reply.

Ben quickly moved on as the man shouted after him, "Impress your friends. Impress your lady. You have a lady, right?"

Ben was in such a hurry he stumbled into a table stacked with murky glass jars and nearly sent the entire stack crashing down.

He managed to get out a hand to steady them before they fell. He recoiled in horror though when he saw what appeared to be human eyes staring back at him from within the cloudy brown liquid. This merchant made no sales pitch, just stared at him from deep within his cowled, undyed robes. Ben prayed it was his imagination that the eyes followed him as he scampered deeper into the market.

A small rack of wire and glass contraptions caught his eye and the plump, colorfully clothed merchant beamed at him as he approached. The devices were a mirrored piece of glass intricately supported above a small metal box. The merchant eyed his sword and purred, "An adventurer, yes? You have come to the right place. My farseeing devices are a must for any hunter, sailor, or soldier. Focus your will and you can see leagues in any direction."

"Really?" asked Ben. He drew closer and leaned down to look into one of the mirrors.

"Now, now," the woman shooed him back, "I only allow testing by serious buyers. Are you serious?"

"I… It sounds interesting, but I'm not sure I have the money for something like this. How does it work?"

"Focus and Will, how do you think it would work?" Her tone had quickly changed. "Move along now. I only have time for serious customers."

Ben moved on and soon found himself in a relatively open space lined with stalls of food sellers and wine merchants. He paused to soak in the strange scents of the cooking food and made a slow circle. He wasn't familiar with many of the items for sale but he at least understood food. He shuddered at the thought of the jars of eyes and decided to take a short break.

A fat, jolly-looking man called out to him from behind a grill covered in long skewers of meats and vegetables, "Ho there, boy. You look like you could use something to eat!"

Ben smiled in return and stepped up to see what the man was

selling. The skewers appeared to be similar to the ones sold by other street vendors at nearly every major intersection throughout the rest of Fabrizo. Ben commented on it.

The man replied, "Ha! Smart boy. Everyone comes to the Stranger's Market for something exotic, but what is exotic to a man from Ooswam? Not ostrich pies, my friend. Fabrizo's finest skewers are! Nice for you, too. The foreign stuff is no good around here. Don't see a lot of live ostriches in Fabrizo, do you?"

Ben was curious about some of the things he'd seen, but the man was right. Where did they get the ostrich meat around here?

He passed the man a few tin bits and got a paper wrapped skewer in exchange. He sat down on a bench in front of the stall and took a bite of the vegetables and greasy meat on the skewer. The crowd in the market was just as interesting and diverse as the wares for sale.

Even from across the bridge, he had been able to hear a deluge of strange sounds. Unknown languages, music, the water, sea birds, and the clatter of commerce. It all contributed to an aural equivalent of the dinner he had the night before. Once on the island, the people seemed to be from a hundred different races and cultures, each with their own unique style of dress. There were shaven-headed, olive-skinned people in long flowing robes that reminded him of Saala, dark heavily scarred men wearing only baggy trousers, pale raven-haired men and women who wore exclusively black leather, a lot of men who must be sailors, women in dresses finer than anything he had seen in Farview, and some women wearing hardly any clothes at all.

He admonished himself for staring but couldn't help wondering what Amelie or Meredith might look like in some of those outfits. One woman walked by in a flimsy dress that covered from her neck to her ankles. When she got close he almost choked on his skewer—he could clearly see through the light material that she had nothing on underneath. He'd seen girl's bodies before in the summer when they'd swim in the rivers around Farview, but that had been much more innocent than this.

The craziest part was that when he was caught staring, some of the women gave him an appraising look right back. The woman in the see-through dress even leaned toward him, winked and in a honeyed voice whispered, "Come find me later at the Barker's tent. Half price for you."

These were the women Cranston warned him to stay away from.

BEN FINISHED HIS SKEWER AND, feeling a bit more settled, headed back into the market. It was early afternoon and he wanted to find Amelie's ribbons then head back to the inn before it got dark. After spending the day navigating Fabrizo's winding streets and bridges, he knew he'd have much better luck finding the place in daylight.

It took him awhile, but near the edge of the Market, he finally found what he was searching for. A kind-looking shriveled old woman was selling ribbons, buttons, and sewing supplies. The woman was only asking a copper for a ribbon, so Ben bought a handful of different ones and still had two of the heavy silver coins and several copper coins left over. He had more ribbons than he could ever imagine the girls needing, but the old woman looked like she could use the business.

His errand accomplished and having seen a good portion of the city, Ben started back to the inn, feeling content. He had daydreamed his entire life about seeing big cities and having adventures, but in the back of his head, he was always nervous about the thought of leaving Farview.

Farview was familiar and it was comfortable. As it turned out, Fabrizo was different, but it wasn't intimidating or scary. Well, aside from the table full of eyes, it wasn't scary. So far, the people seemed to be friendly and helpful.

Ben lifted his head and took a deep breath of the salty air. As he moved, he heard a few small clinks. He glanced down. Around his feet, he saw the contents of his coin purse and a grubby hand scooping it up.

A boy, near Ben's age but shorter and skinnier, jumped up and slashed a knife in Ben's direction before shouting, "Don't try to follow me!"

The boy scrambled backward several steps then turned and bolted down the street.

Ben felt by his hip and realized the boy must have cut the bottom of his coin purse. "Stop, thief!"

A rough looking sailor wearing a loose knit hat and no shirt chuckled as the thief ran past him and called to Ben, "Well, aren't you going to chase him?"

With that, Ben sprang into a run. As his scabbard slapped painfully against his leg, he thought his next lesson with Saala needed to be how to run with a sword on your belt. He grabbed the hilt and tried to steady the weapon as he barreled across a connecting bridge.

Like any boy from Farview, Ben worked for his bread and he was in good shape, but the thief was quick and familiar with the winding streets. Ben found himself hurtling over low carts and dodging passersby all the while yelling for assistance. No one made a move to slow the thief down.

The thief seemed to have no problem navigating the congestion in the streets and was quickly gaining distance. The only thing keeping Ben in the race was that they were moving over more commercial islands that had broad open streets. In some of the narrow alleyways he'd passed earlier in the day, the little thief would be lost in the twists and turns in no time.

Ben knew he had to try something or Amelie's money and his life savings would soon disappear into the back alleys of

Fabrizo. He shouted, "Stop, or I'll put this crossbow bolt in your back!"

It was ridiculous—he didn't have a crossbow and the thief had surely seen that before robbing him—but it was the only gambit he had.

And it worked. The thief glanced back in disbelief, just long enough for an apple cart to roll into his path. He crashed into the cart at a full sprint. Legs kicking in the air, he flipped over the cart, causing an explosion of apples before he crashed down on the ground. The owner of the cart started yelling and kicking at him.

Ben redoubled his speed. He wanted to get there before anyone else claimed his coins.

Suddenly, right before Ben got there, the apple cart owner fell back, gripping his leg and shouting curses. The thief was up again, dashing into a nearby alley with his small blade in hand. Ben paused long enough at the mouth of the alley to make sure the boy wasn't waiting in the dark to stab him, then drew his sword and strode in.

The alley opened up to a small, empty courtyard with several closed doors, probably stairways to people's upstairs apartments. The thief was franticly trying to find one unlocked.

"Stop right there, thief," Ben demanded.

The thief spun around with his blade out. His eyes popped when he saw Ben's sword. Ben dropped into one of the more aggressive fighting stances Saala had taught him. The boy was quick with that knife, but the little training Saala had given him and the unbeatable reach advantage he had with his sword made Ben confident this fight would be a sure thing.

The thief must have felt the same way. He tossed his little knife down at Ben's feet. "Look, I'll give you your coins back. No harm, and all is forgotten."

The thief started digging into his clothing. Ben tensed, thinking he had another hidden knife, but he came out with his own coin purse tied around his neck and emptied it into his palm. "See, all here. Take it. We don't need to have a problem."

Ben had the thief pinned in the alley and thought about calling for the authorities, but considering how little help he'd gotten pursuing the thief out of the market and across several islands, he guessed that Fabrizo was a town where people handled their own business. He felt like he should do something about the thief, but he didn't know what. All of his money looked like it was held in that dirty hand.

"Drop it. Next time, I won't be so nice!"

The coins clinked onto the cobblestones. The thief edged around one side of the courtyard and Ben the other. He spared a glance to confirm all of his coins were lying there, and maybe a little extra. He quickly glanced back to the thief and watched him snatch up his knife before slowly backing out of the courtyard.

Still nervous about the thief returning, Ben laid his sword down on the cobblestones and collected his coins. He was counting them to see if they were all there when the thief appeared back at the mouth of the courtyard, this time, slowly backing into it with his hands raised. Ben quickly slipped his money into his pocket and stood with his sword raised defensively.

The thief was not paying any attention to Ben, though. He was focusing on someone coming down the alleyway after him.

"Nowhere to go this time, Renfro." The shirtless sailor with the knit cap that Ben saw earlier was advancing into the courtyard holding a long, curved knife. It was nearly the size of a short sword and was wickedly serrated along the interior curve. That knife was meant for gutting. Two bulky, menacing looking men with cudgels followed behind the sailor.

"Look, Casper, I didn't know it was protected. I swear. I'll pay it back. Whatever I need to do." Renfro, the thief, kept moving into the center of the courtyard.

Ben held his sword steady. Other than a glance from one of the hulking thugs behind Casper, he was being ignored.

"Doesn't matter, Renfro, and we both know you can't pay back an entire cargo of Ishlanese carpets. The guild's going to pay the coin, but you're gonna pay the blood price."

Renfro glanced back at Ben and pleaded, "You wanna get involved in this? They're going to kill us both! You've got a sword!"

Casper grinned and kept his eyes on Renfro, slowly waving his knife in front of him.

Ben eyed the three thugs and shuddered. All three of the men stepped confidently. From the variety of scars and crooked noses, this wasn't the first time any of them had been a scrap. He knew it'd be long odds, trying to face down seasoned brawlers, but the courtyard was big enough to provide all the room he'd need with his sword. He had the advantage of holding the more deadly weapon.

Renfro still had his hands in the air and wasn't making a move toward the small knife he had tucked in his belt. Ben figured he could count on the small thief to join the fight if it came to it. The boy seemed earnestly afraid for his life.

But Ben had no dog in this fight. The thief had victimized him moments before. If anything, he probably deserved whatever these people were going to do to him. Clearly, they knew each other well, and Renfro had violated some agreement they had.

Ben eyed Casper and asked, "I was just recovering my stolen property. You saw me chasing him. I don't have anything to do with this. Can I go?"

Casper finally spared Ben a glance. "Yeah. Get out of here." He ran his thumb along the edge of his blade to emphasize his point. "I don't need to tell you to forget this ever happened."

Ben nodded and started edging around the courtyard, just the way the thief had done earlier.

Renfro made eye contact. No words were necessary. His look told Ben that he was being left to die.

"Wait!" shouted Ben.

Ben couldn't let them kill the boy. There is right and there is wrong. Ben didn't know what should be done with the thief, but he knew leaving him to be gutted in this courtyard was wrong. And who were these men to decide? What gave them the moral authority to decide Renfro's fate? Before he knew what he was doing, Ben had decided that Renfro should face the law. Renfro would have consequences for his actions, but it would not be determined by these men.

"This man will be turned in to the city guards," declared Ben. "He will face punishment for stealing from me and whatever else he's done, but it will be by the proper authorities."

Casper snorted. "Proper authorities. And who might that be? Renfro is one of ours and he will face our justice. Leave now, and I may not remember your face."

Ben raised the point of his sword. "I am not leaving unless I take him with me."

Casper looked to his companions then back at Ben. "How do you think you will take him? There are three of us, boy. There's no reason for you to die here too."

The two massive thugs finally gave Ben their full attention. One of them started slowly spinning his club, his thick tattooed arms flexing with corded muscle. Too late, Ben realized those cudgels must be filled with lead or some other heavy element. The thug didn't have to strain to swing the thing, but it was clear it was far heavier than a simple wooden instrument. That cudgel swung by that man could easily shatter bones and leave him crippled. Suddenly, the sword didn't seem enough of an advantage.

"I don't know if I can take all of you, but I know you can't take me uninjured!" Ben dropped back into Saala's aggressive fighting stance. He hoped the thugs would see reason. He knew he couldn't win the fight, but he thought they would decide it wasn't worth it.

He was wrong.

The thug on his left, Ben's off hand, suddenly moved around the side of him. Ben turned to face the man, but before Ben could react, the second thug smashed his cudgel against Ben's blade, nearly sending it spinning across the courtyard. The only thing that allowed Ben to hold on was his weeks of practice on the road with Saala.

The man obviously expected Ben to lose the weapon and had quickly advanced after his strike. Ben swung backhanded at him and sliced flesh before the thug jumped away. A long red line spread across the big man's torn shirt.

Before Ben could feel smug for winning the first salvo, a fist the size of a small ham from the first thug smashed into the side of his head. It sent him crashing to the ground with the world spinning and lights dancing in front of his eyes.

The injured thug stepped over to him and Ben saw a steady flow of blood had already painted half of the man's chest. He placed a heavy foot on top of Ben's sword and muttered to his companion, "Bastard's got some fight in him, huh?"

Ben struggled to move his sword before his eyes rolled up into his head. He slid into blackness.

5

THE PHILOSOPHY OF THIEVES

WHEN BEN REGAINED CONSCIOUSNESS, he was lying face down on a damp stone floor. A scent like old wheat filled his nostrils. His head was pounding like it was stuck between a blacksmith's hammer and anvil. His muscles felt like they had the consistency of Edward Crust's holiday jelly.

Briefly, he was back in Farview, and struggled to remember what kind of horrible - or wonderful - night led to such a painful hangover.

But the illusion was short-lived. He elicited a groan as he rolled over to his back. The prospect of sitting was forgotten when his vision swam with streaks of color in the dark room. A wave of bile threatened to fight its way up his throat.

"Awake now?"

The slightly familiar voice brought it all back. The theft, the fight in the courtyard, and now what? He was surprised he still lived. From his back, Ben could see the walls of a dimly lit room slowly come into focus. A sturdy oak door was the only break in the stone walls. The floor was uncomfortably hard, and it was coated in a heavy layer of dust. The rest of it really didn't matter, it was a prison. That's all he needed to know. He wasn't in the mood to discuss their confinement with the person who got him there, so he remained silent.

"I want to thank you for standing up for me," continued the boy they called Renfro, undaunted by Ben's refusal to acknowledge him. "I haven't had a lot of people do that for me, so it means something. Well, it would if we weren't locked in here."

Ben succumbed to curiosity. "And where is here?"

"Basement of the Thieves' Guild. They'll hold us here until they execute us."

Ben groaned again. The details of how and why they would be killed seemed strangely unimportant. Renfro had accepted his fate and Ben was inclined to follow him. He just had another hard lesson that he was no hero in a story. Breaking out of prison, fighting off the pursuing bad guys, and saving the girl—well, thief in this case—that was the kind of thing that only happened in stories. He was learning that real life was much more painful. He couldn't summon the unassailable hope that all of the story heroes had.

Renfro fell silent. Ben suspected he was normally a very talkative fellow, but the depressing circumstances made for difficult conversation.

They sat like that for several bells, Ben staring at the rough wooden ceiling, inhaling the musty scent of the room, and hearing scratches and squeaks of what had to be rats. Over time, the throbbing in his head started to fade. The monotony of the cell crept in on him.

He wanted to turn his thoughts off, but couldn't. His mind raced through the possibilities earlier in the afternoon. Given the result, he felt he must have decided incorrectly, but he still couldn't convince himself that leaving Renfro to die would have been right. Whatever Renfro's crimes, he should face judgment from the proper authorities, not a gang of thugs.

~

EVENTUALLY, the silence in the room was broken by approaching footsteps and a key sliding noisily into the oak door.

Ben was surprised when Casper and a woman entered. The woman sat a white, linen napkin-covered tray on the floor and quickly disappeared back through the open door.

Casper nudged the tray with his boot. "Food and water. We'll keep you alive, for now. I suggest you eat it before the rats do."

Seeing Casper's boot drew Ben's attention to the rest of him. In the streets, he had been dressed like a sailor with torn pants, shirtless, and a dirty knit cap. Now, he was decked out in finery more befitting a lord's throne room than a dungeon. Casper was wearing a billowing snow white silk shirt, snug dark-colored pants, fine leather boots, and a wide silver studded belt. On one hip, he had a wire-handled rapier, and on the other a jewel-pommeled dagger. He had the look of a dashing buccaneer from Ben's imagination.

"I had to come talk to the boy who risked his life to save someone who stole from him. I can only assume you have an interesting perspective on this." Casper squatted down near Ben, unafraid in his own dungeon. "Tell me about it."

"Why should I tell you anything? Aren't you going to kill me?" muttered Ben.

"No, I will not kill you. Your fate has not been decided, but you did seriously injure my friend Balbo. It is he who will decide what is in store for you."

Renfro snorted in the corner. "He will kill you."

Casper offered a wan smile. "Yes, it is likely he will. I suppose a thoughtful man might find out if you had rich or powerful friends, forgive the injury, and attempt a ransom. Balbo is not a thoughtful man though. If I enjoyed betting, which I do, I would bet that when he recovers from his wound he will beat you to death with his bare hands."

Ben grimaced and wondered how he could get out of this. Casper acted polite, but his calm, urbane tone when speaking of murder led Ben to believe he would get no sympathy from him. Lady Towaal or Amelie likely had money to pay a ransom. He didn't want to put them in danger though. They had Saala and Rhys for protection, but Ben didn't know anything about these thieves. There could be hundreds of them for all he knew.

"Regardless of what happens when Balbo recovers," Casper continued, "you are not going anywhere right now. You might as well tell me about yourself. Why did you try to save the boy?"

Ben sighed. Casper was right, he wasn't going anywhere soon. Talking to Casper couldn't make this situation any worse. "I tried to save him because I don't think he should have been killed in the street. He should be held responsible for his crimes, but it should be by the rightful authorities. You are judging him for theft, but unless I am mistaken, you are also a thief?"

"Ha, you are right about that. You have an interesting philosophy, boy. Let me tell you mine. I am a thief and worse, it is true, but so is Renfro. Who better to judge him than his fellow thieves? He entered our society on his own free will and knew the stakes. And like any society, there are certain rules and expectations. Any social organization must have rules. When a person violates those rules, they must be held accountable. If they are not, the organization breaks down, and the society cannot function." Casper paused as if to let Ben ask a question then continued, "Renfro agreed to our rules and now he has broken them. We cannot allow that or everyone will think it is okay to break the rules. We will only have chaos."

Ben responded, "He broke your rules, but he also broke the rules of Fabrizo, along with you and whoever else is in this society of yours. Just because you formed a little group of criminals does not mean you're not all criminals. You're still subject to the law of the land."

"Ah, but what makes us subject to these laws of the land?" asked Casper with a smile. "I don't recall agreeing to anything like that. Why am I subject to the laws of a society I did not willingly join?"

"You are in Fabrizo under your own free will and I am certain that there is a law against stealing here. If you do not agree with that law, but you insist on stealing, you could leave."

Ben felt himself being drawn into the debate with Casper. The man had more depth than the street thug Ben took him to be at first. It wasn't just his clothing, this man spoke like he was part of high society and would have no problem passing as an acquaintance of Amelie's. Ben's perception of a guild of thieves was quickly changing. These were not just alley lurkers and head knockers.

"You are correct again, boy. I am in Fabrizo under my free will and I am aware of the laws of this town, but I do not consider myself subject to them, and so far your 'authorities' have not been able to make me subject to them. If they do not have the power to enforce their laws, then do they have the right to make them? I and the other members of our guild have taken certain liberties with the property of individuals in Fabrizo, and we have the power to get away with it. Are we any more or less right to institute our rules on the people who choose to live here than, say, the Merchants' Guild? But more importantly for our discussion, we have given ourselves authority to serve justice on our own—those who not only choose to live here but choose to join us. Surely you agree, if you conjecture we are subject to the laws of Fabrizo by merely being within its boundary, then certainly a member of our guild who joined voluntarily is subject to the rules of the guild?"

Ben felt himself being outmatched by the thief. He knew in his heart what was right, but this man had a way with words. He was twisting what Ben said and what he thought and turning it into something completely different.

Suddenly, out of the corner of the room, Renfro interjected,

"I'm right here! This talk about rules, law, and whatever is interesting, I'm sure, but what does that change?"

Casper shifted his weight and looked at Renfro. "It doesn't change anything. You will be held here until the Merchant Mallan returns, and then you will be executed. He wanted to see it himself." He gestured to their surroundings. "Unfortunately, you will be stuck in this room until that time. I apologize. We are used to making a decision and doing these things rather quickly. I don't remember the last time we needed a place to store prisoners." He stood and turned to leave. At the doorway, he nodded to Ben. "Interesting speaking with you, boy. Maybe under different circumstances, we could have become friends."

The heavy oak door slammed shut with finality. They could only wait now.

BEN AND RENFRO found water and bread under the napkin on the tray. The tray itself was etched silver. Yet another surprise. These thieves were clearly doing well. Ben's imagination of a gang of dirty miscreants skulking in the city sewers vanished entirely.

Renfro ran a finger along the rim of the silver tray. "We could steal this," he muttered.

Ben raised an eyebrow but didn't reply.

The bread and water on the tray wasn't an ideal meal, but it satisfied. They started to relax as much as possible, given the circumstances.

"So, what exactly did you do to this Merchant Mallan?" inquired Ben.

Renfro rubbed his hand across his face. "It wasn't my fault, really. I found out that there was a cargo of Ishlanese carpets coming into port, unguarded. I also knew about an out-of-work captain who was willing to take a large risk for a large profit. I arranged for a distraction and the captain and his men lifted the carpets. I thought I was sure to be elevated to a full guild member. Turns out, this particular cargo was personally guaranteed by an Elder in the guild. He apparently invests alongside Mallan in his cargoes and handles security.

Ben winced. "You're telling me you stole an entire shipload of goods from one of the most senior thieves in Fabrizo?"

"Yeah. Like I said though, it wasn't really my fault. I just helped with a distraction. I wasn't the one who stole it!"

"You didn't know it was this guild Elder's cargo?" asked Ben with a growing sense of incredulity.

"Well, I guess you're supposed to clear these kind of things with the guild," explained Renfro. "I didn't really know that since boosting ships isn't my normal gig. More of a one-time opportunity thing."

Ben could only shake his head. He still didn't believe the guild should have the right to execute Renfro, but he understood why they might want to.

Renfro continued, seemingly feeling little remorse for the theft. "I almost got away with it, too. Just needed a little more coin to buy passage on a ship and get out of town. Sorry about that, by the way."

"Wait," Ben exclaimed, "you stole an entire cargo of carpets and still didn't have enough coin to buy passage out of here?"

Renfro grunted and stared down at his feet. "The captain I was working with sailed out of port before I could get my payment. I'm getting paid in advance next time."

Ben felt enough sympathy to not bring up how unlikely he thought it was there would be a next time.

AFTER THE FOOD AND WATER, Ben finally felt recovered enough to get up and explore his surroundings. There wasn't much to see. The room must have originally been a storeroom. There were stone floors, stone walls, and the stout oak door. They had a pot in the corner for personal use. The walls had a few weep holes but the squeaks and scratching coming from them turned him away from further exploration. They were too small for him to fit even a hand through, and they had no tools to try enlarging them anyway. It would be no help for escape.

Ben spent a few moments examining the door but he quickly realized it was hopeless. There was a doorknob that wouldn't turn and it had no keyhole to lock-pick like they would have done in a story.

They had a flickering torch stuck in an iron ring on the wall and he briefly thought about trying to burn their way out, maybe through the door or the ceiling. He quickly dismissed that idea once he realized the practical reality of being locked inside a burning room.

He glanced back at Renfro to see if the thief would have any suggestions but he was still sitting in the corner with his head in his hands and solely focused on his feet. And after hearing his tale, Ben didn't have a lot of confidence in Renfro's thieving skills anyway.

Eventually, Ben settled down in his own corner of the room and waited.

HE WOKE UP, startled, to the door banging open. Casper was again standing in the doorway with a grim expression on his face. This time he was not holding a food tray. He gestured out the door and growled, "Come along."

Ben's heart sank. He had accepted he was powerless in this situation, but he held out hope that somehow he would be rescued. He had spent little time with them, but he already thought of Saala, Rhys, and Amelie as his friends. At the very least, he knew he could count on Meghan to search for him. He thought that somehow they might be able to find him and pay a ransom. This Balbo was a thief after all, Ben hoped he'd take the easy coin in lieu of revenge.

"Both of you," ordered Casper.

Ben looked at Renfro and saw he was also surprised that both of them were being called out. The odds that both of their executioners were waiting right at this moment seemed an unusual coincidence.

The hallway outside was similar to the storage room, a series of oak doors down a long stone corridor. Ben noted that there had been no guards stationed outside—a sign that the thieves had also believed escape was futile.

Casper was waiting in the hallway alone, another odd detail. Either he was supremely confident in his abilities or maybe something else was happening. Maybe Casper's grim face wasn't because he was leading two men to their death.

"So, I take it we'll live to see another day?" guessed Ben.

Casper turned toward him and smirked. "You are a bright one, aren't you? Yes, despite my protests, the guild has decided you will be released. Nothing personal. Rule of law and all."

Released. So his friends had come through and paid the ransom. Ben couldn't help a smile coming to his face and the hallway suddenly seemed a little brighter.

They followed Casper up a set of rough stone stairs and into the back of a huge kitchen. It was finely appointed, but had the same feel as the kitchen at the Buckhorn Tavern back in Farview. There were a handful of kitchen workers who all ignored the trio coming out of their storerooms. From the looks of things, Ben could tell they had just finished preparing breakfast for a large group.

As they exited the kitchen, he saw early morning sunlight streaming in through tall, clear windows, and heard the now familiar noises of Fabrizo. He was shocked because they were in what appeared to be a very large, very well-decorated palace. As they made their way along broad hallways, he noticed rich carpets, paintings on the walls, silver candlesticks, and other trappings of wealth. He realized before long that this was, by far, the richest building he had ever been in.

As he eyed the artwork that hung along the sun lit corridors, his perception of these thieves continued to change. Ben knew nothing of artwork. It was a luxury no one in Farview could afford, but someone with a great deal of skill had spent a lot of time painting the pictures and sewing the tapestries. There were gold bowls and silver sconces scattered around as well, but tastefully so. Their wealth was displayed casually, not carelessly.

Renfro, scuttling along behind Casper and Ben, asked, "So this is headquarters? First time I've been here."

Casper looked over his shoulder at him. "First and last. Not even all of the guild members know where this place is. And none of the younglings, of course." He gave Renfro a hard look then waved toward Ben. "Your new friend has his own friend, a bit of a famous friend in certain circles. First I can remember that we've allowed someone not sworn to the guild to walk out of here alive. I'm responsible for the security of this place, along with dealing with a variety of other unpleasant issues. I didn't want anyone to walk out of here this time either." He shrugged. "But I was overruled. Like I said, he is known to us. He made assurances to the Elders, which I'm sure he will explain. Between you and me though, if you ever speak a word of this place to anyone, then we'll be seeing each other again."

"Nothing personal, right?" quipped Ben.

Casper didn't respond.

At the end of the hall, he pushed open two double doors and they entered a plush room to find Rhys relaxing on a comfortable-looking, overstuffed velvet couch. He was sipping a glass of wine. The walls of the room were covered in bookshelves. Ben's eyes popped open at the display. At most, he'd seen the one shelf full of maybe twenty books that Alistair Pinewood kept. There were tens of thousands of them here. He couldn't even begin to calculate the gold it would take to stock this kind of library.

When they entered, Rhys tipped up his wine glass and gulped the rest of the drink before standing. "I spend any more time in this city and I may be sold on the stuff. Great vintage, I suspect?"

Casper nodded his head toward Rhys. "Only the best for our guests."

Ben looked around the room, surprised to see Rhys here. He thought they'd send Saala with the ransom. The blademaster had an air of quiet intimidation about him. He'd be Ben's pick to send into a hostile situation. His skill was likely to be known and respected by men such as these.

Rhys, on the other hand, had weapons, but Ben had never seen him practice with them. He also had a habit of quickly finding his way to the nearest tavern. Ben knew he was hired by Lady Towaal so he must have some talent, but his haphazard and half-drunk manner didn't seem the right fit for this situation. Case in point, when they walked in, he had a drink in hand and his knives and longsword were laid out on a couch across the room. After they entered, he strolled over and buckled his belts while maintaining his affable chit chat.

Outwardly, Casper maintained his calm demeanor when Rhys moved to the weapons, but Ben noticed a slight hesitancy in his speech and his right hand drifted toward his rapier.

Ben scanned the room, looking for any object he could use as a weapon if the situation erupted in violence until he caught Rhys grinning at him then giving a sly wink. The rogue's complete lack of concern made Ben feel slightly silly. The Thieves already had him captured, so bringing him out of the cell and enacting some sort of betrayal made no sense.

Casper, with his eyes still on Rhys, said to Ben and Renfro, "You're both lucky. Do yourselves a favor, and don't come back to Fabrizo. You've been given safe passage to leave the city, but you're on your own if you ever return."

Rhys stepped up to Ben and gripped his shoulder. "Let's get out of here. We've got places to be."

~

CASPER LED them down the opulent hallways of the Guild Head-quarters and they passed without seeing another soul. They exited out two wide, highly polished mahogany doors that stood twice Ben's height. Broad marble steps led through a sturdy iron gate with ornate, finely wrought spikes whose artistry barely hid their deadly nature.

Once on the streets, Rhys led them out of the affluent district they were in and toward the open water and the docks. The streets became shabby and grew more so as they continued. The merchants got louder and the persistent fish smell Ben remembered from the day before grew stronger. Along the way, Rhys explained to Ben that they had arranged passage on a ship and would leave immediately with the morning tide.

"The girls were all worried about you, of course. They wanted me to let you know. Not sure what good being worried does for you, but whatever. Heard you tagged one of them pretty good. I'm sure you'll make Saala proud."

"Yeah, I injured one, but I lost the fight and ended up in a cell with a death sentence."

Rhys laughed. "Good point. All that sword training and look what good it did you. If you'd been just a little better you probably would have ended up dead instead of in captivity."

Ben grimaced. He'd surmised the same, but it hurt coming from someone he now thought of as a friend. Two weeks of training with a blademaster, and he was only good enough to get himself in real trouble.

He broke off the conversation as they approached the docks. He had to focus on dodging heavy carts and quick moving porters who treated him like he was invisible. There was an intricate dance of goods coming in and out of the city and Ben was nearly run over several times before he started being able to anticipate which way to duck.

Still, despite the danger of a collision, the buzz of activity by the ships was a welcome change from the silence and overwhelming dread he had faced in the cell.

Renfro was nervously tagging along behind them. He was at ease with the frantic pace of the workmen, but he constantly checked over his shoulder as if unbelieving there was no pursuit. Finally, he spoke up in the same quaking voice he'd used when they were locked in the cell. "So, do you think we're safe now? I mean, I've never heard of anyone being brought in like that then being let go. Thanks, by the way."

Rhys glanced back at him. "You are safe right now, but honestly, I'm not even sure who you are. When I approached the thieves, I was told they captured two boys together. I negotiated to get you both out because I figured it would throw up confusion about what I was after. The less they know, the better. Whoever you are, they didn't believe I knew you. I'd already started haggling at that point, and I felt silly letting them keep you."

"I, uh, thanks anyway," Renfro stammered.

"No offense, kid. You're welcome to leave town with us and we can keep you out of immediate danger. Maybe if you leave with us it will tweak them a little bit and make them second-guess themselves. Arrogant pricks. Assuming you keep your hands to yourself, that is. If not, you'll find there are worse places to be than locked up in some thief's palace. I don't know what you did to get in trouble with the guild, but I can guess."

Renfro had the look of someone who jumped off a burning ship and realized too late he couldn't swim.

Ben interjected before Renfro blurted out a confession and changed Rhys' mind. "Who do we have to thank? I mean, who paid our ransom?"

"Ransom?" Rhys responded quizzically. "You two were in for crimes against the guild. Ransom wasn't a real option. At least not one I could afford."

"Wait. If it wasn't a ransom, then how did we get out?" inquired Ben.

Rhys gave the same knowing cat-like smile Ben was used to seeing over a half-full pint of ale. "I had a little talk with them. You can thank me next time we get into a tavern. How many rounds is your life worth?"

With that, Rhys started up a wobbly plank onto one of the creaking ships tied to the docks. Ben looked at Renfro, shrugged, and started the next leg of his journey.

6

SALTWATER

FROM THE DOCK IN FABRIZO, the Bay Runner seemed massive. Three broad blue and white stripped sails billowed from masts the size of full-grown pine trees. The deck covered the length of Farview's village green and the ship rose out of the water higher than Farview's tallest building.

Once they left sight of land though, it seemed to be much smaller. The common area below deck was the size of Ben's old apartment. It was used for everything except work, sleep, and the necessaries—which was done hanging off the back of the vessel.

The common area was expansive though compared to the tiny cabin Ben was sharing with Rhys, Renfro, and Saala. They had a four-level bunk bed and enough walking room to squeeze in and out of it sideways. Livestock was given more space than they were.

The size of the cabin was not much of a problem though because he spent almost the entire journey topside. The deck of the ship was the only place to get some fresh air, and it was also where almost all of the excitement was. The sailors were constantly adjusting sails, tightening ropes, taking readings of the

wind and water, and a thousand other tasks Ben did not understand but found fascinating.

The work of sailing the ship required constant attention from
the crew. After the first few days, Ben found if he stayed out of
their way, the sailors paid him no mind and weren't bothered by
him watching them. The officers on the ship spent some time
speaking with Lady Towaal, but the rest of the crew largely
ignored them. Renfro confided in Ben that he thought they were
watching him and he was certain he would be turned in as soon
as they made port in Whitehall.

Rhys, ever practical, was able to spot what everyone else
missed. He pointed out that the sailors constantly had a wad of
herbs stuffed into the side of their jaw. "Leaves from the Xanta
plant. Makes them a little sluggish but the days pass in a haze.
Usually the ship's officers try to tamp down on that kind of thing,
but it does make the crew easy to deal with. If you don't give
them something, men get a little antsy after a few weeks of
sleeping stacked up like cords of wood and eating hard biscuits
and beans every meal. The lure of the sea quickly loses its appeal
for me."

Ben spent bells watching the sailors work and feeling the
wind and salt spray blow on his face. He understood Rhys' point
—a lifetime of this would be tedious and boring, but for Ben, the
adventure was still fresh. He enjoyed every moment of it, while
he was topside at least.

When he wasn't watching the sailors, he spent a lot of time in
close one-on-one discussions with Amelie, Meghan, and Renfro.

Meghan, he had known his entire life. He fell in with Renfro
like they had been friends forever. Spending a day in the death
cell together made for good bonding. Talking with either one of
them was easy and comfortable. He felt like he could tell them
anything and they shared their innermost thoughts with him.

Amelie was different. He felt like he could trust her and tell her anything, but she kept her own secrets closely guarded. She did tell a little, though. He learned her father wasn't just a lord of Issen, he was The Lord of Issen. She said he wasn't called a king, but it sounded just like one from what Ben understood. She had no siblings and didn't speak much about her mother other than to mention she was living and describe her as 'the consummate lady', whatever that meant.

Over the weeks on the water, his relationship with Meghan grew stronger than it had ever been, and with a slight twinge of guilt, he realized Renfro had filled the void he felt for Serrot. With little doubt, he thought all of them would remain fast friends for the rest of their lives.

But as much as he appreciated the friendships with Meghan and Renfro, he felt himself drawn more and more to Amelie. In many ways, she was a closed book to him. He rarely could separate her from Meredith, but when he did, he felt a spark of connection. He kept that to himself. She was a highborn lady, and he was a brewer from a small mountain town. It sounded like a silly story even to him. It was the kind of thing better not to think about. Sometimes the fantastical events in the stories were just that—fantasy.

THE BIG VESSEL rocked gently in the light chop of the bay and Saala judged sword practice impractical. Between the slight movement, the number of people moving around on deck, and Ben's lack of skill, he was sure it would end in an accident.

Lady Towaal took notice, and despite an icy demeanor toward Ben, she instructed Rhys to teach him something.

"Maybe fighting with his hands," she muttered.

Rhys nodded and grinned. "I think I have something useful I can teach him."

"I guess she doesn't want me to go more than a few days without getting pummeled." Ben smirked while he and Rhys cleared deck space to begin.

"You did anger her," remarked Rhys, "and I can't say I blame her. She is very focused on getting Amelie safely behind the Sanctuary's walls as soon as possible. Getting into a scrap with the Fabrizo Thieves' Guild isn't the way to do that."

"When you put it like that..." Ben trailed off.

"Cheer up," replied Rhys. "She didn't exactly encourage me to go get you, but she didn't stop me either. She could have left you locked up or just sent you back home. She sees something in you, and for whatever reason, she wants you to stay with us."

Ben brightened until Rhys added, "On second thought, maybe you shouldn't cheer up. Believe me, being 'useful' to a mage isn't always fun and games."

IN SOME WAYS, RHYS' instruction was similar to Saala's. In others, it was very different. Rhys started by explaining that he wouldn't actually teach Ben any punches or kicks yet. First, he had to learn balance and flexibility. Ben assumed that, like with the sword when he spent a few days learning grips and stances, he would quickly move on, but Rhys spent the entire trip teaching balance.

Rhys would start every lesson doing stretches. They would bend, twist, squat, and pull muscles that Ben didn't realize he had. During the first few days, he felt like he was getting a workout just doing the stretches.

Once they were done stretching, Rhys began teaching him different balance positions when the swells of the sea were relatively calm. At first, it was fairly simple, like standing on one foot or kneeling on one leg with his arms raised straight up. Simple being relative, of course, due to the gentle rocking of the ship.

Standing on one foot becomes exponentially more difficult on a moving platform.

As the days progressed, so did the variety of positions Rhys taught. Before long, several other members of the group joined them. Saala was first, saying the exercise was better than being cooped up downstairs. Then Amelie, Meredith, and Meghan joined as well. With the rest of the young people participating, it was easy to pressure Renfro into it, too. After the first week, everyone in their group except Lady Towaal was spending several bells a day balancing in progressively more bizarre and convoluted poses.

After two weeks, they began tying some of the poses together into a fluid sort of dance. They would begin on their stomachs, push up with their arms while keeping their bodies straight, swing their hips back so they formed a triangle with their arms and feet on the hard wood of the deck, then onto one knee with the other leg up and their chests down. They kept learning new positions and adding them to the mix until they had about twenty of them they would perform in sequence.

Saala was the only one, aside from Rhys, who could make it through the entire routine without spilling onto the deck in tangle of arms and legs. Saala learned the poses with the same smooth confidence he did everything. Ben frequently found himself watching Saala on a particularly tricky move to see how it should be done. Rhys was occasionally helpful with one-on-one coaching, but Ben couldn't help noticing, most of his time was spent directing the girls, particularly Meredith and Meghan.

Anytime one of them wavered, Rhys would appear to place a steadying hand on a hip or whisper soft words of encouragement. At first, Ben felt a flash of jealousy. He thought about warning Meghan, but she was no stranger to dealing with attention. As the attractive and only daughter of the wealthiest man in Farview, she had learned to deal with unwanted suitors. Besides, while Ben was learning the scoundrel did have a few redeeming qualities, Meghan would never be interested in a rogue like Rhys.

~

THE VOYAGE across the Blood Bay to Whitehall typically took three weeks, depending on the wind and water. Their journey was uneventful and in the prescribed time, they were getting close. On the last full day at sea, Rhys threw another loop into their lessons. He made them run the twenty poses in reverse.

This time, even Saala ended up collapsing during one difficult transition. Ben found he had unconsciously learned to make moving between the poses a habit that he had to unlearn when he did them in reverse.

They spent almost the entire day working the moves and by the end of it, Ben was lying exhausted, propped up against a damp coil of rope. His arms and legs felt as limp as the rope.

Rhys squatted down next to him and said, "Good job these last few weeks. You and Amelie are my star pupils." Then he corrected himself, "After Saala, of course."

Ben rolled his head toward Rhys. "I'm glad I'm finally good at something. I still don't know why, though. What's the point of all of this? I seriously doubt we're going to get into a scrape where I end up needing to squat down, roll on my belly, then stand on one leg, all while holding one arm straight out to my side."

Rhys rolled his eyes. "You may not see it yet, but it will help you. All fighting, whether with the hand or the sword requires four things: strength, skill, speed, and balance. These exercises focus on balance, of course. Saala has been teaching you skill. Strength and speed come through repetition and practice. You add it all up, and next time you get into a fight, maybe you manage to not get yourself knocked out."

Ben smirked. "I might be able to balance a little better. We'll have to see once we get off this ship. I certainly don't feel any stronger though. I'll barely be able to lift my spoon tonight."

"That's how you know it's working." Rhys clapped his hands down on his knees and stood to address the rest of the exhausted group. "You are not experts at it yet, but you have learned the first of the Thirty Ohms. If you can learn them all, you will be stronger, faster, and better balanced than almost any opponent. Fighting is about more than just chopping at a man with a sword."

～

RHYS LEFT to freshen up and Ben scooted over next to Renfro and a speculative-looking Saala.

"What's this about the Ohms?" asked Renfro. "And what the hell did he say about thirty of them? I didn't think I'd make it through today. Not sure I could do thirty more of those."

"Twenty nine," replied Saala stoically.

"What?" asked Renfro.

"We have done one," explained Saala. "So there are only twenty nine left."

Renfro rolled his eyes. "I guess I missed that day in the Thieves' Guild mathematics tutoring. You know what I mean. Twenty nine or thirty of them or whatever, what are they?"

Saala sighed. "I've spent years studying various fighting styles around the world and never found anyone to teach me the Thirty Ohms. They're said to be used by a warrior sect in Qooten. The sect is real, I've crossed their path. With reason, they are known as some of the deadliest fighters in the South Continent. Whether the Thirty Ohms were real or not, I wasn't sure. Now I find out that drunk knows them? The world is a very strange place. I'm going to get some rest." Saala stood and retreated below deck to the cabin, shaking his head as he left.

The world was indeed a strange place, thought Ben. Making

small talk with a blademaster and a thief. Travelling with a mage and a lady.

Renfro was thinking the same thing. "Strange company you keep. You've all been pretty closed mouthed about what you're up to, but I think I've picked up on a lot of it. Not sure it's safe travelling with you lot. Course, not sure Whitehall will be safe for me either. Mallan does a lot of business there. You think I could come along with you past Whitehall?"

Ben scratched behind his neck. "It'd be fine with me. It's really up to Lady Towaal though."

Renfro seemed to deflate and Ben realized what he wanted. "I can ask her if you like."

Renfro perked right back up and Ben was struck by how honest and open the boy was, despite his past profession. The reason he was able to make such quick friends, Ben thought, was that the world was such a simple place for Renfro. He wasn't weighed down by concerns on what was right or wrong. He just reacted to what was around him.

When Renfro stole from someone, he didn't consider the consequences to the victim, he only considered his own risk and reward. For the same reasons he had no problems with theft, he had no problems spilling his life story and all his hopes and desires to Ben. He had no mechanism to hold back. He had apparently decided he could trust Ben to help get him out of his troubles, so he jumped into the friendship with both feet. Renfro was all or nothing.

Lying there on the deck of the ship, staring at the billowing sails snapping in the wind overhead, and trying to ignore the stench of the wet rope behind his back, Ben wondered if Renfro's way was better. A life unmuddled by concerns about others. It seemed simpler. Ben had certainly seen his share of trouble trying to help others recently. The fights at Murdoch's and in Fabrizo wouldn't have happened if he'd kept to himself.

~

Ben was still contemplating the simple life of Renfro when he went to talk to Lady Towaal about keeping him in the group past Whitehall. He found her leaning against the rail, staring into the depths of the Blood Bay.

As he approached, she waved him closer and pointed down toward the water. Ben was startled when he noticed several large shapes coursing through the water and keeping speed with the ship.

Lady Towaal explained, "Black sharks. They follow ships all the time this close to Whitehall. No one is really sure why, but the popular story among sailors is that they smell human blood. They say that when the Blood Bay earned its name, these sharks fed for years on the corpses of the losers."

"Blood Bay. Why is it called that?" Ben asked. "I've heard the stories of course, but I don't know how much truth there is to them."

"You might be surprised," Towaal replied. "There is sometimes more truth in stories than there is in the histories. Both the stories and the histories of the Blood Bay are one in the same though. Long ago, almost three hundred years past, the leaders of Whitehall and Issen became upset with each other. They were powerful cities with powerful leaders, much like they are now. It was over some simple offense, a raised tariff or spurned marriage proposal from a cousin. The details of how it started have been forgotten and aren't really that important."

"What happened after is important," continued Towaal, "though its lesson has also been forgotten. The two rulers started collecting allies and making strategic military moves they said to thwart the aggressor. Even at the time, it was difficult to tell which one of them was supposed to be the aggressor and which was the defender."

"They were both powerful enough that eventually nearly

every nation and city state within two hundred leagues of the Bay had been drawn in on one side or the other. One summer, a small skirmish set it off. They called all of their armies together and planned to march to what would have been assured mutual destruction. The forces were so large that whichever side won, the loss of life would have been catastrophic. The land would have been stripped of farmers, wheelwrights, carpenters, fishermen, and all of the other common men and specialists that make our civilization work. Those outside of Whitehall and Issen were extremely concerned of course, but what could they do? Who had the power to stop something like that when both sides had already accumulated so much might?"

"Fortunately, a huge storm came out of nowhere and it rained for weeks. The roads became impassable and the men were washed out of their camps. Critical bridges were destroyed by flooding, mountain passes blocked due to landslides. All of both nation's resources and manpower had been devoted to the military build, so nothing could be quickly repaired."

"The pitched battle had been averted, but both sides were still unwilling to back down. The war took place across this bay. It grinded on for years because neither force could gain a decisive advantage. In the end, it wasn't much better than the catastrophe the storms had delayed. Finally, the people of Issen grew sick of the war and called their troops home."

"The ruler of Whitehall named himself emperor and king and claimed dominion over most of central Alcott. Sadly for him and his heirs, they found that they didn't have the men to work or protect that land. Fields went fallow, nets were left untended, cities abandoned, and so on. The dark forces—goblins, demons, and worse—found a toehold in our world. It took a century to battle them back. In some remote places in the world, they still exist in serious enough numbers to pose a threat. The one we killed in Farview is child's play compared to the demon swarms they faced after the Blood Bay. The lesson was obvious at the time. The victor of the great battles ended up losing more than they gained. The fighting and bloodshed had been pointless. Too few remember the lessons of the past. It's just pages in a book now."

Lady Towaal finished her narrative and continued staring at the black sharks flanking the ship. She appeared to be lost in her thoughts, and Ben was afraid to interrupt her.

Her story surprised him. He'd heard numerous accounts of various battles, the heroism each side displayed, and the glory when it was all over. He had never heard it quite like this. The way Lady Towaal described it, both sides had tasted bitter defeat in the end. In the stories, there was always a winner and a loser. The winner took the battlefield and the spoils. The loser went home in shame. It never occurred to him what happened when the winner went home.

After a moment, he decided to risk a question. "So, does this mean that technically Argren of Whitehall is my king? In Farview, we never really paid attention to that kind of thing."

For the first time Ben had seen, Towaal smiled. "No, the leaders of Whitehall still claim the title of king, but over the years that portion of the map has been shrinking. In reality, their reign doesn't extend much further than the walls of Whitehall and the Sineook Valley by proxy. If you want to be technical, on the maps, Farview falls within the realm of Issen. I suspect, though, that you haven't seen a tax collector in your lifetime. Lord Gregor probably wouldn't remember where to send them if he became so inclined. You are right to not pay much attention. For the common man, it only matters that you are left alone to live your life. Lines on the map, that only matters to scholars and rulers."

She frowned. "Enough history. That's not what you came to ask. What is it? The world is a big and scary place and you're looking to turn back? No one could blame you after what's happened over the last few weeks."

"No, I, uh, I want to continue with you. I want to see this through."

"Good," she replied with a nod.

He thought he detected a hint of another smile. "I, actually, I came to ask if Renfro could continue on with us. Despite his past, he's a good man. I think we could use him."

Towaal paused and gave Ben a long appraising look before answering. "Make sure he keeps his hands to himself."

7

WHITEHALL

THE NEXT MORNING, Ben lined the rail with Meghan, Amelie, Meredith, and Renfro. None of them had ever seen the great city of Whitehall. Even for someone who was used to big cities like Amelie, it was a sight to behold when approached from the sea.

When the shore first came into view, they could only see a long stretch of somber grey cliffs topped with the occasional splash of verdant green forest. Above the forest in the distance, a jagged mountain range tore into the sky.

The city of Whitehall was a brilliant beacon shining out from the grim coastline. In the morning sun, the white of the buildings reflected like a diamond. As they sailed closer, Ben saw that there were virtually no flat areas in the city – it seemed to grow straight out of the water in a dazzling pile of limestone and marble. The buildings were built up from the huge port and stacked in tiers climbing all the way up the cliff. He could see wide boulevards zigzagging up through the city. It wasn't until they were nearly inside the seawall that he was able to make out tiny spots of color in doorways and windows that marked the only breaks in the white stonework.

In the center of the city, the White River poured down through a steep mountain pass into a large reservoir, spilled over a low retaining wall, then flowed more peacefully through the rest of the city and into the Blood Bay. From one angle, the river appeared to cleave the city in two. From another, the two wings of the city appeared to be some mythical beast perched above the reservoir and port.

Surrounding the port was a thick rock seawall that protected the city from the weather and raiding armies. The only break in the wall was framed by two squat fortresses Amelie called the Rock and the Rock Two.

Ben couldn't tell the difference between them, but the huge trebuchets sitting atop looked intimidating enough to scare off all but the most determined attackers.

Once they safely passed through the Rocks, Amelie was able to point out a few other landmarks she'd heard of. "The Great Market there is supposed to be the only flat part of this city, and I believe it now. Beyond that is the cathedral which they say was erected after the Blood Bay War when the leaders of Whitehall claimed they were God Kings. They've since dropped the god title but maintain the building. Way up at the top is the Citadel—King Argren's residence. That's where we'll stay."

"Hold on!" exclaimed Renfro. "We're staying at the king's house?"

"Well, when you put it like that, I guess we are," she replied. "There are hundreds if not thousands of people who live there though. It's not like we're sharing his bathing chambers."

"Still," Renfro nudged Ben. "Pretty fancy."

Ben smiled and tried to take it all in. The port was unlike anything he had even imagined. Where Fabrizo's port was spread out across several miles of mainland and islands, Whitehall's massive docks were all behind the seawall and clustered at the base of the city. Earlier, Saala had explained to Ben that Whitehall, on the western shores of the Blood Bay, was more suscep-tible to fall storms than the eastern shore. The sea wall was built to allow merchants to continue business throughout the year. While several of the cities on the western shores had protected ports, none rivaled Whitehall in scale. Saala said it was the largest port in the known world, and from what Ben could see as they approached, he thought it might be true.

In the port, a veritable forest of ship masts sprouted up. Ben attempted to count the masts but he gave up when he got over one hundred and wasn't a third of the way along. There were large merchant cogs like they were on, small skiffs darting about between ships, and he spied several man-o-wars slowly making their way out of the port into the bay.

One of the small skiffs started toward them at the same time Rhys came to lean next to the young people. He gestured to the little boat and explained, "That's a port pilot. They'll guide us into an available dock. Shouldn't be too long before we tie up. Best go get packed if you're not."

The girls darted off to gather their things. Neither Ben nor Renfro actually owned much, so they had been packed since early morning.

Rhys continued, "I heard Amelie tell you where we are stay-ing. Not my type of people, but you can't complain. We won't find any better accommodations in the city. Good drink, good food, and good beds. Take advantage, lads. Some of these city girls are drawn toward the adventuring type and they're wild. Not like the country bumpkins you're used to. There's more to it than breeding. My advice, find a nice experienced girl and let her teach you a thing or two."

A flush crept into Ben's face and he decided to divert the conversation. Rhys had offered his advice before, and it always carried a similar theme. "Will we meet the king?"

"Not us hopefully. Keep away from lords and ladies, lad. They all play the same game. You're just a piece on the board to them.

All they care about is money and power. If they have one, they want the other. If they have both, they want more. Remember that."

Ben frowned, "Amelie's a lady, and she's not like that."

Rhys shrugged. "We'll see."

BEN TRIED to put the conversation with Rhys behind him as they moved toward the city. The man was an enigma to Ben. He acted like a friend, but he kept plenty of secrets. He worked as a hunter out of the City for members of the Sanctuary, but his open disdain of mages and his disagreements with Towaal didn't seem to match his apparent job. For someone who counted on Sanctuary business for his income, he wasn't very supportive of their activities.

Ben shook his head and slipped below deck to get his pack. Whitehall was one of the grandest cities in the world and he wasn't going to let creeping doubts about his companions ruin the experience.

The first pilot skiff had darted back into the port after they announced highborn guests, and they were now being led in by a second skiff to their dock. The sailors were quickly stowing equipment, tying down lines, and preparing bumpers in a flurry of activity that Ben still could not understand after three weeks at sea. The captain adopted a frosty attitude after he learned the identity of his passengers. Renfro speculated he probably would have tried to charge them double for passage if he'd known.

When Ben returned topside, Meghan was standing at the rail looking up in awe at the city rising before them. The two of them were the only ones who didn't have much experience with cities, and they were both excited and nervous about Whitehall and the rest of the journey.

Meghan told Ben she was growing uncertain about her decision to join the Sanctuary. It had seemed so simple back in Farview. After learning more of what to expect from Towaal and Amelie though, it was more complicated than she'd realized. She hadn't come to grips with how her life would change. After this journey, Ben planned to return to Farview and resume his life. Nothing would ever be the same for her.

Ben's worries about Whitehall were more straightforward and immediate. At Murdoch's, he'd been nearly beaten to a pulp in the common room, and in Fabrizo, he'd been knocked out and imprisoned. So far, his luck out in the world was not very good. His excitement about seeing Whitehall was tempered with concerns around what other kinds of trouble he may find himself in.

At the railing, Amelie and Meredith joined them. "Are you excited about the city, Ben?"

"I think so. I was excited about Fabrizo too and that didn't go well." Ben at least had no secrets from his companions.

Renfro broke in, "Didn't go well? You met me!"

"I see your point, Ben." Amelie gave Renfro a sidelong glance and he effected a hurt expression. She continued, "We shouldn't have any of those problems in Whitehall. Fabrizo is ruled by the Merchants Guild and the lack of a single strong ruler leads to delays and confusion. It allows for groups like the Thieves' Guild to flourish. Some even say the two guilds are one in the same."

Renfro blurted, "They're not the same! The Thieves steal from the Merchants' Guild as much as they steal from anyone. In fact, the Merchants have a bounty out on any known thief."

"Maybe you're right, but Whitehall is different. Argren rules with a heavy hand and he doesn't allow any sources of power aside from his own. At the first hint of something like a Thieves' Guild, he won't just offer a bounty. He'll task his soldiers to root it out branch and stem. They'll turn the entire city upside down before they allow a group like that to exist. The common people don't allow it either. They'd rather deal with the problem themselves than have Argren's men come down on them."

"Have you met the king?" Ben asked.

"No, I haven't," she responded. "My father has and he described him as a hard man. He's had the rule in Whitehall for almost forty years now and many say he's the most powerful man in Alcott. I wouldn't argue against that. When you've had that much power for that long, it can change you, I hear."

"Are you worried about him? I mean, you're going to have to make an appearance, right?"

Amelie blushed. "It's a little more than that. My father sent me as an envoy and asked me to relay a message to Argren."

There's always more to it, thought Ben. "What message? If it's okay for me to know..."

"It's no secret really, not now that we are here. King Argren wants my father to join his Alliance. The Coalition wants us to join them instead. Issen is stuck in the middle and my father is worried that either way he goes, we will bear the brunt of any fighting that starts. I'm here to gain assurances from Argren that if we join him, he will lend us troops and other aid."

Ben scratched his head. "I was born in Coalition territory, before we moved to Farview, and I remember my father telling me it was a horrible place. The Coalition doesn't allow a man to live his life freely. The Coalition says they are building a better world but it seemed to only work out better for the people at the top. They said they were going to make everything fair and provide the people what they need—things like setting up schools, providing medicines, and everyone getting a fair shot no matter how high or common their blood. But someone's got to pay for all of that. Taxes quadrupled in two years. At least, that's what my father said. How could your father want his people to be a part of something like that? Argren is building his Alliance to fight that, right, to make sure people are protected and have the freedom to choose things on their own?"

Amelie smiled a sad smile.

～

As they docked and disembarked, Ben felt like he was still rocking with the waves. He felt the thrill of seeing a city he had heard so many stories about, but the world wasn't as simple of a place as it used to be. Things were changing quickly and he was a small boat on a large open sea.

Renfro pulled him out of his gloomy thoughts. He was close to Ben in age, but sometimes he still acted like a child. In this case, his excitement about getting to Whitehall and escaping Fabrizo was infectious. He bolted down the gangplank as soon as it was lowered and spun back to face the group with a broad smile on his face.

They followed Renfro down and Ben realized that while Renfro had seemed worldly and confident in Fabrizo, his experience with the world wasn't very broad. Renfro had spent his entire life on the islands of Fabrizo. Whitehall was just as alien and strange to him as it was Ben and Meghan.

They dodged through the hustle and bustle down by the docks toward a large structure by the Great Market. That part of the city felt remarkably similar to the docks in Fabrizo, and despite the chaos, Ben found he enjoyed it. A cacophony of languages, sights, and smells mixed into an intoxicating cocktail that tasted like adventure.

The large structure housed the base of something called the funicular. It was the quickest—and most expensive—way to move through the city of Whitehall. The city was built on a steep incline, nearly vertical, and climbing from port to Citadel on the zigzagging streets would take half a day on foot.

The funicular was the way around that. It was a wooden contraption built on wheels, set on a rail, and attached to a pulley system. Once loaded, a signal would be sent to the operators and a team of oxen would pull the heavy cables running through the pulleys. The funicular would roll smoothly to the highest levels of the city, making several stops along the way. Wealthy passengers would board and disembark as the funicular made its way up the steep track.

"Better than walking," said Rhys with a wink.

~

THEIR PARTY BOARDED the funicular with several other passengers and the signal was given. Ben held on tightly when they lurched upward. As they rose, the view was both spectacular and terrifying.

The massive ships in the bay began to look like small toys. The business of daily life in a large city surrounded them. The smells and sounds of the port faded away and the quality of the buildings and shops improved.

The lower tiers of the city were where the commercial business of the port took place, along with warehouses, boarding houses, and taverns for the sailors. Above that were densely packed apartments and businesses like grocers and general stores. The higher they got, the buildings got wider and the type of goods more diverse. There were tailors, jewelers, armorers, and others located past the mid-point.

Above the specialized shops, many buildings were made of marble instead of limestone. Ben caught glimpses of secluded gardens behind the tall walls and thick gates. Toward the top, the only word Ben could use to describe the buildings was 'palace'. Large, statue-filled gardens behind the walls of each residence became commonplace. The streets were nearly empty compared to below. Many of the people that were in the streets were armed guards patrolling or standing watch. Ben wondered if Argren's rule in this city was as secure as Amelie made it out to be.

By the time the funicular reached the highest point, Ben's

party were the only remaining passengers. At the top, the Citadel, King Argren's seat of power, was the only building. As they exited, Ben gasped in awe at the massive, intimidating structure. He didn't know what he expected, but this building was an imposing castle. It had soaring towers, hulking marble walls, battlements crawling with crossbowmen, and a massive double gate. The outer one thick, iron-bound oak logs. The inner, iron grate with bars as thick as one of Ben's legs. They both rose at least ten times higher than Ben's head. It must take several teams of oxen to open or close them, he thought.

The defense seemed unnecessary. Any force that was able to take the entire city up to these gates was likely able to take the Citadel as well. Even if they could not, at that point, the battle would have been lost. These walls and gates were made for a different purpose, he suspected. Intimidation. Anyone who walked up in front of this place couldn't help but feel small and inconsequential. Whether or not Argren himself commissioned the fortress, Ben did not know, but he thought it spoke to the mindset of the rulers of this place.

Hanging from above the gates was a massive banner emblazoned with a royal blue figure. The banner gently flapped in the salty wind blowing off the bay.

"King Argren's sigil?" inquired Ben.

"I believe that is the purported new banner for the Alliance," replied Amelie with a smirk.

"What is that?" he asked. "An elephant? I've heard of them in the stories but have never seen one."

"No," answered Amelie. "I think it's supposed to be a charging mammoth—it's like a big powerful elephant that only lives far north of Northport. It does look a little rotund though, doesn't it?"

Waiting at the gates was a bald, bearded man wearing a plain bleached robe that nearly blended in with the white marble walls. As they approached, he scampered forward and bowed deeply to the ladies. "Lady Amelie, Lady Towaal, welcome to the Citadel. I apologize for the informal reception. I just got word of your arrival."

He raised one eyebrow in seeming rebuke that he was not notified in advance. He glanced between the four women before quickly deciding which were highborn and focusing his attention on them. "I am King Argren's Head of House. You may call me Marrion. Come, let me offer you refreshments and show you to your rooms. King Argren would be pleased if you both are available for dinner this evening. He has much to discuss with you."

The man bowed for Amelie and Towaal, but ignored the rest of the party.

When they made their way through the gates and across the meticulously landscaped courtyard, Marrion waved to another robed figure and purred, "Please, have your female servants come with us. Roland will take the males."

Meghan adopted a baleful scowl after being referred to as a servant, but Renfro grinned at Ben, delighted at being there regardless of his status. Ben had noticed tension between Meghan and Amelie recently, and felt that if the rest of the Citadel had the same attitude as Marrion toward highborn and common, he might be better off staying well away from the women for the duration of their stay.

As soon as Marrion and the ladies were out of earshot, Meredith and Meghan following closely behind, Rhys slapped Roland on the back and belted, "Roland, my man! Marrion I'm sure did not have time to inform you that I am the head of Lady Amelie's household guard. I'm certain she'd be upset if I didn't get accommodations befitting my status. I don't want you to suffer if she were to find me in some mean servant's quarters."

"None of the guest quarters in the Citadel could be considered mean, sir," answered Roland in a condescending tone. "I am confident you will be happy with the room you are given."

Despite Roland's uptight demeanor, Ben could see he was a

quick study and wasn't going to fall for the rogue's deception. As he led them into the Citadel, Ben caught Saala rolling his eyes and giving Rhys a light shove.

~

THE ROOMS they were given were plain and simple, but they were more comfortable than any Ben had ever stayed in, including the inn in Fabrizo. The beds were stout and stuffed with fresh straw, there was a comfortable chair in each room, and they shared facilities to perform the necessaries. To Rhys' delight, the sitting room was stocked with wine and ale. They only had to call and a serving man appeared to fetch whatever they needed from the kitchens.

Saala explained that the expectation for a lord's travelling men was that they always be on hand when he needed something, so the Citadel provided the servants everything they needed. That way they could be at their lord's beck and call. Luckily for them, Amelie and Towaal were unusually self-sufficient for highborn. If they did need something, they had Meredith with them.

Ben quickly stowed his gear in his room, cleaned up, then sat down in the common room to wait. He had nothing to do and it felt odd. They had been travelling for the last five weeks and had reached a major milestone in their journey. While some of their party was busy meeting with royalty, Ben was only there to wait.

After three weeks on the ship, he was restless and ready to stretch his legs, but he didn't know where he could go. If Roland was any example, the staff at the Citadel would be difficult and unhelpful if he asked for directions. Certainly, there were many interesting places in such a large building, but the Citadel was completely outside his experience.

He was saved from having to decide what to do when Rhys and Renfro arrived. Rhys, as always, had an idea.

"Saala went to meet up with some household guard," remarked Rhys. "A man he knows from working for one of the city lords. So, we're on our own. What do you say we go find out what there is to do around here?"

～

To Ben's surprise, Rhys did not immediately lead them out to the nearest flophouse. Instead, he led them on a tour of the Citadel.

When Ben asked how he was so familiar with the fortress, Rhys responded, "I passed through a couple of years ago. Also, all of these places are basically the same. There are areas where the actual work gets done and there are areas where the highborn play. Same kind of work goes on in any castle and the highborn do pretty much the same thing too. Once you've been in a few of them, they all start to look the same."

It may have been the same to Rhys, but to Ben and Renfro, the Citadel was amazing. The more they explored, the bigger it seemed. When they first arrived outside, Ben had thought it was at least as big as the village of Farview. Once he walked around inside, he realized it was much larger than that. The footprint was the size of three or four Farviews, and in some places, it rose seven stories tall. They saw hundreds of people working and there must have been thousands more they did not see.

Of all of the people they saw, very few of them stopped the group and asked what their business was. While there were guards nearly everywhere, none of them seemed to be guarding anything specific.

Rhys speculated, "Argren's pumping up the roster in preparation for war. There's only so much drilling a man can take so he must be giving them breaks with guard duty. The actual guards, the ones he trusts, will be close around his personal quarters and the throne room."

One place they were questioned was the kitchens. They stumbled across several kitchens, and every time they ducked their heads in one, an angry-looking aproned woman would come charging at them waving a spoon. After the third time, Ben asked Rhys and Renfro if they thought it was the same stressed-out cook following the same route they were, or if they hired them all to look the same.

"Maybe sisters?" replied Renfro with a grin.

They quickly learned that the kitchens in the Citadel were the gears that made the place run. The stern women who ran them—sisters or not—brooked no foolishness or visitors.

The most impressive for the two young men, though, was the armory. Arms and armor of nearly every description stretched down narrow corridors as far as they could see. Most of the weaponry was standard issue for the Citadel's guards, but they also had a dazzling array of foreign weapons.

As they were marveling over a rack of wicked-looking exotic axes, a young man approached them and asked, "Anything I can help you with, sirs?"

"Just taking the boys to admire your stock," Rhys responded.

"Finest collection of arms anywhere on the continent," remarked the young man. "We've got weapons from places you've never even heard of. Master of Arms Brinn is a bit obsessed about it, to be honest. Anyone comes in here with a piece he hasn't seen and he'll buy it right off 'em. You have the look of men at arms. Here for the Conclave next week?"

"No, uh…" Ben wasn't sure what to say.

Rhys broke in, "Yes, we're arms' men in the service of Lady Amelie. We're not here for the…what did you call it? Conclave? We're just passing through."

"Lady Amelie." The guard grinned. "Word was she was at the Citadel. I cannot believe she isn't here for the Conclave. Argren called in all of his banner men and they will be discussing the Grand Alliance."

"I'm not sure Lord Gregor of Issen considers himself a banner man. We have been travelling with Lady Amelie and I'm certain she did not know a Conclave had been called." Rhys glanced at Ben. "Crazy timing though, us happening along right before that started. Amelie didn't know and neither did I, but maybe someone else in our party heard about it."

The young guardsman seemed dismayed by the denial. "Well, I'm sure Lord Gregor and his daughter have a lot to think about. While you're here, would you care to spar?"

Rhys pushed Ben forward. "He would love to!"

❧

As BEN STRAPPED on sparring pads, it occurred to him that Assistant to the Master of Arms was likely a pretty boring job. Master Brinn oversaw the training of new guardsmen and the supply of arms for the Citadel. His young assistant's only responsibility seemed to be watching the storeroom and making sure no one ran off with unassigned weaponry.

Ben took a couple of practice swings with the blunt tourney sword and felt comfortable with it. While it didn't move with the same speed as his actual sword, the weight was similar. The sparring pads constricted his movement a little but he supposed it would be worth it when he was struck. He had never used them with Saala. The blademaster was skilled enough to not cause an injury with his real blade, and Ben was never in danger of actually striking Saala.

The young guardsman walked him out to the sparring grounds which were mostly empty in the late evening twilight. The grass was worn from countless feet scuffing and sliding in combat. There was a small group of green-looking guards training in a far corner, but they had the rest of the field to themselves.

Ben and the young guard squared off and started to spar. In

no time at all, it became obvious that the guard was the more aggressive fighter. He came after Ben with a series of quick thrusts and short swings. Ben was able to dance back and avoid a hit. He started to back around in a circle while the guard pursued.

The guard was aggressive and he was clearly practiced, but Ben was faster, which helped him avoid a big strike. Still, the guard was able to get through Ben's defense several times in the first few moments. The blows were glancing, and with the pads, Ben barely felt them. They would not leave the bruises and welts he'd gotten from the flat of Saala's sword.

After a quarter bell of sparring, Ben noticed the guard maintained a consistent, predictable pattern. He moved through forms similar to what Saala had taught Ben, but unlike the guard, Saala's forms shifted with the reaction of an opponent—he called them anticipatory forms. The guard did not seem to adjust once he was set in a pattern. Ben began predicting the next swing and found he was quick enough to disrupt the pattern and was able to put up a real defense.

Before long, Ben gained enough confidence that he switched over to offense and started attacking. The guard fell into familiar defensive patterns and Ben saw he was meeting the blunted tourney blade head on instead of sweeping the attack to the side like Saala had taught. Every time the guard met one of Ben's swings, Ben's arms rang with the impact. The guard's must have been, too. He was getting slower and slower to recover from each strike.

Ben saw his opening and backed up, letting the guardsman get in an attack. Then Ben sent three hard lateral swings in a row which the guard met with raised sword. On the fourth swing, Ben swept his sword down and up, missing the guard's weapon and connecting solidly with his ribs, sending the man crumpling to the ground.

Rhys and Renfro shouted out a cheer and Ben dropped to one knee beside the fallen guard to make sure he hadn't hurt him. He was relieved to see the guard roll onto his back with a grin on his face.

"Surprised me there," grunted the guard. "I thought you were tiring out."

"I was. I knew I had to get it in then or I'd be too worn out to keep going." Ben reached down and grasped the guard's hand, pulling him to his feet.

"Seth, by the way," the young man introduced himself. "Assistant to the Master of Arms of the Citadel. Glad Brinn wasn't here to see that one."

"If he'd been there to see the first part, all he would have seen was you tacking them on and me flailing backward."

"Ah, it was going well at first," groaned Seth. "But as Brinn says, 'it's how you finish a fight that counts.' Which reminds me, I probably ought to get back to the Armory. I've got a little bit more to do before I close up shop today. When the guards spar we normally put a mug of ale on it to make things interesting. I'll honor the same stakes if you want to meet me after my shift. I'll be down at Meggy's on the street of flowers a bell after dusk. It's where a lot of the guards go. Clean ale, good-looking girls, and they don't try to cheat you."

THAT EVENING on the way down to Meggy's, Renfro excitedly described the match to Saala, who had joined back up with them. "Seth obviously knew what he was doing, being a professional and all, but Ben had him down on the ground by the end of it. Nice piece of sword work if you ask me, up against a guard of the Citadel."

Ben was feeling pretty proud of himself too, until Rhys took the wind out of his sails. "That was a good strike at the end. Of course, in an actual sword fight, you wouldn't have made it to the end. He struck you ten or twelve times before you got one on him. In the real thing, it won't last long after the first blood has been drawn."

"He did get me a few times, but he's a professional guardsman!" exclaimed Ben. "He probably trains every day and I've just had a few lessons on the road."

"If he's like any castle-trained guard I've ever seen fight," Saala interrupted, "Then you shouldn't have had too much trouble with him. Sounds like I've got work to do."

"What do you mean? Why shouldn't I have had any trouble with him? I hadn't even picked up a sword until a few weeks ago!" protested Ben.

"Maybe I'm putting too much expectation on you too soon," replied Saala with a sigh. "You're a natural with a blade. You're quicker and smarter than most of the opponents you'll ever face. The reason you should be able to beat Seth or most guardsmen is that instead of training, they drill. He's probably been taught a handful of useful forms and has been practicing them for years now, most likely with people who have been taught the same things as him. If he's like most castle-trained guards, he won't know how to react to something new and different."

Ben thought back to how he had gotten his strike in. Seth had defended only one way against the swing, so Ben had been able to alter his stroke and sweep past Seth's guard. By falling out of the standard form, he'd landed a stroke. When he had been using the forms, Seth was able to meet him with the prescribed defensive responses. He had likely been drilled on them so much that he was able to react without even thinking. Ben realized that he had a lot of work to do before he met an opponent in a real fight.

Tonight, though, he wasn't planning on fighting. They had opted to avoid the funicular and walk through the streets of Whitehall on the way down to Meggy's. It was a balmy night and the lantern-lit streets were teeming with people. The noise of excited revelry poured out of the wine shops and taverns as they descended through the city.

"I can't believe how many people are out tonight. Is it some sort of festival going on?" asked Ben.

"No. It's an influx of people for Argren's Conclave. Delegates, guards, retainers, hangers-on." Saala eyed one exceptionally boisterous group spilling out of a nearby inn. "I'm surprised they're in such good spirits. My friend I met with earlier said the talk is that it will lead to war with the Coalition. Not this year and probably not the next, but the writing is on the wall. Argren is pressing hard to recruit more men, building warships, stockpiling goods... I've seen it before and that road only leads to one destination."

"I don't understand why Argren would want a war with the Coalition. They're all the way on the other side of Alcott. The Coalition isn't a threat to him, is it?"

"It's about balance," Rhys responded. "A buildup of power necessitates a buildup elsewhere. The Coalition has been gathering forces and it's causing a reaction. If it weren't Argren, it'd be someone else. Issen or Venmoor, maybe. No. Once someone starts, it always escalates."

Saala nodded. "Rhys is right, but enough of that. I certainly don't plan to go to war tonight, so let's enjoy it. I hear there is a certain guardsman that owes you a round and I mean to help you collect!"

THE TALK about war was quickly forgotten once they found Meggy's. Seth was true to his word and bought the first round of drinks for their party. Once it got out why he was buying, Ben and his friends drank for free the rest of the evening.

Meggy's was crowded with off-duty Citadel guards and all of

them wanted to hear the story of Seth getting laid out by an untrained country boy. Seth, as the gatekeeper for new arms at the Citadel and one of the few who could bend Master Brinn's ear to keep someone out of trouble, was popular with the other guards. He took the ribbing in good humor. Before the night was over, Ben had a long list of sparring partners that wanted to see what he was really about.

A flushed, bald-headed, heavily bearded guard was already taking bets on the outcomes before Ben knew what was happening. He briefly tried to put a stop to it but the man wrapped an arm around his shoulder and leaned close, sloshing ale all over both of their boots. The guard shouted in his ear, "Don't worry about it none! The only ones that'd be upset about it are the ones who'll lose!"

Ale flowed freely and quickly. Ben was having more fun than he had since leaving Farview. He missed Serrot and his other friends back home, but the excitement of being out at night in a city like Whitehall was overwhelming. He was drunk and giddy with the possibilities of life. One of the last things he remembered before the rest of the night became fuzzy was standing on a table, arm-in-arm with Renfro and Seth, belting out the newly learned marching song of the guards of the Citadel.

THE NEXT MORNING brought a painful reminder of how much ale he drank the night before. His head was pounding and his mouth tasted like sour milk. As he lurched out of bed to the washbasin, he found he was still wearing one boot.

The other men were sitting around a table over breakfast when Ben stumbled out of his room. He got sympathetic looks from Rhys and Saala, but Renfro was slumped over with his head in his hands, softly moaning. Ben thought it was possible someone was having a worse morning than him.

"Try some of this." Rhys gestured to a mug of steaming black liquid. "It's called kaf. They drink it up north, and believe me, it's a critical part of the cure. After that, we'll get some bacon and toasted bread in you then head down to the steam baths. I've been in your shoes more than a few times. We'll get you feeling right as rain by afternoon."

Down in the baths, steam boiled through the dimly lit, cavernous rooms. Ben tipped back a flagon of cold spring water and thought that Rhys really did know what he was talking about. Rhys stated that every drop of water he sweated out had to be replaced by three that he drank. Between that, the kaf, and the food, Ben was almost feeling like his normal self again.

The steam rooms at the Citadel were even more impressive than the bathing room he'd seen at the inn in Fabrizo. There, the copper piping system had fed hot water into a few baths. The steam rooms at the Citadel were made up of a series of honey-combed chambers containing pools going from scalding hot to ice cold. Rhys had them sit on benches in one of the hottest rooms while they poured sweat and drank cold water. When Ben thought he couldn't take the damp heat any longer, they moved down to the coldest of the rooms and plunged into the freezing pool. The change in temperature sent a wicked shock through Ben's body. Rhys claimed it made his blood pump harder and helped clear out the toxins from the night before. Now, they were in the last stage of recovery and were soaking in one of the warmer pools before eating again, and Ben hoped, taking an afternoon nap.

Ben's head was finally clear enough to remember they were supposed to be back on the road this morning. He groaned. "I hope we're not holding off our travel plans because of me getting drunk. Lady Towaal is going to kill me."

"No, we've got plenty of time now," answered Rhys, who was floating gently in the mineral-smelling water. "Towaal and Amelie left word after their dinner with King Argren last night.

They agreed to stay for the Conclave. Sounds like the both of them want to hear what is discussed."

"What does Lady Towaal have to do with the Conclave?" wondered Ben. "I thought it was just Amelie who was relaying a message from her father."

"You've got a lot to learn about politics, kid. I didn't know it before we got here, but the Sanctuary is neck deep in this. I should have realized something was going on earlier. Lords need mages and mages need lords. Think about it. Why else would Towaal have been pushing us to travel so hard? Sure, we need to get Amelie and the others to the Sanctuary, but there's no deadline there. I wouldn't be surprised if Towaal knew about this and was angling to be here before we even left Issen."

"But, on the ship, Lady Towaal sounded like she was against a war. She said in the Blood Bay War there was no real winner."

"She would know that better than anyone," murmured Rhys. "It was brutal after that war and while people have forgotten, I'm sure she hasn't. Her personal feelings and that of the Veil may be different, though. She's a spirited woman but she'll do what she's told when it comes down to the business of the Sanctuary."

"The Veil?" asked Ben, sitting up in the warm water to look at his friend.

"The Veil is head of the Sanctuary," explained Rhys. "Or the Veil is the Sanctuary, some would say. She's their leader and she leads absolutely. If the Veil wants Argren to form his Alliance, then Towaal will support it. That being said, what the Veil appears to want and what she actually wants may not be the same thing. The currents of politics run deep in the City and the Veil plans decades ahead. I've been travelling with Towaal for months now and I couldn't tell you what the Sanctuary's goals are, but there is no chance they'd miss an event like the Conclave."

THE NEXT FEW days were full of more of the same. Ben found eager sparring companions in the younger Citadel guards and they were more than happy to show him their city. Seth, in particular, took a liking to Ben and treated him almost like a little brother. It was an odd feeling for Ben because he quickly realized that in some ways, he was the more mature and worldly of the two. Still, it felt good to make a connection with someone who was close to his own age.

Seth, like many of the younger guards, had never been more than half a day outside of Whitehall. Initially, Ben was the one bubbling over with questions, but soon he found himself spending more time describing the islands of Fabrizo than he did hearing about the towering structures below the Citadel.

The girls, for the most part, stayed in another wing of the keep. Saala, Rhys, and Renfro also kept to themselves. The men would come watch Ben spar and may come out for a few ales afterward, but none of them struck up friendships like Ben did. With the amount of time he was spending with the guards, Ben felt himself being pulled away from his travelling companions.

After one awkward evening at Meggy's where Saala repeatedly dodged Seth and other's questions, Ben asked him about it during the walk home.

"These are my friends. They're good people. They're helping me on the practice field and they're showing us around Whitehall. I don't understand why you are avoiding talking to them."

Saala slowed his pace and glanced around the nearly empty streets. Lantern light reflected off cobblestones still wet from an earlier rain. This late in the evening they were alone, aside from the occasional passerby bundled up and uninterested in them. "They are friendly, but that doesn't mean they are friends. The help they are giving you, the time they are spending with you, it is because they want to learn about you and who you are travelling with."

"What do you mean?" Ben asked Saala. "Why would they have any reason to want to know about me?"

"You are a simple boy from Farview."

Ben glanced at the blademaster out of the corner of his eye.

"I didn't mean that to sound bad." Saala sighed. "I mean that your motives for being here in Whitehall are simple. You are here for your friend Meghan. Maybe you are here because you're enjoying a bit of an adventure. But that is it. These people in this place, they are so used to intrigue that they can't understand you are what you seem."

"I don't think so, Saala. I've spent nearly all of the last four days with these guardsmen. They've heard my story. They know who I am."

"Hearing isn't always believing, Ben. You are travelling with the Princess of Issen, a mage of the Sanctuary, and me, a blade-master. We show up unannounced and claim we are just passing through, but now two of our companions are members of King Argren's Conclave. That is bound to raise some eyebrows. I'm sure King Argren is finding out what he wants to know directly from Lady Amelie and Lady Towaal, but the city is packed full of people with political ambition right now. With tensions rising between the Alliance and the Coalition and now the apparent involvement by the Sanctuary, well, certain information has value in that environment. If the Sanctuary is going to lean toward one side or the other it could make a big difference in the conflict."

"But that's just ridiculous!" argued Ben. "Lady Towaal wasn't even invited to this Conclave, was she?"

Saala laid a hand on Ben's shoulder. "No, I don't think she was. Argren certainly wasn't expecting her at least. Maybe it's just a coincidence Lady Towaal has been pressing to travel so hard and we happened to arrive right before the biggest political council this half of the continent has seen in years. Now that we're here, of course, it makes sense to wait for over a week. Could be Lady Towaal is just lucky she happened to be travelling with one of the couple dozen people who were invited to this event. What do you think—is it luck or design?"

They continued up the damp streets quietly. Ben was mulling over what Saala had said. When put like that, it seemed an awfully large jump to write it off as mere coincidence. But if it weren't, what would motivate the ladies? Amelie's father was actually invited to this thing, so she would have no reason for subterfuge. And even though she wasn't invited according to Saala, King Argren had certainly not turned Towaal away. Travelling all of the way to Issen and back with Amelie in tow seemed like an awfully lot of work and timing just to get into a meeting. Saala worked for Amelie, he had to know something.

Ben glanced at his friend. "If you're worried about sharing some sort of secret information with Seth and the other guards, then why are you letting me talk to them? You've heard me. I've been telling them everything I know."

"Precisely Ben, you've been telling them what you know. Of course, you can't tell them things you don't know. I can assure you that Lady Amelie is not here under some false pretense. I've been with her family for years now, long before this journey was planned. I know it wasn't planned in anticipation of this event. She would tell me if she was playing a deeper game. But Towaal, I only met her days before we left Issen. She arrived early and pressed us to leave quickly. I don't know what she is up to, but there are secrets there. I do not tell you this to concern you. I don't think any of these plans directly involve you. I am just trying to explain why I have been reclusive toward the guardsmen. Keep being friendly with them if you like, it makes no matter to me. Lady Amelie or Lady Towaal would have already stopped you if they were concerned. Just be aware, not everything is always as it seems."

The conversation cut off as they entered the Citadel and headed toward their rooms. The now friendly nods from the guardsmen and glances from the service staff had taken on a new meaning to Ben. He wasn't sure he'd be able to shake the suspicious seeds that Saala planted. He was so lost in thought that he didn't notice a door swing open and he plowed straight into the man exiting it.

Startled, Ben sprawled backward onto the stone floor. The man quickly spun around.

Saala snorted loudly when they saw who it was.

A shocked-looking Rhys stared down at Ben and exclaimed, "Oh damn! You scared the hell out of me. I thought you were..."

Rhys broke off as another person darted out of the doorway. It was an attractive woman with disheveled hair and smeared makeup. She paused to stare daggers at Ben and Saala before turning up her nose and sweeping past them down the hall. Ben watched and half expected her to break into a run before she got to the nearest intersection where she glanced both ways then hurried down one without looking back at the three men.

Rhys reached one hand down and hauled Ben to his feet. He was grinning ear to ear and said, "Well, how was your night?"

THE NEXT MORNING Ben hit the practice field early. The grass was still damp with morning dew and most of the new guardsmen Ben trained with had not arrived yet. The few who had were clustered near the armory sipping steaming cups of kaf.

Ben nodded to a few of the men he had seen before and went to the racks where the practice weapons were stored. He planned to run through some of the sword forms to get warmed up before his normal sparring partners arrived. Saala constantly emphasized the importance of stretching, warm ups, and warm downs before, during, and after practice. It was another thing Saala felt the guards didn't do well. He said that if you didn't stretch, it would leave you sore, tight, and useless when a real fight broke out.

As Ben was working his way through a complicated series of strokes that Saala had taught him, he saw a shape out of the corner of his eye and spun around into a fighting stance.

"Ha!" shouted a large keg-shaped man. "I like it. I wish some of my boys had half your vigor. This early in the morning they're all still in the barracks paying for the celebration the night before. It's like they think war only breaks out in the afternoon after half a roast chicken and pint of ale down at Meggy's."

The man was impossible to miss around the practice yard, both because of his imposing size and wherever he walked there was always a flurry of activity in his wake.

"Yes sir, Master Brinn. I'm still new to the sword so I, uh, need the practice," replied Ben clumsily.

"Right. Maybe so, but you don't look new to me. Must be getting good training from those fellows you're with." He nodded toward Saala, who was strolling into the practice yard. "A blade-master, am I right?"

Ben winced. After his talk with Saala the night before, he was sensitive to questions. "Yes sir. I've been training with my companions." He wasn't sure where this was going or how to deal with it. A diversion seemed like the safe option. "I've really enjoyed sparring with your men, sir. They've taught me a lot."

"Good, good. Care to show me?" Master Brinn stripped off his shirt, lifted a heavy-looking two-handed practice sword from the rack, and gave it a few twirls. He was shaggy as a bear. At first glance, he looked stocky, but Ben could see heavy muscle cording as he swung the practice sword.

Ben nervously backed up, bringing his own sword up. "Uh, sir, don't you want some training armor?"

Brinn grinned widely. "You saying I'll need it?"

Ben was saved from answering by Saala appearing at his side.

"Just a few words of encouragement for my pupil," he told Brinn with a wink. In Ben's ear, he whispered, "He's strong, obviously, but be prepared for him to be fast too. And he's not going to fall for any of the little tricks you've been using on his guardsmen. This is an experienced fighter. Assume he knows the same forms you do plus many more. Your speed and agility are your best friends. Try to stay away from direct engagement because that sword of his is going to put a hurt on you if he makes solid contact. First, you need to shake him up. He's used to ruling this yard and you need to show him you're not afraid. Be aggressive and go on the attack. Hopefully you shake him up a bit and then let him wear himself out."

Saala shoved Ben forward and moved off to the side. Immediately, Brinn lunged and launched a probing jab toward Ben's midsection which Ben avoided by back pedaling. Ben danced a few steps to Brinn's offhand. The Master of Arms easily pivoted to face him. Before his opponent settled, Ben started one of the forms that the guardsmen seemed to favor, and as he expected, Brinn raised his sword in defense. Instead of completing with a high swing like he had seen Seth do numerous times now, Ben dropped to one knee and slashed down at Brinn's legs.

The Master of Arms was caught flat-footed and took a solid strike on his left leg before lurching backward. Ben surged off his knee. Instead of going for a body shot, he took a swipe at Brinn's left arm, slapping his practice blade hard against the exposed skin. The Master of Arms grunted in pain as he lost his grip with one hand and tried to spin out of the way.

Seeing his opening, Ben reversed his swing and leaned in, feeling the satisfying tug of his weapon dragging across the other man's chest. His elation was short lived though, as the Master of Arms continued his spin then dropped low like Ben had and swept his two-handed sword into Ben's legs.

Ben's feet were thrown out from under him with the impact. He crashed hard onto the dew-damp ground. He tried to roll away but was tangled by his sword and Brinn slammed a knee down hard onto his chest. It was painful even through the padded practice armor. Brinn tapped a finger on Ben's forehead. Then the big man reached down and grabbed him by the shoulder, hauling him to his feet and roaring with laughter.

By now, everyone at the practice yard was watching the matchup.

"Got your breath?" asked Brinn.

Ben nodded and quickly fell back into a defensive posture as the bear of a man charged toward him. This time, when Ben tried to slide out of the way and take the offensive, Brinn was ready. He smacked Ben's weapon away hard. To his shame, Ben felt the sword fly out of his grip for the first time since his early days training on the road with Saala.

Ben dove toward the dropped sword and rolled to his feet, but to his surprise, the Master of Arms let him up before advancing again. The next round, Ben managed to hold onto his sword but wasn't able to find an opening in Brinn's defense. Ben took several strikes but none were as powerful as the first couple. He was always given time to recover.

Ben realized the Master of Arms was testing his skills and wasn't interested in causing harm or holding a grudge from the first volley. Ben relaxed into the rhythm of the back and forth and started making a decent show for himself, but still was unable to replicate his earlier success and make contact with Brinn.

After half a bell, Ben was huffing and puffing. The Master of Arms didn't seem worn down at all. The man had gone silent, but he was relentless, constantly pressing his attack, testing Ben. Ben's arms were sagging. Before long, he slipped, allowing Brinn to slide a strike through. It landed heavily on Ben's shoulder and sent him flopping into the dirt again.

Brinn leaned on his two-hander and reached down to haul

Ben up. "Let's take a break son, and get something to eat. I've had enough of a workout today."

Ben grimaced. Brinn's workout was at the expense of Ben's body. Even through the padded practice armor, Ben had felt some blows that would leave nasty bruises.

Brinn waved over Saala, who had been nearby watching, and called for one of his guardsmen to bring bread, cheese, kaf, and water. When Saala arrived, Brinn nodded appreciatively and said, "You've trained him well. Give him a few more months and he'll be one of the best here." He looked over at Ben. "You shocked me, son. I don't know the last time I've had a trainee put a blade on me."

"I may have made some contact," replied Ben, "but I couldn't finish it. You were back on me and I was on the ground before I knew what happened. I never made contact again after that first series."

"Ah, I did get you on the ground and I did manage to redeem myself. I always say it's how you finish the fight, but remember, in a real fight, if those first few swings are good ones, then you will finish it. It doesn't much matter what happens after."

THAT AFTERNOON, Rhys found Ben relaxing in a small courtyard near their rooms. "No more time on the tourney field, huh? I hear you did pretty well with the Master of Arms of this place, if he can even be called that. More like Master of Administering the Arms. Still, the story is the man knows his way around a blade. They say he earned that job by putting down some ugly rebellions a few years back."

"He seemed pretty good to me," responded Ben.

"Ha. There is good and there is good. Swinging sticks at your drinking buddy before you go bed each other's sisters isn't being good with a sword, no matter how nice your uniform looks when you're doing all that drilling and marching."

Ben didn't have a response to that. Sometimes he didn't know how to talk to Rhys. The man acted like a drunk who didn't have a care in the world. Ben had never seen him practice with his sword, but his weapons showed signs of heavy use. He impressed Saala and the confidence he had when sitting in the Thieves' Guild in Fabrizo was impossible to miss. Ben realized he'd hardly seen Rhys over the last few days.

"You seem to know a lot about what I've been doing," remarked Ben. "But I haven't seen much of you. Where have you been?"

"Ah, Ben, surely you know what I've been doing. We're in this big city sharing quarters with the high and mighty. It's a well-known fact that any beautiful city is bound to be full of beautiful women. Why would you spend time on that dirty practice field with a bunch of scruffy-looking men?"

"Scruffy-looking men?" answered Ben skeptically. He eyed Rhys up and down. The man was a born rogue. Even after regular baths and clean clothes, he looked the part.

"I know what you're thinking, Ben. You're thinking that surely these gorgeous highborn ladies must only be interested in foppish court dandies. Judging by the amount of lace and perfume the men of Argren's court wear, that's certainly what they think, but no! You couldn't be more wrong. These ladies are looking for something different. They appreciate a man who's seen the world and can take care of himself. They like a bit of danger, Ben, I swear it's true."

"Is that your line," Ben snorted. "That you're dangerous?"

Rhys guffawed. "Oh, I am certainly not dangerous. Not to any warm willing woman at least. But her husband probably is."

"Her husband! Tell me he's not some lord of this place! What are you doing with a married woman?"

"Don't you worry, boy. Spend enough time with me and I'll

teach you the ways of the world. In fact, I've got some time on my hands now, her husband being recently returned from his voyage to Fabrizo." Rhys stood and stretched. "I've had quite a workout the last few days and I hear you have too, though certainly not as enjoyable as mine. Let's run through the second set of Ohms. That will make us right."

The rest of the afternoon was spent working on the second of the Thirty Ohms. By evening, Ben felt relaxed and refreshed. The light exercise of the movements felt good after several long days on the practice field.

DINNER THAT EVENING was in the small common area adjacent to their rooms. It was just the second time in Whitehall that all of the men in their party dined together. Rhys had been off gallivanting around with his lady friend, Ben and Saala had been spending time with the guardsmen, and Renfro had been occasionally tagging along but mostly vanishing when other people were about. He said it made him nervous being around so many highborn and arms men.

The food was plain and simple, but Ben enjoyed it. He also enjoyed reconnecting with his companions. Even though it had only been a few days, it seemed like longer. He had quickly grown to see the group as part of his family, and over the last month, he'd rarely been away from any of them. He turned the discussion to the women, who they had barely seen since arrival in Whitehall.

"I wonder how Amelie, Meredith, and Meghan are doing?" he asked.

"They're doing fine," Saala responded. "Meghan has fallen in with Meredith and is passing as another handmaiden to Amelie. She doesn't like it, of course, but it's safer that way. An Initiate of the Sanctuary isn't like a full member, but that doesn't mean someone wouldn't want to get their talons in her.

Amelie has been busy meeting with the other princes and princesses in town. Every time there is a gathering like this they size each other up—next generation of rulers and all. They have potential marriages to evaluate, commercial arrangements to negotiate, promises to make, promises to break, spying... It's the usual."

"The usual?" asked Ben incredulously. "That sounds horrible."

Saala shrugged nonchalantly. "It is horrible, but that is the way business is done with the highborn—always something in exchange for something else. And it's better, of course, if you can get what you want without having to give up what the other guy wanted. It's all a big game. A game with consequences, but usually that means pain for someone else. It's rare when the young highborn get out of hand and one ends up hurt or dead."

"Dead!" blurted a shocked Ben.

"Sounds like the Thieves' Guild," added Renfro. "You put enough power or gold on the line and someone always ends up dead. Same as the Merchants Guild. I guess it's the same all over."

"Yep, I gotta agree with the little thief," drawled Rhys. "It's the way the world works up top. Doesn't matter who they are or how they got there. Usually it's by birth, but maybe you're one of the lucky ones who make it big. Once you're there, it's all about the power and the money."

"Well, not always about the power and the money." Saala smiled. He saw the conversation was upsetting Ben. "Someone like Amelie isn't out to do harm, but she still has to play the game. She will do anything to protect her family and her people."

Rhys snorted. "Protect them or use them. I'll give you she seems better than most, but you get that kind of power, it's because you built it off the backs of others." Rhys took a long pull of ale, strangely just his second mug by Ben's count. "It's about leverage, boys. The guy on the top of the pyramid is there because he climbed over everyone else. Look at this Conclave. Argren's already the ruler of one of the most powerful cities on the continent of Alcott, but he's reaching for more. He can't do it with just his armies, so he's recruiting others. It's leverage."

Ben challenged, "If he's just grabbing power, why would Issen and the others join him?"

"Because they're scared or because they think they can grab a little bigger piece for themselves in the process. He's drumming up this threat from the Coalition. Maybe they're a threat, maybe not. Maybe the Coalition is telling all the lords in the east that Argren is the real threat. Either way, there's going to be war. First, the Alliance and Coalition will consolidate their power bases until they just got each other to look at. Then it will start. The reason why only matters to the historians. For us, it's all about how to survive their game until tomorrow and then the next day."

Saala raised his mug. "Survive until tomorrow."

THE NEXT DAY, Ben was back out on the practice field. Some of Seth's friends were eager to try their hand at the man who struck Master Brinn, so there was no shortage of opponents. Ben found quickly that they all tended toward the same patterns and used the same forms and strokes that Seth did. Some were a little quicker, some were a little cleaner in their execution, but none of them were creative fighters.

Halfway through the morning, Seth pulled Ben aside. "Wow, you've improved a lot since that first day we sparred."

"You must be training me well," quipped Ben. Inside, he knew that it wasn't that he was getting that much better. He was just able to anticipate what the green guardsmen were going to try next because they all tried the same thing.

"Oh, I'm not sure how much credit I can take," demurred Seth. "I know Master Brinn was impressed, too. I wouldn't be surprised if he asks you to join us soon. We can always use a good man like you. In a few months you'll be one of the best blades we have!"

Seth was beaming with excitement.

Ben struggled to maintain his smile. This was unexpected and a bit unwelcome. Ben had bonded quickly with the young men of the Citadel but he had no intention of joining them. His loyalties to Meghan and his other companions ran deeper.

"We'll see," mumbled Ben. "He hasn't asked me yet."

"He will! Some of the guys have already been talking about you starting in the guards and skipping the greenhorn class. It's going to be great!"

Ben started to stall. He was saved when one of Master Brinn's other assistants called for Seth. A new class of trainees was starting the next day so Seth said he had a lot of work to do getting ready for them. As he dashed off, Ben slowly walked over to the water trough where they kept cool water for rinsing off and drinking after practice.

Ben stripped off his practice armor and sweat-soaked shirt to splash water all over his face and torso. He felt like the last few days in Whitehall were boiling over. Saala's warnings about questions, the discussion about the power of the highborn the night before, and now the guards were hinting at an offer to join their ranks. His dreams of travelling through big cities had never been this complicated.

"Hi, Ben."

He was startled from his contemplation of the water trough and saw Amelie had quietly approached behind him. Some swordsman I am, he thought. Snuck up on by a lady in an open field during broad daylight.

"Hi, Amelie. How have you been? I mean, how has Whitehall been?"

"I've been busy. I heard you are making quite a name for yourself amongst the guards. One of them asked me yesterday if you were going to stay. Are you considering it?"

Apparently, everyone but him knew about the offer. "Uh, no, they haven't really asked me yet. I won't stay though. I want to finish this with you. And Meghan and the others too," he finished quickly.

"I'm sorry we haven't seen each other much the last few days. There's so much to do before the start of the Conclave tomorrow. I was thinking, are you going to the fireworks show tonight?"

A fireworks spectacular was to be held to mark the start of the Conclave and was going to go off down at the port. The way Whitehall was built, tiered into the side of the mountain, nearly everyone in the city would be able to see the show with no obstructions.

"I, um, some of the guards are going to Meggy's and are going to watch from the roof. Meggy's is a tavern they go to... How about you?" he finished lamely.

"I, well, I was invited to a party on the Citadel's veranda. Argren is hosting a Gala. There will be a lot of people there. I was wondering if you would like to go."

"I-I..." stammered Ben.

"It's ok if you don't want to. I'm sure Miggy's—is that what you called it?—I'm sure it will be very nice."

"No, no. I want to go. I definitely want to go. It's just, well, I've never been to a Gala. What do I even wear to something like that?"

"No way!" shouted Renfro. "I can't believe it. The Lady Amelie asked you on a date!"

"It wasn't like that," protested Ben.

Seth leaned in. "I heard it was like that. I heard she said you looked good without a shirt on, too. Heard it from one of the guardsmen who was walking by."

"She just said I was looking fit." Ben realized that wasn't going anywhere productive. "I've been working with the sword a lot recently. I've put on a little muscle, that's all." He cringed. That was even worse.

Renfro collapsed back into the couch he was perched on, howling with laughter. "It's a fairy tale romance! The poor brewer boy catches the eye of the highborn maiden with his beefy muscles. Unfortunately, this tale ends in tragedy. The poor brewer boy doesn't know what to do with a highborn maiden!"

Ben ground his teeth. He'd rushed back to the rooms and immediately told Renfro what had happened. Seth had shown up moments later, telling how the entire practice yard was buzzing with rumors that some foreign guardsmen trainee was escorting Lady Amelie to the Grand Fireworks Spectacular. They hadn't stopped since. The thing wasn't "Grand" when Seth had been talking about watching it from Meggy's.

He was saved from further harassment when Meredith showed up at the rooms with one of the Citadel's groomsmen. They had the assignment of making sure Ben had proper attire.

She shooed Renfro and Seth out of the door and instructed the groomsman to draw a bath.

"Well," she said with a growing mischievous smile, "are you going to undress or would you like me to help?"

Two bells after being briskly bathed and dressed by the groomsman, Ben was still cooling his heels in Amelie's waiting room. It was a beautiful room, certainly the nicest Ben had ever been in, but it was starting to get boring. There's only so much time one can spend contemplating which farms you could buy in Farview with the pair of gold candlesticks, the crystal bowls, or the finely woven rugs.

A mechanical device with two thin hands moving around a

circular face took up a good portion of his time. It wasn't until both of the hands pointed directly upward and the thing emitted seven chimes that he realized it must be a clock. He'd heard about them, of course, and people in Farview referred to time in bells, but even the Pinewoods didn't have enough money to purchase one of these.

Both Meredith and Meghan occasionally popped in to check on him. Amelie was nowhere to be seen. The girls said she was getting ready and seemed outright offended when he asked how it could possibly be taking this long. Meghan, who Ben felt should have been sympathetic to his plight, was not appreciating the situation.

"A lady takes as long as she needs to. If you just sit here long enough, you will have a wonderful time tonight with your lady friend. I'm sure it will be oh so grand." The dramatic eye roll was a little much, thought Ben.

"Come on, Meghan. What is she doing in there? I've been out here half the evening and this stuff is itching!" He pulled at the snug grey tights the groomsman had foisted on him. He had never worn anything like it and would have thought it was a cruel joke except he'd seen many of the men around the Citadel wearing them.

"She's preparing for a Gala, Ben. I've never been to one, of course, but I'm sure the lords and ladies will all be decked out in their finest. Amelie said there will be more highborn at this Conclave than there were when Argren's daughter got married, although the costumes will be less colorful. There will be banquets, musicians, jesters, play actors, and I heard there will even be a captive wyvern."

"A wyvern!" Ben couldn't believe it. Wyverns were mythical beasts that even after travelling on the road with a blademaster, a mage, and a lady, he still would have bet only lived in the stories. Even Old Gamson claimed they only existed in ancient times. They were supposed to be giant lizards with terrible claws that could fly and breathe fire. Children's stories. "I don't think wyverns really exist. Maybe the play actors are pretending to be one."

"You could be right." Meghan sighed. "You were always the one who knew about the stories. Still, it will be a grand evening and I'm jealous, that's all. I'm sorry I'm giving you such a hard time about it."

"Jealous? What do you mean? I'm just going with Amelie as friends. Why does everyone think it's more?" Ben hoped it was more, of course, but he wasn't going to say that aloud.

"Oh, I know it's just as friends. I'm not jealous of your 'date' with Amelie." Meghan gave another eye roll. "I won't be able to go to the party. There are too many highborn in town for the Conclave for everyone to fit on the balcony. We were told it was just Lady Amelie, Lady Towaal, and their guests. No serving staff."

"Oh. Meghan, you're not really her handmaiden. It's just pretend until we get out of here."

"I know. I remember that very well. I just hope she does, too, when we leave."

A QUARTER BELL LATER, according to the clock face, Ben's jaw dropped. Amelie peeked in before stepping into the room. She looked stunning. She was draped in a flowing green silk gown that left her shoulders bare and spread out across the floor behind her. Her dark hair was raised in an elaborate sparkling jewel studded bun and she was decked in a dazzling array of emeralds around her neck and wrists. As she came into the room, a subtle scent of mountain wildflowers floated around her. The entire impression was breathtaking. He found his eye drawn to her face. Her lips were glistening cherry red, her cheeks were lightly flushed, and around her eyes was a smoky shadow that drew him in and held his gaze, even when he was very interested in the way some other parts of her looked.

"Amelie..."

She twitched her dress and teasingly said, "You're supposed to be telling me how beautiful I am."

"I... You are beautiful. I've never seen anything like this, I mean anyone. I mean, you look good," he finished weakly.

"Ha. You are sweet," she said with a blush. "Argren had a seamstress and jeweler sent and I'm worried it didn't turn out like they envisioned."

"I mean it, Amelie. Really. I've seen girls in dresses and girls with their hair done for a wedding or the spring dance, but nothing like this. No one who looked as amazing as you. I'm not exaggerating. You're the most beautiful girl I have ever seen."

"Well, you'll soon see a lot of girls like me," she said, swishing her skirts around and glancing away from Ben. "Half of Whitehall. Well, half of the wealthy in Whitehall anyway. All of the women will be dressed like this. Thank you for the compliment though, I appreciate it," she finished in a rush, finally meeting his eyes again.

Ben didn't have a lot of experience with girls, and she'd caught him off guard, but he wasn't stupid.

THE CITADEL'S Gala for the Grand Fireworks Spectacular honoring the First Conclave of the Alliance was growing in name and noise as they approached. A wide stone path between splashing fountains and ponds was lit by roaring fires and populated by towering long-legged jesters juggling and cavorting through the crowd. Amelie whispered over the noise of a nearby pack of musicians that the jesters were standing on tall wooden poles called stilts.

As they approached the actual balcony they passed a wave of

men and women loaded with glasses of red, white, and bubbling wines, followed by more serving staff carrying silver trays piled with arrangements of delicate foods. Ben had never had the bubbling wine before. At Amelie's suggestion he plucked two glasses from a passing tray, handed her one, and gave it a try. It was crisp but sweet and tingled and popped in his mouth as he swished it around.

Before he could even comment on the drink, he ducked from a billow of flame exploding in front of a shirtless, sweating man holding a flickering torch. The man cartwheeled off into the crowd. Heartbeats later, another burst of flame leapt into the air to the delighted shouts of nearby revelers.

Ben turned back to Amelie. Again before he could speak, an orange and black-striped beast strolled by with a scrawny turbaned man straddling its back. The animal had fangs the size of Ben's forearm protruding from a head larger than his torso. Its shoulders were even with his. A shudder ran down his back at the thought of that creature attacking, but it seemed tame and calmly sidestepped one of the jesters on stilts who had wandered in from the entryway.

The menagerie only got wilder as they moved deeper into the party. There was an animal that Ben would have called a bear, if it weren't a quarter of the size of ones he was familiar with in Farview. It was balancing on a colorful crimson ball being led around the balcony by a man in a matching crimson vest and short cylindrical hat.

A mage, or at least a woman claiming to be one, held intense concentration on three golden rings in front of her. To Ben's amazement, they looked to be floating freely in the air. As Amelie and Ben paused to watch, she waved her hands under and over the rings then produced a bright purple handkerchief. She bent over the handkerchief muttering words which Amelie said were gibberish then tossed the cloth into the air. The handkerchief hovered briefly then shot through the three rings and into the waiting hands of a young woman who appeared shocked and amazed.

The crowd broke into polite applause as the mage bowed. Amelie sniffed and turned to go. "No real mage would be involved in such a thing."

"It looked pretty real to me," argued Ben. He nodded toward the woman who had caught the handkerchief. She was loudly praising the mage and eagerly showing her trophy to the other partygoers. "She seems impressed."

"They're clearly confederates. I've seen similar in Issen. It was well done, but still trickery. Look," she said, gesturing to the crowd, "don't you think people would be more interested if they thought she was really doing magic?"

Ben had to admit, the crowd had thinned quickly. He and Amelie moved on as well.

A bell later, the experience was becoming overwhelming. As they circled the balcony, the continuous assortment of entertainers started to blend in with the brightly dressed partygoers. Wine was continuously passed by straight-faced serving staff. As it flowed and the last light of day faded, everyone there seemed to merge together into one giant, choreographed show.

Ben was disappointed to find there was no wyvern at the party, though there was plenty else to shock. In one corner of the balcony, they peered into a close-knit circle of revelers to see two bright blue-painted and totally naked men mimicking graphic sexual acts on a similarly naked shimmering gold-painted woman. A red-faced and disgusted Ben quickly pulled Amelie away.

Moments later, he was just as shocked to see a sweating, rotund, and bulbous nosed man pressing a young lady, maybe a third his age, against the stone railing that surrounded the balcony. The man was sloppily kissing the young woman's neck and was pushing her skirts up with one hand above her waist. The woman was giggling uncontrollably and kept admonishing several other girls nearby who must be her friends to go get help. The girls, instead of seeming concerned, kept shouting encouragement to the man. One even swooped in close to slap him on the behind with a closed fan before darting away when he reached for her. He looked back longingly before returning to his original prey.

"Shouldn't we do something? I believe the man is attacking that girl." Ben couldn't help but think back to Murdoch's when Meghan was about to be assaulted like this. He was on unfamiliar ground and didn't want to start another fight, but he had to do something, even if the poor girl's friends wouldn't.

"She's fine," answered Amelie coolly. "That is Lord Rhymer, but I have no idea who she is. If the old man doesn't have a heart attack and is able to finish the job, getting knocked up by him would be the best thing that's ever happened to her. He's the Lord of Northport and the wealthiest man here, aside from Argren himself, of course. He gets too drunk and is rarely able to consummate I am told. From the times he was able, he has just three bastard daughters. His actual wife has never been able to give him child. Any male offspring of his could be heir to Northport."

Amelie's logic was cold. The idea that a young woman would subject herself to a man like that was unbelievable to Ben. The entire event was starting to put him on edge.

They were rescued from more discussion on the topic by the arrival of a short, mousy-looking man with a dark, angular face and hook-beaked nose. His dark unadorned clothing set him aside from the crowd as much as his sour grimace. He appeared to be the only one with no interest in the insane party taking place around him.

"Lady Amelie." He took her hand and bowed over it before rising and curtly nodding in Ben's general direction, without making eye contact.

"Tomas?" acknowledged Amelie with a raised eyebrow.

"I believe the fireworks are about to start," responded the man. "I have Rafael saving us a good spot near the railing. Would you care to join us?"

"Of course, and then you must tell me what you're doing here," replied Amelie. She turned to follow the man into the crowd.

Over her shoulder, she explained to Ben, "Tomas is my father's seneschal. He handles my father's business when he is unavailable, or more often, when it bores him."

When they got to the railing, Ben could see Rafael was Tomas' security. He was dressed in practical, loose clothing similar to Saala, but where Saala was lean like a mongoose, Rafael was stout and hulking like a wolverine. His head was also shaved like Saala's and he had a network of white scars crossing from just above one ear to the back of his head. He quickly scanned Ben before dismissing him and bowed to Amelie.

"Rafael, can you please go get us two glasses of that delightful sparkling wine?" asked the slight seneschal. "We must have a drink in hand to cheers for the—"

"Three Rafael," broke in Amelie.

Tomas glanced at Ben. "It spoils the Man at Arms act when he's drinking, but very well."

"He doesn't need to be my man at arms. He can be my escort."

"Scandalous," replied Tomas dryly.

"Wait. I'm your what?" asked Ben.

"It doesn't do having a lady like Amelie at these functions with no male by her side. It sends the wrong message and some of these gentlemen can get pushy," murmured Tomas.

Ben thought back to the unfortunate girl cornered by Rhymer and realized that made sense.

"A lady alone or a lady with her female attendants is suggesting she's open to advances," added Amelie. "I, of course, am not open to any sort of advances by these men and never have been." She winked at Ben. He felt his heart lighten. After the way she spoke about Rhymer, he felt shocked by her world and was worried about what she'd do to gain an advantage. He understood how one can be part of something but not a participant. He wouldn't want people to judge him solely because he had been adopted by Alistair Pinewood.

Tomas leaned in toward Amelie and started speaking quickly. "Is he safe to speak in front of?" he asked with a look at Ben.

Amelie nodded.

Tomas continued, "While Rafael is gone then. That poor man hates it when I speak business in public. You are prepared for tomorrow?"

"Of course I am prepared, but like I said, what are you doing here?" she asked.

"The Coalition made another offer to your father," answered Tomas in a whisper. "But nothing has changed. I'm here to make sure Argren knows that."

"I'm ready and Argren is aware. At the beginning of the Conclave tomorrow, we'll announce our allegiance and that Issen joins Whitehall. That can't be the only reason my father sent you, though."

Tomas frowned and leaned in closer. "We heard about the Conclave shortly after you left. Weeks after Argren's messenger should have been there. Something happened to him and he never made it. Sending you with little escort in the care of Saala and Towaal was the right decision. It's dangerous for you to be in public like this and we hoped I would catch you before you announced yourself. Your father doesn't know who else to trust." Tomas shot a dark glance at Ben and the nearby revelers.

"Oh, don't worry about it Tomas!" chided Amelie. "Everyone knows I am here already. Our decision will be known from the Citadel to the docks by tenth bell tomorrow. What's the point of secrecy? My father has made up his mind. There is nothing we will do from here to change it anyway."

With that, there was a sharp whistle followed by a massive

boom. The railing shook and the entire night sky was lit a dazzling white as the first firework exploded in the air. Crackling streams of sparks descended toward the city. The first blast was followed by a quick succession of increasingly large flashes. The first salvo of fireworks was an iridescent white. It bathed the entire balcony, the face of the Citadel, and all of the revelers, in a stark white glow.

8

RUINED EVENING

THE GRAND FINALE of the fireworks lived up to the name spectacular. It started with a low, flat explosion of green sparkles that lingered in the air, drifting over the ships in the port far below. Then, behind the guests on the balcony, a cacophony of horns sounded in a thrilling mixture of traditional hunting calls and alarm.

Ben looked back and saw the wall of Citadel was lined with horn players. Argren must have forced out the entire barracks and bought every instrument in the city to put together that many of them, he thought. As he turned back toward the blanket of green sparkles, he saw Amelie smiling down at them. The green light of the fireworks reflected in the emeralds she was wearing and highlighted the gentle curve of her neck. He swallowed the lump in his throat. The moment was interrupted when the tone of the horns changed and a brilliant wave of red and gold arced into the sky.

The fireworks went off with a roar. The crowd took a step back as the entire vista filled with a red and gold beast swooping toward them with wide open maw. The creature would have been nearly the size of Whitehall itself. The crackle and hiss of the exploding lights added to the illusion that the beast was imminently going to rain fire down onto the partygoers.

"Wyvern!" shouted an alarmed and slurred voice from behind them.

Ben and Amelie grinned at each other. Ben had to admit the fire and smoke monster was frightening. As it grew closer, the lights started popping and crackling out until they flashed into darkness. A warm wave of sulphurous air drifted over crowd.

Across the entire city there was silence for several heartbeats then an enormous cheer broke out. From the bottom of the port to the top of the Citadel, the citizens and guests of Whitehall were screaming, clapping, and banging whatever they could to make noise.

Amelie took Ben's arm and leaned against him, staring out down at the city and celebration below. Smaller fireworks shot up sporadically as the citizens who could afford it put on their own version of the show. It almost felt like these hundreds of thousands of cheers were just for the two of them.

When the smoke cleared and some of the excitement on the balcony began to fade, the crowd turned to make their way back through the halls of the Citadel and into the city. For many, the celebration was just getting started, though Ben saw several people he thought should start sleeping it off now. The Conclave was starting early in the morning.

Amelie still had her arm hooked around Ben's as they made their way toward the entry of the building. Ben caught Tomas staring at him with a blank face. The man was the right hand of Amelie's father. Ben thought he understood the look, but he made a note to watch his back.

Suddenly, a man pushed past Ben, heading back out onto the balcony.

"What are you doing? I'm an important guest for the Conclave. I'll have the guards on you!" shouted a tipsy-sounding man behind them.

"Two drunks are about to go at it! I heard they're sending for swords."

Several more of the crowd turned to follow the man who had pushed through. A duel was more entertaining than what the taverns and wine shops in the city had to offer.

Amelie pulled on Ben to keep going. "Stupid men doing stupid things. There's always one or two at parties like this. They probably stepped on each other's toes or someone took the last sparkling wine. Such a waste. Like there isn't more in the world to worry about."

Ben had to agree. No one dueled in Farview, of course, but the stories were full of them. In the stories, it was always over a girl.

Before they made it into the entrance of the Citadel, they saw Saala coming the other way. He nodded back toward the balcony and remarked, "You'll want to see this."

Ben raised an eyebrow then fell in behind Saala. They joined the crowd gathering around two shouting men.

"You will die for this!" snarled a man as the sounds of a scuffle broke out.

"Fredrick, wait until the man is armed or you'll be paying for it also," responded an unseen voice.

Through the pack of people, they could see a short, balding man being held back by two grey-haired men. The grey-haired men had the build of those who had seen their share of battle, but they were struggling to keep the energetic smaller man from rushing forward.

Before they could see the target of his wrath, they heard a man slur, "Whatcha holding him back for? That little sword he's packing couldn't hurt a mouse. Least that's what I heard from his wife."

Ben's heart sank. He'd heard that drunken slur before. Rhys.

The short bald man redoubled his efforts to break loose and howled, "This is to the death. I will not stand for this!"

One of the grey-haired men holding him glared back at Rhys

and demanded, "Stop it. Both of you. A duel has been agreed and you can settle your differences, but I will make sure it's done right or it won't be done. Do you understand me?"

"Yes, general," said the short man in a huff. He was still extremely agitated but he no longer fought to get to Rhys.

For the rogue's part, he was swaying around at the far side of the circle of onlookers and seemed to be having trouble focusing.

"How many of you are there? I see four. I gotta fight all four?" Rhys was squinting toward the three men and holding up his hands in a boxing stance.

"Look now," said the man who had been called general. "This fellow is too drunk to see straight. This is not right."

The crowd chimed in with a chorus of boos until an icy look from the man silenced them. They were there to see blood. If it waited until tomorrow, in the sober light of day, this duel might not happen.

Saala slipped from Ben's side and stepped into the circle. "I believe this man has given Lord Fredrick cause. It is a sensitive matter, and there is a lady involved. We can settle it this evening."

The general appraised Saala. "And who are you?"

"I am the man's travelling companion. I can serve as his second."

"Aye, he's my second. Couldn't have a better man for it either!" crowed Rhys. "Although, I'm not sure it's the little fella's woman I was with. She's a lady right? The wench I was bedding certainly wasn't acting like a lady. Ladies don't have you bend them over and make you call them a filthy whore, do they?" Rhys peered quizzically at Saala.

Lord Fredrick lunged again toward Rhys and was barely caught by the other man holding him.

The general's shoulders visibly slumped and he stepped into the center of the circle. "It appears that despite my reservations, this will happen tonight." He nodded toward Saala. "Since you know this man and have agreed to proceed as his second, I will take the same role for Lord Fredrick. We will continue until both parties are satisfied or one combatant is unable to continue. You may choose your weapons."

A heavy broadsword was passed to Lord Fredrick and a woman hurried forward. The same woman Ben had seen Rhys in the closet with. Ben groaned. It seemed this woman did have a dangerous husband. The man did not appear to have the stature of a warrior, but his sword had telltale nicks in it that only came from use.

"You don't need to do this," pleaded the woman. "This man is nothing! He'll likely be hung as a thief or worse by next week. I was stupid!"

Fredrick backhanded the woman across the face and sent her tumbling into the crowd. "If the man was nothing, it should have been left as a diversion while I was at sea. I will deal with you later."

He swung his broadsword through the air as if to reacquaint himself with the balance and turned toward Rhys. "You should have left it as well. I could understand you thinking you could get away with this while I was gone. I could have understood it as a mistake and maybe just left you a cripple. But tonight? That is too much. For that, you will die."

The general was slowly pivoting, keeping himself between Fredrick and Rhys. He turned toward Rhys. "Do you have a blade?"

Rhys just stared back at him.

An enthusiastic young man from the crowd stepped forward, proffering a slender rapier and smirking. "Use this, good man. She's served me well."

Saala glanced down at the delicate weapon then back up to meet Rhys' eyes.

The crowd was turning nasty.

Rhys swished the rapier back and forth, not hearing the hoots and calls from around the circle. These people wouldn't be satisfied until they got blood.

Ben grabbed Amelie's arm and whispered, "He's going to get killed! That rapier won't stand against a broadsword. It will snap the first time they make contact. I don't understand why Saala is letting this happen. We have to stop it!"

"I think you're about to be surprised," answered Amelie in a hushed tone. She nodded to the opposite side of the circle. "See Lady Towaal over there. I saw her gesture to Saala before he stepped in. Rhys is her hired man and she's been with him for months, if not longer. She doesn't look worried to me. Think about it. He's good enough to get hired by a mage. I suspect he knows exactly what he's doing."

"I don't know," worried Ben. "He doesn't even look like he can see straight. And I'm not sure if Lady Towaal cares about anyone other than herself. And sometimes you," he added. He had to admit though, Amelie made a point.

Towaal was casually chatting with another woman next to her. She held up her wine glass, swirled it around, sniffed it, and pointed to it. The woman nodded and did the same with her own glass before taking a sip and remarking back to Towaal with a smile.

The general brought everyone's attention to the circle when he loudly declared, "When I step away, you may begin. Remember, if one combatant becomes incapacitated, it will stop there." He looked directly at Fredrick when he said it.

The crowd quickly shuffled back a few steps. They may be drunk and blood thirsty, but no one wanted to be too close when Fredrick started swinging that broadsword.

When the general stepped back, Fredrick howled a battle cry and charged. Rhys was barely paying attention and staggered out of the way. Fredrick's first wild swing whistled by where Rhys' head had been a heartbeat before.

"Wanda, Wanda. I can't believe he hit you. I told you he was wrong for you!"

With a start, Ben realized that Rhys was talking to Fredrick's wife.

A man next to Ben started laughing. "That drunk is about to get his head cut off and doesn't even realize it."

The man was right. Fredrick was slowly approaching this time. There wouldn't be another wild swing that missed the mark. He walked up right behind Rhys, who was still imploring the Lady Wanda. Fredrick raised the heavy sword above his head. This was certain to be a fatal blow, and Rhys didn't even realize the fight had started.

"Damn it, man!" shouted the general.

Fredrick started his downward blow and Rhys spun toward the sound of the general's voice. Each heartbeat stretched into a dozen as Ben watched in horror. Fredrick's face was strained into a gleefully wicked mockery of a grin. Rhys looked confused when his gaze caught the man preparing to chop him in two. But as Rhys turned, seemingly almost by accident, the thin blade of the rapier rose in his hand. Ben could barely see the glint of torch light on the narrow steel as Rhys looked from Fredrick to the general.

Fredrick was halfway through his stroke when the rapier pierced his chest. Rhys wasn't even looking at the man, but the motion of his turn had enough force to stick the razor sharp blade deep into Fredrick's body. The crowd gasped in unison when they saw the bloody tip slide out of his back.

Fredrick's broadsword clattered harmlessly to the ground and his corpse slumped onto Rhys' shoulder. Rhys pushed the man away, eyes darting around the suddenly silent circle. He blurted, "What the hell! I think that man was trying to kill me!"

9

THE ROAD II

THE NEXT MORNING, the Citadel was a beehive of activity for the start of the Conclave. Ben, Rhys, and Renfro departed Whitehall in the confusion. Dueling was legal in the eyes of the king and the law when proper procedure was followed. Rhys' duel with Lord Fredrick had been presided over by one of the Citadel's most esteemed generals and had been witnessed by half of the upper class in Whitehall. There was no doubt about the legality. That didn't mean it was smart to hang around town after publicly killing a highborn. There were worse consequences than prison time when a commoner mixed in the business of lords.

The only road out of Whitehall started from an imposing stone arched steel gate on the mountainside of the Citadel. The bulky fortifications made more sense when viewed from the mountain. Though, it would be nearly impossible to mount an attack from that side. Ben supposed it was better than fighting your way up through the entire city.

Just outside of the heavy gates, there was a soaring stone bridge that passed over a river gorge. The water plummeted down an impressive waterfall into the city below. The bridge was sturdy and blissfully short, but Ben shuddered when he glanced over the side. He guessed it was twenty stories below where the waterfall ended violently in a rocky basin, which flowed into the manmade reservoir that supplied the city with fresh water.

Beyond the waterfall, the road was wide and well maintained. In places though, it was covered in a heavy mist from the turbulent White River crashing down over boulders and bends in the gorge. The morning was spent in constant shade and coupled with the mist, it was a damp and chilly way to wake up.

They travelled nearly a full day deeper into the mountains behind Whitehall until they found a clearing near the road and adjacent to a large pool in the river. The country was heavily wooded and mountainous so there was little development. It didn't have the same series of small towns that led up to Fabrizo.

Rhys explained that once the others joined them, they would move up to the top of the mountain range and go through the Snowmar Pass. On the other side was the Sineook Valley which supplied the agricultural needs of Whitehall and many other cities on the Blood Bay. The Lords of the Sineook Valley were traditionally allegiant to Whitehall as all commerce to the East, most of what the valley produced and purchased, passed through Whitehall's ports.

DURING THE EARLY MORNING TRAVEL, Ben had been afraid to broach the subject of the duel with Rhys. He didn't know how the man would be affected by killing another person. He was expecting Rhys to bring it up himself. He had been very drunk the night before and Ben found it hard to believe he had a clear memory of everything that happened. Surely he had his own questions he wanted answered.

But as their journey progressed, he realized Rhys did not seem affected at all and was actually in a pretty jovial mood.

When they took their first rest, Renfro ended up being the

one to break the ice. He collapsed onto a mossy log by the side of the road and complained, "Oh, man. How much more of this do we have until we see a proper city again?"

Ben felt bad for the young thief. He'd never been far out of Fabrizo and it was flat as a pancake. The entire journey for him so far had been aboard the ship.

"Just four more days of this until we reach Snowmar Station. All uphill by the way." Rhys had a wicked grin as he observed Renfro's crestfallen expression. "A little exercise is healthy for you. It will feel good once you get used to it."

Ben couldn't resist saying, "Rhys, I'm surprised you're feeling so well. It was a bit of a rough night, wasn't it?"

"Just go ahead and ask me." Rhys smirked. "I know you've been stewing on it all morning. Let's get it over with."

"Okay, I guess I do want to know what happened last night."

"You know what happened, Ben. The man called me out and he ended up dead. If I recall, you were there to watch it."

"I was there," bristled Ben, "which is why I'm a little surprised you recall anything at all about last night."

"Ah, yes. Well, I wasn't quite as bad as it seemed," acknowledged Rhys. "Word of advice, if you're truly in a state where you can't see straight, then the best course of action is generally to just apologize and worry about fighting later. It's not a good idea to bare steel when you've had too many cups. Better to make friends and have another cup."

"So, it was an act. Why?"

Rhys unstopped his water skin and took a long drink. "It wasn't entirely an act. I had to drink enough to make it look real. As to why, it needed to look accidental. Bad luck for poor Lord Fredrick that his wife's drunken lover just happened to turn at the wrong moment. There were plenty of witnesses and not a one of them will think it was anything other than a crazy, tragic end to one of Wanda's many affairs."

"Hold on. I don't understand. Are you saying you really killed Lord Fredrick for his Lady Wanda?"

"No, Ben," Rhys answered with a sigh. "I killed Fredrick for you."

Ben could only stare back, confused.

Rhys took another sip of water and frowned. "Fredrick apparently got himself into a bit of a pickle with the Thieves' Guild in Fabrizo. Something about a missed payment and needing to make an example. You can explain how that goes, right?" He looked toward Renfro before continuing, "You two had a blood debt to the guild. Takes more money than I have to get out of that kind of debt. Blood though, that is easy enough to spill. The guild and I both had things we wanted and came to an agreement that satisfied both of our needs."

"I-I had no idea," stammered Ben. A friend had risked his life and an innocent man had died because of him. Ben slumped down next to Renfro on the log and stared at the ground. "But why? Why you? I mean, don't they have people who do that kind of thing? Casper…"

Rhys picked up a rock and tossed it into the river. "Aye, anyone can cut a throat in the night, and you're probably right, I suspect Casper has cut his share. Sometimes these things need a little more finesse. Lord Fredrick got into some things he shouldn't have been involved in. He also had a lot of powerful friends—King Argren for one. The thieves may live outside the law, but they aren't stupid. If Argren set his mind to it, he could crush them and everyone in Fabrizo who tried to stand with them—not that anyone would. They needed to get a message across without anyone in power being able to tie it back to them."

"Why you? What if you hadn't come along right when they needed it? And how did they know you could do it?" demanded Ben.

Rhys hung the water skin back on his belt and studied Ben. "This isn't the first time I've been involved in something like this.

The thieves had some suggestions and we spoke about options. They are aware of me and must have thought it was worth the risk to let you two go. They were very concerned others might see Fredrick get away and then start having their own ideas. If I hadn't come along I'm sure they would have found someone else."

"I just..." Ben couldn't summon the words to express his thoughts.

"Give it some time, lad. I know you feel guilty, but that's the way the world works sometimes. You or them. If it makes you feel better, Fredrick was a bad man. He got in with the guild then he betrayed them. He constantly cheated on and beat his wife. He made his choices and he was going to pay for them, whether or not we got involved."

"Well, I for one, am thankful," interjected Renfro. "You saved my life and I owe you. Whatever you need, just ask."

Rhys rolled his eyes. "I'll remember that. If I ever need a pocket picked or someone to make me look good on a hike, you're the one I'll ask for. Come on. Let's get moving. We're wasting daylight."

THE REST of the day was spent in silence except the constant huffing and puffing from Renfro and the occasional bird call. There were few other travelers out because people had either come into Whitehall for the Conclave already or weren't leaving town while all of the excitement was going on.

The terrain reminded Ben of home and for the first time since he had left Farview, he felt a pang of homesickness. He was still excited for what lay ahead, but the real world was turning out to be a much uglier and more dangerous place than he had anticipated. In the stories, the dangers were always clear and everyone knew what was right and what was wrong.

~

BY THE TIME they spotted the clearing, Ben and Renfro were both ready to stop. Rhys seemed just as cheerful as he had been that morning and acted like he could hike all night. But even for Rhys with his boundless energy, the clearing was a good spot to stop and wait for the others. It was within a stone's throw of the road so they wouldn't miss their companions. Nearby, the White River tumbled over a short rapid into a broad, calm pool. It promised an easy water source and the potential for fish.

It was spring in the foothills of the mountains, so while it wasn't hot, it would still be warm enough to camp in the open. Setting up camp just involved unloading their packs and gathering firewood to stack next to a well-used fire pit that must have been dug out decades or even centuries earlier.

They had sausage, cheese, and biscuits they'd brought from Whitehall and shortly after they ate, Renfro rolled up in his bedroll and fell asleep. Rhys packed a pipe full of tobacco and wandered the outskirts of the clearing while he smoked. Ben stared into the fire and thought.

It seemed his world was getting more complicated and deadly. First, there was the encounter with the wagon driver at Murdoch's. Protecting Meghan was clearly the right thing to do, and at worst, he would have taken a beating and been cut up a little. In Fabrizo, helping Renfro had been a more difficult decision because he didn't know him, and the little thief had just tried to rob him, but it had nearly resulted in Ben's death as well as Renfro's. At the time, he thought it had been wrong to leave Renfro to die. He was glad he hadn't, but would he make the same decision again? And he still wasn't sure how he felt about Rhys killing Lord Fredrick. Rhys said Lord Fredrick was a bad man, but even if he was an evil man, would Ben have made the decision to trade Fredrick's life for his? Casper the thief would have argued for that choice, but Ben didn't want to be the kind of man who passed life and death judgment on others.

In the stories, the hero always saved the day and never had to face these types of decisions. You saw the monster, you fought the monster, and you saved the innocent damsel. But what if the person you were trying to save was a bad person—a thief? What if the monster was really your friend and was actually saving you?

Ben was still lost in his own thoughts when Rhys settled down across from him and tapped out his pipe into the fire.

"Still thinking about it?" he asked.

"Yeah," replied Ben slowly. "I just keep going over it in my mind. You said this isn't the first time you've done something like this."

"Like this? If you mean saved someone, it might be," Rhys answered with a snort.

Ben sat up and looked at his friend. "You know what I meant."

"No, Ben, that wasn't the first time. I haven't always been a good person. I've done a lot of things that maybe I shouldn't have. Things I've learned over the years to regret, but saving you at the expense of a man like Fredrick? I don't regret that."

"I'm glad I'm alive. Don't get me wrong, I appreciate you taking a risk to save me and I owe you. But I don't know if I could have made the same choice, even to save my own life."

Rhys slipped off his boots and laid down by the fire with his head on his bedroll. "Well, Ben, the thing about me doing what I did is that you didn't have to make the choice. You couldn't have made that choice. Fredrick's death is on me, Ben, not on you. And I think you're right. If you had the choice you wouldn't have taken it. I don't think you would simply trade another man's life for your own." Rhys propped himself up on one elbow and looked at Ben. "I like that about you, Ben. That's why I did what I did—because I didn't think you would have done it. And this world needs people like you."

THE NEXT MORNING, Ben felt better. The world was still a more complicated and dangerous place than he had dreamed back in Farview, but Rhys was right. Ben had not made a decision that cost a man's life. Lord Fredrick put himself in a situation with the Thieves' Guild and Rhys had bartered for Ben's life. When Ben had been faced with a life or death choice, he had chosen to try and help Renfro. Even though it worked out badly for them both, Ben fell asleep comfortable with where his moral compass steered him.

Renfro and Rhys were both in good moods, too. It was a beautiful day and being back out in nature in a simple camp with a couple of friends was a nice way to spend it.

That morning, Ben and Rhys tried to show Renfro how to set a rabbit trap and look for game trails. Ben had spent countless bells in the woods around Farview with Serrot catching rabbits and other animals. Rhys was surprisingly adept as well. Renfro was proving to be helpless, though. He'd spent his entire life in the docks and back alleys of Fabrizo and didn't know the first thing about woodcraft.

After setting some rabbit traps around promising locations, they spent the rest of the morning trying their luck with the fish. They hadn't brought poles or fishing line, but they were able to wade out into the large pool in the river, stick their hands into the chill water, and wait for fish to swim close. The fish were slippery and it wasn't easy, but after a bell, they'd caught enough for dinner with plenty left over to smoke and keep for the next few days.

By midday, they had restocked their firewood, gathered a few root vegetables and other edibles in the woods, and rechecked the rabbit traps with no luck. It was an active but relaxing morning, and Ben felt the stress of the previous two days fading away.

That afternoon, Rhys continued their instruction on the

second Ohm. The first Ohm had been difficult because it was on a moving ship, but once they'd gotten the hang of it, they could rotate through the positions quickly. The second Ohm was similar to the first but the poses required a bit more balance and had smoother transitions between the steps. It felt more natural to Ben than the first. Rhys explained it was because the first was simply to get your body used to the movements. Each additional Ohm would build upon the others until eventually it was all one fluid movement through a long series of positions. In the end, it was about shifting balance with impeccable control instead of maintaining balance in one static spot.

"By the time you've learned the Thirtieth Ohm, you could do these movements on the mast of a ship, blindfolded, and during a storm. The balance, flexibility, and strength from these poses can help you in a fight or, more likely in your case, plowing a field when you get back to that country town of yours," explained Rhys with a straight face. A glimmer of mirth danced behind his eyes.

Ben rolled his eyes but didn't take the bait.

Renfro rose to the occasion, though. "That sounds great, Rhys. I'd really like to see you do that. Maybe next time we're on a ship you'll show us how you can balance on the mast?"

"Happy to show you. In fact, maybe the next time your ship captain friend is sailing out of port with a load of carpets we could catch a ride?" Rhys glanced over Renfro's shoulder and his eyes grew wide.

Renfro quickly turned to see what Rhys was looking at, forgetting that his legs were crossed in one of the poses. He pitched backward with arms flailing and fell onto his back. Ben burst out laughing as Renfro scrambled across the ground, searching in vain for what had alarmed Rhys.

"It's not my balance you need to worry about." Rhys grinned.

~

THEY FIGURED the girls wouldn't leave Whitehall for at least another week, so the next few days were spent roaming the surrounding forest, ranging further and further from the road. The area was sparsely populated and most of the activity was near the road. They did spy some hunters' retreats and woodcutters' shacks but steered clear of those. Most of them would be only occasionally occupied and the rest were likely people who lived there because they didn't want visitors.

Both Ben and Rhys gave up trying to teach Renfro woodcraft after the second day, though he tagged along and complained good naturedly as they explored.

The week was good for Ben. The woods around their campsite felt similar to what he was used to in Farview, and even though Rhys was a very different friend than Serrot, it still was nice spending time with him. Rhys was obviously comfortable in the wilderness and was able to show Ben some of the tricks he knew. Ben's previous excursions with Serrot had lasted a few days at most. Rhys started teaching Ben how to survive on his own for weeks or months. Their stock of provisions grew as they found different sorts of edibles.

They also spent time working on the Ohms. By the end of the week they had started the third one, which as Rhys said, grew in complexity and difficulty compared to the first two.

Ben felt himself settling emotionally. The first night after Whitehall he had been in turmoil. The more time they spent away from there, the more he felt comfortable with how he had acted and, more importantly, how he would act in the future.

By the end of the week, they started sticking close to camp because they knew the girls could be on the road soon. Traffic was still light on the road but had picked up from the first few days. They heard from travelers they spoke with that the Conclave was coming to an end. With the travelers, bad weather also rolled up from the Bay. The temperature dropped and there were storm clouds on the horizon. They could hear the distant thunder and see flashes of lightning as the front moved up from the coast.

Fortunately, they were prepared. Rhys and Ben found a vertical rock wall and set up treated tarps which would slick away any rain from them. They dug a new fire pit at the back of the tarp structure where the smoke could chimney up against the rock wall. Sleeping out in rough weather was never pleasant, but they had time and made the camp as comfortable as they could.

The sun went down and the wind picked up. They had thick root vegetables stuck into the coals of their fire and had just skewered a brace of fat rabbits when the rain started to pour. Rhys pulled out a wine skin, which he had miraculously not drained yet, and they started passing it around.

Rhys nodded out into the dark. "Could be worse than this."

"Not bad at all actually," added Renfro. He was leaning back against his travel pack and cradling the wine skin like it was a small child. He leaned toward the fire and inhaled the scent of the cooking rabbits. "If I'm honest, this is a damn sight better than what I had in Fabrizo. Most of the time, I slept in the back of a fishmonger's shop. He was one of the successful ones who actually had a shop. Most of them set up down at the Market. The high class didn't like to go down there for their fish, though. Ole Creegar did pretty well on Bon Street. Of course, he had exceptional margins since I stole most of his product for him. It's how I paid my rent. The place was dry, but it smelled like fish."

Ben reached for the wineskin and asked, "How'd you, uh, how'd you end up in the Thieves' Guild? We've never really talked about it."

"It was that or starve. At least, that's what I thought at the time," answered Renfro. "Earliest I can remember, I was an urchin on the streets. Not sure what happened to my parents. Maybe they're dead or maybe they just left me. Stole food and stuff then to stay alive. When you get a little bigger on the streets in Fabrizo, it's keep stealing or go to sea. I was always too small to be anything other than a cabin boy at sea, and there's no future in that. When you get older and you want to keep stealing, you join the guild. In Fabrizo, independents don't worry about the guards, if you know what I mean. But once you're in the guild, they don't much care where you've been, just care where you can go. You do well with the guild and you never worry about having anything to eat. Never have to worry about finding a dry spot to sleep. You saw that palace they had us in."

"That's terrible," responded Ben. "I lost my parents when I was young, too. I got lucky, I guess, and the Town Council put me with someone. There wasn't anyone who could take you in?"

Rhys broke in, "Not everywhere is Farview, Ben. Small town councils look after their own. Their job is the welfare of their people, from the richest family to the orphans. The Merchants' Guild in Fabrizo is there for the money. They don't see people, they see profit. People in a big city, they're on their own."

"Aye, that's the way of it," added Renfro with a shrug. "I'm not saying what I've done is right, just saying I didn't see many other options at the time." Renfro reached out for the skin again, tipped it up then said with a smile, "I'm not there anymore, though."

LATER THAT EVENING, they were scattered around the fire, watching the storm's light show out from under the tarp. They had the kind of lethargy that comes from a rainy evening, a warm fire, a full belly, and a skin of wine.

The conversation trailed off after they ate. Ben was glad he knew more about where Renfro had come from and he thought he understood his friend better now. On the other hand, maybe the thieves were right. It doesn't matter where you came from, it just matters where you can go.

Ben was shaken out of his daze when Rhys sat up and exclaimed, "Now who in the hell..."

"Look!" Renfro pointed where, during the intermittent flashes of lightning, they saw a figure hurrying up the road. They all watched as the person scurried closer in the blowing rain. Still on the road, they saw the shape pause when it must have seen them before making a decision and heading toward the campsite.

A sodden man staggered up outside of their tarps and shouted in, "Ho the camp! That's the most comfortable place I've seen on this road so far. Mind if I join you tonight?"

Rhys shifted around the fire and Ben saw he had exposed the wire-wrapped hilts of his heavy long knives. "Sure, stranger. Come on in."

Their concerns were quickly abated though. They saw the dripping wet man was dressed from head to toe in King Argren's livery. No bandit would be so bold as to wear those colors this close to Whitehall and not expect hard and fast justice.

"Fellow, I have to ask, what are you doing out this late in this weather?" inquired Rhys.

The man sneezed. "Damn, think I'm getting sick in this mess." He looked over to Rhys and answered, "Surely you know about the Conclave going on in Whitehall." It wasn't really a question and the man continued on without waiting for a reply, "Well, they've finished up and Argren wants the news out quick. My wife is the one who wanted me to take this horrible job. Good pay she said. Get to know what's happening she said. Now I'm on the road and she's back in town spending all that good coin and making eyes at the blacksmith's kid down the alley." The man plopped down next to the fire and started stripping off his wet boots and clothing.

"So," asked Ben patiently, "what is the news?"

"Oh, right. The Alliance is official. Naturally everyone in Sineook was already in. Northport, Venmoor, East Bay, Holly-town, and even Issen signed. They're all in. The Sanctuary sent a representative, though she didn't sign the accord. The mages must be neutral, of course, but she was there. I think that says all anyone needs to know. Time to start recruiting and raising arms. It will be war with the Coalition by next summer. Even those greedy bastards in Fabrizo agreed to help with supplies. The fishmongers aren't worth anything in a fight, so I guess that's all Argren thought he could get from them."

"War. They announced war with the Coalition?" asked Ben.

"Didn't announce it, no, but what do you think is going to happen, man? The way they're talking in Whitehall now, it's us or them."

10

SNOWMAR PASS

THE NEXT MORNING was wet and cold. Argren's herald was up early, hacking and sneezing. He'd dried his clothes off the night before by the fire and must have had a chilly evening sleeping out in the open. Ben saw the man's tiny travel pack and felt bad for him. Ben gave him some of their smoked fish. After a week with nothing to do but hunt and fish they had more than enough to share. The man was back on the road shortly after sunrise.

By early afternoon, the sun was out and it had warmed considerably. Rhys, Ben, and Renfro were working hard on some of the more complicated steps of the third Ohm when they saw the girls and Saala coming up the road.

They had prepared to pack up and travel that afternoon, but when Lady Towaal saw the campsite, she suggested they stay the night there. "That will make for three hard days travel to Snowmar Station, but if I remember correctly, there won't be any better places to spend the night."

"You're right," replied Rhys. "After here it gets more and more rocky until you get up to the pass. There are a few spots flat enough to lay a bedroll, but that's the best you can say about them."

"Okay, let's stay here tonight and we'll push the next three days."

~

BEN AND RENFRO spent a moment showing the girls around the camp and made small talk about Whitehall. What they really wanted to know was about the Conclave. Argren's herald had spoken of war, which was something that had not happened in any of their lives. Sure, Ben had heard of border conflicts and the constant troubles up north, but nothing like a full-scale war with the entire continent of Alcott involved.

As they moved back to the rest of the party by the fire, Ben related what the herald had told them.

"Oh, we hope it doesn't mean war, but that is a possibility," explained Amelie. "The Coalition has been getting aggressive. The Alliance is only meant to counterbalance them. My father hopes that with Issen supporting the Alliance, there will be a big enough presence to deter the Coalition. If we do not show them a strong hand, who knows what they will do? Coalition representatives have been coming more frequently and all they talk about is expansion. Lord Jason practically lived in Issen through the winter."

"Lord Jason was there?" inquired Lady Towaal tartly.

Amelie looked abashed. "Yes, he was there."

"I didn't hear that when I was in Issen. I am surprised no one mentioned it." Towaal's tone had acquired a frosty chill.

"I, well, my father did not want to confuse matters. Until we decided if we would join the Alliance, we didn't want people reading into Jason's visit."

"Who is Lord Jason?" Ben whispered to Rhys.

"He's an agent of the Coalition," he answered. "I've never met the chap, but he has a fearsome reputation for being the one who does their dirty work. I'm told he's a blademaster of exceptional ability. The Coalition High Council leads from behind closed doors in their capital Irrefort. Jason is their blade in the night who comes out into the world to make things happen—one way or the other. Though, there is rumor recently that he was elevated to the High Council himself. He's not the man they would send to cool his heels in Issen without expecting some commitment in return. Lord Gregor and Amelie are playing a dangerous game."

〰

THE POLITICS of the Alliance and Coalition were far away, though, and the young people quickly moved past it to catch up on everything else that had happened in the week they were apart. Amelie and Meghan told Ben that Master Brinn had asked about him and wanted Ben to know there was always an opening for him in the Citadel guard. Ben appreciated the sentiment, but after a week away, he knew that barracks life was not for him.

Ben and Renfro showed the girls the second and third Ohms, which they all practiced together. The second and third Ohms were much more strenuous than the first. It wasn't long before they were all sweating in the warm spring sun. Renfro was a little better at some of the poses than Ben, but he was also painfully shy around the girls, so Ben found himself demonstrating over and over the more difficult positions. Before long, he'd stripped off his shirt and was slick with sweat. They'd been going over the forms for two bells and all of them were a bit red faced and breathing heavy.

"Still practicing the sword I see?" asked Amelie innocently before heading over to the pool they had been fishing in to splash water on her face and cool off.

Meredith giggled and Meghan rolled her eyes.

"Practicing the sword?"

"You told her in Whitehall you'd been practicing the sword and put on a little muscle." Meghan smirked.

Ben blushed and snatched his shirt off of the ground.

"Oh don't be a prude," chimed in Meredith. "She's just teasing you a little. I think she'd be disappointed if you started covering up all of the time. I know I would be," she added with a wink and a smile.

Ben wasn't sure how to take that kind of teasing. He'd had a little bit of interest from the girls in Farview, but as the adopted son, everyone knew Alistair Pinewood wasn't going to leave him any money. There was only so far a brewer could go in a small town. The girls in Farview flirted like girls anywhere, but they were practical and everyone knew it was just flirting. After the party and the things he'd seen at the Citadel, he wasn't sure how it went with the highborn.

"Stop standing there like a stumped ox," chided Meghan. "In all of your exploring, did you find anywhere a girl could go for a swim? It's hot. After travelling all morning and doing these Ohms all afternoon, I could use a cool down." She glanced at the pool near the campsite and the road nearby. "Somewhere private would be nice."

BEN LED them back into the forest where they had found a bend in a wide creek that poured into the White River south of their campsite. They'd tried fishing it earlier with no luck but it was perfect for swimming. In the elbow of the bend, it was shallow and deepened toward the center of the stream. It was also clear of trees, so the slow-moving water would be warm in the shallows but cool in the deeper sections.

Ben deposited the girls on the bank of the creek and said, "I'm going to head up toward that hill and see if I can find some mushrooms for dinner. I saw some out there but we didn't know we'd be camping here tonight. We made a rabbit stew that they would go great in. Call out if you need me or when you're ready to go back."

The hill was only a few hundred paces from the creek and they'd seen no one in this area, so Ben wasn't worried about leaving the girls alone in the woods. Also, the rabbit stew really had been a little gamey. Ben hoped the mushrooms would mellow it out. He wasn't much of a chef, but he didn't want to eat badly if he didn't have to.

He circled around the hill, pushing through the thick undergrowth, looking for the mushrooms. The hill blocked the breeze he'd felt earlier and it was sticky and humid. He thought it'd be worth it. They were Goblin's Ear mushrooms he thought he'd seen. They were a little tough, but if you boiled them long enough in a stew, they melted away into a rich savory broth.

He brought his sword along, which felt a little silly since they were just traipsing through woods he had thoroughly explored over the last week, but it was proving handy as he used it to push aside low-hanging ferns looking for the mushrooms. He picked one plentiful patch that had about two handfuls and was looking for a second when he heard a shriek from back near the creek.

Ben spun and ran toward the sound. As he pushed through the thick branches he heard another high-pitched howl and splashing that sounded like a struggle. He started using his sword to hack through some of the foliage when he heard a long cry of, "Help!" His blood ran cold. It was Amelie's voice that was screaming.

He burst through the wall of green that edged the creek and slipped on the muddy bank to land heavily on his rear. Directly in front of him, knee deep in the water and naked as the day they were born, were Amelie and Meghan. Meredith was bobbing deeper in the center and splashing handfuls of water toward the other two girls who giggled and screamed every time a wave hit them.

They all turned toward him as he slid into the mud.

"Damn it, Ben!" shouted Meghan.

Amelie turned to look at him then shrieked again. She raised her hands to cover herself but then realized it was fruitless and dove cleanly into deeper water with Meredith.

Meghan kept shouting and started toward him with a dangerous look. Seeing his naked adopted sister charging toward him with murder in her eyes jerked him out of his shocked state. He scrambled on all fours across the slick mud and back into the bushes.

"What on earth are you doing?" a very angry Meghan yelled at him from the clearing.

"I heard a cry for help!"

"Help! What are you going to do? Help us swim or help us get out of our clothes?"

"Meghan, come on! I heard screaming."

"Maybe we were being a bit loud, Meghan," said a faint-sounding Amelie.

"Well, I think we've had enough of Benjamin Ashwood's help for today," Meghan replied crossly. She then called loudly, "Ben, you run on back to the camp with your mushrooms. I think we can handle getting dressed without your assistance."

ON THE WAY back to the camp, Ben hoped that Meghan would understand how it had been a mistake. He really had heard the screaming and was concerned the girls were under attack. He kept trying to think of ways he could apologize to her but couldn't concentrate. Images of Amelie's lithe body diving into the water kept pushing their way into his head.

She was the most beautiful girl he had ever seen, and not just in Farview. Compared to the other ladies at Argren's party even, she was the sparkling jewel. Physically, she was perfection, but she also had a natural joy to her that drew him in. When they started their journey, it was like looking at the moon. Gorgeous and worthy of admiration surely, but not something you ever thought you'd get close to.

After she invited him to the party, his thoughts started to change. She held his arm and wasn't far away then. It was like looking at the moon every night and then one day finding yourself walking across it. He knew the way she looked standing knee deep in that creek then turning to gracefully dive into the water would be burned into his memory forever.

When he got back to the camp, Saala looked up at him and asked, "Aren't you missing something?"

"I, um, I got the mushrooms. The girls can find their own way back. They're fine," he hurriedly added. He could feel the heat rising in his face and hoped Saala didn't ask him any more about it.

"No, I meant your sword. I'm sure the girls can walk through the woods without you watching them. Didn't you have your sword when you left?"

THAT EVENING Ben was uncomfortably huddled by the fire, trying to ignore baleful glares from Meghan. It seemed she wasn't going to quickly forget. He kept glancing at Amelie to see what her reaction was but she ignored him and seemed unaffected. She was deep in conversation with Lady Towaal and Saala, and he didn't catch her looking his way. Meghan's expression kept growing darker, though.

"What did you do to her?" whispered Renfro.

"I didn't do anything. What are you talking about?" Ben hissed back.

"Meghan. She's mad at you Ben. Can't you see the way she's looking at you?"

"Oh, it's nothing. Just brother and sister stuff. No big deal."

"Are you sure? Every time she sees you look at Amelie she just gets madder. She may be your sister, but she's Amelie's friend. You don't want to come between girlfriends, believe me. Whatever you did to Amelie, you better make right, or Meghan's going to make you pay for it."

"I…" He didn't know what to say. "I need to take a walk."

BEN WAS PACING up and down the road in the low moonlight when he felt a presence approaching from the camp. As it got closer, he saw it was Meredith carefully picking her way through the grass.

"Hi, Meredith. I was just trying to get some fresh air away from the fire."

"Oh, me too. The fire is nice, but it's good to get some mountain air after being in the city. Don't you agree?"

"Yeah, um, it is nice."

She placed her hand on his arm. "I want to thank you, Ben. I know Meghan is mad, but I thought it was very brave that you came running when you thought we were in trouble."

"Oh, it was nothing," Ben stuttered. "I mean, I didn't know what was happening and I was worried."

"I know. That's why I appreciate it. Being Amelie's handmaiden, I am part of the background sometimes. I haven't had a lot of people try to come save me."

"I don't know if I could really save you from anything." He shrugged uncomfortably. "It was just instinct."

"I heard you were a good fighter." She moved closer and looped her arm around his. "Let's keep walking."

"Ok, sure." Ben breathed a sigh of relief. If at least one of the girls wasn't mad, then there was hope for the other two.

Meredith walked close beside him in the cool spring air. The new moon lit the roadway enough to see where they were walking, but the low light made the evening seem close and intimate.

"Some of the Citadel guardsmen came calling for me when we were in Whitehall," Meredith continued. "Not that I would ever pay a guardsman any real attention, of course, but I didn't want to be rude. They spoke about you. They said you had impressed the Master of Arms and that he was interested in you joining the guard. After seeing how brave you were today, maybe I could be interested in you too?"

Ben looked down at Meredith and could see in the moonlight that she was gazing up at him. He didn't know what to say to that.

"I know you like her, but Amelie isn't right for you," she said. "She's highborn and these things are business for her. It's all arranged. Not like us," she purred and drew his arm around her shoulders, "we can do whatever we want."

Inside, Ben groaned. Despite his best intentions, life was just getting more complex.

THE NEXT MORNING they started hiking at the first sign of daylight. As Rhys and Towaal had predicted, it was going to be a hard three days travel to Snowmar Station. Snowmar Station was Whitehall's guard barracks and rest stop atop the Snowmar Pass.

The road itself was broad and well maintained. It was steep, though, and the terrain around it grew rugged as they ascended. They passed a few empty carts that were slowly heading up to the pass and eventually to the Sineook Valley. Many of the large merchant trains must have still been in the city. The merchants made their money bringing agricultural goods to Whitehall from the valley. The more successful ones tried to find a cargo to haul back as well. The cargo might be people, mused Ben, since many would be pouring out of the city now that the Conclave was over.

Hitching a ride in the back of a wagon didn't sound too bad after a long day of hiking.

The climb wasn't any more strenuous than what Ben was used to back home, but the pace Towaal kept was punishing. She rarely allowed stops for breaks and didn't look back to check if anyone was falling behind. There were moments when Ben thought he'd have to carry poor Renfro the rest of the way.

When they finally stopped for the evening, it was in one of the few flat parts off the road that were not already occupied by farmers or merchants. Rhys explained that in the busy seasons many of the merchant trains just pulled to the side and slept right on the road. The party ate a quick dinner and everyone pulled out their bedrolls, exhausted by the brisk pace and long day.

As Ben was arranging his area, Meredith slid in between him and Renfro. She gave a shy smile and asked, "Mind if I sleep here? I promise I don't snore."

Renfro grinned back at her. "Me neither."

She only had eyes for Ben, though, and ignored Renfro's comment.

"Of course you can," sighed Ben.

The next two nights were like that. Right before everyone turned in, Meredith would casually roll out her pack next to Ben. He saw Amelie was pretending she didn't notice, and Meghan's gaze got even frostier. Rhys gave an encouraging nod. Given the rogue's predilections, Ben wasn't sure how to take it. By the third night, even Renfro realized what was happening and shifted his bedroll away to give them more room.

In the mornings, Ben would wake up to find Meredith scooted up almost onto his bedroll. Neither the men or women chose to say anything, but it was clear that she was marking her territory. Ben was embarrassed by the situation and belatedly realized, maybe he shouldn't have kissed her that night.

~

By the final afternoon before Snowmar they were all ready to be done with the rocky mountain road. There were only a few leagues left and everyone, even Renfro, was skipping breaks and struggling to finish the leg of the journey quickly.

With the top of the pass peeking into sight, they passed a tight bend in the road and could see a tower jutting from an outcropping high above them.

Lady Towaal covered her eyes and stared up at it. "It's the guard tower. They have one on each side of the pass. Snowmar Station sits in the middle where it's flat. They use the towers to keep an eye on who is approaching and light signal fires for emergencies. There's a tower down in Whitehall with a looking glass that can see all the way up here for when the signal fire is lit."

Rhys was also staring intently up at the tower. He looked at Saala, grunted then adjusted his pack to free space around the hilt of his long sword.

Saala nodded and did the same.

"What do you see?" queried Towaal. "I see the flag is still flying Argren's sigil. Is something wrong?"

Rhys rumbled, "It's not what we see. It's what we don't see. Where's the guard? Could be he's sleeping or daydreaming about some woman back in Whitehall, but listen. It's just the sound of the wind. There's a hundred men supposed to be barracked up there, and I don't hear a damn thing."

Towaal looked between Rhys and Saala and noted both men's nervousness. "Okay, everyone, be prepared."

Renfro looked to Ben. "Be prepared for what?"

As they drew closer, the silence grew eerie. Ben had not noticed it until Rhys mentioned it, but the only sounds came from the wind and their own footfalls. The group stopped talking entirely and Renfro had gone as far to pull two of his knives out. Ben saw Rhys and Saala still had their weapons in the sheath, so he kept his there as well.

After several switchbacks, they passed the guard tower before entering the pass. The tower was indeed empty with the heavy door left ajar. Rhys silently drew his two long knives, the first time Ben had seen him pull his own steel, and ducked into the narrow open doorway. Heartbeats later he reappeared and quietly reported, "Nothing. No people, no signs of violence. It looks like breakfast was left on the table untouched."

A grim-faced Saala drew his curved falchion with a hiss. "There should be someone here. Even if bandits or someone overran Snowmar, they would have left a lookout on the White-hall Road."

"There's no wealth here for bandits." Rhys frowned. "The barracks only stocks provisions for the men and serves as a way station for travelers. Most of the merchant trains are foodstuffs and not worth stealing."

Ben shared a worried look with Renfro and drew his sword. It was a plain weapon, but the weight of it felt good. If Rhys and Saala were worried, he was downright terrified.

They moved past the guard tower and the group's unease grew. In the distance, they could see the walls of Snowmar Station spreading across the width of the pass. The road ran right through the center and out the other side. The station was designed to be a defense point for Whitehall and it would be nearly impossible for an attacking force to move up the narrow roadway and have an effective assault on the towering stone walls.

Halfway to the walls, Ben's breath caught. Rhys had already seen it and was jogging ahead of the group. On the side of the road were two dark shapes lying on the ground. Rhys had sheathed his knives after exiting the guard tower but now he drew his longsword. When they got closer to Rhys and the shapes, Ben saw they had found the missing tower guards. They were both lying face down in a pool of blood and gore.

"Damn," muttered Saala. He looked to Towaal. "Do we turn around?"

She was scanning the walls of Snowmar. After a quick glance she had ignored the bodies. "This is the only pass anywhere near here. It will cost us a month to turn now.

Rhys nudged a body with his foot. "Karina, this wasn't done by men."

Ben started. He hadn't heard anyone use Lady Towaal's first name since Murdoch's when she introduced herself.

"We press on," she said grimly. "Whatever did this doesn't appear to be here now and I need to see what happened. Saala and Rhys out front," she barked, "and I will take the rear. Girls and boys, stay tight and shout if you see anything move."

Ben shuddered. He saw the spray of gore surrounding the two dead men and didn't think he wanted to see any more, but he couldn't abandon his companions.

The gates of Snowmar were open just like it was a normal day. Through those gates, Ben saw more corpses. Snowmar Station was one big open square surrounded by walls and mountains. The barracks and guest quarters were built into the back of the walls around the square. There was plenty of space for merchant trains to tie up for the night and for the guards to drill in the middle. Now it was littered with dead bodies.

They passed through the gate into the thick walls before coming into the open square. It was a charnel house.

"I count at least fifty of them," said Rhys in a low whisper. "Look, even the horses."

Meredith fell in beside Ben and gripped his arm, whimpering. Rhys was right, a corral for horses at the far end of the square was filled with red and pink chunks of flesh. Ben nearly lost his lunch when he saw it. Renfro did lose his when they had to step around an eviscerated guardsman lying in the center of the path.

Meghan caught Ben's glance and for the first time in days, he saw only concern in her gaze instead of anger. Everything that happened down at the campsite was long forgotten.

Rhys gestured across the square to the other gate. It was also open. "Shall we?"

"No," answered Towaal. "We must find out what did this. You're right, this was not done by men."

"If we must." Rhys sighed and looked around the group. "Okay, everyone to the center of the square. Stand back to back and face out where you have visibility. Saala, will you check the buildings?"

"I'm staying with Amelie," replied Saala. "Sorry, but I am here for her safety."

"All right then."

Rhys slung his pack down on the ground and adjusted his weapons harness until he was satisfied his long knives were easily accessible. He held his long sword out and started toward what looked like the barracks. For the first time, Ben really saw his weapon. It was a twilight grey and appeared to have faint silver etching all along the length of the blade. The steel was darker than any Ben had seen before. The silver etching seemed to fade into the blade the longer he looked at it. It wasn't a blade-master's sigil, but Ben couldn't tell what it was. He didn't have time either. Rhys moved quickly toward the barracks and they huddled into a circle and kept an eye out for any movement.

Nervous moments passed after Rhys disappeared. Nothing moved but they strained their ears trying to hear anything. Finally, he reappeared and trotted over to them, shaking his head.

"Just more dead. And this." He tossed a torn piece of cloth onto the ground. It looked like a piece of tunic from one of Argren's guardsmen. There was a dark purple stain on one corner.

"Damn," whispered Saala.

Lady Towaal glared at the stain then commanded, "We need

to check the pigeon coop. The signal fire wasn't lit, but maybe they got off some messenger birds to warn others."

"Karina, there were a hundred trained guardsmen up here and who knows how many merchant guards. We need to leave. Now."

"I understand, Rhys, but we have to know if they sent a warning."

"Hold on. What is the significance of that stain? We have a right to know what is going on," demanded Amelie.

Saala answered slowly, "It's demon blood. If there was a large enough swarm to take out this entire garrison, then I'm not sure we'll be sufficient. Lady Towaal, I agree with Rhys. We must leave now. Regardless of whether any pigeons got out, we can warn others in the Sineook Valley and they can get word to Whitehall. Others will see what happened with the dead guards on the road and turn around before they get here. The only thing we can do staying is risk ourselves. I cannot let Amelie take a risk like this."

Lady Towaal grimaced. "We cannot go until we check on something. The Captain of the station had an artifact, one that I must recover."

"Bloody Sanctuary politics," snarled Rhys. "You could get us all killed."

Lady Towaal regained her calm and stated, "I insist."

None of them were happy about it, but no one wanted to openly defy Lady Towaal either.

"We stay together then," muttered Rhys.

Rhys again took the lead as they moved toward the north end of the square to the officer's quarters, and hopefully the artifact they needed to find. They moved quickly and quietly. Now that they knew what they faced, the fear was still there, but it was manageable.

The officer's quarters proved to be nearly empty. The men who stayed here must have been somewhere else or must have rushed outside when the attack started. The one body they did find was a half-dressed man lying prone in his doorway. His head had been torn off and tossed into the room across the hall. The scene was surreal. If it wasn't for the destruction outside, Ben would have thought it make believe at first. He made eye contact with Meghan as they passed and saw the sentiment mirrored in her eyes.

Finally, they found what had to be the captain's room. It was the only one in the building that had a seating area. It had a large map of the pass and surrounding territory on one wall. Lady Towaal pushed past everyone into the man's bed chamber while the rest of the group waited. Saala stepped back into the hallway and stood guard.

While they were waiting for Towaal to search the man's room, Rhys began examining the map and called Ben over. "See these pins? These tags on them are dates. It looks like they started up in the mountains here," he pointed to a peak about fifteen leagues from Snowmar Station, "and they slowly moved toward the pass."

Ben nodded. "Yes, but what does it mean?"

Rhys shrugged. "I don't know. Demon sightings maybe? That doesn't make sense, though. They had men to hunt down a lone demon that was loose in the hills. They would have sent for help if it were something they couldn't handle. From these dates, there would have been plenty of time to make Whitehall and back."

They were still examining the map when Lady Towaal returned. "It's not here and neither is the captain. We must find his body. He might have kept it on him."

Rhys rolled his eyes at her back and led the way past Saala into the hall and out toward the square.

By the time they entered the mess hall, they had already searched most of the buildings at the station and had come up empty handed. They were all in similar states as the officer's quarters and the square. In some, it was obvious that the occupants had warning and had attempted to defend themselves. In others, they had simply died.

The mess hall was the first sign of real coordinated resistance. There was a barricade of flipped over tables and benches that had been shoved aside. Ben cringed when he thought about the strength it would have taken to move the pile.

They also found the first dead demons. Six of the creatures lay between the barricade and the back of the hall. The demons were covered in arrows and some had long spears sticking out of them. There were numerous wounds from edged weapons that had come from the piles of dead men scattered around the floor.

Ben stared at the dark shapes. They matched what he remembered from the attack in Farview. They were barrel chested and had thick, overlong arms and stubby legs. Despite the appearance, he knew they could move quickly. The largest one of these would have come up to his chest, but likely weighed twice what he did.

Small wings and horns on the larger ones drew the eye, but the real dangers were the curved claws at the end of each heavily muscled arm and mouthfuls of sharply pointed teeth that sprouted out of powerful jaws. Ben shuddered when he remembered how easily those claws had torn into William Longaxe's stomach.

"Six of them!" exclaimed Renfro. "Do you think they got them all?"

"No," answered Saala. "The men that were stationed here wouldn't have fallen to just six demons. You saw the carnage outside. They were quickly overrun by a large swarm. It looks like they were able to slow them down in here and took some with them, but no one survived this."

Suddenly, Lady Towaal shot ahead and knelt next to a body. The man had taken a raking wound across his face but the sword next to him was stained in purple blood. He hadn't gone down easy. Ben watched as she slid out her tiny belt knife and cut open the man's shirt. It was glued to his chest with sticky blood. When she got his shirt open, she cut a cord and pulled out a small, silver amulet. She pocketed it before Ben got a good look at it. He had no doubt though it was the artifact she had been looking for.

"Are we good?" Rhys was shifting his feet impatiently and looking toward the door. "It will be dark soon, and we don't want to be in this place when the sun goes down."

"Yes," she replied. "Let's get out of here and put as much distance as we can before we stop. I hope everyone is prepared to walk tonight."

They didn't need any convincing. A hot bath and a night under a roof had sounded nice before they got there, but now no one wanted to spend another moment in that butcher shop.

As they exited the mess hall, they heard an enraged animalistic shriek behind them.

"Out, now!" shouted Saala. He spun to cover the door as they rushed into the square.

Ben glanced over his shoulder and saw a squat black shape charging across the floor of the mess. Saala slammed the door and kept backing up into the clear. "It will be through that in no time. Stay behind and give me room."

Suddenly, Ben heard a crash and turned to see Renfro on his back with a corpse at his feet. Ben was about to bend to pull him up when he saw a thin black mass gliding down from the roof of the barracks across the square. "There. Behind us!"

"I've got it. Everyone stay close. Do not break out of the group," demanded Rhys as he swooped in between the fallen Renfro and the demon.

Ben yanked Renfro back upright and heard the first demon burst through the mess door. Saala was waiting and pounced on it before it could get its bearings. His two-handed falchion cleaved into the neck of the demon, spurting a fountain of purple blood that he danced back from. The thing took another step then collapsed to the ground, motionless.

"Bloody hell," yelled Rhys.

Three more demons were gliding down on delicate wings from the roof of the barracks. Saala flew past the group to assist as Rhys engaged the first demon. This one was taller than the one that came through the mess, near the same height as Ben, but it was thin and didn't seem to have the strength of the other. Rhys swiped a taloned hand aside and stabbed his long sword into its chest. He kicked it back off his blade and he and Saala spread out to meet the three new arrivals.

The demons attacked quickly, but with no coordination and no thought of strategy. One charged at Rhys and two came toward Saala.

Rhys jumped forward and Saala flowed to his left, taking one of his demons head-on while the second turned at the last second and crashed into the first. The first demon turned and snarled at the second. Saala took the opportunity to lunge forward, slicing into its throat.

Rhys charged directly at his demon. It did not seem to expect his tactic and kept coming. He slashed it across the face. It stumbled backward and Rhys dropped to one knee, pivoting to swing behind him and cut across the back of the legs of Saala's second demon. Rhys continued the motion and spun around to slice open his demon's abdomen, spraying a horrific tangle of white and purple guts across the square.

Saala stepped forward and neatly lopped the head off of the remaining demon as it dropped, crippled from Rhys' attack behind it.

Before anyone could celebrate the victory, Meredith screamed for help. They saw she had stepped away from the group and was facing across the square toward a charging demon. It was a short squat one and had a single wickedly curved horn. It was bounding in huge leaps across the square toward her. She only had her belt knife as defense.

Ben started to sprint toward her but knew he was too far away to get there before the demon. Suddenly, a dark shape whizzed by from behind him in a blur and sank into the demon's gaping maw as it reached the height of one of its leaps. Ben's heart soared when he saw the wire-wrapped hilt of Rhys' long knife. The demon's momentum kept it going, though. It smashed into Meredith, sending her flying to the ground, the heavy black shape landing on top of her.

Ben kept running toward Meredith but nearly had his head ripped off by another thin black demon that dropped into the square. It flashed in the corner of his vision and he dropped into a roll just in time for the thing to soar over with grasping clawed feet where he had been a heartbeat before. He sprung up to face it, and between its two wings saw three more shapes closing on the other girls and Lady Towaal. Saala hurled himself in between to defend them.

Renfro was to the left of Ben, scrambling to hide under a wagon, but a huge slow-moving monster bigger than an ox gripped his leg and easily started hauling him back out. Rhys appeared out of nowhere and began hacking at its back. Its man-sized wings kept fouling his blade.

Ben didn't have time to worry about Renfro or the girls, though. His demon screamed a primordial howl and lurched toward him. In the second he had time to think, none of the forms Saala had taught prepared him for this, so he slashed quickly in a steady pattern in front of him, trying to keep the blade between him and the advancing nightmare.

He had been right. The thin ones were not as strong as the short ones, but it was quick. He got in a few shallow cuts before it clamped down on his weapon with one hand and raked its claws across his other arm, leaving three parallel bloody gashes. Ben winced in pain but managed to twist his sword and yanked hard, pulling his weapon free and severing several taloned fingers in the process. The demon kept coming. Ben danced back quickly to avoid another slashing attack and a bite.

"Damn it, Karina!" Ben heard Rhys shout.

He spared a second to look to where the ox-sized demon was lying motionless. Renfro had managed to crawl back under the wagon but a new demon was digging and trying to squeeze under after him. Rhys was taking the charge of a muscular-looking squat one and rolled onto his back before kicking with both feet, sending the huge flailing mass of teeth and claws flying over him and trailing a stream of purple blood from his long sword.

That second to look almost cost Ben his life. The skinny demon again caught his blade with its other hand and pulled him closer to its razor sharp teeth. Ben knew he was dead if he let go of his sword. He'd be dead too if those teeth got into him. He held his grip on the sword and struggled desperately.

The creature smacked at him with its fingerless hand. Ben absorbed the blows. The demon wasn't as strong as the shorter ones, but it was at least as strong as a man and it hurt. Better than those teeth sinking into this flesh, though, as he took another blow on the shoulder and struggled to keep his sword between him and the demon's head.

"Karina, now! We're going to lose them!"

Time seemed to freeze for an instant and then the hair on Ben's neck and arms stood on end. There was a thunderous clap and a blaze of brilliant light and heat flashed across the square, impacting the demon in front of him. With a violent, spasmodic twitch and howl, the creature flew back away from Ben, taking his sword with it. He let go in a heartbeat. The leather-wrapped hilt had suddenly become scalding hot.

The entire square crackled with energy as more arm-thick bars of incandescent light flashed back and forth. Everywhere Ben looked, demons were jerking and flailing crazily as the lights coursed through their bodies then arced across to another one. Only moments had passed, but it seemed like half a bell before over the snapping crackle of the lightning, he heard Rhys shout, "Down. Everyone down now! Shit…she's losing control."

Ben dove to the ground and buried his head in his arms. Seconds later, there was a huge pop and the feel of electricity in the air dissipated. When he finally felt safe enough to raise his head, he saw Rhys had somehow managed to cross the square and was lying on top of Lady Towaal's prone body. Saala, Amelie, and Meghan were huddled down in a corner together. The girl's eyes were wide as saucers. Even Saala seemed shaken by the display of pure violent power.

Ben rolled over and saw Renfro was curled up under the wagon still, the iron wheels smoking with heat. He looked like he was crying, but he was alive. Ben looked for Meredith next. All he could see was an arm sticking out from under the demon, which was still on top of her.

He struggled to his feet and stumbled toward her, but realized he was too late before he got close. A large pool of dark blood, purple swirled with crimson red, was spreading from the two motionless figures.

IN THE AFTERMATH of the attack, Ben felt like he was in a bad dream. His companions were like ghosts, all of them moving quietly and using only gestures to communicate. They didn't think anything survived what Lady Towaal had released, but they weren't taking any risks either. The square was now littered with the bodies of upwards of twenty demons in addition to their victims. The charred and smoking demons added an acrid scent to the sickening charnel house odor of the human bodies.

It was a victory of sorts, that such a small party had survived an attack by a large demon swarm. When he looked into the eyes of his friends though, it didn't feel like a victory to Ben.

They bound their wounds and the men quickly built stretchers for the unconscious Lady Towaal and for Meredith's body. Rhys said that aside from a massive headache and a sense of lethargy for the next week, Lady Towaal would be okay. She would likely be unconscious for another day or two, though. What she had done took a lot out of her.

Meredith never had a chance. When they rolled the demon away, they saw its single horn had pierced her chest and its momentum had driven it deep. She was dead before she hit the ground offered Saala. It was little solace to her friends. They would take her away from this place of death and find somewhere peaceful in the Sineook Valley to lay her to rest.

11

SINEOOK VALLEY

IT WAS a solemn procession that made its way down from Snowmar Pass. They were battered both physically and emotionally.

Ben and Saala had bad-looking gashes that ended up being superficial. Some thorough washing and tight binding with supplies they found in the barracks was all the care they needed. It would leave scars, but nothing serious.

The girls and somehow Rhys had gotten through mostly unscathed except for a few nicks and scratches. Renfro had deep lacerations on his leg and a severely sprained ankle where the demon grabbed him. Ben offered to carry his pack and he found a pair of crutches in the barracks infirmary. It was going to be a long, painful walk until they could find a safe place to rest.

Over time, Ben knew the physical wounds would heal. Emotionally, though, it was crushing. Amelie in particular was affected. She had known Meredith her entire life. All of them had gotten to know her well. Two months of travel makes for a lot of bonding time.

That night, they slept in a cold campsite. No one spoke except when it was necessary. The next day, Amelie started to open up to Meghan. Ben tried to give them their privacy and not over-hear, but they were clustered close and no one was interested in walking away from the group.

"She was like a sister to me," started Amelie. "I don't have any other siblings. She was with me from when I can first remember. Her mother was one of my mother's handmaidens. When they fell pregnant at the same time, it was natural for Meredith's mother to become my nursemaid. Meredith was raised right alongside me in the nursery. We stayed that way since. It wasn't until we were older and started to receive different schooling that I even realized she wasn't a lord's daughter. Oh, her mother," she continued sorrowfully. "When we reach a town I must write her mother to tell her what happened. She was so excited for Meredith to accompany me and see Whitehall, Venmoor, the City, all of it…"

"I'm sorry, Amelie," consoled Meghan. "She was such a sweet person and we all loved her. I can't imagine what it is like for you."

Later that evening after Amelie turned in, Meghan found Ben sitting alone by the fire. "I don't know what I can say to her. It's so horrible. We must find a place for Meredith tomorrow. Amelie will not be able to get closure until we do."

The next morning, a groggy Lady Towaal finally awoke. Rhys suggested they wait until she recovered some before they took the road again. The nearest town was only a few bells' journey. They could rest that morning and still easily make it in daylight.

Rhys called Ben over and asked him to help look for a partic-ular bark he thought might grow in the area that could alleviate some of Towaal's discomfort.

"The rest of them couldn't find an oak tree if it dropped an acorn on their head," muttered Rhys.

Ben didn't quite agree, but the thought of getting up and doing something appealed to him. They were all feeling morose, with reason, and it didn't help to sit around and drag each other down.

"Sure Rhys, I'll go," responded Ben.

"Hold on. Before we get out there, I have something for you." He went over to his pack and pulled out a long, narrow bundle. "I picked this up at Snowmar for you, since yours was ruined in the lightning storm."

Ben took the bundle and slowly unwrapped it to reveal a sword. The weapon was plain and unadorned, just like his old weapon, but he could feel the quality was far superior.

Saala was peering over at them. "Venmoor steel?"

"Yes," answered Rhys. "Best forged steel you can find, in Alcott at least."

"Best steel in the world many say," Saala responded with a quizzical look, "although, maybe I'm not as familiar with some of the places you are."

Rhys shrugged. "It's good steel. Better than that stuff you were using before, Ben. In fighting, or any endeavor I suppose, you're only as good as your tools."

"That is true," agreed Saala. "Snowmar's captain, I presume?"

"Yeah. I figured he didn't need it anymore."

Saala gestured for the sword, and Ben handed it to him. He spun it through a series of forms then handed it back, hilt first. Ben wondered if he had a moral objection to taking the weapon. Saala could be funny like that.

Saala nodded. "Good find by Rhys. Well balanced and just the right size and weight. Ben, try to take care of this one. We practiced holding onto it in a fight, but I can't help you if you run into any other ladies in their bath."

The joke was too early, but Ben understood what Saala was trying to do. Meredith's death was a tragedy. There was nothing they could do to fix it now. The world was a dangerous place and they needed to move on.

LATER THAT MORNING, they put Meredith to rest. Rhys and Ben stumbled across an aspen grove half a league from the road and thought it was the perfect spot. It was on a hillside overlooking the length of the valley and far enough from the road that she would not be disturbed. The men quickly dug a shallow grave. They all spoke a few short words.

THAT AFTERNOON they made it to Eastside, the first town at the head of Sineook Valley. A subdued Lady Towaal agreed they would stop for a few days before continuing on through the valley to the Venmoor River. She was still recovering from the energies she'd released at Snowmar and even the half day of travel seemed to wear her out. Renfro was also struggling. He kept up on his crutches, but a few days' rest was needed for his ankle to heal.

Briefly, they discussed spending another night on the road, but realized it was critical that news of what happened got to the right people. All of the demons that attacked were dead, but there could be more lurking in the mountains. Until a full sweep of the area was made, it was too big of a risk to other travelers to delay.

Ben was surprised as they approached Eastside. He wasn't familiar with the town from the stories and had expected it to be a small waystation similar to Murdoch's. When they saw it, it was nearly large enough to be called a city. Saala explained that Eastside was a critical point of commerce. Nearly all of Whitehall and much of the Blood Bay's agricultural products were supplied from Sineook Valley. Any freight from the valley had to pass through Eastside on the way to Snowmar Pass.

The Lords of Eastside had built it into a decent-sized trading hub. They built warehouses and silos to keep goods until they were needed to replenish the stores in Whitehall. Space was at a premium in the port city, so Eastside made a natural staging location. Eastside also had natural defenses and little need to maintain a standing army. With mountains surrounding the valley on the north and south, Whitehall to the east, and the length of Sineook to the west, it would be impossible for enemies to make a direct assault on the place.

For that reason, the actual keep of Eastside was relatively small for a community its size. The bulk of the buildings spread out from it with no protective walls. It reminded Ben of an over-grown Farview.

When they made it to the outskirts of town there weren't even any guards. They had to progress all the way to the keep before finding arms men with Foley's livery.

Amelie took the lead. "Lady Amelie to see Lord Foley. Please send a man to let him know I'm here immediately. We have urgent news about Snowmar Station and must speak without delay."

"Lady Amelie? I'm sorry miss, but I'm not familiar with you. Are you a lady from Whitehall? Coming from the Conclave I suppose. How is that—"

"Sir! Maybe I should have spoken more strongly. Snowmar Station has fallen and every man there is dead. Send someone to alert Lord Foley!" she barked.

Suddenly, the guardhouse burst into activity. It was like Amelie kicked an anthill.

"Dead! How can that be?"

"Wait. Did she say Snowmar Station?"

"It's war! Whitehall is marching on us!"

Finally, a captain appeared, still hastily buckling his sword over his tunic. "Damn it. Get ahold of yourselves! Ma'am, you said Snowmar Station has fallen. Are you sure? What happened?"

"Yes, captain. We passed through there two days ago and there is absolutely no doubt. I believe the details would be better addressed in private with Lord Foley."

"Yes, of course," he replied. The men of Eastside had little experience in actual combat, but the captain had been around long enough to understand a serious situation. He knew how to respond.

"Come this way. Lord Foley is in the gardens. Private Bratch, run ahead and let him know we're coming. Now, man, run!"

The gardens turned out to be a tree-shaded emerald green lawn surrounding a clear sandy-bottomed pond. Lord Foley had recently emerged from the pond and was wrapping a thick cotton robe around himself. He didn't have the posture of a warrior lord like Argren, but he was a large man and fit. Ben thought he would strike an imposing figure if he were dressed for battle and not wearing a bathing robe.

"Lady Amelie." He gave a short bow that was almost a nod of the head then continued, "Bratch here was telling me you'd arrived. Pardon my attire. A swim a day keeps the heart rate up, so my physicians say at least. So sorry we haven't given you a proper welcome. I understand this is urgent?"

It certainly must keep the heart rate up thought Ben as he spied a blond, a redhead, and a brunette ducking into a door at the far end of the garden.

LORD FOLEY TOOK the news of Snowmar's fall surprisingly well. He seemed more interested in their group's battle than he did the casualties to the guard and residents in the pass. He did agree to immediately send messenger pigeons to Whitehall with the news and dispatched a guard captain to take a force up to scout the area.

Before long, they were ensconced in a guest wing of Foley's

keep. At Amelie's insistence, they were all kept close. The keep was not nearly as grand as Whitehall, but the rooms were more than sufficient for their needs. Ben thought he'd come a long way in the world when he saw a pair of silver candlesticks in the keep and wasn't impressed. There was a time not long ago when he couldn't have even imagined owning that much wealth.

THAT EVENING, Amelie and Towaal begged off of a feast that Lord Foley wanted to throw them and they all spent a quiet night by themselves. For Ben, it felt like the first night they were not running from what had happened at Snowmar and Meredith's death. They'd said what they needed to on the road, now it was time to move on.

It didn't hurt that Rhys had been away from the amenities of a town for over a week and made up for it by ordering Foley's staff to keep bringing fresh pitchers of ale and wine.

After dinner, Saala drew his falchion and examined it for nicks. He started oiling it and sliding a small whetstone up and down the blade to smooth out any tiny imperfections he found.

Ben moved over to Saala and brought out the sword Rhys had given him. "I haven't had a chance to look at this one yet."

Saala nodded at it. "Always wise to check your equipment following combat. A small chip can eventually lead to a blade shattering at the wrong moment." He slid his jar of oil and a whetstone to Ben before gently running a finger along one edge of Ben's new blade. "The captain took good care of this."

"More likely he didn't ever use it," snorted Rhys from the other side of the room.

"Do you need to check your weapon Rhys?" asked Ben.

"Nah. I'll be fine." Rhys was in good spirits. A pitcher or two of ale cured a lot of his ills.

"Mage-wrought?" asked Saala.

Rhys sighed and picked up his sword from near his pack and tossed it to Saala. "I suppose we've been travelling long enough together that I can trust you."

Ben asked, "Trust us? What do you mean?"

"Mage-wrought blades are very rare," answered Saala slowly. He drew the weapon from the scabbard and admired its length and heft. The silver etching Ben had noticed before was faded to the point he could barely see it.

Saala continued, "In fact, I've only seen three of them in my time. They don't break, they don't need sharpening, they resist heat, and it's rumored some have other mysterious properties." He raised an eyebrow in Rhys' direction.

"Depends on the mage that crafted it," Rhys responded with a shrug. "At least that's what I've been told. I haven't noticed any worthwhile mystical properties so far. Of course, can't complain about how it cuts. Does that just fine."

Ben wondered, "A mage crafts it? Like a blacksmith?"

"Exactly like a blacksmith," broke in Towaal. She was leaning back in a stuffed chair. Ben had thought she was asleep. "The mages who make weapons are trained in the both arts of blacksmithing and harnessing energies. During the process of heating and folding the steel of a sword, the mage is able to change the nature of the material into something more durable. Occasionally, like you say, the mage is able to imbue something of a different nature into the weapon, which gives it certain properties. It's a difficult process and mistakes can be dangerous. It also takes an incredible amount of skill with one's hands. There are few mages in the world. Even fewer mages take the time to learn a mundane task like blacksmithing, which is why the blades are so rare."

She paused. "Rhys, if you are going to keep ordering wine, can you at least pour me a glass?"

The tension in the room when Towaal spoke quickly dissipated. Magic always seemed like a touchy subject around her. The Sanctuary had its secrets and Ben knew she wanted to keep them. Ben looked at Meghan and could tell she saw an opportunity.

"Lady Towaal, I have never heard of blacksmith mages before. What other kinds of mages are there?" she asked innocently.

"It's all one and the same, girl. It's not a blacksmith mage, it's a mage who happens to know the arts of a blacksmith. People call it all kinds of things; magery, sorcery, wizardry, magic, witch-craft, and more. But it's all the same. At the heart of it is harnessing the energy around you and within you. When forging steel, there is an incredible amount of heat. If someone knows what they are doing and has the strength of will, they can use that heat to modify and improve the metal."

"Is that how..." Meghan paused. "Is that how you did what you did at Snowmar? Harnessed the energy around you?"

"Yes, in essence that is correct. All around us there is friction caused by tiny particles that you can't even see. They are constantly moving and generating heat and energy. The light from the sun or the power of the wind are also forms of energy. The friction is the same thing that causes you a shock when you walk across a wool carpet. That is external energy." Towaal accepted the glass of wine Rhys handed her and continued talk-ing, "I used that friction to create a small charge. I funneled more energy into it and then I directed it at our attackers. There was only so much around us that I could draw on for the charge, though, and I needed more than a little shock. I had to pull substantially from my own reserves—which is why I have been so sluggish the last few days. Channeling one's internal energy externally is taxing and dangerous. But in short, yes, I harnessed the available energy and sent it at our attackers."

"You make it sound so simple," murmured Meghan. "Just take energy and direct it?"

"The concept is simple, child, but the execution takes years or even decades of study. To manipulate physical matter, you must understand it. And I don't just mean know what it is. I mean fully understand to the tiniest detail. Take a tree. Everyone knows what it is and everyone knows what it does, but understanding how sunlight, water, and nutrients from the soil react in the plant to produce the energy to grow is something that very, very few people understand."

"So, at the Sanctuary, learning to be a mage is about understanding how things work?" asked Meghan.

"That is one part of it. A mage must understand what they are trying to do before they do it. There is no short cut to obtaining that knowledge. The second part is difficult as well. The second ingredient, so to speak, is willpower. Anything in this world is possible if one has the willpower to make it happen. Focusing that will in the proper direction and achieving results takes a special person and takes intense practice. Someone might be a natural, like yourself and Amelie, but you will never reach your potential without extensive training. Preparation and ability, they are useless without each other."

Amelie, who had been listening closely, asked, "I'm familiar with the study involved. Lady Greenfoot has been preparing me for the Sanctuary since I was a little girl. She was never clear though about what training goes into directing one's will. She always said that was for another time."

"Study of the world around us is something that anyone can do with the proper instructors or resources. Many of the world's best scholars have no interest in mage craft at all. It is also something that can be done safely from a comfortable chair in a well-appointed library. Focusing will and causing physical elements to react, that is something that cannot be done comfortably. It is strenuous and it is dangerous. Greenfoot is right. That is for another time," Towaal glanced at the men in the room. Apparently her openness had its limits. "And Greenfoot is no lady. She is as common born as they come, no offense of course."

"None taken," Meghan replied quietly.

"I understand your impatience. You are embarking on a journey that will surely change your lives in ways you may have never imagined. You must know though, this path is a long one. Over the course of millennia, the Sanctuary has developed ways to guide girls down that path. But it is a thing best done in the safety and security of the Sanctuary. I only say what I say now because you have witnessed the terrible potential that comes with being a mage. It is not something entered lightly."

Amelie replied, "You speak as if we have not already started. My journey started when I stepped out of Issen and Meghan's when she left Farview. We are on this path, and we are not turning back."

THEY SPENT two more days in Eastside, partly because they needed the rest, but not insignificantly because Lord Foley seemed so offended at the thought of them leaving. He threw a feast as extravagant as he had promised and spent the rest of the time entertaining them with stories of his hunts, musical performances, poetry readings, demonstrations of arms, and the best his court had to offer. It slowly dawned on Ben that this was not a lord who had been at Whitehall for the Conclave. This was a man who had significant wealth, but little political power. The idea that the two could be separated was a new concept.

His loyalty to Whitehall was a given because of the geography his city occupied and the lack of military power he had at his disposal. He wasn't part of the wrangling give-and-take that Argren had done with the other lords. Foley had aspirations, but he was bound to allegiances that his ancestors and nature had made long before his rule. He was a lord, yes, but he was also a vassal of Whitehall and that was how he felt others saw him.

Once Ben realized this, the man's behavior made perfect sense. Any favor he could gain with a Lady of Amelie's status or a representative of the City was more than the scraps he would get from Argren's court.

One of Foley's suggestions that they found difficult to turn down was an escort from two of his hunters. They would travel with them as far as Kirksbane on the Venmoor River to ensure they had, 'no fear of bandits', as Foley said.

"Make sure we don't get lost somewhere in between the cabbage and potato fields? More like listen to every word we say to his neighbors. I can't wait to get out of this inbred valley," grumbled Rhys. "Most of these lords are married to each other's cousins and none of them have anything better to do than look at what the other one is doing. You give a man a little bit of power and he's going to try to find something to do with it. Whitehall won't stand for them making war on each other, and they can't reach anyone else. Makes them compete over silly stuff like taxes on barley, diverting an irrigation ditch, or who threw the best fall harvest party, all while ignoring things like the attack at Snowmar, which took out an entire barracks."

They were in one of Eastside's bare, stone-circled courtyards, working through another one of the Ohms. The calming breathing techniques Rhys had spoken about before weren't having any effect on him today.

"You're probably right about why he wants the hunters with us." Saala smirked. "Lady Amelie and Towaal went public in Whitehall and Eastside. Just because all the fancy lords and ladies joined Argren's Alliance doesn't mean they stopped playing their games. So what, though? We might as well have the extra swords. Amelie is a tempting target and Lord Foley doesn't want any incidents happening anywhere near him, and I agree with that."

Saala winked at Ben. "Besides, some might see our small escort as scant protection for such a highborn Lady."

"Scant protection!" barked Rhys. "Isn't that your job, to protect her ladyship?"

Saala, poorly hiding his amusement at Rhys' frustration, heaped on, "I think it will be nice having some more able bodies with us."

Rhys stumbled out of his Ohm stance and glared at Saala. "Able bodies my ass. Any hunter spending his days on Foley's payroll is either unofficially retired or feeble."

EARLY THE NEXT DAY, with morning dew still clinging to the stone walls of the keep, they departed Eastside and Ben got a clear picture of why Rhys was so upset with their new companions.

"Ah, Rhys! Never thought I'd see you again looking so healthy!" boomed a large man.

"Yeah, Ferg. Nice to see you again too," muttered Rhys.

"Oh, ho ho," chortled the man. "I see you are no longer wearing the sigil? Got a little uncomfortable?"

The man could only be described as pompous. He was wearing a flashing silver breastplate and had a massive two-handed sword strapped to his back. His long, raven-black hair was accented by a silver mustache that drooped from around his mouth and down past his chin. His hair was bound by a silver circlet that matched both the mustache and breastplate.

Surely that could not be intentional, thought Ben.

The man continued, "I earned my sigil a year later, no thanks to you." He patted the hilt of his sword and turned to show a large, brightly gilded blademaster's sigil. "I understand of course, it's an honor and a responsibility. Old Nemil didn't give it up easy, mind you. It was a tough fight. I almost feel sorry for the old chap. Died a couple moons later. A lot of hungry challengers once I beat him. He wouldn't give it up. By the by, it's Ferguson now. I dropped Ferg once I signed Lord Foley's contract. He was paying good gold then because he wanted a man with a proper blademaster's sigil. He'd pay good for a second sigil, I suppose. It's a shame you don't have yours anymore."

Saala had tucked his own scabbard behind his travel pack where his subtler sigil was hidden. He picked up his pace to walk beside Rhys and asked Ferguson, "You earned your blademaster sigil by beating a man named Old Nemil? I can only assume he was, ah, old?"

"Aye, that he was. Did you know him?" Ferguson continued without waiting for a response, "He was cunning, that is for sure. Comes from the wisdom, you know? He'd seen it all. Took some creative blade work to get through that guard. Wasn't my first choice, of course. Good ole Rhys here was carrying a sigil back when we were at Northport together. He disappeared the day after I challenged him. You heard me earlier, right? That's why I said I was surprised to see him. Figured a man who can't protect his sigil is going to get nothing but trouble. Just like Old Nemil did."

"This is going to be delightful traveling with you, Blademaster Ferguson!" Saala slapped Rhys on the back then dropped back, grinning, to walk beside Meghan and Ben.

THAT EVENING they dropped the normal routine of working through Rhys' Ohms and just did sword practice, mostly in an effort to ignore Blademaster Ferguson. The man was an unending fountain of stories about his own bravery. Through the verbal onslaught, Ben determined that he had been in Lord Foley's service the last half decade. Before that, he had been stationed in Northport guarding some lord's household. That's where he had met Rhys.

"The Lord of Northport, is that Lord Rhymer?" asked Ben. "Why did you leave his service? I hear he is quite wealthy and I'm sure would pay better than these valley lords."

"Oh, no, not Rhymer. You're right, Rhymer is the Lord of Northport, but we guarded a lord of Northport. You understand the difference, I am sure." Ferguson gave Ben a knowing wink.

Ben wasn't sure he really did know the difference.

"Lord Allimach got around, that's not secret. He was worried about, well, you know," Ferguson continued. Ben really thought he didn't know.

Amelie saved him the breath and broke in facetiously, "Oh, I have not heard! What was this Lord Allimach so worried about?"

"Jealously, my Lady," answered Ferguson with a serious expression. "He was worried about jealous husbands. He hired a group of us to keep his estate safe, and we did keep it safe. Many tried, but none made it past our guard. Pity him dying of a shell-fish allergy. Such a strange way to go, eating shellfish in North-port and with so many willing to pay good coin to put a knife in him. Anyway, it was a couple days after when a lot of us were looking for new employment that I challenged your friend Rhys here. He skipped town that night and I haven't seen him since."

Rhys grinned back at Ferguson. "That's true. I did leave right after you challenged me. I figured with Lord Allimach dead, my work there was done."

Ben saw Renfro looking at him with questioning eyes.

Rhys continued while tapping his longsword, "If it's been bothering you so much these last five years, maybe we can pick up where we left off?"

Lady Towaal interrupted, "I don't think that's necessary. The man has his sigil now and we need to keep moving. We can't risk someone getting hurt during the contest."

Rhys smiled at her. "That is true. An injury is certainly possible. Oh well, maybe another time, Ferg."

THE HISTORY with Rhys did little to stem Ferguson's loquaciousness. Throughout the length of the valley he regaled them with tales of his exploits. Occasionally, Rhys' sword hand would get a little twitchy, but the rest of them were able to treat it as pure, presumably fictional, theatre. If nothing else, the man had an imagination.

Rishram, the second hunter Lord Foley sent, was Ferguson's opposite. Where Ferguson was big and boisterous, Rishram was small and reserved. He rarely spoke. When he did, it was in quiet tones. Not the silky, slow drawl that Saala had. Just quiet. The one attribute he shared with Ferguson was his bushy mustache. It seemed to take over his small face. Renfro and Ben joked that there must have been some wager involved.

His armaments were also different. He had light leather armor and carried a recurved horn bow, a quiver of arrows, and two hunting knives. When Meghan asked him about a sword, he curtly responded, "We're in the valley. What do I need a sword for?"

Most of the time he spent ranging ahead of them. He said for scouting, but Ben suspected just for the peace and quiet. He was decently skilled with his bow, though. One time when he was back with them, a covey of quail burst out of a nearby field and took flight over the road. Rishram swung his bow off his shoulder and started firing arrows at the flock. In heartbeats, he'd downed two of the birds.

Amelie and Meghan both clapped and cheered for him as he scuttled forward to retrieve the birds.

Rhys snickered while Rishram collected the birds. "Five arrows and he shoots down two of them."

THE NEXT THREE weeks were like that. They travelled down the broad, well-maintained roads of Sineook Valley with little concern for safety and little interaction with the residents. Both Towaal and Amelie preferred to avoid the small keeps of the local lords. In the valley, every town had a lord and every lord was looking to impress passersby with his court. They didn't have time to stop and let each lord try to outdo each other.

The towns were scattered about a half day apart from each other and were well spaced to support the agricultural commerce in the area. There were fields running from side to side across the wide valley and when there weren't natural streams, irrigation ditches had been dug into an interconnected network. It was well organized and peaceful. These people were intent on minding their own business and tending to their fields.

It wasn't so different from Farview, mused Ben. You could replace any one of these small town lords with Alistair Pinewood and it wouldn't make a difference to the residents of the town. From the little they saw when they paused for supplies, it looked like people ignored the men sitting behind the walls of the keeps and proceeded with their lives with little need or want for the protection that the lord offered.

After a few weeks of easy travel through the bucolic pastures and fields, they were passing through a plot of radishes on one side and some sort of small fruit-bearing bush on the other. Ben shared his thoughts with Saala. "It doesn't feel like these people need the lords as badly as the lords need the people. I mean, it doesn't seem like there is risk from bandits, invading armies, or other dangers that you need a lord to face."

"You could make an argument that you don't need a lord for those situations either," replied Saala. "How did Lord Foley handle the demon attack on Snowmar any different than what Farview did? Foley sent word to Whitehall and Farview sent word to Murdoch's. Those types of threats, you either organize or you send for specialists. By the time the lord arrives with all of his arms men, the situation has probably been resolved, for good or for bad. I've spent a lot of time in the company of lords and ladies and I'm not sure there's ever a time the common man really needs them."

"Well, I was thinking that these people don't need standing armies because of the geography, but some areas do," Ben replied after thinking. "What about invading armies? You need more than a couple of hunters to put a stop to that. Without the strength of the Alliance, for example, the Coalition could run rampant. The people here need that protection, don't they?"

"Ah, now for that situation I'll take a different argument," responded Saala. "Yes, a little band like us has no chance of stopping the might of the Coalition, but in that case, are the lords of Alcott helping to solve the problem or are they creating it? Without lords and their like, there wouldn't be a Coalition, and there wouldn't be an army that you needed protection from."

Ben frowned. "Maybe I'm missing something since I grew up without a Lord. If they don't provide protection, why do people put up with them? What value are they adding?"

Saala gestured to the road they were walking on.

"Wait," said Ben. "You are saying that the only reason people put up with these lords is so that they can build roads?"

"I'm saying that is the value they add," replied Saala. "Building a road like this is a massive undertaking and no individual could do it. People can benefit from organization in society, and sometimes that takes the form of swearing fealty to a lord. Sometimes it takes the form of your town council."

"Why do they raise armies then, if it's not something the people need?"

"Fear," responded Saala.

"Fear? What do you mean?" asked Ben.

"There are two ways a lord can stay in power," explained Saala. "They can take the tax revenue they collect and provide services their people need. They can invest it back into infrastructure and building opportunities for their people. This road, for example, allows the farmers of the valley to transport their goods to markets where they can get a good price for their production. The irrigation ditches we've been passing allow water to the fields during a dry spell. These things require upkeep which people see the lord doing. They are projects that the lord spends taxes on, and if it is a good investment, the people will support that lord. But those projects are difficult and take a long time to complete. Inevitably, someone will not be happy with it even when it is for the common good. The farmer on the one side of the road who gets the water is happy, but the one on the other side who didn't get it that year is unhappy with the way his money has been spent."

Saala continued talking as they passed a radish field and started by one full of turnips. "Even though it is difficult and sometimes unpopular, a good lord will do these things for his people. When done right, over time, the people will see that the lord has their best interest at heart and they will trust and support him. Like I said, though, that is difficult and takes years to achieve. Sometimes it is easier for the lord to gain support by inciting fear in the population. Building this road the length of the valley must have taken decades to finish. In a few days, a clever lord could place rumors in the streets and point to signs of how aggressive a neighbor is becoming. Before long, the people are seeing the signs themselves and begging that lord for protection. He has a mandate now to raise taxes, build his army, and collect more power for himself. If one was not concerned with the moral implications, one could argue that is the quicker way to a solid power base."

"Hold on," Ben said. "Do you think that is what Argren has done with this Alliance of his?"

Saala shrugged. "I'm not a lord in Alcott, so it is not my place to say. Argren has gained fealty from Issen, the disconnected cities on the Blood Bay, Northport, and Venmoor. That is certainly not something I think he could have achieved in one generation of public service projects."

~

THAT NIGHT, they stopped a few days out from Kirksbane, a city on the Venmoor River and the official end of the Sineook Valley. They had been camping outside, away from the small towns scattered around this end of the valley. It was late spring and the weather was perfect for being outdoors.

Ben settled next to Meghan, who was stirring a rich-smelling stew over the small campfire. Everyone except Towaal took turns on cooking duty. Meghan favored hearty vegetable soups. Ferguson was already ensconced by her and was regaling Meghan with another one of his encounters.

"It was a brutal fight, miss. There were three of them coming at us like an avalanche. My mates and I, we spread out to meet them and braced for the charge. I drew Panther and made sure I had plenty of room to swing. A girl like Panther needs room to growl."

"Panther?" inquired Meghan innocently.

Ferguson let off stroking his thick mustache for a moment to caress the hilt of his huge two-handed sword. "Aye, my girl Panther."

"Your sword is named Panther?" Meghan quickly wiped at her mouth to cover her grin.

"All blademaster's swords are named, miss. It can seem a bit silly, I am sure, but it is part of the legend we build around ourselves. You can charge more if your sword has a name."

"Oh, of course," agreed Meghan. "Go on."

"Well, like I was saying," he went back to talking and slowly stroking his whiskers, "there were three of them, all coming down on us at once. We met them with fury and steel. I chopped one of the bastards nearly in two with Panther. The other two got cut up by my mates. But before we finished them, they left eight of my friends face down. Horrible scene. You know how it is with demons, they leave a bloody mess behind. You folks were lucky you had a mage with you to take care of it. I don't think we'd be talking now if you didn't. I'm sorry to say it, but it's true. We just had twenty good men and our steel. It nearly wasn't enough."

"You have experience fighting demons?" Ben interrupted.

Ferguson shot him a look.

He was on a mission to impress Meghan, but he knew she was close to Ben, so he didn't want to be rude. "Yes. You see them a lot in the Wilds beyond Northport. It's demon country up there, and worse. It's a good living for a hunter, though. The mines need protecting and there are the artifacts that people find from time to time. Old stuff and worth a bundle."

"Demon country? Is that where they are from? I had never really thought about where they came from," replied Ben.

"Well, I don't know that they're really from anywhere," answered the mustachioed hunter.

"They're just kind of there, you know? I mean, no one's found some place that they all leave from, like a demon village. No one even knows how they're born, if they even are. There isn't any male and female like us, but there are little ones. Probably grow like plants. That's what I think at least, and no one's proved me wrong."

"But," Ben asked, "there are more of them near Northport?"

"Aye," replied Ferguson nodding his head, "they still roam free in the Wilds. Every year the hunting parties go out and try to thin 'em out. They haven't finished 'em yet. It's tough and dangerous work. I was happy to do it when I was up there. If it wasn't for people like me hunting for demon horns, well, people like you wouldn't be safe."

Rhys was dramatically rolling his eyes behind Ferguson's back but didn't speak up.

"I just don't understand," said Meghan. "Someone has to know where they come from and what they want, right?"

Ferguson responded grimly, "The one thing we know for sure, when you see 'em, you kill 'em. Otherwise, they're going to kill you. That's a fact. That's all you really need to understand about it."

12

KIRKSBANE

Two days later, they made it to the low-lying town of Kirksbane. It was situated on the open western end of the Sineook Valley and the bank of the Venmoor River. It marked the border between the fiefdoms of the valley and the territory of Venmoor. The town spread out from a wide oxbow curve that caused a shallow point on the river.

Kirksbane, like the towns of the Sineook Valley, did not have a wall for defense. Ben remarked on it and Saala explained, "Kirksbane is strategically located, but it's not a source of political power in the region. It lives and dies on trade from the river and out of the valley. Kirksbane only facilitates that trade. If someone wanted to cut it off, it'd be easy to do without overrunning the town."

"Well," Ben replied, "it looks comfortable enough to spend a night."

"Right," grumbled Rhys. "I understand why we've been doing it, but I'm ready to get out from under the stars and into a clean bed."

"Ha!" shouted Amelie. "I think we've been travelling together long enough for you to be honest with us, Master

Rhys. I've heard Venmoor's taverns are legendary, and I'm certain you have some favorites in Kirksbane you'd like to show us."

Rhys mock bowed deeply toward Amelie. "I can see why the Sanctuary is so interested in you, miss. A deep thinker like you is certain to go far in this world."

"I'll accept your false praise," she chirped, "in exchange for you showing us to a place that actually does have clean beds in addition to the cold ale."

"As you wish," he answered with a wink.

TRUE TO HIS WORD, Rhys led them to a sturdy, clean-looking inn on the water that overlooked the shallows. After dropping off their gear and freshening up, they met downstairs in the common room. It had wide doors that opened up to a back porch hanging over the water. The porch was framed by massive century old willow trees that drooped down to the water and gave the inn a private feel even though it was near the center of town.

As they settled into seats near the water, a sultry voice called out, "Welcome to the Curve! What can I get for you folks?"

Ben's mouth went dry. The woman's honey blond hair was piled up in a loose bun which accentuated her long neck and bare shoulders. She had on a white, loosely tied top that was hanging on precariously. Her dark skirts fell low enough to hide all but the toes of her shoes and swayed as she walked with a natural dancer's grace. She was stunning. Not the classic, regal beauty of Amelie. She had an earthy, approachable aura. She exuded sensuality.

"A couple of pitchers of ale please," answered Amelie before glaring at the men around the table.

"Sure thing, sugar," purred the woman. "That's our specialty.

Master Taber brews it all in house. We have a golden lager, a red ale, and a barley wine."

Amelie gave Ben a sharp kick under the table before responding again, "Maybe the expert here would like to choose. Ben, aren't you supposed to be a brewer? What sounds good?"

"Oh, uh, yeah. I know how to brew beer," he answered lamely.

The stunning barmaid leaned in, put a hand on Ben's shoulder, and said, "Congratulations. Now, what would you like to drink?"

Ben felt the heat rising in his face as he ordered a round of lagers and ales and barely held his hand from moving to where the barmaid had touched his shoulder. With difficulty, he ignored the hard looks from the girls and turned toward the other men.

"A brewer?" asked Rishram.

The man was so silent that Ben wasn't even sure it was him who'd spoken at first.

"Yes, yes," answered Ben. "I was the brewer at home before I left with Lady Towaal and her company."

"So, not an arms man? I figured you must be, travelling in company like this. I've seen your fine sword. Venmoor steel if I'm not mistaken?" The little man was inching closer to Ben and his voice seemed to be dropping even lower. "With a blademaster in your group and Master Rhys, how could you not be skilled?"

"Oh, no," denied Ben. "I've done some practice with them, but I don't consider myself to be very skilled. We've been travelling so hard that there really isn't time for it. Maybe someday. I haven't figured out what I'll do once all of this is over. I had planned to return home, but maybe I'll find employment with my sword or even open a brewery in the City."

He didn't mean to share so much with the little hunter, but Ben figured it was better he talk than listen to that quiet, creepy voice.

He was saved from further awkward conversation with Rishram by Ferguson loudly slapping the table and near shouting, "A brewer huh! Now that is a profession I can get behind. People drink in both good times and bad. I once saved a brewer in Northport and the man was so grateful that I drank for free in that town until the poor fellow went out of business. Never understood that really..."

Ferguson's monologue washed over Ben as he sat back and looked out over the bubbling water and watched the willow branches dance in the slow current. Three weeks away from the drama at Whitehall, the attack at Snowmar and the awkward interactions with Lord Foley. It felt good to be on the road with his companions and away from the pressures of the large towns where Amelie was known. He wasn't sure what would happen when they made it to the City, but he decided he would enjoy this last stretch of the journey down the Venmoor River.

LATER THAT EVENING, musicians started playing and the staff cleared the tables and pushed them to the edges of the room to make space for dancing. Their party relocated to the fringes of the room. Even though it had been easy travel through the valley, it had still been three weeks constantly on their feet. The music set a lively mood though and the revelry in the room was infectious.

Renfro slid onto the bench next to Ben and scooted close. "You should ask her to dance."

Ben jerked his eyes away from the honey blond barmaid who was gliding around the room, swapping empty pitchers for full and deftly avoiding staggering and sometimes handsy patrons.

"She's working," snapped Ben. "What do you mean ask her to dance? She doesn't have time for that kind of thing now."

"Working?" Renfro guffawed. "I don't think she's worked a day in her life."

Ben glanced at Renfro quizzically and saw he was looking at Amelie. "Wait. You think I should ask Amelie to dance?"

"Of course! Who else do you think I was talking about?" asked Renfro. "Meghan is your sister and Towaal, well, Towaal is Lady Towaal. She knows it wasn't anything serious with Meredith. Amelie knows, I mean. That poor girl was reading into it more than was there. Amelie's experienced with these things and she respected Meredith, even though she was overstepping. She doesn't mind..."

"Hold on!" broke in Ben. "What are you talking about? You sound like one of the old women when they'd gossip over laundry back in Farview. Where did you hear all of this?"

Renfro adopted a hurt look. "It's not gossip. I was just trying to help. Meghan's been so worried about Amelie after the thing at Snowmar. She thinks a little excitement might be the cure and we all know the way Amelie was looking at you before Meredith moved in."

"You've been talking to Meghan!" exclaimed Ben. He was silenced when Renfro dug one of his sharp elbows into Ben's side.

Amelie and Meghan suddenly appeared in front of the two of them.

A flushed Amelie blurted, "This isn't court dancing like I'm used to, but I think I could get the hang of it." The stomping and twirling crowd spun around behind the girls. Amelie reached out a hand to Ben, "Meghan says you know these country dances. Care to show me?"

THE NEXT MORNING, bright sunlight fell directly on Ben's bed and he rolled out onto his feet with a groan. He and Renfro were sharing a room and the little thief was still buried under his pillow and blankets snoring softly. Ben padded out of the room to put on his boots and straightened up in the hall before descending to the common room.

The tables had all been pushed back into place and he spied Saala and Rhys sitting in a corner near the back porch.

Ben plopped down in a chair at their table and held up a hand to shield his eyes from the sun.

"I'm sensing a pattern." Rhys smirked before pushing a mug of steaming kaf toward Ben. "If you intend to celebrate every time we make a new town, you need to learn to pace yourself."

"Funny," answered Ben. "I don't recall you pacing yourself."

"Ah," remarked Saala, "that's because our friend Rhys is a professional. His natural state is sodden. You can't feel the hangover if you never stop the drinking."

"I'll drink to that!" exclaimed Rhys.

After a few more mugs of kaf and a breakfast of biscuits and bacon, Ben was ready to follow Saala and Rhys into the sun and down to the barge moorings to see if they could secure a ride to the City.

"Kirksbane survives on these shallows," explained Saala. "Barges coming down from Northport or up from the City all stop here and move through a series of locks on the far side of town. The depth of the shallows is too low for a loaded barge. Centuries ago, they'd portage around the shallows. Tie up north of town and cart all the goods to just south of town. But that took time and a lot of effort. It was the industry that this town sprung from, though. Eventually, some enterprising fellow built the locks and barges can safely pass through without loading and unloading."

"Why don't they just dredge the channel?" asked Ben. "I mean, it seems like that would be relatively easy to do, right?"

"Ah, and that's why it's called Kirksbane," said Saala. "It means King's Bane in old Vennish. Back in the portage days, the King of Venmoor attempted to fund the project himself. At the time, he must have thought the ease of doing business between his people and Northport was worth the cost. But the town that was here at the time, they refused the king. Goes with their nature. The Vennish have never been ones to listen to authority. Handling those barges was what put food on the tables for the few residents who weren't river bandits. They weren't willing to give up their only source of legitimate income."

"How did they build the locks then?" asked Ben.

"A wealthy family in the City bought up all of the land outside the west end of town and started digging. The river itself is public property, but on their own land, no one could stop them."

"People tried though," added Rhys. "The entire town rose up against the folks building the locks. They had to hire a small army of guards. For about a year it was basically open warfare. Half the able-bodied men in Kirksbane didn't survive that year. There's a little obelisk somewhere around here they raised for a memorial. The same family owns and runs the locks to this day."

Before long, they made it through the low-lying buildings and down to the barge moorings. Even though the town no longer did much portage business, it was still an important port for produce coming out of the Sineook Valley. The center of activity was the barge moorings. The produce would go downriver to Venmoor or even the City. Empty barges were pulled up the river by a team of horses walking along the bank, then they would tie up and wait for enough cargo to fill their hold before floating back down.

Instead of docks, the moorings were sturdy, thick iron rings driven into a sloped stone bank. The barges would toss a rope to shore then be pulled tight to load right there in the shallow water. Narrow gangways were run up to the barges by wheelbarrow men clustered around waiting for work.

This early in the morning, things were still moving slow. A few wagons heaped with vegetables were parked and the drivers were haggling over prices with the bargemen. The only other sounds were the nickers of the horses and the creak of the heavy ropes securing the barges to shore. Ben noted that this time of year, there were more barges than wagons. He didn't think the bargemen would have good news to report back to their lords.

They made their way down toward the long stretch of moorings and Rhys grunted then elbowed Saala. At the end of the line of moorings there was a wooden pier with a sole vessel docked. It was a long, sleek-looking river sloop with two bare masts and a small flag.

"City colors," grunted Rhys.

"Worth a try," replied Saala with a shrug. "She'll make it four times faster than any of these barges."

"Ho the ship!" shouted Rhys as they approached, winding through the maze of hemp ropes strung out from the barges.

Instantly, a wizened, scrawny-looking shirtless man popped up on the deck. "Ho the shore!"

"Are you making for the City from here?" inquired Rhys.

"Where else would we go?" cracked the man.

"Fair enough. We're headed that way also and want to inquire about passage. Are you the man to talk to about that?"

"You need to talk to the captain." The scrawny man scratched himself and stared down at Rhys.

"I imagined we would." Rhys paused and spared an exasperated look with his companions. "Can you tell us where the captain is?"

"He's on shore. At an inn called the Curve. Best ale and best barmaids outside the City. I would've been up there myself last night if I wasn't on watch."

"Of course he is," grumbled Rhys as they turned back toward town.

RHYS' mood didn't improve any when they reentered the common room to find Lady Towaal and the girls sitting across a late breakfast from a well-dressed courtier and a weathered portly man. Ferguson and Rishram were seated behind them at another table, leaning slightly in and clearly trying to overhear the conversation.

"Gentlemen," started Towaal, "I hope you didn't pay for passage yet. Lord Reinhold and Captain, ah, Fishbone are heading back on the morrow. They have a sloop, which Captain Fishbone estimates can make the City four times faster than any river barge. They also have a dozen men at arms, which is a bonus. There is word the river is getting restless again and bandits have reappeared."

"Lady Towaal!" exclaimed Ferguson. "Rishram and myself would be happy to accompany you on the rest of the way to The City. Lord Foley wouldn't like it if we left you at the mercy of river bandits."

"Of course, Master Ferguson. We'd be happy to have you."

"Just what we need," muttered Rhys darkly.

∼

BEN AND SAALA were quickly driven outside by Rhys' grumpiness. Ben didn't blame him. Ferguson was a blustering fool and Ben was always a little shocked every evening they turned in and Rhys had not punched him in the face. Sooner or later, Ferguson was going to say too much. Ben suspected he'd quickly regret it.

"Let's get some work done if we're going to be here all day," Saala said as he tossed Ben his sword. They still used real steel during their practice. While Ben was rapidly improving, he wasn't yet a danger to Saala. The man moved with an unnatural quickness and swirled away like smoke anytime Ben came close.

There was a small clearing in the thicket of willow trees beside the inn where they began to practice. Saala didn't mind instructing Ben around others, but he was always careful to hold back when he did. In towns, he kept his blademaster sigil hidden and none of the company spoke of it. There was an unspoken agreement that the less said to members outside their group, the better.

In the privacy of the willow trees, though, he was like a stalking tiger.

Ben was comfortable with the forms Saala had taught him and after the time in Whitehall with the Citadel's guardsmen, he was learning to adapt. He couldn't match Saala's speed or agility, though. Time and time again, he whirled into an aggressive sequence and Saala would counter until Ben thought he was getting close, then suddenly, Saala would slide out of reach or pivot around Ben's attack to launch one of his own.

For two bells they danced across the clearing, Ben trying futilely to find a gap in Saala's defense. Finally, after one particularly furious series, Ben flopped down on to his back, exhausted.

"You've been training me two months now and I still haven't come close to touching you. I'm not sure I'm cut out for this," panted Ben.

"It might be a year before you manage to score a hit on me in practice. Probably less, though. You are learning quickly," answered Saala in a calm, even tone.

Ben couldn't fathom the fact that Saala wasn't out of breath.

Saala continued, "You must understand, I am the best at this. There are very few men in this world who can defeat me. Certainly there are none that have only been training for two months. When I was young and had only picked up a blade two months before, there were many men who could defeat me. Skill comes with time and practice."

"It's just... you're so much quicker than me," mumbled Ben. "I can practice these forms but it doesn't do any good when you've already moved from where I was swinging."

Saala sat down next to Ben. "Speed comes with time too. It will also come with the exercises Rhys is teaching you. Some people are naturally fast, and you are fortunate to be one. But true quickness like I have, that is from years of training your body to react before your mind processes a threat. It is more than seeing and more than hearing, it is an extra sense that can be learned and developed. I am confident that you will learn it." Saala held one hand down near his waist and one hand high above his head. "Your skill is here today," he shook his lower hand and then looked up, "but your potential is up here."

Ben rolled to his feet. "I hope so."

Saala rose also. "Give it time. Most do not have the potential to be a blademaster. You do. You are getting better very quickly, but you need to think in years and decades and not weeks and months."

They started back toward the inn and there was a rustling among the willow branches and then the sound of running feet. Ben's sword instinctively rose.

"She's running away. And that is not the kind of threat I was talking about," said Saala with a grin.

"Who's running away?"

"The honey blond barmaid you were so taken with last night. She's been watching us for half a bell. As I said, she's not a threat like we were talking about." Saala tapped Ben's sword. "And you'll need more than that to stop her."

LATER THAT AFTERNOON, Ben enjoyed a cold lager in the common room with Renfro. He'd washed up after his practice with Saala and wasn't sure how to spend the rest of the day. Since they'd secured passage on Captain Fishbone's river sloop, there wasn't anything to do but wait.

Suddenly, Renfro bounced to his feet, "Meghan, Amelie!" he called.

The girls had appeared at the foot of the stairs to the sleeping quarters and came over to their table.

"Have an ale with us," pleaded Renfro. "It's really good. Ben chose it."

"Good for him," said Amelie coolly as she looked around the room. "Where is Ilyena?"

Ben blinked. "Ilyena? Who is that?"

"You don't know?" asked Amelie skeptically. "That's the name of the blond barmaid everyone was falling over yesterday. I thought you... well, that's her name. My father always taught me to learn the names of the help. It makes them feel special."

Amelie's cold demeanor was new to Ben, but he'd seen the same thing from the village girls in Farview. The nicest girl in the world turned mean around a rival. He figured it would blow over soon. After all, Amelie was the girl he'd danced with the night before.

"Well, Ilyena, or whatever her name is, isn't around right now. The ale is still good. Care for a mug?"

"I'm sure it's grand," Amelie responded primly, "but I have no interest in drinking ale in the middle of the day. I've heard of the locks of Kirksbane, so Meghan and I are going to see them. They're key to commerce in the region. That kind of thing is important for rulers to understand even if it is not our lands. You two may escort us."

Maybe it wouldn't blow over as soon as he'd hoped.

THE LOCKS, it turned out, were essentially a long trench looping around the west side of town with two massive gates, a windmill, and a water pump. The gates and pumps were used to account for the change in elevation between the river north and south of town. The shallows masked a drop of about five paces which would have made it difficult or impossible to pull a loaded barge up.

With the two gates and the pump, the operators of the locks

were able to raise and lower the water level, so the barges were able to enter, float up, and then exit at the higher level. After they understood the concept and watched a barge make its slow progress through the system, the young people headed back to the inn.

"It's pretty amazing to think how they figured that out. Without those locks, they still would be hauling goods up river by hand," said Meghan.

"Yes, these are remarkable people here in Kirksbane. I wish we had more of that kind of innovation back in Issen," replied Amelie. "The fees and jobs bring a lot of money into this town."

"It wasn't these people," interrupted Ben. "I mean, they weren't the ones who built the locks. It was actually a family down in the City. The people here, they fought it. They used to be in the business of hauling goods by hand. The locks disrupted that and it meant fewer jobs. The people fought the King in Venmoor on it too, but I guess the family from the City had the determination to get it done."

"They had more money than the king," said a quiet voice from behind them.

The young people spun around and saw Rishram standing a few paces behind them.

"Where did you come from!" exclaimed Renfro.

"I followed you from the inn," replied Rishram in his quiet voice. "I wanted to make sure someone was watching you. I saw Lady Towaal deep in discussion with Lord Reinhold before we left. Saala and Rhys aren't nearby, are they?"

Ben frowned. "I'm not sure where they are. Maybe they're back at the inn? We're heading that way if you want to go with us."

"As long as they aren't here."

Rishram then pulled out his hunting knives and started advancing on the group.

"Hey!" shouted Ben. This wasn't right. Why did the man pull his weapons?

"There you are," boomed the loud voice of Ferguson. "I've been looking all over for you!"

All five of them turned to see Ferguson stomping down the street. Rishram was the first to move. He launched himself toward the big man with his knives held low.

"What are you..." stammered a wide-eyed Ferguson.

He didn't have time to finish his sentence. Rishram was on him, one knife going low and plunging into Ferguson's unprotected side. Rishram pulled back with his other blade and stabbed at Ferguson's neck. The big man got his arm up in time and the flashing silver weapon punctured his forearm and slid all of the way through, leaving a hand's length of bloody steel jutting out of Ferguson's arm.

Ferguson jumped back, spinning, the knife lodged in his forearm. His side spurted a fountain of blood as Rishram wrenched the first knife free.

Silently, Rishram turned toward the young people and charged. The little mustachioed man was headed straight for Amelie, ignoring the injured Ferguson and the rest of the party. Amelie started running backward down the street. Her heel caught an uneven stone and she went sprawling onto her back.

Rishram picked up his pace with a murderous glint in his eye and was full on sprinting toward her when Ben arrived just in time, crashing into Rishram's side and sending him flying to the ground. Ben had little time to set himself before Rishram flipped off his back onto his feet with an acrobat's grace.

He snarled at Ben, "Poor decision, brewer boy. I would have let you live."

Ben couldn't keep his eyes off the bloody knife as Rishram stalked toward him. He cursed himself for not bringing his sword and searched in vain for a weapon.

He was temporarily saved by Renfro hurtling at Rishram with

a cobblestone in his hand, but Rishram barely paused. He ducked Renfro's charge, caught him in the midsection with a narrow shoulder and then tossed Renfro over his head like a rag doll. Renfro crashed to the hard ground, stunned. Ben could see he was okay, but Ben knew he wouldn't recover in the heartbeats before this fight was over.

Rishram darted forward toward Ben, who slid to the side in one of Saala's signature moves. He almost wasn't quick enough and Rishram's knife sliced open a tear in his shirt. Any slower and that razor sharp blade would have emptied his guts onto the street.

Suddenly, a pained bellow erupted from Ferguson and he charged into the fray, swinging his two-handed sword Panther at Rishram's head. The smaller man easily ducked the wild swing and came in close to cut a deep laceration in Ferguson's thigh.

Blood bloomed along Ferguson's new injury. His entire side was now covered in blood from the first wound. He kept coming though with a vicious figure-eight attack. Rishram's knife was still sticking out of Ferguson's forearm and he could barely hold his heavy two-handed blade. It wavered in his grip, giving Rishram an opportunity to come in close again. Ferguson was able to twist at the last instant and the knife slashed along his shoulder instead of stabbing into his heart, but he was nearly finished. He dropped his two-handed sword with a clatter and gripped the much smaller man's wrist.

Rishram's face twisted into an evil grin. He started a series of quick punches into Ferguson's injured side, dropping the bigger man to his knees. Rishram then chopped a hand down on Ferguson's shoulder, causing a pained cry and springing Ferguson's grip on his knife hand. Ferguson slumped back, his injured arm with the knife still embedded in it raised to protect himself.

Rishram whipped back to give a killing blow, but Ben had seen his chance. He slammed into Rishram's back with his entire body weight, pushing them both onto Ferguson, and sending all three men crashing to the ground. Ben landed on Rishram who landed on Ferguson.

Before Rishram could recover, Ben stripped the knife from his hand and scrambled to his feet. The little man didn't follow. He lay still on top of a heavily breathing and profusely bleeding Ferguson.

By now, Renfro had recovered and was back up with his cobblestone, and the girls were cautiously moving around to put Ben between them and Rishram. There was no reason to fear though, Ben knew. In an eerie similarity to Meredith's death, Ben bent down and pulled Rishram's body away from Ferguson, and the wounded arm that still had the knife lodged in it. As Rishram's body rolled off, they could see where the knife in Ferguson's arm stabbed into Rishram's chest. Ben's body weight on top of the little man had sunk the knife deep into his heart.

"Shit. That hurt," grunted Ferguson before his eyes rolled up and his head thumped down on the paving stones.

THE CURVE INN that evening was a bustling hive of activity. Kirksbane was a decent-sized place with its share of rough characters, but it wasn't every day that a group of strangers fought to the death in the middle of town during broad daylight. Locals and visitors alike packed the common room and were whispering to each other and staring. Ben felt like livestock at an auction. This must have been what Amelie and the others felt like in Farview.

Ferguson had been rushed near death to the local physic and Lady Towaal had gone to see if she could assist. The rest of the group clustered in the common room under the watchful eyes of Saala and Rhys. They had plenty of bumps and bruises, but thanks to Ferguson, none of the young people had suffered any serious injuries.

The constable spent half a bell questioning the companions before Amelie cut him off. Once he realized she was the daughter of Lord Gregor of Issen, he backed away from the investigation. As several witnesses could confirm, she'd been attacked and the attacker had been killed. She was satisfied that the man was dead. No further action from the constable was needed or wanted. When it came to highborn, the constable had a policy learned over the years—he stayed out of it.

Shortly after the constable left, a tired-looking Lady Towaal cut through the crowd to their table. "He'll live, but it was a near thing. I expended all of the energy I was willing to, which was enough to save his life. He will be under the physic's care for weeks." She glanced at Rhys. "The body?"

"Nothing. His knives were decent quality but he could have picked them up at any major city in Alcott. The clothes were in the style of Sineook Valley and he had no identifying marks."

"The room?" inquired Towaal.

"Same story. All locally sourced provisions. No significant stock of coin and no artifacts."

"Of course. He would have known he was travelling with a mage before we left Eastside. How did you miss it? Is he not known to you?"

Rhys grimaced. "He's not a member of any guilds I know, and he didn't have any of the customary signs. He threw me off with his pitiful bow work. I thought he was just some hack who'd managed to impress Foley and get on the payroll."

"Do you think Foley would have..." Towaal glanced between Rhys and Amelie.

"No," answered Rhys quickly. "It's too obvious. Rishram leads directly back to him. He would never risk blowback from Argren, the City, and Issen with something so stupid. I'm sure it wasn't Foley, but I have no idea who could have hired the man."

"If I didn't have experience with your work, I'd think you were slacking off," snapped Lady Towaal.

Rhys shrugged angrily, his frustration at himself was evident.

Towaal continued with a hiss, "So, we don't even know who he was working for. Not Lord Foley certainly, but who else has the pull in the valley to direct something like this?"

"This is my fault." Saala sighed. "I am here to protect Lady Amelie and I let my guard down. We must be more diligent."

"Hold on!" interjected Amelie. "We all travelled with that man for three weeks and none of us suspected a thing. You all protected me well for three weeks and the first time you weren't around, he struck. Let's stop the blame and focus on what we need to do next. Keep in mind, none of you failed. I'm still alive, and aside from a sore tailbone, I'm uninjured." She smiled, attempting to break the tension and continued, "Before we figure out what's next though, when a lady is assaulted, it's customary for her to thank her hero." Amelie leaned over a planted a kiss on Ben's cheek.

Ben flushed at the sensation of her soft lips on his skin.

"A lady and a hero, is it?" breathed the barmaid Ilyena. She was flushed from the excitement going on in the inn that evening and breathing heavily. Ben couldn't help but notice the effect the deep breaths had on her full chest. "I'm sure Master Taber will agree," she crooned, "drinks on the house tonight for you folks. I'll be back with some ale."

"Now when did she show up?" muttered Amelie.

"I, ah, noticed her just before you started kissing Ben," said Rhys.

"Oh, you noticed her, did you!" quipped Amelie.

They all laughed and the rest of the tension faded away. The concern over who hired Rishram and what motivated his attack was still there, but they knew they could trust the people left in the group. With nothing to do until morning when Reinhold's sloop left, it was time to celebrate the fact that they were all still alive and uninjured.

~

LATER THAT EVENING, the ale was flowing and the entire room seemed to be in on the celebration. Just like the first night, a band started playing raucous tunes and they pushed back the tables and chairs to make an open dance floor in the middle of the room.

Ben, Amelie, Meghan, and Renfro all paired up again and were soon swinging and skipping to the beat. A tipsy Rhys and smooth as silk Saala joined the fun. Only Lady Towaal remained seated. The ale kept flowing and Ben felt himself becoming quite drunk.

Two bells after nightfall, the dances changed from partner dances to circle dances. The entire dance floor spun around in two giant circles, women on the inside and men outside. They rotated around to different partners in an endless progression of smiling, laughing faces. The faces and lights began to blur around the edges, and Ben was having the time of his life.

After several rotations, he found himself across from Ilyena the barmaid. She was beaming up at him but he found it hard to keep eye contact. As they held hands and danced, she bounced mesmerizingly with the steady beat of the music. He was entranced by her movement, and when he did pull up his gaze to meet her eyes, instead of the expected accusatory glare, he saw she was enjoying the attention. They danced around the room in a circle and his gaze kept falling down to her body. He had to force himself to look back up at her face. Her full rose-colored lips were parted slightly and her heavy breathing was somehow worse than concentrating on the rest of her.

As they neared their starting point, where the inside circle would rotate and they would change partners, Ben wasn't sure if he should pull her close to kiss her or turn and run.

She made the decision for him. She caught him staring again, pulled him close, and whispered in his ear, "How about I give you a better look, hero?"

Her hot breath on his ear sent tingles down his spine. He found himself not resisting when she pushed him out of the circle and into a narrow hallway in the direction of the kitchen.

"Here," she said. She tugged him into a dark storage room then closed the ill-fitting door. "No one will come in here this late."

Ilyena pulled him close. Her tongue fought past his lips and she curled her hands in his hair. They kissed hungrily. Ben felt his body responding to her warmth. She reached down below his belt with her free hand.

"Good," she whispered, "I've been waiting for this since I saw you practicing the sword in the willows earlier today. I was so worried you'd bed that lady you saved tonight, but you're all mine now, and I can't wait any longer."

She shoved him back and he flopped down on pile of burlap sacks. Must be beans was the only coherent thought his mind could process. In the dim light, he watched her strip off her top, exposing her smooth skin. Without another word, she yanked down his pants and hiked up her heavy skirts before straddling him. She settled down and his mind swirled with sensations he'd never felt before.

"Oh-Oh..." he stuttered. His entire body tensed. He shuddered over and over again as she rocked back and forth on him, sucking and biting at his lips and tongue. Time froze until finally, the shudders stopped, his muscles turned to jelly. He fell back on the sacks, utterly drained.

Ilyena broke the passionate kiss, a hand still grasping his hair, and whispered in his ear, "What was that? Your first time?"

"I, uh..."

"Don't worry. The second time is much better." She wiggled off of him and dropped down to her knees. As she worked her lips and tongue, he found he wasn't quite as drained as he thought. And she was right, the second time was even better.

THE LOUD CLATTER of pots and pans in the nearby kitchen startled Ben awake. As his senses slowly caught up, the unfamiliar surroundings came into focus.

The smell of baking bread and the sharp sounds of metal on metal meant he was near the kitchen. Light streaming under the door meant it was morning. The scratchy, lumpy bed was a pile of sacks filled with dried beans. The pleasurable, soft warmth beside him was the barmaid Ilyena. He could feel her smooth skin wrapped around him.

His stirring woke her and her eyes popped open. In the dim light of the storage room, he could see a smile break out of on her face. She tilted her head and kissed his jawline, sending a shiver through his body. He felt himself start to respond to her nakedness.

"Good morning, my lord," she whispered.

"I, uh, good morning," he mumbled barely coherent.

She slid her hand across his bare chest and said, "I'm not scheduled until lunch shift." Her hand started to drift lower toward his stomach. "I've heard that lords are not early risers, but you seem like you could, mmm, get up, this early."

"Lords? Early risers?" asked a bewildered Ben. He knew it was rude, but her perfect body was distracting. He could barely focus on what she was saying.

"Don't be offended, my sweet." She kissed his neck and her hand continued to rub lower down his torso. "That's what I've heard from friends who've been in bed with a highborn. No need for you to get up when a servant will bring everything to you. I can only imagine how wonderful that must be."

Ben's mind was foggy from the drink the night before and the sensations he was feeling. "Yeah, I guess lords don't need to be early risers. I've never really thought about it."

Her hand was resting on Ben's belly button. He fought to keep from grabbing it and pulling her to where he wanted. He involuntarily shifted his hips toward her and felt her snuggle closer in response.

In his ear she whispered, "I know this isn't a lord's bed, but I like it just fine. Maybe we should stay awhile. You don't think your lady friends will be mad, do you? I saw the way the pretty dark-haired one looks at you. She isn't your betrothed, is she? You seem like such a good man. You wouldn't do that to me, would you?"

"The pretty one? You mean Amelie." Ben had no interest in talking but he didn't want to upset her. "No, of course she's not my betrothed. I'm certain she'll marry some lord someday."

"Marry a lord. Aren't you a lord?" She had stopped moving abruptly. Ben's need was becoming irresistible. He had never wanted anything more than to stop this conversation and start what they had been doing the night before.

"No, I'm not a lord. Didn't I tell you when we first met? I'm a brewer."

She bolted upright, and he couldn't help but stare as her pert breasts bounced with the sudden motion. "Not a lord? What do you mean? I thought brewing is a highborn hobby. I've seen Taber work and no one else has time for that. This Amelie is a lady, right? You fought for her and I saw her kiss you. I saw you practice the sword with a blademaster. Do not tell me you're not a lord!"

"Ilyena..." Ben's mind raced but all he could think about was getting his hands on her soft skin again. "I'm so sorry. I didn't mean to lead you on. Really, I didn't even know you thought that. I'm not a lord, but I'm still a good man. A better man probably. That doesn't change what we did last night, does it?"

"That doesn't change last night," she fumed, "but it changes what we're going to do this morning." She snatched up her clothes, spun around, then stormed out of the storage room door, naked as the day she was born.

Ben sighed and lay back on the lumpy burlap sacks of dried beans. He could only manage to pull up his pants and give a small wave when one of the cook's assistants peered curiously through the open doorway.

13

VENMOOR

Lord Reinhold's river sloop pulled smoothly away from Kirksbane's dock and Ben leaned against the gunwales, staring morosely into the murky water below. He felt awful.

"I heard there was a bit of commotion this morning," drawled Rhys. He hitched his sword belt and looked back at Saala and Renfro, who were clustered on the other side of the ship. "I've been asked to talk to you about it. Give you a shoulder to cry on or something. I feel like I should be buying you an ale. I'm not sure why you're so whiny about this."

Ben sighed. "I don't need to cry, Rhys, and I'm so, so glad you're the one they sent over."

"Despite his silky smooth and bald charms, the blademaster isn't as experienced with women as you'd think. Spends a lot of time with his sword. And Renfro, well, I think he messes his pants every time he even talks to a woman, so you're stuck with me. Now, what the hell is the problem? You got laid by a beautiful woman. Enjoy it. That doesn't happen every day."

"She thought I was a lord, Rhys. That's the only reason she did it, because she thought I was someone else."

Rhys snorted. "That's the way it works, mate. Perception is the reality when it comes to how other people see us. You got lucky and it worked out for you last night, even if you didn't mean it to happen that way. Think about this. You weren't trying to deceive her. She got whatever impression she did because of what she saw. The person she saw acted like the kind-hearted, heroic, highborn lord that she wanted to share her bed and probably a lot more with. Is what she saw, your actions, is that a better reflection of who you are than whether or not you were born into a family with a title?"

"I see what you're saying," muttered Ben. "But what she wanted isn't what she got. She wants the title and the gold and lifestyle that come with it."

"Ah." Rhys gripped Ben's shoulder. "And that's where you're really lucky. With a woman like that, you got what you wanted last night. Now you're better off leaving on this ship without her. Enjoy the memories, but you don't want a woman like that in your life worrying you. I'm sure you'll get plenty of worry from the women who are in your life now. Once they hear about this, at least."

Ben groaned and his head slumped down to his folded arms on the gunwale. He hadn't thought about that yet.

THE RIVER SLOOP, true to Lord Reinhold's and Captain Fishbone's word, practically flew down the river. They darted around the slower-moving barge traffic with Fisheye, the first mate on the vessel, deftly handling the tiller and steering sweeping turns around the slower-moving obstacles.

Towaal, Amelie, Lord Reinhold, and Captain Fishbone had been shuttered in Reinhold's cabin all morning. Ben had barely seen them as they'd breezed out of the inn to depart. By lunch, they emerged onto the deck, which was the most pleasant place to sit on the vessel. The speed they were moving kept a steady breeze moving across the deck and the tall sails provided shade.

Ben, Renfro, and Rhys were sharing a loaf of hard bread and jerked meat. Rhys nodded to Ben. "Watch it. Here she comes."

Ben turned to see Amelie striding across the deck with a look of determination on her face. "Do you have a moment, Ben?" she asked and then beckoned for him to follow her across to the other side of the ship.

"Yesterday in Kirksbane made me realize something," she started.

Ben grimaced. He had hoped this conversation wouldn't happen. When he imagined how it would go if it did happen, it was never good.

"I need to be able to defend myself," she said. "Saala, Rhys, and you have been there to watch over me, but you can't be there all of the time. I may not be able to become a blademaster, but I can learn enough to help. I can do something."

"Wait," responded Ben. "You want to learn the sword? I thought you were..."

"Going to ask about Ilyena?" she finished for him with a harsh look.

Ben blushed. "Yes. That's what I thought you wanted to talk about."

"What is there to say?" she asked bluntly. "I am highborn and you are not. It's nice to think otherwise, but those are the facts. I should have listened to Tomas when he... Well, when I heard this morning, I was reminded that we come from different worlds. You have the freedom to choose whom you love, and I do not. I don't understand why you wanted to be with that awful slut, but that is your choice. Maybe it was for the best."

Her eyes glistened and Ben swallowed hard.

"Amelie, it wasn't like that. I was drunk and..."

"I know, Ben." She sighed. "Let's not talk about this now, okay? With going to the Sanctuary, Meredith's death, the attack by Rishram, there is just a lot going on. I'm not myself and I'm not thinking clearly. I can't add another thing to my list of worries. I need a friend, Ben. Despite last night, I know I can trust you. I'd like you to be that friend."

"Of course, Amelie. Of course we can be friends." He didn't know what else to say.

"That is why I came to talk to you. I need your help and I am asking for it as a friend. Saala is in my father's employ and he will train me with the sword if I ask. I am certain I can convince Rhys as well. When we get to the City though, both of them will eventually leave. That is what they do. I would like it if you stayed. I can set you up with a business and we can practice the sword together. Because of my birth, I will be treated differently at the Sanctuary. With Meredith gone, I have no one else to turn to."

"I-I hadn't thought about what I'd do once we got there," stammered Ben.

"Do you need time to think?" she asked.

"No." He really hadn't decided what he would do once they arrived in the City. At the start of the journey, he'd planned on returning to Farview. But now the thought of making that trip back alone and rejoining life in the small town where nothing ever really changed didn't seem very appealing. Compared to living in the City and being friends with a lady, what was he thinking? "I'll stay if you're sure you want me to."

"Good," she said and placed a hand on his arm.

SHORTLY AFTER LUNCH, Lady Towaal called everyone together for a quick meeting on the deck. "We'll be in the City in a week according to Reinhold," she began. "I've asked him to push hard down the river with no stops. I don't want another incident like we had with Rishram. After signing the Conclave agreement, the risk is too great for Amelie. When we arrive, Amelie and Meghan will begin training immediately at the Sanctuary. Rhys, you know what to do and who to check in with. The rest of you are free to remain or go as you please. If you remain, I'm sure Rhys can recommend some places to stay in the City."

"I think I'll stay for a bit," Ben said to an encouraging smile from Amelie. He ignored Meghan's bitter look. She wasn't happy about the Ilyena thing.

"I as well," added Saala, "at least until I know Amelie is secure and I get further instructions from Issen."

Lady Towaal scowled. "There is no doubt about security once we make the Sanctuary, but suit yourself. It is your time."

"I'll stay too!" exclaimed Renfro before glancing around the group sheepishly. "I don't really have anywhere else to go."

That evening, they got back to practicing the Ohms. It was difficult on the ship, but they could do the first Ohm which required the least amount of balance and skill. It felt good after the long pause they'd taken in Sineook Valley. Ben missed the stretching exercises and felt more energized once they'd finished, but he was glad they hadn't done it in front of Rishram.

Afterward, the young people sat near the bow of the ship, enjoying the breeze and watching the sun set over the country-side as they passed.

"So, what will you do in the City, Renfro?" asked Meghan. She had been pointedly ignoring Ben since they'd left Kirksbane. Sisterly affection came with sisterly disapproval.

"Oh, I don't know. Find a trade I suppose," the young thief answered, scratching absentmindedly at his arm. "Is there much fishing around there? The City sounds grand, and for me, it is just as good as anywhere. Fabrizo is the only place I've known and I can't go back there."

"Oh, I don't know about fishing," replied Meghan. "It's on a river, isn't it?"

Renfro glumly looked down at his feet. "Yeah, I guess it is.

Since I was a little one, it was go to sea or join the thieves. Not sure what else I can do."

"Maybe Ben will hire you at this new brewery he's starting." Meghan smirked.

Ben enjoyed Renfro's company, but his work ethic was questionable at best. Renfro was probably the last person he'd consider asking for help with a business. Meghan meant it more as a barb for Ben than a knock on Renfro. She was always kind to Renfro.

Luckily, Renfro didn't pick up on the subtext. "Oh really? That would be great! Ben, we could be partners together."

Ben raised an eyebrow.

"Well," allowed Renfro, "You could be the senior partner, of course, since you know about brewing already and I'd just be starting."

"I think that would be wonderful," chimed in Meghan.

"Sure Renfro. We can see how it goes when we get to the City." Ben hoped the idea of how hard the work will be to start a new business in a new city would eventually creep into Renfro's thoughts and he'd drop it. A change of subject seemed best for now though. "Amelie and Meghan, how about you? Are you excited to begin at the Sanctuary?"

"I think so. Maybe," hedged Meghan.

"Lady Towaal has been explaining some of the training regimen," added Amelie. "It sounds... challenging."

Meghan sighed. "There is a great deal of study involved and successive tests of willpower. I'm sure Lady Towaal is exaggerating to mentally prepare us, but yes, challenging. I think that's the right word." The two girls shared a glance. "Lord Reinhold also said something to Amelie that worried us a little," she continued. "He said it when he first heard we were joining. He said, 'The Sanctuary? Who would commit two decades of apprenticeship just to become the Veil's stooge? There are shorter paths to power, girl.' I'm sure he didn't mean it like it sounded."

Ben blanched. "Surely not."

~

LORD REINHOLD KEPT to himself aside from the occasional discussion with his captain or Lady Towaal. His and Towaal's communication was strained. It seemed she was paying him a very large amount of gold to get them to the City quickly, and they weren't moving quickly enough for her. The two would not remain friends after the journey, Ben was sure.

He was able to gather that while Reinhold was a landed lord, his primary business was various merchant banking interests up and down the Venmoor River. He spent most of his time on the river sloop checking up on things.

Ben watched him stalk around the deck peering intently at the countryside as they passed. He constantly mumbled under his breath, and, from what Ben could overhear, seemed to be tallying figures in his head. Unlike the merchants Ben was familiar with who had wagons or ships heaped with goods, Reinhold dealt in coin.

Before Amelie stopped him, Ben considered asking Reinhold for a loan to start a business for himself in the City.

"That's not his kind of business, Ben. Men like him, they think on a grand scale. He's not a moneylender like you would know. He's out here looking to see if there's a bad wheat crop in one area then he'll buy up all the rest of the wheat elsewhere or have it imported in. He's not going to loan money to an individual for a business. He's going to finance a moneylender who will do the hard work of collecting loans for him. Men like him, they wait for situations like this with Argren's Alliance. He will buy goods to support the war effort, swoop in, and buy land or other war spoils on the cheap afterward. Besides, you know I will give you the money to get started. You don't need to worry about doing business with some chiseling lender."

"I know you said that, Amelie, but I feel bad taking money from you."

"Don't think about it as taking then. We can make it a loan or an investment. Really, I trust you'll do well for me. I don't want you to have to get tied up with lenders. Many of them are unsavory people."

After that, Ben watched Reinhold with a certain fascination. Alistair Pinewood used similar tactics on a smaller scale in Farview. Men like these only cared about the gold. Ben had never understood Alistair and his desire to always have more. He wondered if Lord Reinhold motivated by the same things.

One afternoon, Rhys caught him watching Reinhold.

"Thinking about getting into merchant banking?" quipped Rhys.

"No, just wondering what makes the man tick," responded Ben. "How does someone like that only care about having more gold and more power? If I had all of the resources he does, I would help people. A man like him could change the world and make it better, or at least a part of it."

"It isn't always as simple as that. He's helping us after all, isn't he?"

"Only because Lady Towaal paid him," replied Ben.

"Sometimes paid help is the best help. And changing the world, well, when this war between the Alliance and the Coalition breaks out, people like Lord Reinhold will be the first ones there with medical supplies, food, and other things people need. The lords and ladies have other concerns and are looking at a different picture. Don't get me wrong—you pay him, pay a very high price maybe—but when the need is the greatest, it's men like him who will be there. Trust me. When you're on the front lines and you're starving, you don't really care how much the food costs, you just know you need it."

Ben shrugged uncomfortably. He hadn't thought about it like that.

Rhys continued, "Those locks around Kirksbane? If it weren't for men like Reinhold, they wouldn't be there. You don't have to like it, but it's worth understanding. Things happen and progress is made when there's profit at the end of it. Making grand speeches, fighting off the bad guys, and giving alms to the poor isn't the only way to change the world. Something to think about." Rhys pointed down river to a grey cloud hanging low on the horizon. "Speaking of which, we're coming up on the town of Venmoor. How do you think a brewer boy from the country knows all about this roughneck former bandit town on the other side of the continent? The people here found a new and better way to make steel, and in their way, they changed the world."

VENMOOR HAD the earmarks of a former roughneck town just like Rhys described. As they glided past, Ben could see squat stone buildings spreading out from the river. Dark smoke was belching out of many of the buildings where the famous forges of Venmoor produced the steel the town was so famous for. The art of forming the extra strong Venmoor steel was a closely guarded secret of the Blacksmiths' Guild. The stories were full of tales of the length the blacksmiths went to keep that secret.

In addition to the forges, there was a sturdy-looking keep built up on a low rise. The sprawl of one and two story stone buildings scattered around it had little organization Ben could see. He'd heard all the buildings in Venmoor were stone due to fire risk.

In the distance, there was a huge structure carved into the side of a hill. Ben craned his neck to see and thought there were hundreds or even thousands of seats built up around a flat space at the bottom. From the river, he couldn't tell what it was for.

"What is that?" he asked Rhys, pointing toward the large structure.

"Venmoor's College Arena. They have one of the more famous Colleges of the Sword and that's where the students show off. There are regular competitions, examinations, and what not. Of course, the most attended events are trials to become a blademaster. Most of the students are highborn and fail the test, which makes it popular with the common folk." Rhys shrugged. "The king built it years and years ago when they first created Venmoor steel. They needed a place to demonstrate the superior quality. They keep it up now because the competitions lead to some pretty lively wagering and the king takes his cut."

Other than the College Arena and the forges, the town itself was unexciting after seeing Fabrizo and Whitehall. It was just as large but it didn't hold the romance the other two did. Venmoor was about industry. They passed under a series of ugly-looking bridges then drifted downriver away from town. Maybe another time, Ben thought.

MORE TRIBUTARIES JOINED the river and it widened south of Venmoor. The barges still cluttered the waterway but other vessels began to join them.

The barges hung close to the shoreline where on one side they were pulled up river by horsepower. There was a well-worn path that dray horses slowly plodded along. Long ropes were tied to the empty barges and a lone man would be stationed at the tiller to keep the shallow-drafted ships from butting against the bank. On the other bank, the loaded barges floated down at the speed of the current with just a few bargemen on board to steer and keep watch over the goods.

In the center of the river were wind-powered vessels or

rowboats. Fisheye, the first mate, explained that closer to the City, they would see more of the smaller craft.

"Keep an eye out," drawled Fisheye. "Going to see the big country estates soon too."

"The big country estates?" asked Ben.

"Aye, where the people like Lord Reinhold live," explained Fisheye. "At least when they want to get away from the noise in the City. Richest place in the world they say, just north of the City. They got these big pieces of land called estates. It's like a farm, but the only crop they have is grapes for wine making. Gentleman farming they call it. They build their big mansions and castles there of course. You'll see."

Before long, Ben did see. Subtly, the countryside gained a manicured look. The trees and terrain remained the same, but it was cleaner and more orderly looking. He wouldn't have noticed if Fisheye hadn't mentioned it. They came around a wide bend in the river and Ben saw a large manse that must have been three times the size of the Buckhorn Tavern back in Farview.

"Look," exclaimed Ben. "I think I see the first one."

"Pssh," replied Fisheye. "That ain't nothing, son. Probably some gardener's cottage. Wait 'til we get a little closer. The City is still a two-day trip from here on land. The real money guys ain't gonna travel that far."

Rhys joined Ben and Fisheye at the tiller. He was using one of his wicked-looking long knives to peel a withered apple and tossing the peels overboard. Fisheye glanced at the long knife, which was clearly designed for combat and not apples, and gave a wounded grunt.

The sailors during their off time liked to get drunk on rum and play cards. They all got drunk enough that it turned into a game of chance instead of skill. Ben saw they ended up just handing silver back and forth. By the end of the voyage, a lucky one or two might end up ahead, but there were no hard feelings. Fisheye hadn't counted on Rhys being able to handle his liquor better than the rest and lost more silver than he had on the ship. He repeatedly assured Rhys he'd be good for it as soon as they got their harbor wages. Rhys found it amusing to intimidate the poor first mate.

Fisheye swallowed uncomfortably and stuttered, "T-Telling the boy about the country estates we'll pass. The big ones." The little beads of sweat forming on his forehead made Ben wonder how easily he'd really be able to pay Rhys.

Rhys took a big bite of his apple and grinned at Ben.

"Why are all of the big estates on this side of the City?" asked Ben. He didn't really care, he just wanted to break some of the tension.

"Well, rich folk like to be near other rich folk. They don't want to be near the common class. They don't like the way we talk," Fisheye started to explain.

"And no one who's halfway intelligent lives down river from a major city," snorted Rhys. He zinged his apple core close by Fisheye's head and into the water to make his point. He must have felt a little guilty when Fisheye cowered from the apple because he added, "Fisheye is right about what he said earlier, though. The estates are pretty impressive. Space in the City is limited, so the lords and the most successful merchants have places out here. Gives them room for their summer galas, fireworks shows, hunts, and so on."

Rhys pointed up to another building they were approaching. "Lord Merley's new country estate." A white limestone-clad building close to the river was under construction. "The family's fallen on hard times. Bet a fortune on a gold mining venture that didn't produce any gold."

"How do you know who's estate that is?" asked Ben.

"It was all over the Sanctuary when we left," replied Rhys. "Large scale miners will pay a cut to the Sanctuary to borrow a mage and they delve the ground to see where it makes sense to dig. Merley thought he had a sure thing and tried to cut some corners, but all he had was dirt. The rise and fall of these lords and merchants is half the entertainment in the City. Ask in any tavern on the island and they can tell you who's on the way up, and who's on the way down."

"If he's on the way down, how is he building a new estate?" Eyeing the swarm of workers around the structure, Ben added, "It looks pretty expensive to me."

"Oh, I'm sure it's expensive," responded Rhys. "But it's way out here. He had a larger estate closer to the City but was forced to sell. Sold the mining interest too. Any further and he'll be laughed out of town."

"He should be out already," remarked an urbane voice behind them.

Ben jumped in surprise and saw Lord Reinhold had silently joined them.

"His property was run down and the structures will likely be demolished by the new owners," added Reinhold. "I haven't heard that last bit about his mining interest, though. Any fool knows there isn't gold in the Shallock Range, but there could be iron ore. It's close enough to Venmoor it might be worthwhile. Where did you hear he sold it? You've been on the road for months, right?

Rhys showed none of the surprise Ben did. He must have seen Reinhold coming. "Oh, we heard somewhere on the road. With all of the travel we've been doing I'm really struggling to remember who it was…"

Reinhold grimaced and flipped Rhys a shining gold coin.

"Ah, it was definitely someone from outside the City. Maybe it was a lord?"

"Come on man. It's just a potential iron mine!" Reinhold grudgingly flipped another gold coin toward Rhys who winked at Ben.

"That's right. It was Lord Rhymer from Northport. He's the one who picked up the interest. It was brokered from someone in the City, but before you dig another coin out, I really don't know who."

"Rhymer! What is that fool doing?" Reinhold muttered to himself. He started away before quickly turning back and barking at Fisheye, "Run close to the bank when we pass. I want to see how the new wing is looking from the river."

～

RHYS FLIPPED and caught one of his new gold coins as he and Ben walked away from Fisheye and the tiller. "That's life in the City for you. Gold and power, the only two things anyone cares about there."

"Don't you live in the City?" challenged Ben.

Rhys grinned and tossed the coin again. "Like I said, gold and power."

"It can't be all bad. The Sanctuary helps a lot of people," said Ben.

"It's a generalization, but I've found it to be more true than false. Certainly truer than other places I've been. And the Sanctuary only helps those who help them hold onto power. Think about Towaal in Farview. She helped that brother of yours, but it came at a price. I'm not saying there is no good in the people of the City, there is some. Just be prepared. Everyone there knows where they stand relative to everyone else. That's all that matters for some of them. Don't play their games if you don't want, although that's harder than it sounds. My advice, get good at the games and play them only when it benefits you." Rhys smiled as he tucked the gold coin into his purse.

Ben shook his head and went to join the other young people and Saala at the bow of the vessel. He knew Rhys meant well with his warning. Maybe the City was worse than most, but the money and the power, that sounded like everywhere else he'd been.

14

THE CITY

THE REST of the country estates did not disappoint. They were grand affairs that sprawled across the hillsides and bluffs overlooking the river. Further out, they were built of limestone, granite, and other field stones. Closer to the City, they were uniformly clad in marble and intricate stonework. Ben marveled at the time and resources that went into building these massive edifices solely to house one family and only part of the time.

As Ben stood on the deck watching the buildings go by, they swept in close to one particular estate and he realized it must be Reinhold's. A veritable army of workers were erecting a new wing just like Reinhold had stated. The scale of the place was unreal. Ben struggled to connect the overwhelming sense of wealth of the place with the fact that he was on a boat with its owner. Even after taking Alistair's money to watch over Meghan, Ben still had more fingers than gold coins. A man like Reinhold could probably spend the rest of his natural life counting and still not know how many coins he had.

"What's the point?" Ben wondered to himself.

"That's how they keep score," answered a gruff voice.

Ben turned to see Captain Fishbone had come up behind him.

"I-I didn't mean any offence to Lord Reinhold," stammered Ben.

"Ha. Don't worry about that. Lord Reinhold knows just as well as you and I that it's silly. Don't get me wrong, the lord enjoys the finer things in life, but he's building rooms in that estate that he'll never even see."

"So, why does he do it?" wondered Ben. "You said it's about keeping score. Score with the other lords and merchants?"

"Aye," answered Fishbone. "Lord Reinhold isn't married, doesn't have any kids that he admits to, and spends most of his time on my boat. The only reason he keeps building on that estate is to show the other lords that he can. He builds a little, they build a little more to keep up, and he builds again. By the end of it, you have these damn big houses that no one can even use. It's all about keeping score, showing who's most successful or who's the most powerful. You stop expanding one season, don't buy a faster vessel, don't buy your mistress a bigger diamond, and suddenly everyone thinks you stopped because you have to. You've played cards, right? Sometimes you gotta keep putting more money into the pot if you want to stay seated at the table."

"That sounds awful," grunted Ben.

Fishbone shrugged. "I suppose it is awful. Awful and addicting. The most exciting game out there, if you ask Reinhold. It's certainly not about the money at this point."

They sailed on. Ben and Fishbone watched Reinhold's estate disappear around a perfectly manicured emerald green bend.

THE GRANDEUR of the country estates though, even Reinhold's, did little to prepare Ben and the other young folk for the first sight of the City itself.

The City was located in a natural basin where the Venmoor

and the smaller Razen River met. It comprised a huge island in the center of the river basin but over the centuries had expanded to the banks surrounding it. Technically, the City referred to just the buildings on the island. Most used the term for the entire sprawl.

Rhys explained, "In the past, each of the little towns on the bank had its own name, but they've all kind of grown together now. Some of them still have their own town councils and the like. I have no idea how they keep straight which is which."

Ben silently agreed. The 'towns' were the size of about one hundred Farviews all strung together in a huge circle around the water. It was impressive, if only for the size and the number of people Ben thought must be living there.

They saw the towns first and didn't get a full view of the City until their sloop entered the river basin. The island on which it sat was huge. Ben estimated at least two leagues long and a league wide. All along the length there were massive buildings, delicate palaces, and, most striking, thin towers soaring into the air. Ben had seen nothing like it before. Some of the towers must have had the elevation of Whitehall, but where the port city was built on a mountainside, these towers reached into the sky with no support at all. Many of them looked like a strong wind could send them toppling.

As they drew closer, Ben's breath caught. Linking the towers was a network of barely visible bridges. Some towers had numerous connections and some only had one or two. He thought that many of those bridges were fifteen or twenty stories above the ground. A few rose even higher than that. He almost had to look away as he started to pick out tiny figures making their way across the bridges.

"The sky bridges of the City," said Rhys. "It looks crazy, but think about it. If you walk twenty stories up one of those towers, you don't want to walk back down just to chat up your neighbor and borrow sugar. They say there are people who get up there and never come back down."

"Oh my," said Amelie in a quivering voice. "We have towers in Issen, but nothing like this. How is it even possible these do not fall over? Is it something the Sanctuary does with magic?"

"I'm not the person to ask about that. The masons of the City are more close-lipped than the blacksmiths in Venmoor. I do know it doesn't have anything to do with the Sanctuary. You can't tell from here, but The Sanctuary doesn't have any buildings over four stories. This is all done by hand. Look." He pointed to one squat tower near the waterfront.

Scaffolding and ropes dangled from the sides of the structure and Ben saw they were still building it. A pallet of stones lifted into the air. There was some sort of loop and rope apparatus a handful of men were using to pull it up.

"Amazing." Amelie gasped. "I've seen artist renderings of what it looks like, but none of them do justice to this."

"Why do they build them so high?" questioned Renfro. "That's great some genius figured out they could do it, but that doesn't mean they should do it. A serious storm or a little earthquake and this whole place is coming down."

"Space," replied Rhys. "Like we were talking about with the estates, space is very expensive here. Every inch of that island outside the Sanctuary grounds is built on or designated public space. You want more room, you build up, or you move out. As for the safety of it, in my time here there haven't been any incidents. The City and some of these buildings have been around for millennia, I suspect they will be around for many more."

"Where is the Sanctuary in all of this? Is it away from the City?" asked Ben. "I pictured it in some reclusive setting off by itself. You know, like a sanctuary…"

Rhys grinned and pointed to the north end of the island. Easy to overlook with the rest of the vista in front of them, there was a large patch of green dotted with low white buildings.

"Physically it's not far from the rest of the City, but believe me, it sure feels it."

～

THE DOCKS of the City seemed pedestrian compared to the rest of the place. They didn't have the hulking war galleys and merchant ships that populated Whitehall's harbor. There were personal river craft and other small vessels. The barges they'd seen on the river must tie up elsewhere. Still, it was a place bustling with activity and First Mate Fisheye did an impressive job steering them past the clutter and dropping sail before a small pilot skiff darted out to meet them.

The pilot eyed Lord Reinhold's colors then tossed up a heavy rope which Reinhold's crew expertly looped around the hawsers. A handful of men leaned hard on the oars in the pilot skiff and started inching them toward Lord Reinhold's open dock.

Lady Towaal appeared from below with Amelie and Meghan in tow. "Rhys," she ordered, "show the boys some lodging and report before nightfall. No carousing!"

Rhys winked at Ben and mock bowed toward Towaal, which elicited an indelicate snort and eye roll from her.

"At your command, my lady."

Amelie stepped over to Ben and waved Saala close. "Lady Towaal says we're confined to the grounds during the first few months of training but usually Newday is a free day. She says you can come visit us in the Sanctuary's parks. We won't be able to do much sword training there, but maybe that can come later. After we obtain enough rank that we're not green Initiates, we're allowed off the grounds on the free days so I can come visit you. Here," she said, and passed Ben and Saala each a small pouch. "Your pay, Saala, for another three months. I know you plan to stay for a while, but I want you to have this now in case we don't see each other for a bit. Ben, hopefully that is enough seed money to start your business. Face time is limited, but you're allowed to write, so I expect regular updates on my investment!"

Her bittersweet grin told Ben she wasn't serious about her investment. He saw she already was missing the time they'd spent together. He felt it as well.

"Of course, Amelie. I'll come every Newday, and write you plenty. I can't wait until you can get out and we can explore the city together."

"Watch out for him will you?" a watery eyed Amelie asked Saala.

Saala nodded. "I'll keep an eye on him. I'll be in town until your father's agents in the City tell me otherwise. You know you only have to call and I will come running."

The goodbyes were interrupted when the sloop nudged up against the dock and Lord Reinhold's men slid a narrow gang-plank down. A brisk Lady Towaal was the first one on the gang-plank. She gestured for Amelie and Meghan to follow. A quick peck on the cheek from each girl for Ben and rushed hugs for the other men and they were off.

The men lifted their few belongings to follow but were stopped by Lord Reinhold.

"Rhys," said Lord Reinhold as he glanced to where Lady Towaal was vanishing into the crowds around the dock, "I'd offer you a position, but I suspect you're already well compensated by the mages. I have work for a man of your talents. If the Veil ever lets you off the leash for some part-time work, I can make it worth your while. In addition to the gold you got earlier, I have many other special items a man like you would find useful. You too," he said to Saala. "If you get bored watching Lord Gregor's daughter, I can find you something more interesting."

Rhys grinned. "Well, we both love a challenge, of course, and I'm sure you'd be a great boss, but like you say, we're already happily employed."

Reinhold shrugged. "Employed now doesn't mean employed

tomorrow. It's an open offer. Good luck." He nodded curtly and stalked off toward his cabin.

"What? No job offer for me?" Renfro chuckled.

Rhys gave him a light shove and said, "Come on. Let's go see The City."

~

WHAT HAD LOOKED from a distance like a disorganized jumble of soaring towers, grand arenas, and palaces was actually well delineated in clean grids when they saw it up close. Broad tree lined avenues were laid out neatly and small parks dotted the major intersections.

Rhys talked as they moved along the smoothly-paved streets. "Long ago, before even the current Veil can remember, this entire island was owned by the Sanctuary. They must have realized over time that it made sense to have staff and services nearby, so they sold off pieces, but still retain leadership of everything on the island. They kept a lot of open public space. They collect all of the taxes on the island and pay for the maintenance. It's all planned and managed from within the Sanctuary." He breathed in deep. "You'll notice it's the greenest and cleanest city you've ever been. I have a lot of problems with the way the Sanctuary does its business, but I've got to admit, they know how to run a place."

"Problems? Don't you work for the Sanctuary? Or at least for Lady Towaal?" asked Renfro.

"Aye, I work the Sanctuary," nodded Rhys. "They pay the best. Doesn't mean I always have to agree with what they do. You didn't agree with everything the thieves were doing in Fabrizo, did you? Don't answer. Let me guess. You and your little thief buddies spent most of your time complaining about that guild and its policies?"

"Hmm." Renfro scratched his head. "You're right. When you explain it like that, it makes a lot of sense."

"So, what exactly do you do for the Sanctuary?" asked Ben. He had his suspicions, of course. Rhys was slippery when it came to certain topics so he hoped to catch him off guard while he was in a talkative mood.

Saala perked up as well. He'd been studying the architecture they passed but he was obviously also curious about what Rhys would say.

Rhys laughed. "A little bit of this and a little bit of that. Most of this town is somehow involved in Sanctuary business, but some things don't need to be discussed in public, you know? Let's just say they send me where I need to be to make sure their interests are being protected. In some cases, that means making sure threats to their interests do not manifest. Just like our friend Saala, right?"

Saala frowned. "I'm not sure what I do is just like what you do. But if you say so, I'll go along with it."

"Right," continued Rhys. "So what do you want first? The bawdiest boudoir, the sweetest singing minstrel, the brightest wine, the coldest ale? The City isn't cheap, you may quickly run out of coin, but you'll never run out of things to do."

WITH A LITTLE NUDGING FROM SAALA, Rhys was persuaded to show them some comfortable beds before he took off to make his report to the Sanctuary. He picked an airy-looking plain stone building ringed by arched windows. It was a few blocks down from his apartment, and he knew the owner, so he said he could get them a better rate than they'd find elsewhere. It was small and simple compared to some of the places they'd stayed on the journey, but it was a good sight better than the bushes and rocks they'd slept next to. Even the discounted rate gave Ben pause, but

Rhys assured them that it was a better deal than they'd find elsewhere.

That evening, bathed and refreshed, Ben, Renfro, and Saala sat in the common room to dine and to plan. Now that they had finally made it to the end of their journey, they had to answer the question of what came next. Ben and Renfro were committed to starting a brewery as neither had any other marketable skills. Saala had graciously agreed to assist. With Amelie safely ensconced in the Sanctuary and no further instructions, he was free to help until he got called away.

"Location, equipment, supply of materials, and customers. Those are the four problems we'll need to solve," started Ben.

"I can help with the customers I guess," offered Renfro. "I don't know too much about the other things. With the guild in Fabrizo, one of my roles was sizing marks. This can't be too different, can it?"

"Sadly, it's probably not." Saala smiled. "If you tell me what you need, Ben, I might be able to help with a location. Showing the blademaster sigil occasionally has some perks. People tend to be a little easier in negotiations."

"Okay," stated Ben. "That leaves the equipment and materials to me. Once we get the location and that lined up, we can start brewing."

THE NEXT TWO weeks were a blur of activity getting the brewery set up. They received a message from Amelie and Meghan that their first two free days were cancelled for extra classes, so the men focused on the business. In that time, Saala was able to find a suitable location, Ben got the equipment and materials, and Renfro scouted some potential customers. No one wanted to commit without tasting the beer, as Ben suspected would happen, but they'd found some people unhappy with their current supplier.

They accomplished a lot in two weeks Ben thought as he surveyed the dimly lit room. The location Saala found was a large cellar under one of the towers. It was crisscrossed with heavy arches and supports. In some places, the ceiling only cleared Ben's head by a hand, but it had room to grow into, it had accessible water in large supply, and they could afford it. There was poor lighting and the owners of the tower didn't need it for storage, so they'd been able to pick it up quickly and cheap by City standards.

Ben walked by the rack of twenty sturdy kegs where the first batch was fermenting. He had poured nearly all of his resources into these kegs. He found simple usable equipment but splurged on high quality ingredients. He hoped it was worth it. Within two weeks, he'd bottle a small amount to shop around to local taverns. When they had a buyer, they'd wheel the entire keg—or hopefully kegs—over. In the meantime, he didn't have much to do.

While he was still surveying their work, he heard a squeak near the entrance to the cellar and turned to see Saala shutting the heavy doors.

"You might want to get in the habit of keeping these shut," he called out. "The City isn't nearly as lawless as Fabrizo and some other places, but there are still people who you don't want coming in here uninvited."

"Good point," replied Ben. "I guess I'm used to Farview still. It wasn't much of a concern there."

"You're not in Farview anymore. Speaking of which, since you've got some downtime, I saw these at the market and picked them up." Saala tossed Ben a long object.

When he caught it, he saw it was a practice sword. It had nearly the same heft as his long sword but it appeared to be a bundle of long reeds.

"It's weighted in the center to give you the real feel of a sword, but the reeds will soften a blow. I'm thinking it's going to leave a wicked welt, but that's better than a cut or broken bone. I want you to get real practice without that play armor they used in Whitehall. It limits your range of motion, and unless you're marching to a battle, you won't be wearing full armor anyway."

Ben swished the practice sword around a few times to get a feel for it. The weight felt familiar, but it was thicker than a real sword so there was more air resistance.

"Looks like you're ready." Saala grinned before lunging at Ben with his own practice sword.

Ben was caught off guard but managed to dance back before Saala landed a blow. The next two bells they fought in the dim cellar. The low ceilings and arches kept getting in Ben's way. He felt like he was nearly back at step one. Over and over again Saala struck him. He found himself constantly on the defensive.

"The next two weeks," said Saala, "you'll spend mornings with me and afternoons we'll both be with Rhys. I convinced that scoundrel to continue teaching us the Ohms."

Ben hoped Saala's talking would distract him, so he ducked low and advanced with a spinning attack he'd invented to use on the men at arms at Whitehall. Saala smiled and deflected the first strike then glided out of reach.

"Good thinking," he continued. "That was the perfect time to get aggressive. Any time your opponent gives you an opening, use it." Saala kept giving pointers as they fought. How he had any breath to speak was beyond Ben, who was panting and wheezing from the exertion.

After another bell, Saala stepped on an empty sack causing his foot to slip and Ben saw an opening. He quickly swung an over-head attack before Saala could reset, but nearly lost his sword when it smacked into one of the low hanging arches. Saala chuckled and instantly reacted. He poked his own sword into Ben's stomach, just hard enough to send him crashing to the ground.

"You got very close that time," Saala said with a short bow.

Ben grunted from the floor.

"The next two weeks, we'll take the time to find and practice in new terrain. I can see we spent too long in flat open fields." Saala reached a hand down. "Get up. Rhys will be here soon."

~

"WHERE'S RENFRO?" asked Rhys that afternoon.

"I'm not really sure," replied Ben. "He said he has some things to do. I think he's trying to come up with another option if the brewery doesn't work out."

"He should be." Rhys nodded. "He's living on Amelie's gold and your skill making ale. Not a bad life, but it always pays to have a backup plan. That being said, you should keep an eye on him. The guild in Fabrizo is dangerous, but in some ways, they made it safer for someone like him. The guild gets away with their petty theft and doesn't rock the apple cart for the major merchants so they are tolerated. There's no guild here and no protection. He gets caught doing something he shouldn't, and it could be off with his head."

Ben gulped. "I don't think he'd take up thieving again. I think he's looking for honest work."

"Maybe he is." Rhys shrugged. "But once you've had a taste of easy money, it's hard to turn it down the next time."

~

LATER THAT EVENING OVER DINNER, Ben asked Renfro about it.

"Oh, I was down by the docks," Renfro explained. "I had to learn to fish in Fabrizo. It was the only way I ate some days before the guild took me in. I figure with this big of a river, there's got to be fishing around here too. I was looking into it."

"Any luck?" inquired Ben.

"Not so far." Renfro sat back. "There's some old folk scattered around the water front, but from what I could tell, it's more of a past time than a profession. I went down to the docks where Reinhold's boat is and couldn't get in there. There are some guards and they say it's all private vessels. You have to prove you've bought passage on one to get in. I'll keep at it though. Like I said, it's a big river, and there's got to be fish."

"Good," said Ben. He was satisfied with Renfro's answer and didn't think there was any reason to bring up Rhys' suspicion.

~

Two weeks later, it was time to find out if they could sell their ale. Despite Renfro's prospecting, Ben thought Rhys had given them the best shot and that's where he wanted to start. Rhys swung by for 'a small taste'. Several mugs later, he had convinced Ben he needed to sell to the Flying Swan Inn. It had a small number of rooms and a large tavern with a reputation for quality.

"Tell 'em it's a foreign style and produced in small batches," advised Rhys. "They eat that stuff up there. Tell the owner, Mathias, that I sent you. I think he'll like this." He took a sip. "Maybe I should have another, just to be sure."

The next morning, Ben and Renfro stood in the near empty common room of the Flying Swan and asked to see the proprietor.

"No solicitations," barked a gruff serving man. "The manager only sees vendors once a week on Newday. And we already have plenty of ale and only serve the highest quality product. You're wasting your time here, young fellas."

Ben and Renfro looked at each other nervously.

"Well, thank you for your time." Renfro sighed. To Ben he added, "Might as well try the Gnarly Dog next."

Ben saw the wicked smirk the serving man gave when Renfro mentioned the Gnarly Dog. He knew that would be a dead end as well.

"Hold on," Ben broke in. "We know the owner Mathias. Can we see him instead of the manager?"

The serving man blinked. "Well, why didn't you say so? Normally he doesn't bother with this kind of thing, but if you really do know him... What did you say your name was?"

"Uh, Rhys," replied Ben.

～

MOMENTS LATER A HAIRY, burly-looking man emerged from the back. Ben immediately began checking escape routes because the man moved like a swordsman. Those scar and muscle-sheathed arms didn't come from wiping tavern tables.

"Ho," he boomed. "I didn't think I'd find Rhys out here hawking ales. That man is solely on the other side of the transaction."

"Sorry sir," muttered a nervous Ben. "Master Rhys had directed us to this inn, and I couldn't think of another way to avoid getting kicked out of here."

"If you know Rhys well enough to drop his name and you aren't face down in the river, then I suppose you're worth my time," the man answered. "Let me see what you've got."

Half a bell later, Ben and Renfro walked out of the Flying Swan Inn with an order for five kegs and five more kegs in a week. After that, Mathias told them they'd see if the patrons drank it and go from there. Ben felt buoyant. When they mentioned they had twenty kegs of stock, Mathias suggested they ramp up production immediately.

Mathias kept all of their sample bottles to pass around to his staff for tasting. Ben thought that they didn't need any more samples though. At five kegs a week, they'd need to start brewing now just to keep up with that order.

～

THREE MONTHS in the City and the brewery business was going well. In the last week alone they'd sold twenty kegs to Mathias and several more to individuals. Mathias started offering a premium if they kept him as their only public customer. Ben was happy to keep their product exclusive for the time being and make fatter margins, but Renfro was pushing for expansion and wanted to capitalize on the excitement people had for something different.

"I don't know what to tell you about that," Rhys drawled. They were meeting him at the Flying Swan Inn, and were enjoying some of their product. "It depends on what you want to do I suppose. You expand, that means adding employees and a whole lotta headaches. Might get the notice of some of the big guys, and competition in the City isn't always friendly. Of course, if you plan to settle down here and make a life out of this, then maybe it's worth it to build a serious business."

Ben shrugged. "That's just it. I don't know what I want to do. Things haven't worked out so far like we planned and I don't know if I want to stay here."

"What do you mean you don't want to stay here!" interjected Renfro. Ben ignored him.

"Give it some time," said Rhys. "The Sanctuary is always like this, secrets and more secrets. They'll let you in when it's time."

"We've been here three months and I haven't even gotten to see them!" complained Ben. "They've barely written. How do we even know they're okay?"

"I told you they're okay." Rhys sighed with a shake of his head. "I saw them two weeks ago and they're both fine. Tired, but fine."

Ben sat back glumly. The promised free days at the Sanctuary had not happened for Meghan and Amelie. Aside from a few brief notes, he had no communication with them. Rhys visited the Sanctuary irregularly, and he'd been their only source of news about how the girls were doing. Lately, it had started sounding repetitive. Tired, but fine.

Rhys placed a hand on Ben's shoulder. "I'll go by tomorrow and see what I can find out, but I can't make any promises. I'm pretty much straight in to see my handlers, then I'm back out. Not a lot of time for sightseeing. I've been working for them for three years now, which isn't a lot of time in the eyes of the Sanctuary. They think long term. It's not like they let me wander around the Initiates' Quarters on my own."

"It always sounds like you hate the place," said Renfro. "Why do you keep working for them?"

Rhys grinned and answered, "Gold."

Ben leaned in. "You've got enough gold, don't you? I never see you spending it. Can't you quit if it's that bad?"

"Oh, it's not really about the gold." Rhys smirked and his expression darkened. "I pretend it is, but you know me well enough by now. I'm not a good man. There have been times I've been a very bad man. As I've gotten older, I've thought about it more and more. What if I could do some good in this world? The Sanctuary was the way I was trying to do the right thing for once. Doing good, doing what's right, it isn't always as easy as it seems."

"What do you mean?" asked Ben. "Don't take what isn't yours, help others, don't put your needs above someone else's... That's a start, right?"

"Remember when I helped you two out of that jam in Fabrizo? Bargained you right out from under the knives of the Thieves' Guild. It cost poor Lord Frederick in Whitehall his life, though. Two for one, does that make it a good act? Or maybe because I know you and we'd been getting to be friends. Is that good to protect your own at the expense of someone you don't know?"

"Oh," replied Ben, sitting back. "I see."

Rhys tapped the worn handle of one of his long knives. "You live by the sword and have the power to make life and death choices, sooner or later, you will. I was getting tired of it. That's why I joined with the Sanctuary. Figured I'd trust them to call the shots and maybe I'd end up doing some good for once. Problem is, I'm not so sure that good is what they're doing."

THE NEXT NEWDAY, Ben finally got a chance to go to the Sanctuary and see Meghan and Amelie. Rhys had returned with the news after his last visit. Ben was nervous. It'd been three months since their emotionally charged goodbyes. A lot could change in that time. What Rhys said was weighing heavily on him as well. Would they be the same two girls he travelled with from Farview, or younger versions of Lady Towaal?

Renfro said he would stay behind to check on some business leads, but Ben figured he just wasn't as close with the girls and wanted a day off. They'd been working hard recently and he didn't think anything of Renfro needing a break.

THE SANCTUARY WAS LOCATED in a high-walled compound on the north end of the island. It was a half bell walk from the brewery and Ben's apartment. He had made the trip twice already when he was waiting to hear from the girls and wanted to see what he could see, which wasn't anything from the street. Some of the taller towers around the north end certainly had views over those walls, but on casual checking, he found most were private residences and none seemed open to a young man trying to spy on girls in the Sanctuary.

It was a pleasant walk to the Sanctuary. All of the streets in the City were broad and well maintained. As you got closer to the seat of power, fountains, statuary, and open parks became more common. The south end of the City was where most of the commerce took place and also where most of the bridges to shore landed. The north end near the Sanctuary was where the government buildings were, a college of the sword, the wealthier citizens, and something called a university—although Ben was a little vague on what that was.

When he drew near the Sanctuary, he found himself on a verdant green, tree-lined boulevard that led directly to imposing copper gates. The gates were the only break in the high walls that opened to the city streets and were polished to a brilliant shine. On his first trips around the area he noticed the walls appeared to be a seamless grey stone that crossed the entire width of the island. Their construction was a mystery to him. He suspected it was a small wonder, though, compared to what the mages inside were capable of.

Despite their height, it was clear these walls were more for privacy than protection. No army on the continent of Alcott would be willing to challenge the power concentrated behind them.

Since it was Newday, the copper gates stood open for visitors. Two huge smiling faces representing an ancient woman and a young one were embossed on the gates. Below them, a small handful of guards stood and directed the few visitors where to go. They were armed and armored. While they were alert, they did not appear to be concerned with who came and went.

"Reason for your visit?" one blond-haired man called out when Ben drew close.

"I'm here to see Ame... I'm here to see two Initiates. They're expecting me." Rhys had instructed him on what to say and Ben had memorized it like it was a secret passcode. He winced as he fumbled, but the guards took it in stride.

"They'll be at the Initiates Garden then," the blond man replied. "Straight ahead to the breezeway then follow it to the right. About five hundred paces and you'll see the hedgerows surrounding the garden. Ask anyone you see there for the Initiates by name and they can point you to them. Direct to the garden, of course."

"Of course! Thanks," replied Ben.

The guard nodded and turned his attention back to the streets beyond the gate. A second guard kept his gaze on Ben as he started toward the breezeway, not in an unfriendly way, just watchful. These men may not be expecting trouble, but they weren't shirking their responsibilities either.

The inside of the grounds surprised Ben, though, he wasn't sure what he had been expecting. Along the outer wall were ungroomed trees, tall grass, and wild flowers as far as he could see. Compared to the planned and manicured nature of the rest of the City, it seemed odd. The amount of unused space was also shocking to someone who'd spent the last three months in the City where they built towers thirty stories into the air because they'd long ago run out of land.

The way to the breezeway was a straight pebble-strewn path about ten paces wide. Compared to the wild flora around him, it was meticulously kept weed free and clean.

Interesting, thought Ben, as he made his way into the famous home and training grounds of Alcott's mages. Unlike the bold, striking entrance to Argren's keep in Whitehall, the Sanctuary was almost aggressively unassuming. The mages were making a statement to their visitors. They wanted to show they had no need and no desire to impress.

It was powerful. Where King Argren put towering gates and walls, plush carpets, glittering gold fixtures, tapestries, crystal bowls, trumpets, and liveried staff to greet and fawn over arrivals, the mages had pebble walkways, untrimmed grass, and wild flowers.

The breezeway was merely a junction in paths he found. Beyond it, he could see the path led into more open spaces and three or four story white stucco buildings further along. The breezeway had a large open arch where the path came through. Then it went off to the right and left to connect to more of the white buildings a thousand paces from where he was standing.

Anyone entering the Sanctuary had a bit of walking to do before they found their destination.

Another guard was meandering around the arch in the breezeway, but he merely nodded a greeting when he saw Ben turn to the right. A few other men were walking ahead of Ben. They and the guards were the only other people he'd seen since he entered.

A gentle wind stirred the long grasses around him and rustled the leaves of the scattered trees while he walked. He had to admit it was a very peaceful place. He found himself lulled into forgetting that this place existed to train mages. Mages like Lady Towaal who called lightning out of thin air to burn a score of attacking demons.

He shook himself and regained focus when he saw the other men duck out of sight behind a low green wall. It was the hedgerow the guard had mentioned and so far the only sign of human cultivation.

A thin, wire gate stood open in the hedge wall. The pebble path narrowed and continued into a large garden. Here, there were blooming flowers, fruit trees, and small fountains. The kind of things he would have thought to see. A large bird with a rainbow hue of tail feathers walked by and he saw Meghan and Amelie sitting on a bench near the entrance to the garden.

"Hi," he said.

"Ben!" Both girls sprang up from the bench and rushed over to give him hugs. A confusing barrage of questions started about how he was, was his apartment clean, was that really his handwriting in the letters, did he need money, was he okay?

"Hold on," he interrupted. "I haven't heard anything about you two! I came to ask how you were doing. With all of your free days cancelled, I didn't know if you needed my help."

The two girls looked at each other but they didn't laugh in his face like he was suddenly worried they would.

"We're tired, but fine," said Meghan.

Ben rolled his eyes. "That's what Rhys always says."

"It's true," added Amelie sheepishly. "The studies are very taxing and it takes a lot out of you to focus on something for so long. It's not easy to learn what we need to learn. But we're not hurt or anything like that, if that's what you were worried about."

"I don't know what I was worried about I guess," he admitted. "I just knew it couldn't be good if you didn't get your free days. Can you tell me about it?"

"Let's walk," said Meghan. "This is the Initiate's Garden. That building over there," she gestured to a long three story white building, "is the Initiate's Hall. It's where we all stay, take our meals and have the little free time that we do. We can't take you in, of course."

"Of course," he responded.

He looked over the building and eyed the garden. There were several clumps of young women in plain but well-made dresses escorting either young men or older couples around the garden. Initiates with their boyfriends, brothers, or parents, he guessed. Curiously, there were no male initiates he could pick out.

As the girls led him deeper into the garden, he asked, "Is everyone studying here a, ah, a girl?"

Amelie smiled and Meghan responded, "Thinking about joining, Ben?"

"No. I just didn't see any guys," he remarked.

"That's because you are right. There aren't any male trainees," explained Amelie.

Trying hard to hide a broad grin, Meghan added, "Males have a more difficult time learning control, which isn't a surprise to any woman who's had to deal with men. Some years ago, the Veil decided this place wouldn't train men. You saw what Lady Towaal is capable of. It was determined to be too dangerous to have men wielding that kind of power on the island."

"So, there aren't any male mages?" queried Ben. He'd never really thought about it. It was always ambiguous in the stories.

Meghan shrugged. "There aren't any here. Men lack control, but they do have the capacity to learn magic."

"Where would they learn though?" questioned Amelie. "I can't think there are many men who are able to learn it on their own. Our instructors shared that it is possible to learn on your own but unlikely one would achieve any notable ability. It can be rather dangerous. Without proper guidance that is," she added quickly with a sidelong glance at Ben.

"Dangerous how? What can happen?" He knew they were in good hands, but all of this discussion on danger made him nervous for the girls.

"It's not really something the Sanctuary likes to share outside the walls, so we can't talk about it much. Don't worry though, we are fine and they take it slow. We're not rushed into anything we're not ready for. It's just, intense. We can't talk about the training in detail, but we can show you the gardens. They really are lovely, and unlike anything else in the Sanctuary."

Ben had to admit she was right, the gardens were lovely. They had an astounding variety of plants and flowers and all of them seemed to be in full bloom. Each one had been placed with precision to accent the flora around it. Bright blues with loud oranges, vibrant greens, and buttery yellows. Each arrangement felt right. There were also a variety of fruit trees scattered around producing apples, pears, and orange-, green-, and yellow-skinned fruit the girls called citrus. They said it made an excellent juice and plucked and peeled one of the orange ones for Ben to try. The fruit came apart in segments and was very tender. When he took a bite, sweet liquid filled his mouth. He thought about snatching a couple more to take back with him.

"What are these called?" he asked around a mouthful of the fruit.

"Oranges," replied Meghan.

He looked at the bright orange skin. "Okay." He looked at Meghan to see if she was teasing him, but she looked back with no trace of the expected mirth. He frowned down at the fruit, swallowed, then continued the conversation, "Tell me about your training, or at least what you can. What are you spending all of that time doing?"

"It's a lot on theory so far," answered Meghan. "The theory of how different forces in the world act. Physical, social, political..."

"There is a lot of political theory. A lot," affirmed Amelie with a crisp nod.

Meghan grinned. "Amelie doesn't always agree with what our teachers have to say. That's been part of the struggle and why we haven't had as much free time as planned. Every time she disagrees with Mistress Eldred, we get another reading assignment or essay to complete. At first, there were a lot of disagreements."

"You've started coming around to her point of view?" Ben asked Amelie.

"Let's just say I've seen the futility of debate. The Sanctuary has some very strong opinions on certain subjects, and one way or the other, they expect you to fall in line. It's better if I just go along with it, for now."

"I for one am delighted," chirped Meghan. "Every extra reading assignment that Amelie got, I got too. It's part of the Sanctuary's teaching method. Don't get me wrong. Lord Velson's musings on the benefits of the categorical denial of rights to the peasant class and the tradeoff with the effort to enforce breeding standards in that class is fascinating. But after a while, a girl is ready for a break."

"Wait," said a confused Ben. "The categorical denial of rights, breeding standards? What does that mean?"

"Oh, don't worry about it," answered Meghan. "They have us read opposing viewpoints then argue the merits. Not every position can be the most sensible one."

"It's really quite droll," said Amelie. "The Sanctuary feels it's important for Initiates to understand the political climate before continuing their studies in the art. There's a certain responsibility that goes along with becoming a mage, and on that subject at least, I agree whole heartedly."

"Yes," concurred Meghan. "It wouldn't do having people running around slinging lightning bolts with no understanding of the consequences."

15

CONFLICTING INTERESTS

Ben's feet kicked up little puffs of dust as he circled around the stone-rimmed fountain. His sword was held steady in front of his face and his breathing was even. Shirtless in the hot, still summer air, he could feel beads of sweat work their way slowly down his back. The heat was stifling and seemed to have sucked the energy out of the city. The normal sounds of life that would have floated their way to the empty courtyard were absent. The only sound was the low scuff of bare feet on dusty stone.

Outwardly, he appeared solely focused on his movement and the other man across the dry fountain from him, but in his head, he was constantly calculating and recalculating odds. What were his chances if he darted to the right? How about if he went left? Moments before, he'd tried stepping back toward the narrow alleyway that was the only entrance to the courtyard to give himself an advantage, but his opponent grinned, moved toward a tight corner, and signaled he was willing to wait.

In a snap, his decision was made. He scanned the rim of the fountain with his periphery vision. He was looking for a flat spot in the rough mortar. He would step there, then launch himself straight over the fountain. He hoped to surprise his opponent and gain precious time before he could react. So far, they'd been dancing around the edges of the fountain with minimal engagement.

Just as Ben tensed to make his move over the fountain, Rhys shouted, "Come on! I'm sweating to death out here just to see you two walk in circles. Forget the wager. The first round is on me if we leave right now."

Saala dropped out of his fighting stance and smirked. "If you're satisfied Master Ashwood, I am as well."

"Sure," replied Ben. "If Rhys is buying then we both win."

To make things interesting and get motivated in the oppressive sticky heat of late summer, they'd started wagering that Saala would buy a round for every time Ben landed a strike. If Ben couldn't land one, he'd buy all of Saala's ale that evening. About half of the time recently, Saala ended up buying a round or two. It'd been a week since Ben had been unable to score at least one strike on him. One strike during the course of one or two bells practice didn't seem like much, but it was a big improvement from what he could do a few short months before.

"Finally," grunted Rhys. "I don't think I've ever been more bored by a sword fight. It's too hot for this strategic nonsense. You stick them with the pointy end. What else do you want to know?"

"Some fighting is speed and flash. Some is strategy," voiced Saala. "Knowing when to attack is just as important as how to attack, although I'm sure Ben and I both would benefit from your extensive experience. Maybe tomorrow you could participate instead of just watching and complaining?"

"Yeah," encouraged Ben. "Why don't you join us? For a man who makes a living with his blades, shouldn't you practice some?"

Rhys grunted again. "I only start it when I mean to stop it. You two hope to gain an edge by practice. I keep my edge because there is no holding back. Besides, I've done my share of practice over the years. I've been doing this for a very, very long time."

"How long could you have been doing this?" challenged Ben. "You aren't much more than ten or fifteen years older than me."

"Longer than you would think possible," retorted Rhys before sharing a long, direct look with Saala.

"Interesting," said the blademaster.

Ben felt like he'd missed part of the conversation. He was interrupted from further questions though when they got to the entrance of the Flying Swan Inn and were nearly trampled by two massive, grim-faced and block-shaped men who pushed their way out the door.

An angry-looking Mathias was standing near the entry when they got in. "Who were those men?" inquired Ben. It was clear Mathias had been upset by them.

"Trouble," grunted the barkeep. "More for you than me, though."

"Trouble for me? What do you mean?" asked Ben.

"Let's sit down." Mathias motioned to an empty table near the back of the room away from the afternoon crowd. "Claudia, a pitcher of Ben's lager please."

Saala and Rhys had both gone into alert mode when their friend Mathias mentioned trouble, but the threat had obviously passed for now.

"Those were Gulli's men," explained Mathias when they sat down.

"Gulli?" asked Ben. He looked to Saala and Rhys but Saala was as confused looking as he was. Rhys, though, looked concerned. Unusual for him.

"I suppose it's really Lord Gulli," continued Mathias, "although he doesn't act like any lord I've heard of. He runs a lot of businesses in the City. Everything from gambling dens and brothels to a team of masons and a linen factory. Most importantly for you, though, he has the largest brewery in the City and supplies ale to over half the taverns on this island. You must be getting a lot of interest in your brew for his boys to start making house calls."

"Business has been good," replied Ben cautiously. "We sell to you and a few other taverns now, but it's not like we're any threat to an operation like that. I'm only doing about forty kegs a week."

"You're selling to more places," broke in Rhys. "I thought you were going to keep it small?"

Ben frowned. "Renfro really pushed to expand. He's been so unhappy here that I thought it'd give him something to keep occupied."

"Well, it must have been enough," added Mathias. "Gulli's goons were asking about you and whether I'd consider switching to another supplier—that being Gulli of course. Don't worry about me. I've got enough friends that I'm not intimidated by his thugs, but some of the other tavern owners might be. More importantly, you better watch your back. I've heard stories about Gulli before and he plays dirty. Competitors have had their stores trashed and there are rumors people have turned up badly injured or missing. He's tight somehow with senior members of the Sanctuary, so even though there are a lot of rumors, the City Watch hasn't stepped in. He thinks he's outside of the law and he's very, very dangerous."

"We can be dangerous too," muttered Rhys darkly.

THE NEXT NEWDAY, Ben sat slumped in a corner of the Flying Swan Inn going over his ledgers. In addition to being his biggest customer, Mathias had become one of Ben's best friends in the City. The man was an excellent listener and appreciated complexities and qualities in ale that was beyond even Ben. He offered Ben a spot at a table whenever he wanted and the serving girls had learned to leave him alone when he was working.

The Flying Swan Inn was a well-run establishment that benefited from its proprietor's sole focus on running the place. The common room was constantly in a state of being cleaned, and Mathias spent extra for comfortable tables and chairs. He lined the walls with memorabilia from other people's travels and added other little touches that created a welcoming ambiance. It was a far step above the Buckhorn Tavern in Farview in terms of quality, but it held the same feel of home for Ben, so he was happy to do work there instead of in the dimly lit cellar he did the brewing.

Today, he was having trouble focusing on getting the ledgers done. It wasn't long before Mathias stopped by his table to ask what was wrong.

"Visitation day is cancelled again. I heard it from a meat pie seller down the street," grumbled Ben.

Mathias, who was familiar with Ben's relationship with Amelie and Meghan, asked, "What, the girls acting up in class again? Hold on. You said a meat pie man told you. It's cancelled for everyone?"

"Yes, that's what I heard. I was still going to walk over this afternoon during my normal time but it's probably a wasted effort. Supposedly some important visitors showed up in the night and they don't want any strangers on campus."

Mathias surveyed the room before pulling up a chair at Ben's table. "This is just rumor, but there is word that representatives from the Coalition are here. I heard it from a man I used to work with, someone I trust. This kind of thing usually is all over town, though, and I haven't heard a peep from anyone else. I'm not sure what to believe, but it would explain why the Sanctuary doesn't want any outsiders behind those walls."

Ben frowned. "The Coalition? But the Sanctuary is aligned with the Alliance. I was there with Lady Towaal at Whitehall. That doesn't make any sense."

Mathias rapped one scar crossed hairy knuckle on the table and replied, "What the Sanctuary says they do and what they do aren't the same thing. Take anything they show to the world with a grain of salt. Lady Towaal was at the Conclave, but I heard she didn't sign the agreement, right? I don't claim to know the mind of the Veil, but this wouldn't be the first time she played both sides. Like I said, I'd expect that news to be everywhere and it isn't, so that means it's not true at all, or it's very true and it's serious."

"What would the Coalition want with the Sanctuary anyway?" wondered Ben. "I heard the mages never participate in war. That's why Lady Towaal didn't sign the agreement."

"You're right. They don't participate in war. Too great a risk to their pompous selves I guess. But there's still a lot a mage can do without fighting. Healing, telling the weather, farseeing, and so on. Could be gold too. Running a war costs a lot of money and the Sanctuary has more of it than anyone. Borrow some money now and pay it off afterward with concessions the Sanctuary wants. One thing about the Veil, she plays the long game."

Just then, Ben heard a familiar sound and looked up to see Amelie and Meghan speaking with one of the serving girls and looking his way.

"Ben!" shouted Amelie. She flew across the room to wrap him in a tight embrace. Meghan followed close behind.

"Meghan, Amelie, what are you doing here?"

Both girls began to talk excitedly at once before Meghan deferred and Amelie took the lead. "They let us out for a free day! We're not due back until two bells after nightfall! Mistress Eldred came to the dormitory last night and told us we've progressed so well that we could leave the grounds. We found Rhys' apartment this morning and he said you'd probably be here, so we came to find you." She gave a long pause before finishing, "And here we are. Are you busy? Can you show us around? I don't want to interrupt your business meeting."

"Oh no." Ben turned to Mathias. "This is my first customer and friend, Mathias. He runs this place. Of course I'll show you around. Wow. I'm just surprised. Giving an extra free day doesn't sound like the Sanctuary I know."

"There was some talk of important visitors on campus so many of the classes were cancelled. I think we just got lucky," said Meghan.

"Lady Amelie," said Mathias with a deep bow.

"Yes." Amelie blushed. "But I prefer not to talk about that here. Right now I'm just an Initiate at the Sanctuary like all of the others."

"Of course," replied Mathias. "You can trust me and that's the last I'll say of it. I was just surprised to hear you were studying at the Sanctuary. I figured Lord Gregor would want you home with all of this Alliance and Coalition business starting up. I can't imagine he, or anyone else, would want you accidentally running into members of the Coalition." Mathias looked to Ben and tilted his head slightly.

"Oh, I don't think there's any chance of that. Maybe I shouldn't say this to a stranger, but if you're a friend of Ben's... I was at Whitehall in the Conclave when the Alliance pact was signed—I was one of the signatories. Lady Towaal was there as an observer from the Sanctuary. I can't imagine anyone from the Coalition would come near here."

Ben looked back at Mathias and quickly decided to keep silent about the rumors he'd shared. Amelie was a long way from home and none of them were close to the halls of power in this place. If this Mistress Eldred had sent Amelie away for the day, maybe it was for the best.

"Well, in that case, let's go see the City!" Ben exclaimed with excitement that managed to sound only slightly forced.

During the previous few months, Ben spent much of his time working on his business in the cellar brewing and then ducking in and out of taverns to make sales calls. In his free time, he'd been with Saala and Rhys practicing the sword or the Ohms. Renfro spent a great deal more time exploring the City, but Ben didn't feel like tracking him down for this.

"What do you want to see first? The sculpture gardens and the bone museum are the most famous. They say the theatres are the best in Alcott, but it's a little early in the day for that. There's also the pleasure pier or the tea houses on the east side. I haven't been there much. I'm told it's nice if you like tea. There are musicians in a few of the busier markets, but if I'm honest, I have no ear for music and I can't tell you if they are any good. If you're feeling adventurous, we could go up in one of the public towers and cross some of the sky bridges."

"Whatever you suggest." Amelie grinned. "We don't know when we're getting another free day outside the grounds, so let's take advantage of it."

"Let's go to the sculpture gardens first then," suggested Ben. "The Issen Consulate is on the way and we can pick up Saala."

"The Consulate? Oh, please keep me away from that today," begged Amelie. "Is there another way to get Saala? I do need to see him."

"I know a back way in and I can get him. They've seen me there before."

"You know your way around the Consulate building? Very fancy. You're coming up in this world." Amelie smiled.

Ben blushed. "Only because Saala is staying there. It's not like I'm some highborn or something." Ben winked at Meghan. "Now those people are fancy."

Amelie rolled her eyes and started toward the door. "Let's go see these sculpture gardens of yours. You know how us highborn get if we aren't dazzled by artwork at least once a day."

∾

THEY PICKED up Saala at the Consulate building then bought some meat pies to eat while strolling through the gardens. Ben had come by once before and he was impressed again by the statues and the greenery surrounding them.

The gardens extended across several blocks in a serpentine pattern. They were designed to be seen along a looping path that circled the park. The statuary had been commissioned from many artists over the years. It was all supposed to tell the story of the City. Some of the figures represented grand moments in history but some told everyday stories of the common folk. Several were made up of many pieces and a few could have filled a decent-sized building on their own. The oldest were little more than worn down lumps of rock with small brass plates detailing their origins—thousands of years before in a couple of cases.

In addition to the hard stone of the statues, the gardens were filled with a profusion of plant life. The gardeners put just as much care and attention into their creations as the sculptors had. Thickly planted bushes and deep green ferns gave the gardens a sense of privacy in the middle of the busy city. Tall wooden structures supporting bright flowering and hanging vines blended into the back drop of the City's soaring towers. It felt like it was all part of the same tapestry.

The sculptures though were the highlight. The flora fell into the background and served as a pleasant accent to the history and artistry that unfolded around them.

"Here, Winged Victory," said Saala as he pointed out a slightly larger than life figure.

It was one of the most famous works in the park, and a small crowd was milling around it. It depicted a headless and armless woman leaning forward, her garments flowing behind as if she was pushing against a strong wind. She had two expansive wings spread out from her back and one foot was set in front of the other in mid stride. It was remarkably realistic for a work of stone, but Ben saw immediately the reason it was famous was how the sculptor had captured the essence of the woman's triumph.

"Breathtaking," pronounced Amelie. She hung back from the work as if afraid it'd fade away if she drew too close.

"It's very good," replied Meghan, "but what is she supposed to be victorious over? Is this in dedication of some battle or something? I like some of the others better where it's clear what is going on."

"It could have been after a battle," remarked Saala. "No one is quite sure. The sculptor and the reason behind the work have been lost through time. I'm not even sure the work was originally commissioned for display in the City. Many people think it was moved from somewhere else and that's where it could have been damaged." He gestured to the missing head and limbs.

"It's powerful as it is now. I can't imagine how beautiful it would be whole." Amelie sighed.

"Less impressive, maybe," offered Ben to a quizzical look from Amelie. "Think about it. What face could match the grandeur of the rest of the work? In your mind, you think about what expression the woman could have, you conjure the strongest woman you can imagine. The sculptor might have had something different in his head. Without the face, the work is a question as well as a story."

"Maybe," Amelie pensively admitted. "But still, I'd like to see what she looked like. Surely there must be records kept somewhere for something like this."

"No written records exist from what I've heard at least," replied Saala with a shrug. "Supposedly, not even the oldest of the long-lived remember anything other than this statue being right here. Possibly the Veil knows more, but who is going to ask her about it?"

It wasn't until later that night, when the girls had gone back to the Sanctuary and he was tucked away in his cot, that Ben started to wonder what Saala had meant by 'the oldest of the long-lived'.

Before that, they had a full afternoon exploring the City together. After the sculpture garden, they climbed one of the towers and spent a bell wandering the sky bridges. The bottom levels of the tower were dedicated to residences and about ten levels up, where the first bridges connected, it had shops that catered to people living in the tower. There were small grocers, apothecaries, taverns, and other places people would visit regularly.

After crossing the first sky bridge with its narrow wooden slats and slight swaying when the wind blew, Ben shakily declared he needed a drink. They settled down at a large tavern which took up an entire floor in the next tower. Tall windows were left open to catch a cross breeze that made it much more pleasant than the street-level venues Ben normally visited.

"How'd you like to carry your kegs all the way up here?" teased Saala. He lifted his small glass in toast. "To Ben's successful brewery, and to our two Initiates who've finally gained enough trust to be let out of sight for a day!"

Ben and the girls raised their glasses as well.

They were drinking a clear liqueur with squeezes of juice from the sour yellow and tangy green fruits Ben saw in the Initiates garden. The liqueur packed a punch, but with the juice, it was a refreshing combination and perfect for the hot day.

WITH A LITTLE LIQUID COURAGE, Ben was able to enjoy the sights from the bridges and appreciate the massive scale of the City. From the higher vantage points, the island spread out below them in an organized swirl of streets, parks, and buildings. Unlike Whitehall or Fabrizo, which grew up naturally, the City was planned. The result was a clean, sensible, and beautiful design, but it lacked the spontaneity and excitement of the other cities.

From the bridges, the people filling the streets below looked like tiny bugs scurrying about their day, but to Ben, the most amazing part was the forest of towers that rose around them. The time and energy involved in creating the structures staggered him, particularly when he thought about the boundless open land just a day or two's journey away from the island.

He mentioned it to Amelie as they stared down from one of the sturdy masonry bridges and she responded, "People like being near other people."

"But look at this," he said gesturing to the nearby towers. "A lot of these people live in tiny apartments that they can barely afford. Their kids have nowhere safe to play and they're always looking over their shoulders at what the neighbors are doing. They could sell their places here and move out to the country where they'd have a roof over their heads and more than enough land to raise crops and support themselves."

Saala smiled and countered, "But that's all they'd have, which is better than good for a lot of folks. These people, though, they want more. They want excitement, they want entertainment, and most of all, they want to win some imaginary competition that they all play with each other. That's the culture of this place, it's what makes them feel good. They're all looking over their shoulders because they compare themselves to their neighbors, and in some way, they want to win. More wealth, a better view from their apartment, famous friends, secret knowledge, and of course, power over others." Saala shrugged. "Having enough just isn't enough for some people."

Amelie wrapped an arm around Ben's waist. "You're a simple man, Ben. Which is to say, a good man. One who knows himself and knows what he wants. Not everyone does."

"I don't think I always know what I want," replied Ben as he felt Amelie's arm around him.

"You do. You just don't know it yet!" Saala laughed.

The night ended at The Flying Swan Inn with Mathias personally suggesting and serving his favorite dishes. Mathias' first love was ale, but he had a knack in the kitchen as well. He brought out heaping plates of food for them to share. It wasn't the fancy fare they'd eaten on their journey in Fabrizo or Whitehall, but it was good, and it fit.

"So, tell me about my investment. Going well I hope?" Amelie jokingly asked Ben.

"It is going well," said Ben. "Mathias here is my first and best customer, but we're expanding across town. We had to hire two full-time porters to keep up with deliveries. I'm worried we'll need more in a few weeks. I'm making a trip off the island tomorrow to look for additional materials. I hear they're cheaper if you're willing to walk a bit."

"Really?" broke in Meghan. "You never needed help like that in Farview. I just... I thought you were going to be doing the same thing here."

"It is the same thing. It's still ale," replied Ben sardonically. "There are just a lot more people here to drink it."

"I'm so proud of you!" exclaimed Amelie. "I've heard the City is a tough place to do business and I think it's just great you're doing so well." She looked to Saala. "Why didn't you tell me it was going so well? You'll be a major player in no time Ben!"

"Well, I don't know about that." Ben replied with a grin. He thought back to the conversation earlier in the day about having enough. It seemed everyone from Renfro to Amelie now was pushing him to keep expanding. Every time they added a new customer or hired someone, it was a little more work, and a little less free time for him.

"Keep your respect for the craft, enjoy what you do, and the business will take care of itself," advised Saala. He knew what Ben was thinking. "You're young still and you have options. This is just one of them. It will feel less like work if you think about it as exploring an option."

~

THE NEXT DAY, Ben, Renfro, and their two porters made the trip off island to buy more wooden kegs. By asking around over the course of a few weeks, they'd found a cooper who only charged half of what they were paying on the island. Ben figured with those savings they'd be able to put away some of the gold and silver they were bringing in instead of pouring it all back into the business.

"We should be in the business of selling empty kegs," grumbled Renfro as they helped the porters pull two overloaded handcarts up a short hill.

Ben laughed. "It'd certainly be easier than hauling around the loaded versions."

Martin, one of the porters, grunted in assent.

At the top of the hill they paused to catch their breath. "I really think we're going to need to hire some more men once we fill these up," said Renfro. "Poor Martin over there is going to collapse on us one day."

Martin grunted in assent again. Ben looked his way and then nodded toward a nearby bar that opened to the street. Martin took the hint and gestured at the other porter to join him for a break.

"I think you might be right," started Ben. "This batch is going to be half again bigger than the last one. I'm not sure we'll be able to sell it all though. I don't want to bring on a lot of people then find out we don't need them, or worse, can't pay them."

"You know we have more than enough coming in to pay a few more guys," argued Renfro. "And we won't have any problems selling the stuff. Now is the time to expand because Gulli is up in Venmoor and no one is minding the store."

"Gulli is in Venmoor? How do you know that?" demanded Ben.

"I've been talking to some of his people. They're not happy with the way he's running things recently. Let's just say they're open to new ideas. Anyway, he's got bigger fish than stocking barrooms in the City. They say he's up there trying to buy up what's left of the arms market. Trying to get ahead of the build-up with the Alliance and the Coalition. Good luck I say. Reinhold and his ilk are three or four months ahead of him."

"You've been talking to Gulli's people!" exclaimed Ben. "Damn it, Renfro. I don't care if he is out of town. That's reckless. Someone's going to tell him. He's dangerous Renfro. We can't risk doing something stupid."

Renfro leaned back against one of the handcarts and crossed his arms. "We're dangerous too. Let's put that blademaster friend of yours to work. Finally get something out of it. Maybe go talk to Rhys too. I'm not convinced he's not all talk, but we can throw him a little gold and put him on the payroll. His name means something in some of the circles in this town."

Ben ran his hands through his hair. "Renfro, the last thing we need to do is escalate this business with Gulli. His goons went and talked to a few of our customers. Most of them ignored him. The ones who left us weren't good customers anyway. We should leave it at that. Pulling Saala and Rhys into this isn't fair to them."

"You know he's going to make a move, Ben. All I'm saying is we should be smart and think about it. Do we wait for him or do we move first?"

"I can't believe you're even talking about this. What has gotten into you, Renfro? This is crazy. Gulli's been leaving us alone and no one's 'making a move'. Besides, he has a small army of thugs working for him. Even with Saala and Rhys, that's not a mess I want to get involved in."

"Your business, your call," muttered Renfro.

"We'll look for new customers and we'll get some more porters, but that's it. No more talking to Gulli's people!"

A FEW WEEKS LATER, Ben was still mulling over what to do with Renfro. Their business was doing well and his friend had gold in his pockets, which he'd never had before, but he still wasn't content. Renfro spent most of his days meandering through alehouses and worse, usually around the rougher areas of the City near the waterfront. He said he was prospecting for customers and networking, but those places rarely paid the premium Ben asked for his ale. They were most successful in the respectable taverns. Those places had clientele willing to pay up for ale that wasn't watered down or soured.

Ben tried to put it aside as he neared the Issen Consulate. Amelie was getting her regular free days now and they'd agreed to meet there. That allowed her to check for messages from her father that Issen didn't want to pass through strange hands on the way to the Sanctuary. Also, Saala was staying there, so it was convenient to practice the sword with him.

Amelie, true to what she'd said after the attack in Kirksbane, had begun studying with Saala and Ben. She was still a novice with blades, but learning the Ohms with Rhys had improved her strength and balance. Like Ben, she was quick and had the natural grace of a dancer, or a blademaster.

Ben was lost in thought as he ducked into the back door of the Consulate building and nearly ran over a small, mousy man who crashed onto the floor. A meaty hand shot out from the side and slapped against Ben's chest, sending him stumbling back a pace.

"You," a high-pitched voice said with a lisp.

The owner of the hand stooped down to pull up the mousy man and Ben saw it was the bodyguard Raphael and Lord Gregor's seneschal Tomas.

"I'm so sorry!" Ben scrambled to help Tomas up, but Raphael gently lifted him to his feet as if he was light as a feather.

"I suppose I shouldn't be surprised you're still around." Tomas sighed. "Got a taste for the good life did you?"

"What?" asked Ben. He thought he should be offended.

"No worries. Amelie is a big girl now and can handle her

affairs. She's in the courtyard with Saala. Since you're walking in here so confidently, I'm sure you know where that is. Raphael and I were just about to head out to tour some of the City's baths. They're really quite splendid. Have you been?"

"Oh, no. I've been focusing on getting a business started," mumbled Ben in response.

"Of course you have. Amelie is an investor I assume? The only investor, perhaps? I'm certain it will be a profitable venture, whatever it is." Tomas breezed out the door without waiting for a response, the hulking Raphael following close behind.

Ben was certain now that he should be offended. The diminutive Tomas obviously didn't like him, but he supposed that made sense. The man was, after all, the right hand of Amelie's father. He had a right to be protective and suspicious of anything involving her.

The clack of reeds on reeds drew his attention back to why he was there and he strolled out into the courtyard to find Amelie trying to hold onto her practice sword as Saala casually, and almost lazily, swatted at it. The scene brought back memories from his first few days with the sword and he silently hoped he didn't look half as awkward as she did when another swipe from Saala sent her sword spinning across the open space.

Amelie saw Ben standing there when she turned to retrieve her practice blade and panted, "Sorry to start without you. Maybe you'd care to take a turn. I think I'll watch for a little bit."

Ben grinned at Saala, stripped off his shirt, and drew his own practice sword. They'd gotten to the point where they would spar for bells with no breaks, but he remembered how early on he felt exhausted after half a bell.

THE ADVANTAGE of being with Amelie at Issen's Consulate was that they treated her like the lord's daughter she was. There was no anonymity for her in that place, which was nice when a veritable swarm of staff brought out a light lunch of meats, cheeses, and fruits along with chilled water and white wine.

Ice was barged down from Northport, but at this time of year, nearly two thirds of it may melt before it got to the freezer rooms in the City. It was not a luxury Ben could afford and not one that was even available outside of winter in Farview. It was a luxury he was happy to enjoy, though, as he sipped on a delicate crystal glass of the cool, refreshing wine.

"It shouldn't take more than a month, maybe a month and a half," said Saala. He was discussing a trip he would take with Seneschal Tomas to Akew Woods, the westernmost city on the continent of Alcott. The forest around Akew Woods was rumored to be populated by lawless tribes of primitive peoples. No one really knew though because there was limited commerce over land and little reason to travel there.

Tomas' mission wasn't explained to Ben, but Saala and Amelie both thought it was worth the extra protection the blademaster could provide. Amelie, behind the walls of the Sanctuary, was as safe as she could be.

"Well, I'm sure Ben would be happy to continue my tutelage in your absence," Amelie said.

Saala replied, "I'm sure he will also. That's a whole new level of skill, Ben. To be able to teach, you must know something very well."

"I'm not sure how well I can teach the sword, but I am happy to try." Ben was confident he could help teach Amelie to hold the blade and she really wasn't far advanced past that yet. He also looked forward to having one-on-one time with her. He enjoyed Saala's company, but the man had little sense of humor—particularly when it came to Amelie.

"Do you think Meghan will come next week?" Ben asked Amelie.

"I'm not certain," she said. "She says learning to become a mage will make the sword an irrelevant skill. Maybe she's right, but harnessing energy takes a lot out of you and I think knowing practical skills will always be beneficial."

"I do not claim to know much about these things," started Saala, "but I do know that understanding your own physical limits and gaining control over your body will be helpful to you. Magic is about willpower and control. Skill with the blade can improve both of those things."

Amelie smiled at him. "I hope you're right. Meghan, and many of the other girls, spend their free days studying. I worry I will fall behind."

"From what I have seen with mages in the past, it is not a talent only learned behind walls and closed doors. Few talents are. Experiencing life is just as important as knowledge from a book."

BEN GROANED as he lifted another sack of barley out of the hand-cart and tossed it onto a pile of identical stacks against the cellar wall. He winced as a fresh cloud of dust puffed up from the impact of the barley sack. Keeping the cellar clean was getting to be a near impossible task with the amount of work they were doing down there. He or one of the growing number of employees swept it out daily now. He knew he'd regret leaving this place with it's cheap rent, but soon they would need to find a place that was less apt to collect dust.

"That's the last of this load," announced Martin as he wiped sweat from his brow. It was early fall and starting to cool, but the humidity had not quite broken yet.

"Thanks, Martin," responded Ben.

The man waved and rolled the cart off. They had found space in a nearby merchant's warehouse to store their carts because they'd run out of space in the cellar. Ben started rearranging the barley sacks against the wall.

"That's a lot of material. How much ale will it make?" called out a confident voice from the cellar stairs.

Ben turned and blurted, "Lord Reinhold!"

"Yes, that's what they call me," drawled Reinhold with a sly smile. He nodded to the stack of barley sacks. "How much will that make?"

"Uh, about sixty kegs, sir."

"And how often do you produce that much ale?"

"It takes a couple of weeks to ferment, but we're starting a batch a week."

"And you have no problem selling that many?" quizzed Reinhold.

"Oh, no. We could probably sell a good deal more, but we've run out of room. This is the biggest batch we can make in this space."

"I see," said Reinhold, peering around the room from the entrance. "What kind of margin are you making on each of these kegs? Ale is almost entirely water, of course, but surely it's expensive to purchase these wooden barrels and transport the stuff across the City. There are a lot of taverns on this island, but I see sailors drinking whatever swill they serve down by the docks and the highborn and other wealthy citizens are inclined toward wine. How do you compete in that market profitably?"

"We do okay," answered Ben slowly. "Excuse me, sir, but why are you asking all of these questions?"

Reinhold stepped the rest of the way into the cellar and made a show of examining its contents before responding. "I'm considering going into business with you."

"I, uh…" Ben was stunned and didn't know how to answer.

"I'll pay fair value for a stake, of course. If what I've heard is true, then it's certainly more gold than you've ever laid hands on. I also have access to capital for expansion and networks you could leverage to get into places you are currently not welcome. The Foreigner's Barracks, for example. The visiting soldiers spend more on ale than the rest of the city combined. I can get you on their taps if you can stomach a lower price than what you've been asking. Most importantly, I can offer protection from Gulli."

Ben eyed Reinhold suspiciously. The man seemed to know a lot about the business.

Reinhold continued, undeterred by Ben's silence. "I'm aware of what your current partner has been doing, and you and I both know it's dangerous business. Your friend the blademaster is leaving town and while Rhys is dangerous, he's unreliable. When Gulli sees an opening he will take it. You are not prepared for the type of competition that man is. Partner with me, though, and you have no worries."

What the hell had Renfro gotten them into now? Ben hadn't even seen the former thief in days. Renfro spent most of his time down by the docks from what Ben had heard. Recently he had only been coming by to collect his share of the profits and encourage Ben to keep hiring more strong-backed porters. Renfro had taken to treating the men to a night on the town and always footing the bill, which Ben knew was a tactic to buy their loyalty. He just didn't know why. When they'd last spoken, he confronted his friend about it, but Renfro blew him off, saying it was just a way to recognize the help everyone had been on their way to success.

"I see you need time to think," declared Reinhold. "I can accept that, but do not take too long. Gulli is sticking his nose in business that does not belong to him. He's reaching outside of the City and disrupting trading arrangements that have been in place for years. His income is still almost entirely on island though, so it's time to send him a warning. With you, I plan to take his ale business from him. That is the way I do things. His way of dealing with competition is more violent. Keep that in mind when you decide what to do."

Reinhold swept up the stairs and Ben heard a clatter of arms and armor move as the lord made it to the streets. He had a team of heavily armed guards up there, Ben realized. He looked over at his sword leaning against the wall and felt like things were spinning out of control.

THAT NIGHT at a candlelit table at the back of the Flying Swan, Ben shared a pitcher with Mathias. His thoughts swirled around the earlier conversation with Reinhold, but Mathias brought him back to the present with news.

"Well, I hate to be the one to mention this, but since you haven't brought it up, I guess you haven't heard." Mathias stared down at his thick hands wrapped around a tankard. "The Coalition is mobilizing. I'm hearing there will be a spring offensive."

Ben shrugged. "We knew that was coming, right? I mean, that's been the talk at least. Both the Coalition and Alliance are building up armies. You don't do that unless you're planning to use them."

"Aye." Mathias sighed. "But the expected target will be Issen. Lord Gregor's going to get hit, he's going to get hit hard. The Coalition is gearing up to make an example. At least, that's what the rumor is."

Ben slumped back in his chair. They'd worried about that too. Issen was in between the centers of power for the Coalition and the Alliance. Amelie said her father had to join one of the other. In a war like this, there is no room for the middle ground.

"They've got half a year to prepare," continued Mathias. "Maybe this one won't be so bad."

Mathias was a veteran. The network of scars across his body and the limp he had when he stood after sitting too long spoke to what he knew about war. His grim face spoke to what he thought the chances were that this one 'won't be so bad'.

"Amelie will want to return to Issen and be there for her people," stated Ben.

"I'm sure she will. That doesn't mean they'll let her go. Gregor had to know what was going to happen and I suspect that's why she's here in the first place. The City is far from the conflict and no one would be stupid enough to come here with an army. Gregor's no pushover. With support from Argren and the rest, he could make a stand. If he does, Issen will be a bloody mess next year. He wouldn't want that for his daughter."

Mathias didn't know Amelie as well as Ben, but he knew people. His assessment of Lord Gregor was likely spot on, thought Ben.

~

THOUGHTS OF LORD Reinhold and his offer were forgotten until Ben saw Renfro early the next morning.

Ben was sitting at a quiet café across the street from their cellar having a cup of kaf and a fruit and soft cheese-stuffed pastry. The cool of the fall morning felt good compared the sticky heat that marked summer in the City. He'd taken to rising early to enjoy the quiet moment while the sun was rising and the city had not yet fully awoken. Unlike life in the country, the City did not really get moving until midmorning.

"Renfro," called Ben.

His scrawny friend spotted him at the café and crossed the cobblestone street to join him at the table.

"I was just coming to see you," said Renfro.

"Kaf?" asked Ben. "You look tired."

"I've been up all night," responded Renfro, shaking his head. "I wanted to catch you, then I'm going home to crash. That stuff just makes me jittery."

"You've been up all night? What for?"

"There's a gambling den over near the Sunset Tower and the owner is interested in us." Renfro scooted his chair closer to the table and laid his elbows on it. "If last night was any indication, they'd easily be our best customer. The place was packed until just a bell ago. Raffe, that's the owner, said he's trying to attract heavier-pocketed clients so he's improving his offerings and likes what we're selling. The ale he has now is piss water. It could be a big deal for us."

"That's great," agreed Ben. He inhaled some of the bitter steam off his kaf then took a sip. "What's the next step?"

"We send over a couple of kegs and if it sells well, he'll put in a serious order. Maybe forty or fifty kegs a week if it goes really well."

Ben grimaced. "We don't have room to brew that."

Renfro frowned at his friend. "We can find another place. That cellar was good for low rent, but that's about it. We need to move out anyway."

"Moving takes coin and that's something we don't have a lot of extra," challenged Ben.

"I can get us a loan," growled Renfro. "I've met some people who are connected. They can get us whatever we need."

"There might be another option." Ben sighed. He'd thought about not mentioning Reinhold at all, but he was certain they didn't want to get involved with any of the shady characters who'd loan Renfro money. "Lord Reinhold came by yesterday. He offered to take an interest in the business."

Renfro bolted to his feet. "Perfect!" he shouted then glanced around the café before quickly sitting back down. "He'll probably try to screw us on the share, but if we negotiate hard, that could solve all of our problems."

"I'm not really sure we have problems if we don't want them," murmured Ben, "but I think he'll be just as interested as you in expansion. Tell me something. Where is this Raffe getting his piss-water ale from?"

"I knew you'd be worried about that," snapped Renfro. "He gets it from Gulli of course. Where else? Look, Ben, we can't run this thing out of fear. I've been making some friends and Gulli isn't as secure as he acts. He's getting pressure from some people who invested with him and he's making mistakes. We've got friends in this town now too. With someone like Reinhold behind us, Gulli is nothing to worry about."

Ben's head sank into his hands. "That's what Reinhold said."

16

THE SANCTUARY

THE NEXT NEWDAY, Ben headed to the Sanctuary to meet Amelie and Meghan. Their free days had been curtailed again. The note he got from the girls said they could see him in the garden for a few bells though.

He wished he were in a better mood to see Amelie. He knew she'd be worried about her father, but his concerns about Renfro, Reinhold, and Gulli were weighing on him. He wanted to brew good ale, drink good ale, learn from Saala and Rhys, and make enough to afford the little apartment he'd rented. Expanding the business so quickly, taking on a potentially dangerous competitor, it just wasn't worth it to Ben. It seemed silly though when compared to what Amelie must be going through. Before long, an army could be marching on her home.

"I don't want to talk about it," was the first thing she said when he spotted her.

"Okay, uh, sure," agreed Ben.

"We were worried this would happen and it is not a surprise. My father will be prepared, whether the rumors are true or not. There's no use us talking about it. It's best I focus on my studies here and not things I have no control over."

"Alright Amelie. I want you to know I've been thinking about you though. I'm sure this is tough, so if you change your mind, I'm available to talk when you need to."

"Thank you for that, Ben. I knew I could count on you."

"I'm just glad you're still here," teased Ben with a grin. "I thought you might be stowed away on a boat or something."

Amelie blushed furiously and Meghan fidgeted uncomfortably, eyes darting around the garden to see who could have overheard.

"You did try to escape!" accused Ben.

"Just the night I heard about it," replied Amelie sheepishly. "I've realized now that wasn't a good idea." Amelie surreptitiously rubbed her backside.

Ben wondered how she came to decide running away wasn't a good idea. The mages of the Sanctuary were famously strict.

"Let's not talk about it," continued Amelie. "Let's talk about something to cheer us up. How is the business?"

"It's great, I guess," answered Ben. "We're finding new customers and we're keeping the current customers happy. It's grown enough that we're looking for more space too. We can't decide if it makes sense to move off island and pay more porters to make deliveries or stay close and pay more rent. Oh, and Lord Reinhold wants to invest in an ownership share."

"What!" both Amelie and Meghan cried out.

"We haven't agreed on any specifics yet," added Ben. "I was going to check with you first, of course, Amelie. Since you were the first investor, I want to make sure you are on board."

"Lord Reinhold is one of the most successful merchants in the City, probably one of the most successful in all of Alcott. Of course I am on board!" Amelie exclaimed.

At the same time, Meghan asked, "Reinhold is the one we rode on his boat, right? The one with that huge estate north of town?"

"This is what we needed to cheer up," gushed Amelie. "Tell us more Ben. How did it happen?"

"Well, he just came by one day and said he was interested." Ben didn't think it was prudent to mention the situation with Gulli. "He thought with our ale and his connections there were some good opportunities. It makes sense. With his capital we have plenty of gold to expand, and he does have access to certain markets that we just can't get into by ourselves. I talked to Renfro and he supports it. We were just waiting on your okay and need to work out some final details with Reinhold."

"Oh my, that is amazing Ben! I can't believe how well you're doing with this. When I suggested you start a business here I was thinking small. I never thought it could grow this quickly."

"I'm impressed too," admitted Meghan. "Back in Farview, I didn't know you had the business skills to do something like this."

Ben shrugged. "it might be more luck than skill. I'll take what I can get though."

ON THE WAY back from the Sanctuary, Ben walked with a little more pep in his step. Having the two girls gush over how great his business was doing made him feel silly for being so upset about it earlier. Gulli was a concern, but with Reinhold backing them, he wasn't a big one. Renfro would come around too. Ben thought that finding this Raffe might be the confidence booster the former thief needed. He wondered if part of Renfro's dark mood was because he was thrust into a foreign place with no idea how to succeed here. A big sale could pull him back to the old Renfro.

When he turned onto the pebble path from the breezeway, Ben caught one of the guards out of the corner of his eye. The man was about one hundred paces behind Ben and staring intently at him. He didn't look familiar, but it was obvious his entire attention was focused on Ben.

Ben tried to brush it off until he saw all of the guards at the gate looking his way also. They spared only a glance at a new arrival who strolled in from the city. The guards all found something else to look at when Ben drew close. Ben shot a glance over his shoulder before he passed through the gate and saw the first guard had come to a stop, still about one hundred paces behind him. The man's hand was lightly resting on his sword and he hadn't lost his focus on Ben.

No one tried to stop him or speak to him, so Ben thought he must be imagining things. He'd never had any trouble with the guards at the Sanctuary and couldn't recall meeting any of them outside the friendly nods when he came to visit. Maybe they were on edge since he'd come to visit Amelie. Surely they had heightened protection around her knowing she was Lord Gregor's daughter.

The hustle and bustle of the City quickly washed over him once he got away from the high walls of the Sanctuary and he forgot about it. He was headed to the Flying Swan to meet with Rhys. Rhys seemed to be growing busy recently and frequently vanished for a few days at a time. Ben wanted to run the Reinhold idea by him before accepting the merchant's proposal.

Rhys wasn't a businessman, but he had an uncanny sense for trouble.

~

"Reinhold?" Rhys asked incredulously. "As in, the Lord Reinhold?"

"I must have made an impression by gawking at his estate when we passed it on the river," joked Ben.

"Well, you could certainly do worse. The man has more gold to throw at a business than you'd ever know what to do with. I'm sure you're doing a great job and all, but I'm a little surprised he's interested. I figure he's got bigger fish on the line than a small brewery."

Ben shifted uneasily. "Well, that's where I have the question. He's doing it he says to thwart Lord Gulli. He says Gulli is reaching too far so he wants to give him some competition locally and cut into his sources of income."

"Hmm," said Rhys before reaching over to the pitcher, refilling his mug, and, without asking, refilling Ben's too. "I'd hoped this situation with Gulli was over with. He's a dangerous man, as I'm sure you know."

"As far as I know, we are out of the situation with Gulli. His men came by just once and we heard he spoke to most of our customers. A few begged out of their deals with us but the majority stayed on. There hasn't been any trouble since then, at least that I know of. I'm worried that Renfro is stirring the pot down by the docks. He said he's spoken to some people who work with Gulli and that they aren't very supportive of the man."

Rhys unconsciously tapped on the hilt of his long knife and paused before speaking again. "If Renfro is going to get himself in trouble then he's going to take you with him. If Renfro won't stop, then I think you have two choices. You may not like either one."

Ben frowned and leaned forward on the smooth oak table.

"One, you disassociate yourself from Renfro," suggested Rhys. "Buy him out of the brewery, sell him the brewery, whatever it takes to cut ties. Gulli is a thug, but he's also a businessman. If he sees you're not involved then he will leave you alone. You may think you have nothing to worry about now, but if Renfro is talking to Gulli's men, then you should be worried."

Ben sighed. "Renfro is still enough of a friend that I can't do that to him, not yet."

"Option two then. You do this partnership with Reinhold. I don't think Gulli is stupid enough to cross his path. Reinhold is a fair man and he will do what he says with you. He's a hard man too with nearly unlimited resources. He won't back down from a fight if Gulli makes it one. He's the protection you need."

"I can't abandon Renfro and I don't think he'll stop," replied Ben with a grimace. "So it's not much of a choice. We partner with Reinhold."

Rhys smirked and raised his mug in cheers. "To bigger and better things."

He took a long pull of his drink then smacked it down for a refill. "Now, let's talk about something important. When I was downriver last week there was this barmaid with the biggest…"

THREE DAYS LATER, Ben grinned and shook his head as he followed Rhys and Renfro up a wide dirt track into the hills. The early autumn heat and humidity of the City was fading as they ascended away from the river. The quiet of the road would have been a welcome change for Ben after the constant noise and commotion in town, but Rhys and Renfro hadn't stopped talking since they left.

Each one was comparing exploits that had grown more and more lurid as the sun rose higher. By now, Ben was certain that everything coming out of the former thief's mouth was a lie, but it didn't stop Rhys from cackling at the tales and then coming right back with another to top it. By their accounts, there couldn't have been an unspoiled barmaid or wash girl within two days walk of the City.

Ben suspected Renfro had been a virgin when they'd finished their journey, but it seemed since then he'd grown in experience, or at least expanded his imagination.

"What about you, Ben?" called Renfro. "Did you ever manage to close the deal with that sweet lady or the country girl? What's her name? Meghan? I bet the Sanctuary is locking those two up tight."

Renfro had never made it to the Sanctuary to visit the girls and it had been five months since they arrived in the City, but that was just ridiculous. "Renfro, that country girl is my sister."

"Oh, right." Renfro paused to catch his breath and pull up his pants, which had been slowly sinking as they walked. "I guess I knew that. It's too bad really. I bet she'd be a handful."

Rhys caught Ben's eye and mock slapped his forehead. Rhys glanced at Renfro and said, "Maybe you should get a belt, Renfro. Or are you staying prepared for any wayward wenches we stumble across?"

"A belt?"

"Your pants are falling down. It's not befitting a man of your carnal aptitude," explained Rhys.

Renfro looked down and asked confusedly, "My what?"

"Don't worry about it. Let's get moving. We've got business to do and I want to see the legend in action once we get to the tavern."

Renfro flushed then scrambled after Rhys.

It dawned on Ben that Renfro was trying to be like Rhys. He probably saw the older man as a role model, but where Rhys flouted all conventions because he had self-knowledge and confidence in his abilities, Renfro seemed to be doing it because he thought that was the way to gain respect.

"Why can't I find some normal friends," muttered Ben as he fell in behind them.

THEY WERE HEADING to the small village of Vis, which was in the hills a two day walk from the City. Rhys vaguely mentioned he had business there and invited them along because it was a logging town with a bevy of timber mills, carpenters, and coopers. They hoped that by going further out from the City they could find a better price on fresh, empty ale kegs. They collected, washed, and reused the old ones when they could, but Reinhold's investment would launch another round of expansion and they needed new materials to keep up.

Contrary to Ben's hopes, Renfro continued to spend more and more time in seedy establishments by the docks. The few times Ben had stopped in some of the places, he'd immediately wanted to leave, and was always a little surprised when he checked his coin purse and found he hadn't been robbed. Ben hoped a short trip away from there and amongst real people outside of the City would do Renfro good.

The dirt track they were on was wide enough for a wagon and not much else. If two of them were to meet on this road, one would need to pull off into the tall grass on the side. The road followed a broad zigzag that gently rose and cut through thin stands of small trees.

"There can't be much of a lumber town up there with these trees," Ben shouted to Rhys.

Rhys held back to walk beside Ben then answered, "They've got bigger trees. Used to have big trees down here too. They cut them all down." Rhys gestured to low lumps in the grass that Ben hadn't noticed. "Tree stumps. This land isn't much use to anyone until the forest grows back some."

"Wow. So who logged all of this? People came down from Vis to do it?"

"This was Vis, or near it. Over the years the town has moved with the tree line. Three hundred years ago the forest ran almost down to the river. Back then, lumber came to the City from Venmoor. It was further but easier to ship on the water. Then someone invented Venmoor Steel. They all started making swords and using the lumber to fire the forges so Vis got started in the logging business. They come back through down here from time to time when the trees grow big enough."

The lumpy fields of tall grass spreading out around the road looked different all of a sudden. It had looked peaceful and open before. Now Ben couldn't help imagining what it had been when the forest extended for days in all directions.

"You know a lot of history. How did you learn all of that?" queried Ben.

Rhys smirked. "The world changes. I just know enough to say we've got to change with it."

~

THAT NIGHT, they camped near one of the stands of young trees and collected a pile of fallen branches to make a small cook fire.

Renfro was worn out from the physical activity and his blustering finally faded. As soon as their dinner of ham and beans was done, he curled up on his bedroll and was snoring before they finished cleaning up and putting away the frying pan.

"How is Amelie taking the news about the offensive on Issen?" Rhys asked in a quiet voice.

Ben flipped out his bedroll and answered, "She's not taking it well, I don't think. I got a note from Meghan saying the Sanctuary is keeping Amelie busy with studies to distract her but I know she wants to be home. Her family and all of her old friends will be at risk when the Coalition moves. Her father moved her to the Sanctuary because that's the one place she'd be out of harm's way, but you know her. She's not worried about her own safety."

"Stay close to her, Ben. Be the friend she asked you to be. That's what she's going to need. I have a weird feeling about all of this. It just doesn't feel right."

"Do you think the Coalition will prevail against Issen? I thought with Argren and the Alliance behind them they'd be safe. At least, that's what Amelie seemed to think in Whitehall."

Rhys rummaged around in his pack and produced a short tobacco pipe, which he took his time stuffing and lighting before replying. "No man knows what will happen in battle. That's why they have to fight the things. Just because a few overdressed frumpy old men signed some papers in Whitehall doesn't mean anything. Keep close to her and be there when she needs you."

~

IN THE MORNING BEFORE BREAKFAST, Rhys was up early and prodded Ben and Renfro to show him how they'd progressed with the Ohms. Renfro collapsed in a tangled heap after the fourth one. Ben got to thirteen before he reached the end of his knowledge.

"Very nice," acknowledged Rhys. "I see I need to come by and teach you some more. A little shaky toward the end. You've got the idea though. The movements get progressively more difficult, but once your mind and body fully understand what is needed, you will learn them quickly."

Renfro sat down to breakfast of hard crusted bread and a hunk of cheese. He griped, "I don't get it. If you want to fight, you learn to use a sword, a spear, or an axe. What's the point of these Ohms? Shouldn't you be practicing your sword? While you sit there stretching, the other guy is going to come up and chop you in two."

Rhys grinned. "I haven't been chopped in two yet."

Around a mouthful of cheese, Renfro snorted. "Yet, he says."

Ben remarked, "It's for balance, Renfro. It also builds speed, strength, stamina, and flexibility."

"Aye," agreed Rhys. "Holding and swinging a sword is one thing. Swinging it faster, harder, and more accurately than the other guy is how you win a fight. As for practicing with the sword, I've done that. I've learned over the years that the better I know how to move my body, the better I'm able to move my sword."

"Speaking of moving, let's get going and eat on the road." Ben gestured toward a dark cloud moving down the river valley. "I've gotten used to city life and don't relish the thought of what that rain will do to this dirt road."

～

WEEKS later and back in The City, Ben surveyed their new building. After the Vis trip, they'd finalized the deal with Lord Reinhold and moved the operation from the musty cellar to a spacious warehouse off the island. It was near the foot of one of the bridges, so Ben didn't think it'd be an issue getting back and forth. The area of town was a little rough, but as Reinhold said, the price was right.

With the new space and an influx of Reinhold's gold, Ben had been able to get proper fermenting tanks and other equipment for a full-scale brewery. They'd also hired new staff including assistant brewers and several more porters. It felt like they had a small army at their disposal and now Ben spent more time managing the people than he did actually brewing. He was responsible for the brewery operation and the money. Renfro was handling sales and deliveries. Renfro kept mentioning that he was willing to do the accounting, but without saying it outright, Ben declined because he didn't fully trust his friend.

Still, the partnership with Reinhold and the rapid expansion seemed to have lifted Renfro out of his dark mood. He was spending more time visiting reputable alehouses and less time in the sinks. He hadn't brought up anything about Gulli in a week, and Ben silently hoped that episode was behind them.

The assistant brewers did most of the activity now, following Ben's recipes, but he still liked to walk the floor and monitor the quality. He felt like none of them cared about it as much as he did. Then again, it was just a job for them.

While he was circling the room, one of his assistants caught his attention near the entrance and waved him over. A strange young man was standing with him. He had shaggy, unkempt hair and ill-fitting, nearly worn-through clothing. Prospective employee, thought Ben. It wasn't uncommon now that they'd expanded. Young men saw the growth and wanted to be part of it.

"Hi, what can I do for you?" Ben asked. Now that he was close, he noticed the boy kept fidgeting and glancing around the wide-open room like he thought someone was watching him.

"Can we speak in private?" the straw-haired boy croaked.

"Sure. Come on to the storage room," Ben said and then shot a quizzical look to his assistant. The man just shrugged. "What can I help you with? What's the secrecy about?"

"I... I saw you visit the Sanctuary, right?" The boy was sweating and hadn't lost his anxiousness as they stepped into the storage room. It was half-packed full of bulging sacks of barley and hops.

"Yes," replied Ben tentatively.

"Who are you visiting there?"

The question and the attitude raised Ben's hackles, but the boy didn't appear to be a threat. "I visit my sister and a friend. They are Initiates there."

A wave of relief swept through the boy's scrawny frame and he rubbed a hand over his face. "Your sister, good. I thought so."

"Why? What is going on? Is Meghan in danger or something?"

"Oh, I don't know. I don't know her," replied the boy. "Maybe."

Ben's concern grew. "What do you mean, maybe?"

"My sister Issabelle. She is an Initiate too, but I haven't seen her in weeks. She's stopped writing. When I ask about her, the guards tell me maybe she doesn't want to talk to me anymore, or they tell me maybe she's left. They tell me to forget about it and leave. She's my sister. She would never do that to me! What could they have done to her?"

The emotion painting the boy's face told Ben all he needed to know about his story.

"Maybe she's just been busy," answered Ben lamely. "The studies there are taxing. Sometimes my sister tells me all she wants to do is sleep on her free days."

They both knew that didn't explain why Issabelle would stop writing. There had to be an explanation, though.

"Tomorrow is the next free day," Ben continued. "I'll ask my sister about her. If they're both Initiates, surely they know each other."

"Yes, thank you!" the boy cried out and moved to embrace Ben.

After the boy left—Segor was his name—Ben couldn't shake the image of his tear-streaked face. Segor was assuming the worst, and based on what he said the guards told him, Ben thought something unusual must be going on.

THE NEXT MORNING, Ben left early for the Sanctuary. He usually arrived mid-morning and found the girls waiting for him, but he couldn't wait today. He had barely slept the night before, mulling over what Segor said and thinking about his encounters with Meghan and Amelie over the last few months. There was no question they were healthy and didn't seem to be in immediate danger. Now that he thought about it though, he realized they'd shared nearly nothing about what they were doing there. Lots of studying, that was all they'd told him.

He approached the massive copper gates that marked the only opening in the outer wall of the Sanctuary. The two faces—one old woman and one young—seemed to sneer instead of smile down at him.

One of the four guards posted at the entrance stepped out and rested a hand on his sword hilt. He wasn't blocking the path through the open gate, and the other guards didn't move, but his wide-legged stance was clearly meant to intimidate.

Ben strode close and the man grunted. "Worried about something?"

"What do you mean?" asked Ben.

The man's eyes flicked down to Ben's belt and Ben suddenly noticed the weight of his sword. It wasn't exactly illegal to carry weapons in the City, but it was frowned on in most establishments.

"Oh, I, uh, didn't even notice I was wearing it. Is there a rule against being armed here?"

"No," the guard answered coolly, "there's no rule against it. There are more dangerous things than steel inside these walls, boy. You try to start anything and you're going to find out what."

Ben flushed and skirted around the guard who stood rooted on his spot in the middle of the gate. The man left a hand on his sword and slowly pivoted on one boot as Ben passed. Ben broke eye contact and cringed as he imagined the guard's sword slicing his back.

Once in the gates, though, he felt some of the tension dissipate and had an unimpeded walk to the Initiate's Garden. He only spotted a few guards scattered loitering in the distance and they made no move toward him. There were certainly more of them than usual, but none spoke, and none seemed overly concerned about his sword. He cursed himself for thoughtlessly strapping it on. If he wanted to lay low and avoid suspicion, coming into this place armed was the exact opposite of what he should have done. Besides, the guard was right. Any of the mages here could fry him to a crisp before he got close. What did he think he was protecting himself from?

In the garden, Meghan and Amelie had not yet arrived, so Ben strolled around watching the other initiates and visitors out of the corners of his eyes. The guard presence here was increased also. There were two of them now as opposed to one. They both seemed bored and uninterested and were playing some sort of head-to-head card game.

Despite his watchfulness, he was surprised by Amelie when she came up behind him.

"Ben, when did you get here? I'm sorry I wasn't out earlier. Usually you come half a bell later."

"Oh, I haven't been here long," he started. It was hard to drop the polite conversational conventions. He took a deep breath and started again, "I came early because I was worried. Speaking of which," he peered around behind Amelie, "where is Meghan?"

"She studying," griped Amelie. "She doesn't do much else these days. We have a test later this week and that's all she's concerned about right now. Lady Towaal is briefly in town and has taken time to personally tutor her. It's rare we get time with a mage other than our assigned instructors. I'm sorry, Ben. I'm sure if it wasn't such a big test she'd be happy to come see you."

"No, that's all right. I'm just glad she is okay."

"What do you mean?" questioned Amelie. "Why wouldn't she be okay?"

"I heard there is another girl that might not be." He looped his arm in Amelie's and led her away from the guards and other people in the garden. "Issabelle?"

He caught Amelie as she nearly stumbled. She hissed, "How did you hear that name? I don't think it's a good idea to speak about her here. Or outside of here either."

"Her brother," he quietly responded. "He came to find me."

"Oh," said Amelie. She covered her mouth with her free hand. "I didn't know she had a brother. Why... How did he find you?"

"He hasn't been able to reach her and no one is talking to him," said Ben. "So he followed me back from here one day. He said it took him a week to work up the courage. He asked me to find out what happened. He's looking over his shoulder and afraid of talking to anyone."

"I don't think he needs to be afraid." She sighed. "But then again, maybe he should be."

"You do know her, then. What happened to her?" asked Ben.

Amelie carefully scanned the garden to be sure they were out of range for anyone to hear them. "You mustn't speak too freely about this. Not even in front of Meghan. The Sanctuary wouldn't look kindly on it, and they deal harshly with those who upset them. But if he's her brother, he has a right to know. Not all of our tests are in books, Ben. As we've spoken about, there are two parts to being a mage. One is knowledge. We are tested on that regularly. There are examinations, essays, debates, and other things that aren't so different from what my father's tutors had me do as a child. The other part, will, is tested differently. Sometimes, it can be dangerous to not pass the tests."

"Dangerous. How do you mean?" asked Ben.

"Things can happen when your will breaks. It might be a short depression that you quickly get over. Sometimes it's worse. In the very worst cases, you may not want to go on living." She looked at Ben out of the corner of her eye and he knew Segor's worst fears had come true.

His grip tightened on her arm. "You and Meghan are taking these tests too?"

"Don't worry. Both Meghan and I are strong-willed. It is hard, very hard, but we both have a natural ability for this sort of thing. Issabelle was a sweet girl, but she was not made to be a mage. She shouldn't have been here. Once Issabelle realized it, it was too late for her to leave. I know you must tell her brother something. Tell him it was a terrible accident. The less he knows... maybe it will be better for him. He needs to stop asking questions."

"Why? What will happen to him?" worried Ben.

"The Sanctuary doesn't like to admit failure. A girl like Issabelle should have been let go by the instructors before... before what happened. They made a mistake, or even worse, maybe they knew. These kinds of things are kept behind the walls. If this brother wasn't told a story or paid to vanish, well, he must not be someone they consider important enough to bother with. He must not be someone they think would be missed. Ben, you know Rhys and what he does. Not everyone who works for the Sanctuary is a nice person."

Ben was sickened at the thought his friends may participate in this kind of thing. If this girl Issabelle knew the risks and took them, he could understand that, but keeping it from her brother, it just didn't make sense.

"Are you saying that they'd hurt her brother if he knew about this?"

"Not if he knew about it. If he spoke about it. Really, I don't know what they would do. I just know what they are capable of doing." She glanced at Ben. "You do too. Think about Lord Frederick in Whitehall and what happened to him. If it was something that mattered to the leaders here, like the reputation of the Sanctuary, there is nothing they would stop at."

BEN MANAGED to leave without further encounters with the guards and breathed a deep sigh of relief when he turned his back to the scowling faces on the copper gates.

The City swirled by in flashes of movement and color as he walked, but his thoughts were moving even quicker. He felt terrible for Issabelle and Segor, but there was nothing he could do. Meghan and Amelie were still at risk, though. He wracked his brain, trying to think of anything he could do to help them.

Crossing the bridge from the island to the bank where their new warehouse sat, he saw a small boat drifting in the shallows. A ragged fisherman was hauling in a net and Ben saw when he lifted the tangle of twine out of the water that it was empty.

He passed over the bridge and his mood soured further. There had to be something he could do. Amelie seemed unconcerned about her own safety, but that's the way she always was. The rumors of secret meetings, what happened to Issabelle, and even his friend Rhys—everything he learned about the Sanctuary pointed toward it being a place he didn't want Amelie and Meghan involved with.

"Ben, come on!" A shout startled him out of his winding thoughts.

Renfro was leading two of the porters, Evan and Red, up the street toward him. They were hauling an empty handcart and were moving quickly.

"One of the carts broke a wheel and we have five kegs sitting unattended down by the granaries," huffed Renfro.

"The granaries?" Ben was trying to comprehend what Renfro was saying.

"We made a sale to a dive down there earlier this week. It's a rough area, Ben. If someone hasn't already rolled off our kegs they're probably sitting in the street drinking them. Come on!"

Ben fell in behind Renfro and the porters and saw Red give him an odd look. The man was big, but unlike most of the porters, it appeared to be blubber instead of muscle. He was named after his wild spray of red-gold hair that stuck up oddly and responded poorly to his constant efforts to pat it down. He was sweating profusely and nearly tripped forward into his cart when he saw Ben watching him.

"Let's get moving," encouraged Ben with a friendly grin. Red never really fit in with the rest of their team, and Ben felt bad for the man. He was regularly the target of rough teasing from the others.

The granaries were towering stores for grains, beans, and other foodstuffs and were all clustered along one section of the riverbank. No one typically lived or worked near them because the dust had a bad habit of exploding when a careless worker would introduce open flame in the enclosed spaces. During harvest times they were a hive of activity. During the other seasons, it was quiet with just the occasional wagon of product being hauled off.

"How did you find this place? I can't believe there's anyone down here who'd want to order five of our kegs," asked Ben skeptically.

They were surrounded by towering silos and bins. The hard-packed dirt streets were deserted.

"I didn't find the place," replied Renfro. "Red did. You think I'd be wandering around down here by myself? Evan, where did you say this wagon broke down? I don't see anything or anybody around here."

"It wasn't me," mumbled Evan as he walked ahead to peer down a cross street. "Red told me someone lost a wheel down here."

Renfro turned. "Red?"

The man stared straight ahead.

"Uuaagh!" cried Evan.

They all spun and saw a bald, thickset man standing over the prone porter. The man had a rag tied around the bottom half of his face and was holding a stout club.

Suddenly, Red lifted the heavy handcart over his shoulder and swung it with all his might at Renfro.

"Watch out!" yelled Ben.

The cart crashed into the side of Ben's little friend and sent him flying across the street. He landed in a heap, but before Ben could run to check on him, another masked man stepped out, also brandishing a club.

"There were supposed to be two. The little thief and one employee," growled the new man.

Red quaked. "This one is the other owner. He saw us walking over here and followed."

The man met Ben's eyes then menacingly raised his club. "Well then."

Without thinking, Ben smoothly swept his sword out of his scabbard and set his feet. There were three of them, but he had the superior weapon. Still, he thought, those heavy-looking clubs would do serious damage.

"Drop it son, and we'll let you live. This is just supposed to scare you a bit. You want to get serious though," the second masked man slapped his club against a meaty palm, "then we'll get serious."

Ben waited.

Red made the first move and charged, wildly dragging the handcart behind him. Ben rushed forward before Red could raise the cart, startling him and slowing his charge. The big man didn't expect Ben to charge and didn't move quickly enough to prevent Ben from smashing the hilt of his sword into the side of Red's sweat-streaked face.

The two masked men weren't surprised so easily. Both were quickly closing when Ben stepped over Red's limp body.

He had heartbeats to observe their movement before they closed. The first man who'd assaulted Evan moved a bit slower and had a slight limp with his right leg. The second man was the more dangerous of the two. He carried his weapon like he had plenty of experience using it.

Ben knew there was no use waiting anymore and rapidly sidestepped several times to his right to put the first man between him and the second. The man grunted and pivoted, giving Ben an opportunity. While the man was still turning, Ben darted in and slashed at his weapon arm. Ben felt the blade slice through flesh. The man screamed and flailed backward, dropping his club.

Splatters of crimson blood painted a dark pattern on the dirt streets.

Without his club and injured, the man shouldn't be much of a threat. He would live though. Ben hadn't intended to kill him. He wasn't sure who these men were or why they were attacking. By wounding one, he hoped he'd be able to question him later.

Renfro stirred in the street and Ben felt a trill of relief. The heavy cart had crashed into his friend hard.

The second man shoved his companion out of the way and

set himself to face Ben. He held his club upright with firm hands. The way he set his feet told Ben he was no stranger to combat.

The injured masked man stumbled across the street to lean against the wall of a granary. He gripped his injured arm. Blood leaked around his fingers in a steady flow. He was recovering from the shock. Judging from the blood, it was a deep cut. He wouldn't be returning to this fight.

"What are you waiting for, pup?" snarled the man.

Without speaking, Ben held back and assumed a defensive posture Saala had taught him. The more the man talked, the more he might learn about what was going on.

The man took half a step forward and paused, looking back at his bleeding friend and then at the unconscious Red.

Suddenly, Renfro staggered to his feet and let out a curse. "I think the son of a bitch broke my arm!" The former thief used his good arm to yank out a small razor-sharp knife. His other arm hung limp and twisted at his side. "I'm going to cut that bastard's throat and use him as fish bait."

"Shit, Arnold. Let's get out of here," barked the bloody man leaning against the granary.

The second man, who must have been Arnold, glared at his companion then back at Ben. "I'd love to stay and finish this, but my friend here needs to go. Follow us and I'll crack your skull open." He swished his weapon back and forth a few times as if to show he meant it and then gestured to the still unmoving Red. "You can have him."

Both masked men started slowly backing down the street before getting nearly a block away where they turned and ran.

Ben looked at Renfro, who was angrily scowling at their backs and muttering foully under his breath.

"You think I should chase them?" asked Ben.

"No, I think they may turn and fight. That wouldn't do us any good. The little I saw, he looks like he knows what he's about.

You probably couldn't injure him like the other. You would have to kill him, and we don't need that."

"Well, we have him," replied Ben, gesturing to Red. "You weren't serious about the throat and the fish bait, were you?"

"Oh, I want to. Believe me, I want to." Renfro stuck his knife back behind his belt with a cringe of pain. "But not as much as I want to know what the hell just happened."

THAT EVENING, their warehouse resembled a fortified camp more than the brewery it was. The former porter Red was still unconscious. The physician they brought in said he would survive. Renfro got a splint on his arm and bandages wrapped around his torso. It turned out he did have a broken arm and several ribs to go with it. He was ordered to rest and remain stationary. Instead, he was stalking around the warehouse, swilling from a skin of harsh liquor.

Renfro would heal with little permanent damage, but Evan was not so lucky. He passed shortly after they got him back to the warehouse. The physician said his skull was cracked by the blow and that he didn't have a chance. The mood was somber, but they had to understand what happened before they could take time to mourn Evan.

Saala was still travelling for at least another month, but Rhys had arrived quickly when he heard what happened. He gathered the details and then helped Ben set up buddy systems and arms for their work force. They were sure Renfro had been the target of the attack, but they didn't know if it was directed at the business or him specifically. Until they knew more, no one was to move around alone. They would monitor the warehouse in shifts. Those with families were encouraged to bring them in or send them elsewhere for safety.

Rhys was about to leave to investigate what he could at the scene when Lord Reinhold arrived.

Reinhold marched up to the doors, which a porter quickly swung open, and walked in without slowing. He brought a heavily armed squad of guards who spread out around the building and disappeared down side streets. A few followed him in and casually started examining the entryways and windows.

Reinhold saw Rhys and gave a hawkish smile. "I offer you a job and you turn me down, but when I really need it, I see you are here before me."

"Just here as a friend," responded Rhys.

"Very well," replied Reinhold. "Your presence is appreciated." Reinhold turned to Ben. "So, we are assuming it is our business that is under attack?"

Ben shrugged. "I'm not really certain, but I think it must be. The attack was planned and they used our own man to set us up. I wasn't supposed to be there, but they knew who I was. What else could it have been?"

Reinhold looked to Renfro. "Our partner has been known to be involved in under the table dealings. Despite that, being set up by our own man and continuing the attack against you, we must consider this an assault on all of us. You will have my full support in this. The warehouse will be watched by my men and any of our employees who wish it may stay at my barracks with their families. There is no better protection outside of the Sanctuary."

"The men will be glad to hear that," acknowledged Ben.

"I understand this Red is still unconscious. Is there anything we've been able to find out?"

"Well," Ben answered, "the attackers were masked and did not leave anything behind. All we know is that they know us and that one of them was named Arnold."

One of Reinhold's guards politely coughed and the lord scowled darkly. "I know," he said to the guard. To Ben, he continued, "I suspected, of course, but it's good to get confirmation.

Arnold is one of Gulli's thugs. He is well known to people who soon have their merchandise smashed, businesses burned, and customers threatened."

"So it is Gulli!" exclaimed Ben. "I thought so as well. I was worried that it could be, uh, someone else. It didn't seem like their style though. Do we go to the authorities now?"

Ben breathed a sigh of relief. He knew it was irrational, but after the latest dealings with the Sanctuary, he was worried they were behind this. It didn't make sense, of course—a mage could easily wipe out him, Renfro, and their entire warehouse. Gulli was dangerous, but he was a man just like the rest of them.

"Who else would it be?" asked Reinhold quizzically, then kept talking without waiting for a response. "No, there is no use bringing the Watch into this. Gulli isn't any better than a common criminal, but he is a lord, and that offers certain protections from the law. The name Arnold is definitely not enough for the Watch to even speak with him. Besides," Reinhold laced his fingers and glanced around the room, "sometimes these things are better settled outside of the law."

17

ENGAGEMENT

THE NEXT FEW days were both tense and boring. They continued to serve their customers and conduct normal business, but unless necessary, no one left the protection of the warehouse. Even when making deliveries, Reinhold's men went in force and provided support. They barricaded some entrances to the warehouse and added observation points on the roof. No one could easily approach without being seen. Racks of arms now stood by the door and squads of Reinhold's men were always nearby.

The City's Watch paid scant attention to the small bands of armed men roving the streets.

"It's not unusual for lords to take matters into their own hands," explained Rhys. "The privilege of having a title. Normally it's knives in the dark, so it doesn't make a mess in the streets and doesn't disrupt Sanctuary business."

BUT DESPITE THEIR PREPARATIONS, nothing happened.

There were no more attacks and they found out Gulli appeared to have fled the City. Renfro crowed with success, "We ran the bastard off. He must have realized he bit off more than he could chew. We're going to own this town!"

Ben wasn't so sure. Gulli knew before the attack that Reinhold partnered with them. The attack made no sense if Gulli was afraid of conflict with Reinhold.

Ben exchanged letters with Amelie and Meghan and they expressed the expected shock and dismay at what happened and offered condolences for Renfro. Ben was looking forward to seeing them in person on the next Newday but finally that morning, they got their first bit of activity. Red woke up from the week-long coma he'd been in.

"Water!" he called coarsely over and over again. They had trickled water into his mouth while he was unconscious to keep him alive, but now that he woke, they wanted him to be uncomfortable. He was locked in a storage room in the warehouse and they were waiting on Rhys to arrive to begin questioning him.

When Rhys got there, he tersely asked, "How is he?"

"He wants water and he's alive. We haven't asked him anything yet," answered Ben.

"Good. Come in with me and bring a water skin," instructed Rhys.

They entered the dimly lit storage room, which was bare except for a pile of empty sacks they had laid Red on. The big man was huddled in a corner of the room, staring remorsefully ahead.

Rhys tossed the water skin down next to Red and drew one of his knives, which he placed across his knees. He squatted down in front of the man.

"You are welcome to drink as much water as you need while you answer our questions," stated Rhys.

Red snagged the skin and took a long drink before looking back at Rhys and shuddering. "I know who you are and I know what you do. I'll answer whatever you need, but I don't know much."

"You better know something," growled Rhys menacingly.

Red sighed and leaned his head back against the rough wall. "I have a problem. I like to gamble. Sometimes I go down to one of Gulli's places, the Red Door. I, uh, I haven't been doing too well recently. Maybe longer than just recently."

Rhys slid a finger along the blade of his long knife and nodded for Red to continue.

"Well, some men, I guess they are Gulli's, they found me down there one night. Said they had a way I could wipe out my debt. All I had to do was get Renfro to a spot over by the granaries. That was it. I didn't know what they were going to do, I swear!"

"Surely you had to suspect what they were going to do," snarled Rhys.

"You're the one who hit Renfro with the cart!" exclaimed Ben.

Red flushed enough that his red face was visible in the dim room. "I didn't know for sure! I hoped, though. I never liked that little shit. Always running around like he's something special. Everyone knows he was some two-copper thief in Fabrizo. He just got lucky hooking up with you. And, yeah, I hit him. Once it started, I figured that was my shot to get personal."

Despite himself, Ben gained a sliver of respect for Red. The man was their captive and had to know Renfro was lurking around somewhere nearby. He still said what he did. He must really hate Renfro.

"How did you know they were Gulli's men? If they were going to wipe out your debt, they had to give you some assurance, right?" asked Rhys.

"I didn't know for sure," implored Red. "I mean, so what if they weren't? I wouldn't be any worse off than I was. Being in debt to Gulli, that's a tight spot."

"You don't think this is a tight spot?" Rhys gripped the hilt of his long knife but left it resting on his knees. "You said you know me. Are you certain you're not in a much worse situation now? I want you to think about that. Think about what you could say to me to get out of the spot you are in now."

Red sighed. "I don't know nothin'. I was just supposed to lead Renfro to the granaries. They said after I did it they'd send word to Gulli and my debt would be wiped clean. I don't even know the guys. I think they were the same ones who attacked you." He looked at Ben. "I'm pretty sure it was them."

"Send word to where?" asked Ben. He looked at Rhys, who rolled his eyes. They'd spent time planning how to get Red to talk. Now he was singing like a bird, but had nothing useful to tell them.

"I guess wherever Gulli is," muttered Red unhelpfully.

FIGURING out where Gulli went proved to be harder than finding out he was gone. By the next Newday, they still didn't have any promising leads. His business associates all claimed he was in the hills around the City. There were plenty of small villages scattered around and none of them made sense as a hideout for a lord on the run. His home in town and modest estate to the north on the river were both empty. Even the household staff had vanished.

Reinhold was fuming. He had moved into the brewery business to cut into Gulli's profits and erode his ability to do business in Reinhold's other markets. Ben realized that Reinhold now relished the idea of violence with his smaller rival. Whether he'd planned for this conflict all along or whether he was just seizing the opportunity, Reinhold was prepared and ready for anything except waiting. The man was a master strategist. Not knowing what his opponent was doing was driving him mad.

Ben tried to remain calm as he left to make the regular Newday visit with Meghan and Amelie, a pair of Reinhold's guards in tow. During the actual fight, he'd felt a weird sense of peace. The confusion of the last few months had been gone. There was only one direction he needed to move. Now, he was back to the nervous indecision he'd felt before the partnership with Reinhold. They were all ready to act, but they didn't know how.

When the tall copper gates of the Sanctuary came into sight, Ben looked back at the two guards following him and decided he needed to let them know the tension he'd felt recently from the Sanctuary guards.

"These guys are pretty wary. They haven't given me any real trouble, but you two with me and heavily armed, they might."

"Really?" asked one of the guards. He was clean-shaven except a thin blond mustache that matched his closely cropped hair. He was typical of one of Reinhold's guards—self-assured, neatly dressed, and always proper with someone he considered his better. He didn't think Ben was. "That's strange, having trouble with the Sanctuary. I can understand Gulli. I've been here count-less times though, and these guys don't give a rat's ass who comes and goes. What are you going to do in there, attack a mage?"

"Well…" Ben regretted speaking up. "I'm just saying to be aware. There's something going on around here and I don't know what."

"Okay, whatever you say. Maybe you're on edge about the other situation. I'm just saying, think about it. You've got reason to keep an eye over your shoulder, but this place ain't it."

At the gates, the old and young women's faces stared out stoically. It was funny, thought Ben, how they seemed to change in the sunlight. An overcast day lead to an overcast expression, maybe? He'd have to pay more attention next time he was there.

The guard's expressions had gone from watchful to uninter-ested. Ben slowed his pace expecting trouble, but one of the men merely lifted his hand to wave them on. "Visiting an Initiate, right? Take the path to the breezeway then five hundred paces to your right."

He didn't recognize the guard, but surely they had all seen him by now. There weren't that many Initiates or that many people to visit them. He'd been to the Sanctuary plenty of times.

"Glad you warned us," snarked Ben's blond companion.

~

MEGHAN AND AMELIE were both there when he got to the gardens.

"Oh, Ben! I hope you're okay. How is Renfro?"

"I'm fine." He was glad to see the girl's friendly faces. The warehouse had gotten to be a place full of angry glares and curses when another lead came up empty. "Renfro is alright too. We had to nearly tie him to the bed for a few days, but after some rest, he's back up again. He'll have his arm in a sling for a while though."

"What about your men? Some of them were hurt as well, right? A knock on the head?" asked Amelie.

Meghan stared over Ben's shoulder at Reinhold's guards. The two of them were looking around and pretending not to be eavesdropping.

"Uh..." He couldn't remember what he'd written about Red. Red had been press-ganged onto one of Reinhold's long haul merchant vessels with strict instructions to the captain that he be left far away and copperless. It was better than it could have been. Rhys had seconded Renfro's idea of cutting his throat and dumping him in the river. Reinhold was only interested in Gulli and didn't much care what happened to his minions. Ben found himself arguing to save the traitorous former porter, if only because the man wasn't the one who'd struck the blow to Evan.

He thought more than once that maybe the other's ideas of how to deal with Red would have been best. At the time, he couldn't bring himself to do it, though.

"They're not good. I don't know if they'll fully recover," he hedged. He didn't like talking about Evan's death, but he felt bad sugar-coating it with his friends. The girls didn't know the details and he hoped they never would.

"Maybe there's something we can do to help," replied Amelie tentatively.

Meghan shouted, "Amelie!"

"I know! But these are friends of ours."

"They are not your friends. You don't even know them!" chastised Meghan. "And even if they were, it wouldn't matter."

Ben looked between the girls in confusion.

"It matters to me," challenged Amelie.

Meghan simply rolled her eyes and stalked off to sit on a nearby bench. She stared back at Ben and Amelie impassively.

"This place is getting to her," muttered Amelie.

"I don't want to be a source of strife between you two. Aside from me and Saala, you just have each other."

"There's a lot of stress here, Ben. And the Sanctuary has some strong opinions. It's hard to stay true to yourself and not get absorbed in their philosophies."

Ben shifted uncomfortably on the pebble-strewn path. "What kind of philosophies?"

"I suppose I should just tell you since I already offered my help." Amelie sighed and spared a look at Meghan. In a whisper to avoid the eavesdropping guards, she continued, "We've been learning to heal. A little bit only, but maybe enough to help your friends. The Sanctuary takes a dim view of expending ourselves unless it is for Sanctuary business. Of course, Initiates are never supposed to practice off the grounds." She shrugged. "If someone is hurt, it's worth a try."

"I..." Evan was dead, and Red, wherever he was now, didn't need that kind of help. "Reinhold hired the best physicians. I think they did everything that can be done. Honestly, I've seen what Towaal can do, and even she couldn't help with this. Thank you for offering, though. I appreciate it."

A relieved-looking Amelie nodded quickly and brushed an errant strand of hair back over her ear. "Okay then. I had to offer."

"So, healing. Are you a mage now?"

The spark of the old Amelie, before the Sanctuary, shined through briefly. She smirked back at Ben. "I'm a mage like you were a blademaster the day we left Farview."

BEN FELT a little better as he walked back through the busy streets of the City. His two guards shadowed him several steps behind. He almost felt alone, and like things were back to normal. Whatever that meant anymore.

He hadn't lost the watchful edge that he gained over the last week, though. He spied Rhys heading toward him through the crowd while he was still a city block away.

"Come on. I want to show you something," called Rhys.

Ben fell in beside Rhys.

"You two can head back to the warehouse," Rhys said to the guards.

"You sure?" asked the blond to Ben.

"It's broad daylight and I'm with him." Ben smiled as he gestured to Rhys.

"Right." The guard eyed Rhys up and down then said to Ben, "The name's Henrick. Everyone on Lord Reinhold's staff knows me. Get the word to someone and I'll be there if you need me. The lord wants you protected."

"What's going on?" asked Ben as he and Rhys moved off into the current of people in the street.

"I've got to leave," answered Rhys. "A little bit of work. Nothing serious, but it's urgent. The damn Veil herself requested both Towaal and I go and that we leave tonight. Terrible timing with what's going on. I hate to leave you while Saala is out of town too, but I can't say no to the Veil. I want to show you a few things before I go."

"Lady Towaal is in town?" inquired Ben. He hadn't seen her since they arrived in the City.

Rhys nodded. "She never stays long. I think she just got back yesterday."

They arrived at The Flying Swan Inn. Mathias saw them from behind the counter and waved them back. Ben followed Rhys through the busy kitchen and out to the yard behind the building. He'd been back there before making deliveries. This time of day it was empty except for two practice swords leaning against the wall of the inn.

"Practice swords?" asked Ben. "I thought you never practiced."

"I don't," replied Rhys, "but you do. The blademaster taught you well and you're on your way to being a perfectly adequate swordsman. There's more to it than memorizing some forms, though. You do that and you're just waiting for the guy who learned one more than you. Then it's over."

Ben picked up both of the blunted weapons and tossed one to Rhys. "So, what will you show me then?"

Ben swished the sword back and forth a few times to get a feel for the weight and balance then started loosening up. In the months he'd known Rhys, he'd never seen the man practice.

He had seen him in combat at Snowmar, though. Rhys had a smooth elegance with his weapons that surely came from experience. The rogue moved like a powerful wind. Even Saala was impressed, so Ben was both excited and nervous about what would happen next.

Suddenly, Rhys surged across the space between them and slapped Ben's practice sword from his hand before he could react. Ben dove across the hard-packed dirt, snatched at his sword, and rolled to his feet, ready to face Rhys.

Instead of the expected attack, he saw the rogue's jaw drop open. The swordsman pointed over Ben's shoulder and Ben spun to face the new threat, only to the feel the painful slap of the practice sword against his bicep, sending him stumbling to the side.

He angrily turned back to Rhys and demanded, "What are you..."

Rhys launched a cloud of loose dirt at Ben's face and he felt his practice sword yet again violently smacked away from him while he tried to shield his eyes.

"Come on!" Ben shouted.

"Get your sword," responded Rhys coolly.

"Not until you tell me..."

Rhys jabbed his own practice sword hard into Ben's midsection and Ben collapsed to the ground breathless.

Rhys squatted down next to Ben, who was still gasping and painfully clutching his stomach. "I will tell you. I am teaching you how to fight."

"By throwing dirt at my face?" grumbled Ben.

"It was effective, wasn't it? I won that round. You should appreciate what Saala has taught you, he is very skilled at what he does, but fighting isn't sparring, dueling, or some refereed blademaster qualification. A real sword fight is about maiming or killing your opponent. And when someone is trying to kill you, you do anything you can to get an advantage. You distract them. You throw dirt in their face. You attack when they aren't looking." Rhys stood and gestured for Ben to get up. "Saala and his ilk bring honor to the profession of swordsman, but it isn't about honor or following some set of rules. It's about winning and staying alive until tomorrow. You can worry about your honor then."

Ben sat up slowly. His stomach really hurt from where the blunted point of Rhys' wooden blade hit him.

"Why are you telling me this now? Saala spent months practicing with me on the road and you just watched."

"You didn't need it then. You were with me, Saala, and

Towaal. What more protection could you have?" He grinned. "Of course, at the time I didn't expect you'd get captured by the Thieves' Guild in Fabrizo, face a swarm of demons at Snowmar, or anger a lord of the City enough that he sent a hit squad after you. I think, despite yourself, you've chosen to live a rather dangerous lifestyle." Rhys reached down and hauled Ben up to his feet. "We don't have much time and the blademaster made a good start. I will teach you as much as I can about winning a fight. It's about taking what you've learned so far and adding creativity and ruthlessness. Knowing all of the proper forms does you no good if your opponent knows them all too. The forms Saala taught are the most efficient and powerful strokes or defenses you can make in a particular situation, but they don't take into account that your opponent might anticipate that, or might react some way other than swinging his sword."

The rest of the afternoon was spent with Rhys landing strike after strike. By the end of it, Ben was sure he had more bruises and welts than he would have with a month of training under Saala. Rhys was fast, strong, and efficient with his movements. His real advantage though was that Ben could never guess what he was going to do. Rhys anticipated Ben's movements before they even happened. Even when Ben attempted some creativity and modified a swing, Rhys was ready.

"Every movement that is taught by master swordsmen also has a counter that is taught," said Rhys while he circled the hard-packed dirt courtyard. "Inventing your own movements can help, but don't expect that to always work. I suspect everything that can be done with a sword has been done. Instead, you need to go beyond the forms and teach your body to adapt to the moment. You are most effective when there can be no expectation of what you will do next. If the most efficient stroke from a position is high, that only makes sense if your opponent doesn't know to counter it." Rhys continued probing strikes at Ben while he spoke. "If your opponent is in position to parry your high swing, then you go low. Do not plan a complicated sequence of attack. Instead, attack your opponent's vulnerabilities and weaknesses. Use your environment. Skilled swordsmen are taught to read your eyes to anticipate a movement, so try tricks with the eyes to confuse them. Shift your balance when it won't throw you off and yell at them or taunt them. Make them emotional. If you're not willing to fight dirty, then you shouldn't be fighting."

Finally, as the sun began to drop behind the slender towers of the City, Ben flopped down by the wall and leaned back exhausted. He was too tired and in too much pain to even remember the sword forms Rhys was trying to shake him out of.

"Where did you learn all of this?" panted Ben.

"Experience. Lots of experience. Come on. I'll buy you an ale."

Mathias was on the way to their table with a pitcher and mugs before they even sat down.

"He teach you anything?" the gruff barkeep asked as he plunked the ale down on the table.

"I spent most of the afternoon falling down and getting hit. So, too early to say," replied Ben with a pained groan. Mathias had grown to be a good friend. He seemed to never leave the Flying Swan, and was always willing to make time to speak to Ben.

"My first lesson with him was the same. Pissed me off at the time, but it kept me alive through some pretty nasty situations."

Ben frowned. Rhys had maybe a decade on Ben, but Mathias had at least the same on Rhys.

"He trained you? Uh, when was that?" inquired Ben.

Mathias snorted. "You don't ask an old war dog like me specifics. We like to talk in generalities. Everything before I bought this inn is 'back then'. Whether I was a young pup or making my last march, it's all the same time to me now."

"I told you I had experience," added Rhys with a wink. Then he grinned and said to Mathias, "I don't remember you ever being a young pup."

~

EARLY THE NEXT MORNING, Ben was rousted out of bed by a heavy banging on his door. He, Mathias, and Rhys had put down a few more ales. He got a little tipsy, but he stopped himself before he could be called drunk. As he stretched out the soreness from Rhys' training and winced at the more severe bruises, he was glad he'd learned at least one thing from his time with the rogue—don't try to match the man drink for drink.

"I'm coming," he cried coarsely. He crossed his tiny apartment in a few steps to the door.

He peeked through a gap in the doorframe and saw Reinhold's mustachioed blond guard, Henrick, standing impatiently.

When Ben opened the door, Henrick barked, "Glad you survived whatever it was he put you through yesterday. Get dressed and pack for travel. Bring your sword. We found where Gulli has been hiding."

Against Henrick's protests, Ben swung by the warehouse on the way to Reinhold's estate north of the City. Renfro and many of the others clamored to go with them, but Ben insisted everyone stay and continue to work like any normal day. The customers weren't going to care about a delay to settle scores.

Renfro pulled Ben aside. "Come on, Ben. If anyone is going, it should be me. They nearly killed me!"

Ben smiled then poked a finger into Renfro's newly healed arm. The little thief winced in pain.

"You can't go out there with that," declared Ben. "If anyone came at you, there's no way you could defend yourself."

"We'll be behind Reinhold's men," argued Renfro. "They're professionals and I have no intention of getting in their way." Renfro sighed and rubbed the spot Ben had poked. "But I get your point. Just promise me, we'll get justice for Evan and what they did to me."

"I don't think we need to worry about that. I think Reinhold wants to use this to settle things with Gulli once and for all."

"You better go." Renfro nodded toward Henrick and clapped his good hand on Ben's shoulder. "I think he's going to have a heart attack if he doesn't get you to the estate soon. Good luck Ben."

~

REINHOLD'S ESTATE was two bell's worth of brisk walking from the boundaries of the City.

"I'm surprised Reinhold comes out here very often," muttered Ben as he matched Henrick's quick pace. The guard didn't have any sympathy for the sword practice or drinking Ben had done the previous day.

"This estate is closer to the City than most," replied the guard. "He keeps a place in town and only comes out here when he wants to relax, or marshal forces, I guess. Besides, when he comes out he rides a horse."

Horses were almost exclusively used for commerce. It was too expensive to keep and feed one for any other purpose. Keeping one stabled in the City was ludicrous. Ben imagined spending the gold wasn't really a problem for Reinhold, though. He decided he was right when they finally made it to the expansive manicured grounds of Reinhold's country estate. It was even more impressive on land than it had been from the river. The entire thing was encircled by a low stone wall and it must have covered the same area as the Sanctuary.

As far as Ben could see across the gently rolling hills, there were little bits of carefully placed trees and bushes with the occasional small structure he supposed was for resting while strolling the massive grounds. He could also see little foot bridges that may have been crossing unseen streams meandering through the property.

The path to the estate was behind an imposing stone and iron gate that rose ominously up from the low walls and a thicket of colorful flowers that surrounded its base. A cobblestone path led to a huge building that Ben thought was more appropriately labeled as a castle than a country estate. Ten Flying Swan Inns could fit inside the thing. The marble-clad walls looked like they could withstand a barrage of trebuchet or catapult fire for a week.

Ben was so focused on the estate that he missed the handful of guards standing by the gate. To Henrick, one called, "Glad you made it. Looks like the lord will be ready to march in half a bell. They're staging over by the festival grounds." To Ben, he smirked. "First time here?"

"Uh, yeah. Nice place," replied Ben, peering through the gate at the massive palace.

"Come on," said Henrick. "Bodas was supposed to bring my pack but he's a lazy ass. I need to check things over before we leave. Shouldn't be gone more than a few days, but if I get on the road with no socks, I'm going to kill that fool."

THE FESTIVAL GROUNDS turned out to be a wide-open flat grassy area. It was packed full of milling men adjusting packs and checking weapons. There were about one hundred of them and they were all decked out in Reinhold's livery. Most wore light chain mail and had swords strapped to their sides. A few carried spears and bows as well. One massive, brutish-looking man leaned against a wicked battle axe that was taller than Ben.

"Stay away from him," advised Henrick. "That's Gra. Reinhold got him from some western island and they haven't really tamed him yet. He carries that damn axe everywhere and is always looking for excuses to use it. After the first week he joined, Reinhold banned him from the City and keeps him up here. There were some incidents. When things get hot, he's just as likely to take your or my head off as he is Gulli's."

The rest of the men seemed friendly enough, though, and Henrick turned out to be a squad leader. Ben surmised he'd been with Reinhold for many years and was now trusted with more than keeping trespassers off the property.

"You'll march with my squad. If it gets hairy, you stay behind us," explained Henrick. "I know you think you know how to use that blade, but leave this to us. Of course, I expect Gulli's thugs will throw down their weapons as soon as they see us, but you never know."

"Of course," answered Ben. "I have no problem watching from the back."

"Good," said the guard with a nod.

SHORTLY, Reinhold appeared out of the palace and they started to march. With a glance, Ben saw how Reinhold wanted this to end. The lord was decked out in chainmail, just like his men, and had an elegant-looking long sword strapped to his back. Whether he really knew how to use it or not, Ben didn't ask. His grim face told all that needed to be known.

Ben wasn't comfortable with how this expedition was going, but he didn't think there was anything he could do to stop it. In the City, Reinhold was a polished urbane merchant banker. Now, he looked every bit the bloodthirsty warlord. Ben hoped Gulli's men did throw down their weapons quickly, because Reinhold was going to take any excuse to slaughter all of them.

They had gotten a report that Gulli was holed up in a town called Arrath. One day into the march, they got confirmation from a second rider Reinhold sent immediately after hearing the first report. Gulli only had a dozen of his thugs with him and his household staff. The rest of his men were assumed to have quit and run for the hills when they realized who they'd pissed off.

The rider rested with the group then started scouting ahead on his horse. Reinhold rode at the head of the column. The rest of them walked.

Arrath was another two days' travel. The plan was to move into the woods surrounding it and gather further intelligence on where exactly Gulli was. With one hundred heavily armed and trained men, they could easily overrun the entire town if need be, but no one thought that would be necessary. The town people of Arrath would be happy to give up Gulli in exchange for Reinhold's good will and gold.

The first night on the road, Ben huddled around a small campfire with the men in Henrick's squad. They had the confidence of men who were with one hundred of their peers, but there was still a little nervous excitement in the group.

"The pay is good but you don't see much action with Reinhold," explained one of the younger men. "I spend most of my time patrolling the border of the estate. Been doing it a year and haven't seen anyone trying to come in yet. Unless you count deer and birds." He snorted.

"Working in town isn't any better. You spend all day in the lobby of the lord's tower or following him around to meetings, which is even worse," chided another of the men.

"Yeah, but at least there's something to do at night! Go out, meet some friendly ladies, and show 'em a good time. There's only so long you can spend watching Gra practice with that damn axe before you start to lose your mind."

"Well, at least this will be a little excitement. Who knows? Maybe they'll try to put up a fight."

THE MORNING of the third day, the squad leaders strode around the camp, kicking awake the late sleepers and shouting for everyone to get ready. They stopped early the previous night and were two bells outside of Arrath, far enough that word of their approach wouldn't be known in the town yet. "Look alive, boys. This is real action. We're not hiding the mistresses from each other today!"

Henrick gestured to Ben and the young guard who'd been speaking the other night. "You two, stay back at least a hundred paces. Soan, make sure Ben doesn't engage."

"What!" exclaimed the young guard with a scowl on his face. "I'm supposed to be at the front with the rest of the squad."

Ben had never seen a heavily armed and armored man pout before. It wasn't very becoming.

"You're supposed to do what I say," growled Henrick. "How about this? You keep Ben out of it, and you get City duty for a month when we get back."

Mollified, the young guard looked at Ben and shrugged. "Sorry. Guess we walked up here for nothing."

∽

BEN KNEW where Henrick's orders were coming from but he didn't know what he could do to change them. Ben had been the voice of reason before. He'd argued to keep Red alive and he'd hesitated about some of Reinhold's methods of interrogation when they were still looking for Gulli. He suspected Reinhold wasn't interested in hearing a voice of reason today.

Fair enough, he thought. Gulli's men had tried to injure or kill Ben and Renfro. If they were too stupid to see how outnumbered they were today, they'd pay the price. He hoped they threw down, but this situation was out of Ben's control.

His thought was confirmed when Reinhold made his rounds to encourage the men.

Reinhold placed a hand on Ben's shoulder. "After today, Ben, you will become a wealthy man. The ale trade in the City is going to be wide open and we're positioned to take advantage. Whether it's with a quill and ink, or a sword and spear, there is nothing like beating an opponent and relishing your success. I'll teach you this. Tonight, we drink the finest wine and ale Arrath has to offer, and we discuss our partnership. You're a little soft, but I like you. I see a young me in you. We're going to do great things together."

Reinhold's glassy eyes spoke to the fine wine he'd already been enjoying that morning. The perfectly polished silver pommel of his sword peeking from above his shoulder spoke to how little he was involved in real combat. One thing Reinhold said was true, though, he didn't care if it was quill and ink or sword and spear. He just truly enjoyed beating someone. Today, he was going to beat Gulli and he was already celebrating.

Soon after he spoke to Reinhold, Ben saw a rider come into camp. Suddenly, shouts went up for everyone to get their gear and get moving.

Henrick jogged back from a meeting with the other squad leaders and explained, "We sent a man into town last night and he spotted Gulli at the inn. Our man says Gulli is holed up there and seems to think no one will notice him. We'll be done with this by lunch," he finished with confidence.

The troop started marching. Ben and the young guard dutifully fell back a hundred paces. Ben decided he was fine with that. The men were psyching themselves up for blood, and whatever Gulli's men did, their lord was unlikely to survive this day. The certain and unnecessary bloodshed made Ben queasy. He, Renfro, and Evan had been the victims of the attack, but Reinhold had taken to the cause like it had been him. The situation had escalated too far on both sides to turn back now. It had never needed to come to this place.

"I hear you brew an excellent ale," began the young guard. "Maybe when we get back you can show me around to some good taverns. These older guards just sit around the barracks dicing all evening. I want to go out and meet some women. You've got to be in the taverns all day, right? You can show me which places have the pretty girls."

"Sure, when we get back." Ben sighed.

The terrain around Arrath was heavily wooded. The rolling hills near the river turned into steep ridges and valleys. The road to Arrath humped over the ridges as it skirted the foot of a small mountain range. Arrath itself, according to Henrick's sketch in the dirt the night before, was located in a narrow valley. It was a small tin mining town. Business couldn't have been very good, thought Ben. They hadn't seen another traveler or a merchant in two days. All the better for their purposes, though. They needed the element of surprise to prevent Gulli from running away into the forest.

A hundred paces back, they started losing sight of the troop as the road climbed and dropped over the ridges. Ben wasn't worried. There was only one way to go and no one was getting around all of Reinhold's men.

If it weren't for the mission they were on, it would be a pleasant walk. The early fall weather was refreshing after summer in the City and the woods around them were peaceful.

"Hurry up," pressed the young guard. "We may not be able to engage, but I want to watch."

They crested a hill and saw the troop strung out on the road before them. Reinhold and the other rider, his scout, were in the lead. Everyone else was marching in rows of four. The household guard was making a good show of looking like a real army unit, thought Ben.

Then he paused. He caught a glimpse of movement in trees below them on the ridge. Ben grabbed the young guard's arm and pointed down.

"What?" asked the guard.

A dark grey clad man stepped out of the trees and flapped a bright red handkerchief.

"Who is that?" continued the guard.

"I don't..."

An animal cry broke the quiet of the forest. Ben saw Reinhold's horse buck upward, sending the lord tumbling over its back.

Instantly, the forest became alive with swarms of grey clad figures bursting from the undergrowth and charging into Reinhold's men. A volley of arrows arced over their heads as they hit Reinhold's line.

Ben swept his blade from his scabbard and stepped forward, but the young guard pulled him back. Without saying anything, they both saw the fight was over before it started.

Reinhold's men were outnumbered, surprised, and overwhelmed quickly, but they didn't all go down without a fight. Ben saw the axe man Gra step out of the line and meet the charge head on. Muscles bulging, he cleaved through the first wave of the grey-clad men like they were blades of grass. Within heartbeats, though, he was surrounded and sprouting several arrows from his back. He kept churning and surged forward into the midst of his enemies to cut down several more.

"Oh shit," the young guard mumbled. "Lord Jason."

A pony-tailed blond man walked up to Gra and smoothly ducked under the spinning axe. He then casually sliced the big man open from groin to neck. Without pausing, the newcomer plunged into the thick of the battle. Reinhold's men perished in his wake.

Ben turned to the young guard but the man had broken into a full sprint back down the road and away from the battle.

"Lord Jason?" Ben asked himself aloud. "The Coalition's Lord Jason?"

He looked back to the battle and quickly realized he needed to move too. Reinhold's men, in the span of a few breaths, had been wiped out. The grey-clad men were covering the road and ruthlessly dispatching any survivors. Ben jumped to the side of the road and sank down amongst the tall grasses there. He started wiggling closer to the forest but could still clearly see the road below.

The man who must be Lord Jason was dressed the same as the others, but he stood out like a wolf amongst a pack of lap dogs. Even if Ben hadn't seen how easily he put down Gra, he would fear this man. Lord Jason moved to the head of the column and knelt beside a body before rising again, holding a scabbarded sword with a flashing silver pommel. Reinhold didn't even draw his weapon realized Ben.

Ben slid on his stomach into the thick undergrowth just in time. A handful of the grey-clad men appeared on the hill where he had been standing. One called out, "Look. Someone dropped a sword."

Ben cursed himself until he realized he was still holding his own sword. The damn guard must have dropped it to run faster.

"Go tell Lord Jason one got away," called another voice.

Cringing down amongst the low-lying bushes and grasses, Ben was afraid to move. The men were close enough that they were sure to hear him pushing through the leaves and branches. He could only hope he was deep enough that they wouldn't spot him.

"Someone got away?" asked a strong, even voice.

"We think so, sir," answered the original speaker. "We found a sword and belt in the middle of the road. They could have dropped it to run."

"Strange," replied the voice. It sounded like silk whispering over steel. "They didn't have scouts out, so why a rear guard? Regardless, we must move quickly for the City now. Brons, send a runner to alert the Sanctuary we're coming and let them know someone got away. Whoever it is, they probably aren't stupid enough to return to the City, but if they do and they start talking, well, that will be handled by the mages." The voice trailed off ominously.

"Should we dispose of the bodies, sir?"

"No, there isn't time for that now. We must move faster than planned. It makes me nervous that this person wasn't part of the column. I don't like not knowing who it was. If somehow they understand what they just saw, they could alert the girl. Without Reinhold in the way, Gulli can take our gold to lock up the arms supply from Venmoor then cut off Issen and the rest of the Alliance. Lord Gregor is too hard headed to break just because of that, though. We need his daughter."

18

FLIGHT

DAMN IT. Damn it. The words ran through Ben's head over and over as he followed behind the Coalition forces. He had stayed in hiding while they gathered up and started marching. Now he was as close behind them as he dared. He had to get to the City and warn Amelie before they got there.

He knew he could pass them in the night, and one person could move faster than a party of hundreds. His biggest concern was how to contact Amelie and Meghan once he made it to the City. Lord Jason had mentioned sending a runner to the Sanctuary so they must be in cahoots. The Sanctuary was at Argren's Conclave, but apparently that didn't mean much to them. Being involved in a kidnap plot for one of their own members was unexpected but not surprising given what he'd been finding out over the last few months.

The slaughter of Reinhold's men weighed on him also, but not as much as he thought it would have. It was a tragedy, and he couldn't help but think of the men he'd gotten to know and their families. Henrick and others had been friendly to Ben, but they were the ones who had marched and they had intended to engage Gulli. None of Reinhold's men that Ben met were unwilling to do violence. Many of them were eager. Live by the sword and die by the sword, he figured.

That evening brought his first chance to get around the Coalition men and nearly got him caught. As the sun set, he started moving more cautiously, but not enough so. It was only a flick of light on top of a nearby hill that alerted him to a sentinel. These men were professional soldiers behind enemy lines. They had sentinels stationed around the camp and were eschewing fires or other signs that would give them away. The lone sentinel lit a pipe just in time for Ben to see him before drawing too close.

He looped wide into the countryside and walked well clear of the boundaries of the Coalition camp. It cost him a bell to get by, but caution ruled over speed.

Once in the clear, Ben set a ground-covering pace. Fortunately, the moon was only a few days away from full so light was not a problem. The open road was easy to navigate for a single person. The solo hike through the darkness reminded him of when he left Farview. The sense of dangerous excitement he felt that night wasn't too far different from what he felt now.

Two nights of long marches and cold camps later, he made it back to the City in the afternoon. He shaved a day off the time it had taken to get to Arrath with Reinhold's men. Whatever he was going to do had to be finished by morning, though. After that, the Coalition men may be there. Jason would push his troops hard. Once they made it to the Sanctuary, there would be nothing Ben could do.

He thought about going straight to the warehouse to enlist the help of Renfro and their men, but attacking the mages would be futile and likely a death sentence for anyone he spoke to. Stealth was the only option, and more men couldn't help him with that.

He would have gone to Saala of course, but he was out of town escorting Tomas. Rhys had left with Lady Towaal. The Issen Consulate was another choice, but they were unlikely to believe Ben. If they did, they'd probably send a representative for an official discussion with the Sanctuary. The Consulate would also be the first place Jason checked if Amelie escaped.

That left Mathias. The barkeep was his friend. He may be willing to help. He wasn't directly tied to Amelie, so no one would suspect, but what was Ben even asking him to do?

The Flying Swan Inn was crowded as usual when he arrived. He peered around the room nervously. He chastised himself when he realized he didn't know what a Coalition man would look like. They wouldn't know him either.

Mathias approached him and instantly saw something was wrong. "The kitchen or my room? Let me get some ale."

"Your room," replied Ben tersely. "And no ale tonight."

Mathias frowned, but led Ben through the common room without further questions. "Tell me what's going on," said the barkeep when they were out of earshot of the common room.

It burst out of Ben in a rush. "Reinhold and all of his men are dead. There are Coalition forces within half a day of here intending to kidnap Amelie or worse. And somehow, they are working with people in the Sanctuary."

"Wait. What?" The war-scarred veteran fell into his chair and stared incredulously at Ben. "Are you sure? How could you be sure? Never mind. You wouldn't make this up."

"I am sure. I saw the ambush on Reinhold and saw all of his men killed. Just me and the one other who was guarding me got away. I hid and overheard the Coalition men talking about their plans. One more thing. Lord Jason is the one leading them here."

"Damn!" exclaimed Mathias. "We have to get that girl out of there tonight."

"I know," Ben responded quietly, rubbing his hands over his

face. The pace to get back had been punishing and he was exhausted. "But how?"

~

FOUR BELLS LATER, full dark had descended on the City. Ben and Mathias were bobbing in a small dingy in the river just north of the island.

The gates to the Sanctuary were heavily guarded and not worth considering. The walls surrounding it were high and smooth as glass. Even with a grappling hook, it would be noisy and maybe not even possible to climb up. The hook could just slide off. Getting back out with Amelie and Meghan would be even worse.

Once Mathias calmed down, he pointed out that the water side was the only option for stealth. There were parks open to the water, which rarely had people in them during the day, and they both hoped would be empty at night.

They rowed closer. Mathias silently dipped the oars into the water. Muscles bulged as he propelled them toward the bank. The small boat glided through the slow-moving current.

"I don't see any guards," whispered Ben. He was perched at the bow and scanning the grounds intensely for any signs of life.

"They must think no one is stupid enough to assault this place. That, or they have some magical ward we're about to trip,"

Ben stared back at Mathias. "A magical ward?" he hissed.

Mathias shrugged as the boat bumped up against the thick grass of the island. He whispered back, "I don't know. I've heard about them in stories."

"Shit." Ben cursed his friend for not saying something sooner, but what other choice did they have? No other entry point was feasible.

"If I trip some ward, if you see something happen, get out of here," instructed Ben. "There's no use both of us getting caught.

This isn't your fight. Worst case—you can alert the Consulate tonight and maybe they can do something."

"Those political hacks?" Mathias snorted. "I'm sure they'd manage to get a meeting called by the end of the week. This is it. I will wait out here as long as I can."

Ben nodded curtly and slithered off the bow of the boat onto the gently sloped riverbank. He had a good idea of where the Initiate's Quarters were. For a boy used to navigating the woods and hidden landmarks around Farview, it would be no challenge to keep that fixed in his mind. The problem was that neither he nor Mathias knew what else was in the compound, or how he would find Meghan and Amelie once he got to their building.

Worry about that later, he told himself. For now, he was in an open park with three squat buildings visible. It was late evening, so lights were still on in some windows. He didn't see any people. They hoped that coming now instead of the middle of the night would disguise any noise he made as normal activity.

He set off in a low crouch for a wide gap between two of the buildings that he thought would lead in the direction of the Initiate's Quarters. So far, so good. No alarms were raised and no rush of guards with weapons drawn.

Well into the park, he found a path and started following it, but quickly jumped off when he heard the telltale jingle of a man in armor.

Ben squatted down next to the thick trunk of a tree and waited. Near two of the buildings he'd been about to pass between, two figures popped in and out of the intermittent light from the windows. Two guards on their rounds. From their pace, they were in no hurry. They drew closer and he heard the low rumble of their voices in conversation. Before they came close to his hiding place, they turned around another building and kept walking into the darkness.

So, they did have guards and they worked on patrols, Ben

realized. It would make it easier to see them coming, but he had to be aware at all times.

With the guards out of the way, he scuttled forward and moved between the two buildings right where they had passed.

Halfway there, he stopped and stood upright before continuing at a normal, if somewhat hurried pace. If anyone caught a glimpse of him it would be better to look like he belonged than sneaking around.

Staying on the path he found worked well. It was well maintained, so there was no risk of noisily stumbling over something, and it seemed to go in the direction he needed. Away from the river, the grounds became wilder with tall grasses and stands of trees similar to what he saw at the front gates. It made sense. If the mages were interested in strolling on the grass they would do it near the fresh air at the north of the island by the water.

Luckily, the buildings of the Sanctuary were spread out and the place had more space than they needed. He encountered people two more times but these groups were carrying some small object in their hands that emitted a low, steady yellow light which they shined in front of them. It made it easy for him to move off into the darkness and avoid detection. The guards must intentionally be in the dark to not give away their positions or spoil their night vision.

The buildings he could see were nondescript and it was impossible to identify their purpose from the outside. One did give him pause. It emitted a noxious sulphurous smell. An angry red light pulsed behind closed doors and shuttered windows. He stopped and observed for a few heartbeats then hurried past that one.

In only half a bell he'd moved all the way across the grounds and found his way to the Initiate's Quarters. He was confident he was in the right place because the hedge-walled garden was the only one like it he had seen during his normal visits or this night.

Three stories of white stucco and the length of a city block.

Staring up at the building he still couldn't figure out how he was going to find Meghan and Amelie inside without alerting anyone else.

He began to circle the building, peering in the lit windows, hoping he'd get lucky. Maybe both girls will be together and sitting alone in a room on the first floor. He ruefully shook his head at the stupidity of the thought, but right now, he didn't have anything else.

After a couple of windows he saw that the first floor was all common areas. There were rooms that looked like they were for studying, a mess room, a large steamy washroom, and other open rooms with no obvious purpose. Most rooms had the lights on still and he saw several young women going about their evening tasks. Many of them were reading books and he saw some small groups debating chalk writing they'd put on a blackboard.

He made it around one side of the building with no sign of Meghan or Amelie, but he was hopeful. A lot of girls were awake, so he might see them. If he could at least find where they were, a plan might materialize.

On the far side of the building he had to pass a brightly lit entrance. He counted to one hundred and hadn't seen or heard anyone. He held his breath and walked through the light, hoping he looked like he belonged there.

Almost to the other corner of the building, he thought he was safe until he heard a soft voice loudly and pointedly clear its throat. He paused mid-step.

"Excuse me. Do you care to explain yourself?" demanded a young female.

"I…"

"Don't bother. I saw you looking in the washroom window. Hoping to catch a peek?"

Running wasn't an option. She would simply raise the alarm if he did anything other than turn and convince her she didn't need to.

"I'm sorry, ma'am. I believe I am lost. Are the guard's barracks near here? I wasn't sure, so I was trying to figure out which building this is." Maybe if she thought he was trying to reach the guards she wouldn't think she needed to call them herself.

She crossed her arms and scowled at him. "You are not out for a casual stroll deep in the night looking for the guard's barracks. This is the Sanctuary. Do you think I am stupid? Let's try that again, and if you lie, I will know."

She was standing in the light of the entry way. She was a pretty young woman, close to his own age. She wasn't screaming for help yet. That was something.

"I-I'm looking for my sister," he stammered. Could she really tell if he was lying? He didn't know, but he did want to find Meghan in addition to Amelie. It was at least partially true.

"Your sister?" she asked disbelievingly.

Might as well go for broke. "Meghan Pinewood. She's stopped answering my letters and I've heard stories about this place. I did a lot of asking around after she left. I came to see if she was okay."

"Meghan Pinewood is your sister?" The scowl remained on her face but her tone lightened. "Then know that she is okay and that you shouldn't be here. The mages do not look kindly at tres-passers. I suggest you go out the way you came in and thank the stars it was me instead of a guard who saw you. You can visit her in the gardens on the next Newday."

"I need to see her now, tonight," implored Ben. "Do you know her? Could you send her out to talk to me?"

"You should go," advised the girl. "You should go now before someone else does find you."

"Please. I came all of the way here to make sure she is safe. I promise, I will leave as soon as I know she's safe." He was skirting the truth as closely as he could.

"This is a bad idea." The girl was wavering.

"If you know her, she must have told you some about her

family or her past. Ask me anything and I can prove I'm her brother."

"Where is Meghan from? Wait. Wait. That is too easy." The girl flipped a twist of wet hair back over her shoulder then asked, "What caused her to come to the Sanctuary?"

"I was injured in a demon attack. A mage, Lady Towaal, came to our village of Farview to kill the demon. She healed me as well. She was with Lady Amelie, Lady Amelie's handmaiden, a blade-master named Saala, and a hunter named Rhys. Meghan and my adopted brother left with Lady Towaal as payment for my healing. Please, she is here because of me. I must talk to her to know she is safe."

The girl sighed. "Very well. There is a hedge-walled garden on the other side of this building. It's locked at night so you will need to climb in or wiggle through the brush. If you got this far without being detected that should be easy. Our curfew is in half a bell. Meghan will sneak down after that to meet you in the garden. I will tell her you came to see her, Brandon."

The girl turned and disappeared back into the Initiate's Quarters. Ben almost collapsed in relief.

THE HEDGE WALL turned out to be thick bushes surrounding an iron fence. Ben scrambled over it then dropped behind a tangle of shrubs. He'd been lucky so far and he wasn't going to risk a stray guard or Initiate peering into the garden and spying him.

The bells rang dutifully on time. He squirmed in the damp, slightly chill earth while he waited. He peered through the leaves and strained his ears to hear anything. There was nothing to see and no sounds.

Finally, he heard the scrape of a door and whispered voices. He remained still and silent, waiting for the footfalls to draw closer.

"Ben!" hissed Meghan's voice.

He poked his head up from the brush and saw both Meghan and Amelie staring at him from near the building.

"Damn it, Ben! I knew it would be you. What are you doing out here? You're going to get us in a lot of trouble and yourself thrown in prison!" exclaimed Meghan in a low voice.

The girls were still standing near the door to the garden. Ben risked further wrath from Meghan and waved them deeper into the plants and flowers. They followed reluctantly.

"You've got us out here and violating our curfew. What are you doing in the Sanctuary at night?" demanded Meghan.

"Really, Ben, this was a very bad idea," added Amelie, glancing over her shoulder at the building.

Ben grimaced. It wasn't a good way to start. "I know this is risky, believe me, I know. I came because I had to warn you, Amelie. You are in serious danger."

"This better not be more cow shit about some bumpkin you met who's worried about his sister," muttered Meghan.

"No," growled Ben. "It's about how two days ago an army of men from the Coalition slaughtered Lord Reinhold and one hundred of his guards outside the town of Arrath. They are coming here next and they plan to take Amelie."

"What! That is ridiculous," replied Meghan incredulously.

"Hold on. What are you talking about Ben?" Amelie asked and shot a concerned look at Meghan. "How do you know this?"

"I was there!" Ben was exasperated. For the last two days his head was spinning with plans to sneak into the center of power for all of the mages in Alcott and spirit away two of their precious Initiates. In his plans, though, Meghan and Amelie had believed him.

"We thought Gulli, the man who arranged the attack on us, was in Arrath. So, Reinhold assembled his men and we marched up there. But it was an ambush. A Coalition army was waiting for us in the woods. They killed them all. They are on the way here. I can't be more than half a day ahead of them. They're going to take you, Amelie."

Amelie sat down on the ground, stunned. "The Coalition?" she asked in a small voice.

"Ben," chided Meghan, "if there was this big battle and everyone was killed, how are you here?"

"I was behind them," replied Ben. "Reinhold wanted me away from the action. I got to the top of a hill and saw them attacked. I watched it until the end."

"So then what?" pressed Meghan. "These men, Coalition you said? I guess they just let you go after that. How do you know they are coming here?"

"I overheard them while I was hiding. Meghan, I am not lying. Amelie is in grave danger." Ben ran his hands through his hair in frustration. He was exhausted from the frantic march back to the City and couldn't find the words to explain himself.

"You lied to get us to come out here didn't you?" accused Meghan. "Be serious, Ben. This story makes no sense. And even if it was true, and these men want to harm Amelie, what do you expect us to do? There is no safer place for her in Alcott than behind these walls."

"No, the men, the Coalition men, are working with the Sanctuary," explained Ben. "The Sanctuary is part of this. I heard them dispatch a man to come here and give news of what happened."

Meghan dramatically rolled her eyes and threw up her hands. "Oh, now the Sanctuary is in on it? Really? You're saying the Sanctuary is involved in some crazy plot to assassinate a lord and then kidnap someone who is already here?"

Appealing to Meghan was going nowhere. Whatever trust they shared as adopted siblings was vanishing quickly.

Ben sat down next to Amelie and ignored the glowering Meghan. He placed a hand on Amelie's shoulder. "Amelie, Lord Jason led this Coalition army. He ambushed and killed Lord Reinhold so that Lord Gulli could buy up all of the arms from

Venmoor and cut off your father and the rest of the Alliance. He plans to come here next and kidnap you to put more pressure on your father. He wants him to surrender from the Alliance. I do not know what they plan next, but I can imagine the offensive planned against Issen will turn into an offensive with Issen. This Lord Jason believes you are the key, He thinks your father will bow to the Coalition demands if they have you."

"Oh please," grunted Meghan.

"Lord Jason," squeaked Amelie. "You saw him?"

"Yes, I did," answered Ben.

"What did he look like?"

"I only saw him from a distance. He is around my height and had long blond hair pulled into a ponytail. He was wearing the dark grey of the Coalition and he moved like I have never seen. He made Saala look like the city watch. I heard him. His voice was smooth and strong, like a razor-fish in the water."

Amelie looked to Meghan and whispered, tears filling her eyes, "I know Lord Jason, and that describes him. If he is coming, I need to go. Ben is right. My father would do anything for me. I came here because he knew I would be a target. He thought I would be safe in this place. If I'm not, then I could be a pawn in the Coalition and King Argren's games."

"Amelie." Meghan squatted down next to her and put a hand on her other shoulder. "You are safe here. The mages would never allow anything to happen to you. Surely you know that by now."

Amelie looked between the two, torn. They all sat there in silence. Ben looked to Meghan. She stayed focused on Amelie and didn't meet his eyes.

"I have to go." Amelie sighed.

"Amelie…" Meghan objected.

Amelie placed a hand on Meghan's and interrupted. "No. The risk is too great. Not for me, for my father and for Issen. I cannot allow even the smallest chance of the Coalition capturing me. My family, my father, my people, my home would all be at risk."

"Amelie," Meghan started again, "this is your home. You may not feel like it yet, but you are already part of the Sanctuary. Our old ties have been severed and we belong here now. We have no fathers anymore. The Veil is our mother, she will protect you."

"I have to go." The whisper was barely audible. Amelie resolutely rose to her feet before looking back down at Ben and, in a stronger voice, declaring, "I will follow you out." She turned to Meghan. "Please understand. There is more at stake here than just me or even my family. My father's weakness is me. I have no doubt he would cave if I were captured. My people would suffer. Hundreds of thousands, Meghan. They would suffer under the Coalition if Argren didn't make an example of us first. Issen as I know it would be no more. The Sanctuary has existed for millennia. It will continue to do just fine without me."

"You are making the wrong choice," snarled a steely voiced Meghan, "but it is yours to make. I wish you the best of luck, because I believe you will need it."

Amelie looked back down at Ben. "We should go."

"Do you, uh, do you need to get anything?" he asked.

"If we go, we go now," she answered with determination.

Ben scrambled to his feet and motioned for Amelie to follow him to the hedge-wall. He kneeled down to make a stirrup for her feet and boosted her over the fence.

He looked back at Meghan and held her gaze for three long breaths. A year ago, they were siblings, adopted but still close. He felt like this night, their relationship had been sundered. He would never call her sister again. As she said, her family was the Sanctuary now.

TAKING quick strides along the pebble path, Amelie looked to Ben. "You have a way out, right?"

"I do. Amelie, I want to you to know, this is real. The things I saw..."

"I know, Ben. I wouldn't have left otherwise. We will talk later. This is not the place."

With that, a clanging erupted through the still night. It sounded like a giant banging a steel spoon over and over against a cook pot.

"Damn it!" screamed Amelie. She grabbed Ben's hand and they started to run. "That bitch didn't even give us a head start."

"What?"

"Meghan, Ben. Meghan just found a guard. Or a mage."

Ben steered them down a fork in the road and between breaths said, "We have to get to the water. There's a lot of brush ahead that I don't think the guards would ever spot us in. Should we run, or hide until the alarm dies down?"

Amelie, already panting, replied, "We're trying to escape the bloody Sanctuary. The guards aren't what we need to worry about. We fucking run!"

~

AND THEY DID.

The buildings Ben had passed between earlier were lit up like fall festival jack-o-lanterns. They'd be spotted within heartbeats of passing between them. Instead, Ben pulled Amelie toward the exterior wall and through the waist-high grass. They started a wide circle around the populated areas of the grounds.

He glanced back and saw the trampled path they were leaving. Someone tracking them wasn't the problem right now, though. Movement was their only option. Running into a guard or worse would ruin their escape attempt.

They made it to the outside wall and paused. Amelie was

breathing heavily and leaned against the cool stone that encircled the city side of the grounds.

"So, how are we getting out of here?" she asked between deep rasping breaths.

Ben grinned. The stress of the last few days had weighed heavily on him, but the confusion from earlier was done. Now they just had to execute their escape. Whatever had happened between him and Meghan could be dealt with later. Amelie was the one in danger and she was the one who had trusted him.

"Boat," he said. "If he can wait long enough. I know you're tired, but we've got to move."

Amelie pushed off the wall with a groan and a broad gesture. "After you."

Ben started again, tracking the outside wall to get to the river-bank, which he hoped they could move along until they met Mathias. He kept a quick pace, but not the run they started at. Amelie clearly was no longer used to physical activity. The last thing he needed was to wear her completely out.

The clanging sirens continued, and in the distance, Ben could see bright spots of light moving throughout the grounds. Their possible saving grace, he thought, was that the entire complex wasn't lit. It looked like individuals carrying the lights which were easy to see coming. As long as they could avoid them, they should be fine.

But as they neared the water, Ben saw they had a problem. A bobbing light was making its way toward them. From a distance, it looked like it was tracking the outside wall as well.

"I should have thought of that," muttered Ben. "Of course they'll check along the walls to see if we're climbing out some-where." He glanced behind them. A thousand paces back, and behind a stand of trees, another light flickered in and out of sight.

"Can we climb out?" whispered Amelie.

Ben brushed a hand along the wall and said, "I thought about that before I came in. This wall is some sort of mage-fused stone.

It's completely smooth. There's nowhere to get a finger grip. Any hooks you could throw over the top and try to climb would just slide off. We have to make it to the water, it's the only way out."

"There." Amelie pointed to a low, dark building. "That should be deserted this time of night, and there's something in there we can use."

They scurried through the high, dewy grass. Ben frowned down at their feet then looked back to the first light. It was steadily moving closer.

"It won't be long before they see these tracks."

"We run?" asked Amelie.

Ben nodded.

Quickly, they made it to the dark building and slipped inside the unlocked door. It was one long open room. Half of it was entirely glass and filled with a stunning variety of plant life. The other half held sturdy tables covered in an array of objects Ben didn't understand. There were liquid-filled brightly colored glass tubes, a profusion of massive leather-bound books, strange metallic devices, and other objects he wasn't even sure how to classify. Some of them bubbled and hissed strangely.

Amelie plunged into the room and kept straight ahead, Ben scrambled to follow her. If they made it out of here alive, he was very curious to ask her what this place was.

Halfway through the room, Amelie paused and then darted to the wall to snatch two slim vials off a rack on a shelf. She yanked a cork stopper out of one, passed it to Ben and then opened her own vial.

"Cheers," she whispered then downed the contents.

Ben drank his as well. It tasted like water. "What was that?" he asked.

"I'll explain later." She quickly turned again and rummaged through the shelves until she found a palm-sized wooden disc carved with strange symbols. She tucked it into her dress and nodded back to Ben. "Let's move."

The building was long, but there was a walkway down the center, so even in the dark, they were able to move fast. The door at the far end came into view and Ben saw reflected lights on the river through the wall of glass windows.

"Almost there," he whispered excitedly.

"Not quite," called a stern voice that sent shivers down Ben's spine.

He and Amelie spun around and saw a plainly dressed, stern-faced woman standing in the center of the aisle they just walked down. Two armed guards stood behind her. One was wearing the dark grey of the Coalition and the other the emerald green of the Sanctuary. The men contemptuously hadn't drawn their blades. Without a doubt, Ben knew the woman was a mage.

"Where do you think you are going, Initiate Amelie?" she continued in the same firm tone. "You know that at this stage of training it is forbidden to leave."

Amelie gestured to the Coalition man. "I think you know why I am leaving."

The woman smiled and stepped forward. "That is a fair point. It's too bad it ends like this, you would have made a good mage."

"Eldred..." Amelie started.

"That is Mistress Eldred, girl," the woman corrected. The woman took another step forward.

Amelie looked to Ben. He placed a hand on his sword and his body tensed. He was willing to challenge the two guards, but he would be helpless against the mage.

Eldred took a final step closer and placed a hand on Amelie's shoulder. "I am sorry about this. I truly am. You would have been one of the great ones, but it is politics, girl. It is bigger than any one of us. We must do what we must for the greater good."

Amelie looked down and to her side, "I am sorry too." She glanced back at Ben and said, "You shouldn't have come here, Ben. But even if we wanted to, there's no going back now."

Ben met her eyes.

Amelie turned back to Eldred and swept her hand out over one of the sturdy tables, snatching up a heavy glass beaker full of steaming liquid. She maintained her momentum and spun with the glass, raising it up and crashing it straight into Eldred's face. The mage's head snapped back in a spray of glittering glass, white teeth, and bright red blood. Smoke boiled off Eldred's skin where the liquid poured over her. She collapsed silently backward. Ben whipped out his sword and leapt over Eldred's falling body before she even hit the ground.

The Coalition man was the first to react, reaching for his sword, but he was too late. Ben plowed into him, slapping the man's hand away from his weapon and slashing his blade across the man's throat. The man dropped to his knees, clawing futilely at his ruined neck. The Sanctuary guard stumbled backward, still fumbling to draw his blade and staring down at Eldred with wide eyes.

Ben paused for a heartbeat. He saw a streak of iridescent yellow light through the glass windows arc into the sky from the direction they came.

"They found our trail," moaned Amelie.

Ben grimaced, darted forward, and pounded the hilt of his sword into the side of the Sanctuary man's head. The man fell like a limp rag doll. "No reason to kill him if they're already onto us," Ben said with a frown.

"I understand," replied Amelie before they both turned and ran for the door.

There was no pretense at sneaking now. It was a race to the riverbank where they could only hope Mathias was still waiting.

THE SPRINT to the water took no more than one hundred heart-beats, but it felt like an eternity. Shouts were rising throughout the compound, and bright disks of white light began to rise high above from all sides. Ben wasn't sure if it was his imagination, but they seemed to start floating slowly toward them.

"Don't get below one of those!" shouted Amelie.

Ben didn't even want to think of what would happen if they did.

They flew down the pebble path he'd come in on. The lights drift closer, but Ben didn't think anyone has seen them. Paces from the riverbank, his heart sank. Mathias and the boat were missing.

"Damn." He stared out at the water.

"Are you sure this is the right place?" asked Amelie. "We've been running around a lot. Maybe you got turned around?"

He looked back. The park and buildings were exactly like he remembered. "This is the place," he answered, teeming with frustration.

A swarm or lights were in the glass building they just left and he saw them begin to pour out the exit. The floating discs began to converge more quickly. They were out of time.

"Can you swim?" he asked out of desperation.

"How far?" she answered while kicking off her shoes.

"The far bank is half a league away."

"I've never swam that far before," she admitted nervously. "I saw the man from the Coalition. We killed him for sure, and maybe a mage. What choice do we have?"

Ben kicked off his boots, tore his shirt off his back, and looped his sword belt over his shoulder. He grabbed their shoes and other clothing and hurled it into the river before they both stepped off the bank and dove into the water.

The water was cold, but the current was lazy this close to the island. After a furious moment to get distance from shore, they settled into slow and steady strokes. Behind them, they heard angry shouts and bright lights bloomed along the riverbank to light it up like it was day. The clanging of the siren finally let off. The ensuing silence was eerie. Ben cringed and kept swimming.

Amelie's strokes began to get sluggish before they were a quarter way across the channel. Ben started to worry she wouldn't make it. He kicked with his feet to rise out of the water, scanning for nearby boats. There was one narrow sailing skiff rounding the north side of the island that might pass near them. It had a softly flickering lantern on the bow, so he could easily track it while they swam.

Whoever was on it, it couldn't be worse than who they'd left. It was a long shot, getting spotted in these dark waters, or even making it close enough to the fast-moving boat, but they had to try something. They weren't going to make the other side with how quickly Amelie was fading.

Amelie's strokes continued to slow, but Ben encouraged her. "I see a boat coming our way. Keep going the way you are and we should be able to wave them down."

Without looking up, a little burst of energy coursed through her and she kept swimming. A moment later, though, her pace fell off again. Her arms churned sluggishly through the water. Ben knew she had moments left before she started to sink. He'd try to help, but he knew she'd likely take him with her as there was no way he could pull both of them through the current for long.

Ben bobbed up again to get a bead on the skiff and almost got run over by a little rowboat that he hadn't seen.

"Ho there!" called a muffled but familiar voice.

Mathias reached over the side, and, with strong arms, hauled a sodden Amelie out of the water and rolled her into the bottom of his boat. Ben swam over and grabbed the side before Mathias pulled him in as well.

"Now, that is two drowned looking rats if I've ever seen them," exclaimed the barkeep. Glee and excitement filled his voice.

Amelie lay wheezing at the bottom of the boat, too tired to talk.

Ben reached up and slapped a wet hand on Mathias' arm. "I thought we were done." He panted.

"Ah, I know that must have hurt when you saw I wasn't there. I had to move, though. I could see the guards sweeping the bank and they would have spotted me easily."

"I understand. I'm glad you stayed out here watching for us!"

They both paused as a sharp snap split the night air. Amelie sat up and all three of them watched a blaze of energy arc out from the Sanctuary and soar over the river.

"We need to get out of here. Now," demanded an exhausted Amelie.

Mathias nodded and sat down to the oars, but none of them could take their eyes off the swirling red light as it crackled and popped closer. Several hundred paces away, it struck the deck of the sailing skiff Ben saw earlier. The red light exploded in flames and heat. Screams from the doomed vessel filled the night air, but were quickly choked off as the unnatural fire consumed the boat.

The oars dipped into the water and their tiny rowboat surged forward, cutting through the low chop of the river.

SEVERAL MOMENTS PASSED IN SILENCE. Mathias steadily rowed them further from the island. They watched behind his silhouetted figure as more crackling lights arced out from the Sanctuary and torched nearby ships.

Ben and Amelie could only watch in shock as the brutality of the Sanctuary was displayed in full force.

The disks of white light drifted out aimlessly over the water, but their rowboat was too small to be seen from the shore. Everything larger was already burning. After a long and tense half bell, Mathias had gotten them far enough away they could breathe a sigh of relief. They moved out of the river basin and upstream into the Venmoor River. The Sanctuary and the island disappeared around the bend.

"Where to?" croaked Ben.

"The only place that could be in more chaos than where you left," answered Mathias grimly. "Lord Reinhold's estate."

Amelie slumped against Ben and laid her cheek against the bare skin of his chest. He wrapped his arms tight around her shivering body and sat back to watch the water glide past while Mathias rowed.

REVIEWS, ACKNOWLEDGEMENTS, AND NEWSLETTER

I WROTE this book for myself. It is the book I always hope to read when I pick up something new. I hope it is a book you enjoyed reading as well. If you did, I encourage you to leave a friendly review and share with your friends. Books sell by word of mouth, and I'm counting on you the reader to help spread that word.

For the first edition of this novel, I had no acknowledgements. That edition was a solo endeavor written in isolation. I took full credit for the good, the bad, and the ugly. Turns out, there was a lot of ugly. Since that first edition, I've gotten help from some wonderful people who made this thing look like an actual professional book.

My cover and social media package were designed by Milos from Deranged Doctor Design (www.derangeddoctordesign.com). Milos did a great job of creating a cover that matches the feel of the book. And inside the cover, I must thank Nicole Zoltack (www.nicolezoltack.com) for her proof-reading services. She took this book from 'business major English' to something I am not ashamed to put in print.

Finally, and most importantly, I would like to thank the early readers who took a risk on an unknown, self-published author.

Most books fall flat on their faces. I honestly expected mine to do that as well. I consider myself lucky that I've had some small measure of success. It is you early readers who inspired me to keep writing instead of tucking the Benjamin Ashwood word file away and pretending that chapter of my life never happened. So, from myself and from anyone who is interested in reading further, thank you!

Thank you for your interest in the book,

AC

To STAY UPDATED and find out when the next book is due, or to receive **FREE Benjamin Ashwood short stories**, I suggest signing up for my Newsletter. In addition to the short stories, I stick in author interviews, news & events, and whatever else I think may be of interest. One e-mail a month, no SPAM, that's a promise. Website and Newsletter Sign up: https://www.accobble.com/newsletter/

Of course I'm on **Facebook** too: https://www.facebook.com/ACCobble/

If you want the really exclusive, behind the scenes stuff, then **Patreon** is the place to be. There are a variety of ways you can support me, and corresponding rewards where I give back! Find me on **Patreon**: https://www.patreon.com/accobble

ENDLESS FLIGHT: Benjamin Ashwood Book 2 is available now! You can find it at nearly any online book retailer.

Made in the USA
Lexington, KY
30 November 2018